CEILYN DREW HIS SWORD....

He did not hear the door at the foot of the steps burst open, but he felt the wind sucked up the tower and he saw the torches flicker in their cressets. A terrible racket surrounded him, like the screeching of a thousand cats at a Tagharim, and a dark tide swept up the steps, a mass of small misshapen creatures that threw themselves against him in a frenzy. . . .

Ceilyn struck at them with his sword, slashing and cutting to left and right, but as swiftly as he slew them, worse things came to replace them.

The Work of the Sun

Book Three of
THE GREEN LION TRILOGY

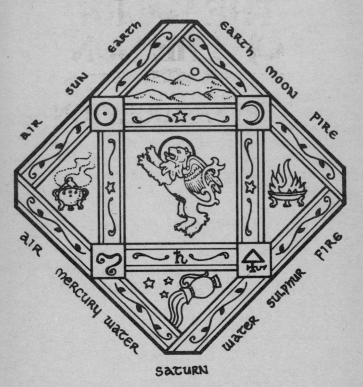

THE ELEMENTS

THE WORK OF THE SUN

TERESA EDGERTON

ACE BOOKS, NEW YORK

This book is an Ace original edition,
and has never been previously published.

THE WORK OF THE SUN

An Ace Book/published by arrangement with
the author

PRINTING HISTORY
Ace edition/March 1990

ISBN: 0-441-90911-6

Ace Books are published by The Berkley Publishing Group,
200 Madison Avenue, New York, New York 10016.
The name ''ACE'' and ''A'' logo are trademarks
belonging to Charter Communications, Inc.

PRINTED IN THE UNITED STATES OF AMERICA

10 9 8 7 6 5 4 3 2 1

Ace Books by Teresa Edgerton

THE GREEN LION TRILOGY

CHILD OF SATURN
THE MOON IN HIDING
THE WORK OF THE SUN

ACKNOWLEDGMENTS

I would like to thank my parents, Jack and Eleanor Waller, for aid and comfort throughout the writing of the trilogy, and my friends—most especially Pat and Yoko—for encouragement. The Whensday People provided valuable insights by critiquing this final volume while it was in progress. Gwyneth, Daisy, Megan, and John-Miles provided incentive, if not peace and quiet to work in. And finally, I would like to thank my husband, John, for without his patient help and support, and his indispensable assistance in writing the fighting sequences, The Green Lion could never have been written.

CUAN DORAIGHEN

SKELLI

N

FALIAS

LETH

DUN FIORENN

MURIAS

GORLAS

FARGADUISGE

YNYS GLASTIG
YNYS YREG

DUNN DESSI

LETH SCATHACH

EINNI

COBLYNAU hILLS

ARG

R. ARAON

COILL DORCHA

TREGALEN

DOL TAL CARREG

YSCRAD PALAGUR

CAMBOGLANN

REGANN

CAER CADWY &
TRELEDIG

CREDENHALL

BAY of CAMBOGLANNA

PEFYNS GRAVE

DINAS TRACHMYR

TEIRWAEDD MORFA

GOLCH

LEGEND

Journey to Caer Wydr — · — · —
Return to Caer Cadwy — — — —
Marshland . . . . \w/ \w/ \w/
Gravesite . . . . †

25

A SCALE

A GUIDE TO THE PRONUNCIATION OF THE NAMES OF PRINCIPAL CHARACTERS AND PLACES MENTIONED IN THE GREEN LION

Generally speaking:

c and *g* are always hard.
f is pronounced like *v* in English.
ff is just *f*.
ll is the Welsh *ll*, except in Draighenach names.
dd is a soft *th*.

Vowels are usually the same as in Welsh, except where the names look Irish, or where I decided to pronounce them differently.

With only one exception that I can think of, the accent is on the penultimate (second to the last) syllable.

Specifically:

Teleri ni Pendaren (Tel-AIR-ee nee Pen-DARE-en)
Ceilyn mac Cuel (KAY-lin mac KILL)
Cynwas fab Anwas (KIN-wass vab AN-wass)
Sidonwy (Sid-ON-wee)
Caer Cadwy (Kair KAD-wee or Kair Kah-DO-ee)
Camboglanna (Kam-bog-LON-nah)
Diaspad (Dee-AH-spad)
Calchas fab Corfil (Kal-kass vab KOR-vill)
Fflergant fab Maelgwyn (FLUR-gant vab MEL-gwin)

Tryffin (TRIF-fin)
Garanwyn (Gar-RAN-win)
Gwenlliant (Gwen-HLLEE-ant)
Glastyn (GLASS-tin)
Tir Gwyngelli (Tear Gwin-GELL-ee)
Mochdreff (MOCK-dreff)
Rhianedd (Hree-ANN-eth)
Cadifor (Kad-EE-vor)
Llochafor (Hllock-AH-vor)
Daire mac Forgoll (DARE-eh mac FOR-goal)
Derry (the way you think it is pronounced)
Morc (Mork)
Prescelli (Press-KELL-ee)
Caer Celcynnon (Kair Kel-KIN-non)
Manogan fab Menai (Mann-OH-gan vab MEN-ee)
Gwdolwen ni Dyffryn (Goo-DOHL-wen nee DUFF-rin)
Arfondwy (Are-von-DO-ee)
Tiffaine (Tiff-ANE)
Anwe (AHN-wee)
Castell Maelduin (CAS-tell MEL-doon)
Dyferdallben (Duff-ur-DALL-ben)
Teirwaedd Morfa (TIRE-wayth MOR-vah)
Celydonn, Celedon (Kel-UH-don)
Donwy (Don-OO-ee)

A note for the linguist: The Celydonian tongue and its dialects are not intended to represent any real-world Celtic tongue or dialect, nor any mixture which would be historically or linguistically possible. Rather, it is an intentionally fanciful combination of Welsh, Irish, and pseudo-Celtic elements, which derive any coherency or consistency they may have by a loose adherence to a pattern of migrations, intermarriages and inter-tribal cultural exchanges which could only have taken place on Ynys Celydonn and nowhere else.

CONTENTS

0.

The Stuff of Legends

Ceilyn mac Cuel disappeared one day from the King's grand castle at Caer Cadwy. The young knight had been a disturbing presence, whether he was standing stiff and disapproving at the Queen's side, or hovering on the edge of a crowd, dark-eyed, passionate, like a thunderstorm about to happen. At the beginning, most of the castle inhabitants were glad to be rid of him.

Off on another quest, folk said, a secret mission for Queen Sidonwy, and wild tales began to spread: tales of a grey wolf that was more than a wolf . . . of the great white fairy stag that lives in the deep woods waiting to lure the overeager huntsman into perils and adventures . . . stories of holly and oak and a mysterious magician clad in green and scarlet who came and went secretly with a brown owl perched on his shoulder . . . tales of giants and trolls, of riddles and gold rings. . . .

There had been a time when such stories were commonplace, and every one of the King's knights was the hero of some quest or deed of daring, but of the present generation, only Ceilyn seemed to qualify for the status of hero. It was not surprising, then, that he served as a kind of lodestone for all the bits and pieces of older tales floating around loose, attracting them to him until a body of legends began to form and a glamor grew around his name that would have astonished the young knight had he been there to learn of it.

Only Teleri ni Pendaren knew the secret behind Ceilyn's disappearance—and whom would she have spoken to? The castle folk shunned her, or perhaps she shunned them. Her separation from the others had been a fact for such a long time that it was no longer possible to remember just who had rejected whom. Her old companions: the stone gargoyles come to life, the banner beasts and heraldic monsters grown remarkably voluble in the presence of Teleri's undirected Wizard's talent, all the friends born of her vivid imagination . . . all had deserted her. Of necessity, the little sorceress kept what she knew to herself.

So the stories grew not only stranger but more elaborate with every new telling, until gradually the little bit of truth at the heart of them was obscured, then buried, and at last completely lost. And no one but Teleri suspected that the true story, though simpler, was nearly as strange and wonderful as all the wild tales.

. . . therefore, he who would become wise must first gain knowledge of the four elements, their seasons and their qualities, their conjunctions, dissolutions, and their adaptations, but principally of their metamorphoses, mutually and reciprocally changing and changed.

—*from* The Testimony of the Philosophers

1.

The Language of Foxes

Ceilyn moved through a colorless world of altered shapes and distances, buffeted by intense sounds and scents, stirred by terrifying impulses. Fear made him dangerous in those days, fear that caused him to cringe away from every moving shadow, to snarl and snap at everything that came his way.

He dug a den for himself under a leafless bush, and lay there, trembling, belly to the cold earth, until hunger drove him out again. He caught a rabbit and tore it to pieces, man-sense and beast-sense so at war within him that he knew not what he was doing. There was not much meat on those fragile bones, not much blood after he had ripped the tiny body apart. He returned to his den, still hungry, still confused and frightened.

But gradually, the world began to right itself. Black and white, near and far, taste and touch and scent, all became comprehensible again. As he adjusted to his altered senses, the panic and confusion faded. Creeping out of his den, he explored the glade thoroughly; after a few more days, he ventured farther afield.

There were other wolves in the forest: He heard them, caught glimpses of them at a distance, came across their scent markings on rocks and bushes. He avoided them at first, torn between fear and the first painful stirrings of . . . something. . . . It might have been the awakening of an instinctive pack-sense. At last the need became so great that he gathered his courage and walked boldly, more boldly than he felt, into a clearing where the pack lay at rest.

They surrounded him and mobbed him, tearing at him with strong white teeth, throwing the weight of their lean bodies against him. They were not out for blood, not out to kill him, only to drive him away. Sensing that, Ceilyn stood his ground. He knew that he was bigger and stronger than any of them, with a man's weight and mass wedded to the strength and agility of a wild beast. So he growled and bared his teeth, and eventually they retreated, leaving him in possession of the frosty glade.

His fear of the pack met and mastered, Ceilyn set out to explore this new world he lived in.

The snow fell and the wind wailed dismally among the bare branches, but Ceilyn ranged ever farther afield. He learned that he could run for a long time without tiring. Hunger was an almost constant presence, but he could go for many days without eating and suffer no ill-effects. When he did kill, he ripped out the entrails first, ate until he was gorged, then retired to his den or some other sheltered spot to lick the blood from his fur and sleep until hunger roused him again.

One day, he met another lone wolf, a big rangy male with a silver pelt. With stiff-legged posturing and snarling they took each other's measure. Finally, the old wolf walked away, but leisurely, to show that he had merely lost interest, that Ceilyn had not intimidated him.

The next evening he came back, trotting boldly into Ceilyn's glade. He paused to sniff at a bush, then lifted his leg and dribbled a scent marking. Ceilyn growled, but he did not contest the action. When he went hunting that night, the silver wolf ran at his side.

Under a full winter moon, they sought their prey: field mice and other small nocturnal creatures. Other predators inhabited the night, foxes and wild cats, slant-eyed pookhas and headless yell-hounds, but these the wolves instinctively avoided—hunters, for the most part, do not prey on each other.

After that first night, Ceilyn and the old wolf hunted together often. Ceilyn was happier as part of a pair, and a pain somewhere inside of him eased.

Another day, another loner joined them, a dark young female. She was lighter and faster than either of the males, which was an advantage when they went out after larger and fleeter game: deer and elk and bagwyn. Ceilyn communicated with her and the silver male after the manner of wolves, but he suspected they were neither of them what they appeared to be, no more than he was.

One evening, out on his own, the old disorientation assailed him, the sense that the world and all his senses had gone awry. After a long time, he recognized the problem: He had returned to the man-shape. He did not like it; it was so helpless and awkward and oddly fastidious, hunting with rocks and sticks, gagging and retching when it tasted raw meat. He was relieved when the episode passed.

Yet in the days that followed, the change came over him again and again. Fighting the transformation at first, he soon learned that resistance was futile. The periods he spent as man and wolf began to assume a pattern, and as he stopped resisting, his passage from one shape into the other flowed more smoothly. He still preferred the wolf-shape, but he was learning to tolerate the man. Out of curiosity, he tried to consciously initiate the transformation, and found that he could.

As a man, Ceilyn built a hut out of dry, leafless branches and gathered heather for a bed to sleep on. He kindled a fire and roasted a rabbit whole in the coals. His clothes, made of wool and linen—the matter of living things—which were somehow included in the transformation, grew ragged, so he fashioned a tunic out of deerskin and rabbit fur, using tiny splinters of bone to hold the pieces together.

When the other two wolves joined him in his little house, curling up comfortably beside the fire, he was more certain than ever that they were not ordinary wolves. He knew the old silver-grey male now, beyond any doubt: It was the same beast who had pursued him in his flight north last year, who had followed him all the way to the Coblynau Hills.

"For the love of God," Ceilyn said aloud. His voice sounded strange and harsh, grown rough and awkward with disuse. "You have me here now, just as you schemed all along. But what do you want of me?"

The old wolf yawned and licked a lean grey flank, pretending not to understand, but Ceilyn was not fooled.

"God damn you to an eternity in Hell, Glastyn," he said another time. "God damn you and your damned uninvited meddling in my life."

But the old wolf refused to be provoked into revealing himself. About the other wolf, the female, Ceilyn continued to wonder:

Who she was, really, and why she was there. Sometimes when he was with her a dim picture came into his mind, a picture of a dark-haired woman with a cold stern face, softened by a pair of compassionate grey eyes. Allowing his fancy free rein, he imagined her as a woman of power: a mighty sorceress or a priestess of the old pagan religion. But either way, Ceilyn could not understand why she should take an interest in him, why she was there in the forest as his companion.

As a man, Ceilyn wondered about his companions; as a wolf, he did not let such questions trouble him. His needs as a wolf, though just as urgent as the needs he knew as a man, were simpler, more elemental. He knew what he wanted and what he must do to get it, and there was no agonized weighing of choices, no conflict between duty and inclination, those twin devils that had tormented him when he was a man among men.

Yet if his needs were simpler, his experiences were richer and more complex. Learning to live with his keener senses, he gained a new awareness of the land, an intimate knowledge of other living creatures. The wind brought him scent from a herd of deer: an aging buck, two does, and an ailing youngster. His nose and his ears shared the same fine discrimination; moving through a wood, he knew all the trees where squirrels guarded their hoarded nuts, the burrows where the little palpitating rabbits crouched waiting for him to pass by, even the place where other wolves had made a kill two weeks past.

Through the pads of his four feet, he felt the changing textures of earth and stone, grass and forest mold. He felt the heartbeat of the Isle of Celydonn throbbing restlessly. He learned the languages of foxes and badgers, and of the blackbirds and ravens roosting in the winter woods.

But sometimes, something, the swift movement of a startled bird, or a gleam of sunlight on the snow, would nudge at a memory at the back of his mind. One day, chancing on the silver shimmer of a frozen waterfall, he was suddenly, forcefully, reminded of Teleri.

Teleri . . . passing from light into shadow, always elusive, unattainable. Without thinking about it, Ceilyn shifted from wolf into man and sat in a bank of snow, remembering.

Air and water, quicksilver and ice, melting away whenever he reached out to touch her—that was Teleri. Yet there had been tears in her eyes the night he had left her—how long ago?—and she had begged him to stay at Caer Cadwy and by her side, if only for a little longer.

Perhaps she had need of him. Ceilyn remembered other things: the Princess Diaspad and her complex plots . . . Sidonwy, the Queen, who was wont to depend on him . . . his little cousin Gwenlliant and her troubling dreams . . . blood on the grass down in the meadow on All Hallows Eve . . . the suspicion and implied accusations of witchcraft that Teleri had faced in the chapel the next morning. He had been at her side then, lending her such countenance as he, with his almost spotless name, had to bestow. But she was alone now. Alone, if it came to that, to face the rabble, the cowards who would not hesitate to bring down a helpless woman, though they lacked the courage to face a man with a sword and a reputation for knowing how to use it.

Yet Teleri had never been as helpless as she looked. She had summoned ancient powers the night in the meadow, and before that . . . all the little tricks of camouflage and misdirection that had teased and puzzled him . . . she was adept at avoiding trouble. He felt a rising resentment, remembering that talent of hers, and all the times he had made a fool of himself, attempting to protect her who needed no protection of his.

Well, she would have to rely on that talent now, lacking his help. Because Ceilyn was not ready to go back to Caer Cadwy for a long time yet. He was contented as he was, and had no desire to return.

"The matter of metals," said the wizard Glastyn, "requires lengthy treatment before it be transmuted into gold: calcination, congelation, solution, digestion, ceration, fermentation . . . these and many other processes may take months or years. And in that time a man's entire wealth may be expended—all for the sake of a handful of gold."

"Why then," the young girl at his side asked him, "do men seek gold in the laboratory, when it may be taken cheaper from the earth? Why do Alchemists beggar themselves in this profitless quest."

"The quest for gold," said Glastyn, "which the True Alchemist undertakes, is not a quest for riches or for power. The medium on which he experiments is not the metal only, but mankind in general, and specifically, the Alchemist himself. If he boils the matter, subjecting it to great heat and turmoil, so, too, the man is exposed to similar turmoil. And as the matter progresses through the nigredo, the dark phase, the Alchemist explores his darkest, most secret nature.

"The Alchemist seeks wisdom, which may be defined as: knowledge of nature, knowledge of God, and—primarily— knowledge of self. For the joy he gains from this knowledge, and from this knowledge only, the seeker of wisdom undertakes the quest."

2.

A Season of Ice

So cold and mean and dirty a winter Teleri could scarcely remember. It snowed and it snowed and it snowed, big wet flakes that melted as soon as they touched the ground, forming slushy puddles of hay and mud and ice. The wind did not howl, it whimpered, a ceaseless driveling complaint that wore on Teleri's nerves. And whenever she opened her bedchamber door, a spattering of snow blew in and puddled on the flagstones.

By day and by night, the pale Wizard Fire burned on her hearth, the fire that burns steadily though it consumes but little fuel. Teleri fed it with twigs and bits of straw, and when the wind came down the chimney and snuffed her fire out, she rekindled it without the aid of flint and steel. Yet the Wizard Fire offered more light than warmth.

When Teleri went out to fetch water from the well, the damp air crept under her shawl and her full skirts, between the layers of wool and the linen she wore next to her skin. Her face, hands, and feet ached with the cold. And that was very strange. All last winter she had walked abroad without any gloves, her shoes and her stockings full of holes, and never heeded the cold or the damp—yet here she was in stout boots and thick stockings, with grey woolen mittens upon her hands, and still she was wretched and tormented by the cold.

Teleri watched her oak bucket descend into the depths of the well, reflecting that last year she had not known Ceilyn, last year she had been able to *imagine* such petty discomforts away. For months she had pretended to be the Princess Essylt trailing through the castle in a fur-lined cloak and tiny jeweled slippers. The Princess Essylt had never suffered from cold feet, so neither did Teleri.

And when she tired of that game, she had only to devise another: She was St. Niamh walking barefoot through the snow, St. Niamh who was mad and given to holy ecstasies, and therefore beyond mere physical discomforts.

The windlass creaked as Teleri began to haul up her bucket.

This year, she thought, everything was different. This year, she was hopelessly mired in the present moment, imprisoned in her own small shivering body. And who was to blame for that, if not Ceilyn mac Cuel?

Teleri unhooked the bucket and trudged back to her stark bedchamber in the Wizard's Tower. In spite of the fire, the room was dark as well as cold, and the lion-maned gargoyle above the fireplace, the figures carved around the door, watched her with icy disapproval.

"But it is your fault quite as much as his," Teleri said, returning scowl for scowl. "And now you have deserted me, too."

There was no answer. Teleri sat down on a three-legged stool by the fire. "Perhaps I have simply outgrown you. But if that is so . . . what have I grown *into*? What am I to do now?"

As if in answer, there was a sharp rap at her bedchamber door.

Teleri jumped to her feet, knocking the stool over. But then she heard voices on the other side of the door, a man's and a woman's, and neither was the voice she wanted to hear.

She righted the stool, crossed the room, and reached for the door handle, just as somebody knocked again. Teleri took a deep breath, steadied herself, and threw open the door.

Three men, two of them in armor, and a slender woman in a dark green cloak with a wide, fur-trimmed hood stood on the doorstep.

"May I come in?" the Queen asked, and Teleri, not trusting herself to speak, nodded and stepped aside. To her relief, the guards remained on the doorstep and only the Earl Marshall followed Sidonwy into the room. He closed the door behind him.

"I should have preferred to come alone and not daunt you by arriving in such state," the Queen said with an apologetic smile, as the Marshall helped her to remove her cloak. "But the King insists. . . ."

She crossed the room, sat down upon the stool, and looked around her curiously. "It is long since I last visited the Wizard's Tower . . . not since Glastyn left us. I meant to come last spring, to thank you for—" She stopped, frowning at the Marshall.

"I shall not hear a word that passes between you," said Manogan, laying the green cloak and his own crimson velvet across the bed. "I am here merely as decoration, and I see and hear nothing." He positioned himself, arms folded across his chest, by the door. The pose was a familiar one, though Ceilyn, in imitating it, had always lacked the Marshall's lazy elegance.

Apparently resigned to Manogan's presence, Sidonwy went on. "I meant to come, but Ceilyn told me that you did not welcome visitors. I thought, perhaps, that might have changed?"

Teleri nodded shyly, at a loss for words.

"It seems to me," the Queen continued, "that you and I might be of mutual use at this time. For my part, I am in need of a household physician, for the King's physician is far too busy, these days, to attend to all the little ailments that arise in the Mermaid Tower. At first, I thought I would appoint some reputable doctor from the town, but then I thought how much easier it would be for the young ladies to confide their problems to another woman. Brother Gildas had never been sympathetic toward complaints of a *female* nature. Then, too, you could be useful to me in countless other ways as well."

Teleri frowned thoughtfully. "I do not see—"

"In most households the chatelaine keeps a stillroom and brews simple medicines, she knows how to bandage wounds, treat simple illnesses. . . . Perhaps it was so at Castell Aderyn, where you lived before?"

Teleri shook her head. "There was no chatelaine at Castell Aderyn. The Lord was widowed, his sons kept their wives in Golchi, and there were few women of any sort at the castle."

The Queen nodded understandingly. "I was also raised in a household of men, and my education in these matters suffered. Until recently, that has not troubled me, but now I realize that being unable to teach these things to the maidens of my household, I have not prepared them for the time when they will have households of their own to oversee. Brother Gildas tells me that your knowledge of herbs and medicines equals or excels his own, and there is a charming little chamber in the Mermaid Tower that might serve you as a stillroom.

"And there is another way you might serve me." Here, Sidonwy hesitated. "The truth is . . . your abilities as a wizard might also prove useful. Do you remember how it was before Ceilyn came—how I was in the habit of going about with an escort of armed men? But when Ceilyn was with me I could dispense with the others. He was so watchful and so alert, and he was better than any six men-at-arms. He could protect me without constantly reminding me of the need for protection.

"Now that he is gone . . . well, you have seen the escort the King has burdened me with, even when I venture from my apartments such a short distance as this. And I should not be allowed even so much privacy as we enjoy now, had not the Marshall consented to accompany me. And yet, though I am so well protected, I do not feel so safe as I did when Ceilyn was here."

Sidonwy sighed, and she held out her hand with such an appealing look that Teleri, in spite of herself, took a few steps in that direction. "I meant it for the best when I told Ceilyn to do whatever was necessary in order to make peace with himself. But I do miss that boy, and the young women miss him, too, though they were a long time admitting it. We *all* depended on him in more ways than we knew.

"He cannot be replaced, of course, but I think I would feel safer with someone like you watching over me: someone unobtrusive, but gifted with the sight to see what others cannot. And as you, too, may feel the poorer for Ceilyn's absence . . . what more natural than that we two should aid one another?'' She took Teleri's small cold hand in her smooth warm one. ''Will you serve me, as Glastyn once served the King?''

Teleri looked around her bedchamber, so cold and lonely before, so much warmer and brighter now, thanks to Sidonwy's presence. And was not Sidonwy suggesting the very thing that Ceilyn had so often urged Teleri to do: to make a place for herself at court, exactly as Glastyn had done before her, to serve the Crown directly as the old wizard's true successor? The Queen's offer was appealing, and yet . . .

''It is difficult for me to intrude where I am not wanted. And I fear that the young ladies in your household would not welcome me.''

''But they will welcome you,'' Sidonwy assured her. ''They are very eager to learn what you can teach them, and besides . . . well, they feel, as I do, that certain debts are owed, debts they may never be able to settle in any other way.

''Will you come, Teleri?'' she asked plaintively. ''I have such need of you.''

Teleri took a deep breath. ''I will come. I will come—and gladly.''

Down on the cobblestone streets of Treledig, a sallow youth and a veiled woman in a long cloak and a dark gown that had obviously seen better days threaded a cautious path through the dirty lanes and alleys in the poorest part of the town.

''But why was it necessary to come ourselves?' Calchas kept asking. ''Dressed in our oldest clothes . . . mud to the ankles . . . on what must be the beastliest day of the whole long year . . . when Bron or any of the other dwarfs might have come instead.''

''Ah yes.'' His mother's melodious voice issued from beneath the inky veil. ''That *would* have been secret and subtle. To send a hunch-backed dwarf—now, who would take notice of that? Or noticing, connect the fellow or his errand with either you or me? Indeed, why not send one of the woodwoses . . . or better, Pergrin the giant?''

They turned a corner and entered a narrow alley. The walls of the buildings on either side blotted out most of the light, and the alley stank of urine and rotting fish.

''Well, you might have sent Prescelli, anyway,'' Calchas amended. He pulled a scented handkerchief out of his sleeve and waved it under his nose.

"I believe I told you," his mother replied, her voice taking on a sharp, impatient edge, "this errand is tremendously important. Too important to trust to the likes of Prescelli. I wish to examine the merchandise myself before I decide to buy."

Calchas sighed. "Yes. Well, I hope it will prove to be worth our while." He slipped on a patch of melting ice and only just regained his balance in time to prevent a tumble into one of the dark, malodorous puddles. "I cannot say that our time at Caer Cadwy, until now, has been particularly rewarding. What have we done this past year that hasn't been undone these last disastrous months? Cadifor and Llochafor are back at court, as much in favor as they ever were. Lord Dyffryn returns in the spring. And Fflergant and Tryffin are to be knighted on New Year's Day. Our enemies flourish, while we—"

"We are here, too," the Princess reminded him. "For all our *real* enemies have done to dislodge us. And if we have gained nothing, there is nothing we have lost."

"Not anything of value, I suppose you mean," said Calchas. "No doubt Derry and Morc valued their miserable lives which they lost in service to our glorious cause, but as *you* account their sacrifice of such little value, why then—"

"Nothing that was ours when we arrived, I should have said. We have gained nothing and lost nothing. We have simply to make a fresh beginning, just as we did a year ago today.

"And we begin right here, at the Toad with Colors." She paused beneath a faded sign depicting a repulsive member of the species painted in bilious shades of green and yellow.

The interior of the tavern was even more noisome than the outside; the stench of unwashed bodies and sour beer augmented the stink from the alley. The Princess Diaspad, forgetting she had come there in disguise, sailed grandly on, right through the smoky room and up a rickety flight of stairs at the back. The crowd, recognizing the arrogance of privilege, even when it came veiled, instinctively parted before her, allowing Calchas to trail along in her wake.

On the landing, a ragged sailor—perhaps drunker than the rest—failed to move quickly enough. There was a hiss of indrawn breath, a flash of claws, and the sailor staggered back with a terrible cry. The left side of his face was scored with bloody lacerations from forehead to chin.

Calchas's stomach, already rebellious, gave a sickening lurch at the sight of blood. "I don't like this place," he whispered weakly. "I want to go home."

"Nonsense," said his mother. She pushed aside the door at the top of the stairs and passed into the room beyond. Reluctantly, Calchas followed her in.

The air on the other side of the door was better, thanks to the sweet scent of an applewood fire blazing on the hearth. The long, low-ceilinged chamber was sparsely furnished, with a scarred table, two or three unreliable-looking benches, and a high-backed chair beside the fireplace. A thin man in travel-stained grey leather slouched in that chair, apparently asleep.

"Well, Penfyngon," the Princess spoke in a sweet, carrying voice.

The man came awake with a visible start, opened a pair of lustrous dark eyes, and proceeded to unwind himself from the chair. He stumbled to his feet and continued to go on unfurling himself until his head brushed the rafters.

Calchas stared at him, open-mouthed. He understood now why his mother had chosen such an out-of-the-way spot for this meeting, for the lanky Penfyngon—with his passionate, tragical, noble face and his ludicrous proportions—was, in his own way, as conspicuous as any of the Princess's other freaks. Yet everything about him suggested the last sort of person one might expect to meet in a vile hole like the Toad with Colors.

(*"But do not let Penfyngon's face deceive you,"* his mother had warned Calchas earlier. *"A more rapacious, more thoroughly venal man I have yet to meet. The face has its uses, of course, especially for a man in his particular profession—which happens to be relieving other men of their most valuable possessions, sometimes in broad daylight, but more usually by stealth in the middle of the night."*)

The Princess threw back her veil, revealing a pale, passionate face and a pair of bitter green eyes. "I had your letter this morning," she said briskly. "We have already agreed on a price should the book prove genuine, so if you will just produce the volume and allow me a few minutes to inspect it, we can conclude this business swiftly."

With a graceful gesture, the thief indicated the table, on which a battered volume bound in faded blue leather lay open.

Diaspad raised a skeptical eyebrow. "The book is not even sealed."

Penfyngon shrugged. "Unnecessary. You will see why, when you examine it more closely."

The Princess glided across the room, picked up the book, and turned over several pages. A frown creased her snowy brow; it was evident she was not pleased by what she saw. Curious, Calchas edged closer and craned his neck to look over her shoulder. He saw that the parchment was old and brittle, crumbling at the edges of the pages, and the writing was small, crabbed, and faded.

Diaspad leafed through the book, her displeasure growing more and more pronounced. "The hand *appears* to be Atlendor's and the book is old enough. . . . The diagrams, too, indicate something more than a journal or a book of household accounts. Nevertheless, I had expected something quite different."

"Had you so?" Penfyngon murmured. "And yet . . . the price agreed on was scarcely munificent, considering the risks I took in obtaining the volume."

"The price was more than fair. And I doubt this was the only or the most valuable item you took with you from Boadhagh's library," the Princess replied icily. "I am certain you compensated yourself *quite* handsomely for your time and trouble."

But then she appeared to change her mind, to become more gracious. "Well, as you say . . . you incurred some risk on my behalf, and the volume will make an interesting addition to my collection of curiosities." She closed the book and tucked it under her cloak. "Give the man his gold, Calchas."

Calchas obeyed her, then wordlessly followed his mother out of the room, down the creaking staircase, and through the tavern. But when they passed through the door and out into the stinking alley, the boy could contain his surprise no longer.

"But *why* did you buy it? *What* collection of curiosities? I never knew you collected worthless old books."

"Nor do I," said Diaspad, adjusting her veil. "And if I did," she continued in a low, excited voice, very different from the cool tones she had used in bargaining with Penfyngon, "then I do not think this particular volume would belong with them. I believe this book was Atlendor's Grimoire, and that it contains all of his most potent spells.

"Think of that," she said, as they made their way back toward the light at the end of the alley. "The secrets of Atlendor, Glastyn's old master. Soon, I will know everything Glastyn knows, and if my will be stronger, I shall emerge victorious from our next contest.''

''But the book is written in cipher, as you surely noticed,'' Calchas said, as they emerged from the alley and turned down another narrow lane. ''And without the key to that cipher, the book and its contents are worthless.''

''If it were not written in cipher—a cipher which others have labored in vain to decipher—were it not for that reason *accounted* worthless, the man who owned the book before might have guarded it more carefully.''

Calchas digested that. ''Yes, but you can't read it either,'' he said at last. ''Or can you?''

''I am not altogether certain, but there is something . . . decidedly familiar,'' Diaspad replied. ''It is possible that I may be able to read it after all, and that Altendor's secrets may very soon be my secrets as well.''

And the Great Lords of the realm gathered together on Christmas Eve to hold a feast at Dinas Moren. And the question that everyone asked was: "Who shall be King in Celydonn? Too long have we contended, too long has the Kingdom been divided. Shall we not, from among our own ranks, choose one to rule, swearing fealty to that one and peace and brotherhood among us all?" Yet there was no agreement among them as to who would be King.

Now, the wizard Glastyn had come to the feast, bringing with him Anwas, his foster son, and through all these discourses the wizard held his peace. But when the feasting was done and many were preparing to leave the hall, Glastyn rose from his place and, taking Anwas by the hand, presented him to the company, saying, "Here is one in whose veins flows the blood of many kings. Sinnoch's heir stands before you, for this boy is the last of Cynwal's noble line."

Then there was a great uproar in the hall, and many lords spoke in protest. "We do not know this boy or where he comes from. How could the line of Cynwal survive and we not know of it? Surely this is some jest or deceit of the wizard's."

But Glastyn silenced them all by raising his hand, and those who wished to speak found that Glastyn's spell was on them and not one word could they utter.

"Neither jest nor deceit," said the wizard. "And the truth of all I tell you shall be revealed through many signs and portents, for this is the season of miracles, and those who have eyes to see and wisdom to recognize the truth shall be satisfied."

Then Anwas opened his cloak, and on his breast blazed a great white jewel, and that was the Clach Ghealach (moon stone) the mightiest of sidhe-stones, that in times past had been the chiefest treasure of the High Kings. And the Lords of Celydonn were amazed and the power of speech returning to them they all cried out in wonder.

"That is but the first sign," said Glastyn.

—from The Great Book of St. Cybi

3.

A Season of Miracles

On Christmas Eve, the wind rose and the cold intensified. A hard frost formed on walkways and walls, on naked tree limbs and marble statues. Water dripping from eaves and overhanging turrets froze into bizarre, dreamlike figures of ice, and the snow piled up in high white drifts, until the castle and the town below took on the appearance of some fantastic confection lavishly adorned with marzipan and sugar icing.

Down in Treledig, the common-folk feasted on cockles, whiting, and plum porridge, on gingerbread, frumenty, and mince pies. And in stables, paddocks, and innyard, hostlers mixed up a steaming hot mash which the little stableboys, staggering under the weight of heavy wooden buckets, carried to the horses and cattle—for on Christmas Eve, the animals feasted, too.

Up in the castle on the hill, the guards toasted the season with hot elderberry wine. Cooks refeathered and gilded whole roasted peacocks and swans; the castle craftsmen wassailed the apple-trees in the kitchen garden, and throughout the castle children played noisy games of Hoodman Blind and Hunt the Slipper.

The Queen and her young attendants sat in the Solar sewing for all they were worth, putting the finishing touches on costumes for *The Masque of Three Shepherds* that was planned for Christmas day.

In the courtyard down below, there was an unusual amount of foot traffic moving between the dormitory assigned to the King's Esquires and a set of tiny rooms behind the Scriptorium. Squires and pages loaded themselves down with pillows and feather mattresses, furniture and assorted household goods. Balancing their awkward burdens carefully, they staggered up a long slippery flight of stairs, across the battlements, and through a series of doors and tunnels and gateways, many built so low that it was necessary to bend at the waist when passing through. Then the boys went back to the dormitory and loaded up again. Tryffin, Fflergant, and Garanwyn were moving into quarters better suited to their new status, and their friends had volunteered to help them.

"... though I don't see how I am to engage in any *serious*

debachery, with you and Tryffin on hand and everything so crowded,'' Fflergant said, as he and Garanwyn entered the bed-chamber. He deposited two stools and a small table in one corner. ''If that was what I had in mind, I might just as well have stayed in the dormitory.''

Garanwyn paused on the threshold. ''These rooms are certainly cozy and I daresay we'll have grand times here—imagine the luxury of coming and going exactly as we please!—but there is no denying that you and Tryffin fill up the place.''

He put the pewter plates and wine cups he had carried in down on the table, brushed the snow off his blue wool cloak, and wandered over by the fire. A pile of driftwood, carried up from the beach below, blazed on the hearth, bathing the rough stone walls in colored light: crimson, sapphire, gold, and sea-green.

''There is a well just outside the door,'' said Fflergant. ''Convenient for you, bringing in the wash water in the morning. I like mine tepid, if you please.''

''Yes, of course,'' Garanwyn replied absently, staring into the flames. Then, coming back to the present moment with a jolt: ''What did you say?''

''I said I like my wash water tepid. In a crystal ewer. And my clothes laid out neatly while I eat my breakfast.'' Fflergant dodged as Garanwyn took a playful swing at him. ''And here I thought you would appreciate the honor of waiting on the two of us hand and foot.''

''*After* you are knighted, and even then I shouldn't expect too much—I'm to be your squire-of-the-body not your bond-servant. And the pair of you such junior knights. . . .''

His voice faded out and his gaze returned to the fire. Fflergant regarded him, frowning. This sort of thing was becoming all too common. Fflergant took him by the shoulder and shook him gently. ''Wake up, for the love of God. I've never known such a lad for daydreaming and mooning about.''

''Sorry.'' Garanwyn took a deep breath. ''I was thinking . . . well, I was thinking these little rooms were well suited to our friends in Teirwaedd Morfa, and I was trying to imagine Arfondwy sitting there by the fire with her spindle and flax.''

''You are certain that was all?''

Garanwyn smiled. ''What else could there be?''

Fflergant shook his head, somehow unconvinced. But now the voices of other boys could be heard in the garden outside, and Fflergant was forced to let the subject drop.

Kilraen and Gofan came into the room, carrying between them a massive oak chest bound with heavy ropes.

"This just came . . . by wagon from Castell Maelduin," Kilraen explained breathlessly. The two boys carefully lowered the chest to the floor. "The men at the gate . . . hailed Tryffin as we went by. Tryffin said he would skin you alive '. . . if you opened the chest before he came."

"*Tryffin* said that?"

"Well, perhaps not in so many words," Kilraen admitted. "But there was something in his manner . . . I'm certain skinning alive came into it somewhere." He sat down atop the chest. "It's an odd thing about your brother: As good-tempered and soft-spoken as he is, he has only to smile in a certain way and chills crawl down my spine."

Fflergant nodded knowingly. "Yes. And dragons are also soft-spoken, I've heard—so long as it suits their purposes."

His brother appeared in the doorway a few minutes later. Kilraen moved from the chest to one of the beds and Tryffin took out his dagger, knelt down, and began sawing at the ropes that bound the chest. The ropes parted, Tryffin lifted the lid, and everyone crowded around to see what the chest contained.

"Your mother and your sisters have been busy with their needles," Gofan said, as Tryffin lifted out bright padded surcotes and richly embroidered banners, torses, mantling, and trappings for horses—all beautifully worked with appropriate heraldic devices: the dragon of Gwyngelli suitably differenced with the orle of an elder son for Fflergant, and Tryffin's own dragon and sunburst.

At the bottom of the chest were two oblong packages swathed in white silk. "Our swords," breathed Fflergant, and he and his brother exchanged a radiant glance.

They stared at the wrapped swords for a long moment, then, without touching them, Tryffin began methodically to repack the chest.

"But aren't you going to take them out and look at them?" Kilraen asked.

Tryffin shook his head. "That would be to invite the direst ill-fortune. Aye, laugh if you will, but these blades were forged in Tir Gwyngelli by our father's own swordsmith, and all the old rituals attended their making. In the Hidden Country, work on the sword a prince will carry begins on the very day he is born. We don't *need* to look at them, for the swords and every incident and portent that occurred during their making have been described to us a hundred times by the smiths at Castell Maelduin. And we aren't about to tempt fate by allowing anyone to tamper with them until just before the knighting ceremony.''

"Oh bother!" exclaimed Fand. "This thread has snapped again. I told you it would never do for working with these heavy velvets.''

Teleri looked up from her book and heaved a great sigh. It was difficult for her to study in the Solar amidst so much activity and noise, but the Queen had requested her company that afternoon, and she was determined to make the best use of the time that she could.

"I don't know why," Fand went on, "but I am incapable of setting a straight stitch today. Look at this hem. . . . It will all have to be taken out and done again.''

"Let me do it." Red-headed Megwen put her own needlework aside. "My gown is nearly finished and my eyes aren't tired. I would love to work on yours. . . . The rose and peacock-blue are lovely together.''

Teleri looked down at the page she had been studying, but her mind was not on the heavy copper-bound volume in her lap. She thought, instead, of the last ten bewildering days, and the unexpected kindness of the Queen's handmaidens.

There was no doubt that the other girls had gone out of their way to make her feel welcome. On the first day, there had been smiles and friendly words; on the second, Gwenlliant had offered to lend her a pretty gown, and Finola had begged for an opportunity to comb and dress her dark blond hair. By the third day, all the young ladies were offering to lend her their clothes and their jewels, and insisting that she accompany them into town on their quest for needles and cloth. Teleri began by rejecting these offers with a frightened shake of her head and an inarticulate protest, suspecting . . . she knew not what. But the offers had continued, no ulterior motive had immediately appeared, and so, finally, timidly, she responded to their overtures.

By now, however, she had a fair idea what it all meant—and none of it was motivated by the flattering interest they all displayed during the lessons she taught in her new stillroom. The Queen had said something about debts to be settled, and everything seemed to revolve around Ceilyn—whose name was mentioned frequently and whose sterling qualities (it seemed to

Teleri) were better appreciated in his absence than they ever had been before. *"When Ceilyn was here,"* the young women often said wistfully. When Ceilyn was there, no one had lacked for a dance partner, a willing messenger, or an escort into town. Under Ceilyn's watchful eye, the pages were cleaner and better behaved, the servants more respectful, and *"we never lacked for candles, or firewood, or the best wines."*

The girls were evidently suffering from guilty consciences because they had not treated Ceilyn well while he was there, had assumed (erroneously) that she and Ceilyn were betrothed or the next thing to it, and had adopted this remarkable method of making amends. *"Do try on this dress. If you like it you can keep it. I am certain Ceilyn would find it vastly becoming."* Teleri did not like to accept their favors under false pretenses, but she was too embarrassed to disillusion them.

Remembering all this, Teleri absently smoothed the skirt of her new blue gown, a gift from the Queen. It was a plain gown, but the cloth was good and the color brighter than anything she had worn in years. It startled her, sometimes, the feel of soft cloth against her skin, the flash of color, still unexpected, whenever she moved. But the shock was not an unpleasant one. She hoped she was not growing vain.

She looked up again when Fand left her chair, wandered over to one of the deep, arched windows, and stood frowning down at the snowy courtyard below.

"Is it another headache?" the Queen asked.

Teleri closed her book. "Have you tried drinking willow-bark tea?" she asked shyly.

"I will try anything. I am tired of feeling ill and out of sorts," said Fand, and she followed Teleri upstairs to the stillroom.

The stillroom was like and unlike the laboratory at the top of the Wizard's Tower. There was a large fireplace with a frieze of scallop shells, dancing sea-trows, and fish worked in white plaster above, and a brick furnace built into the wall to one side. Bundled herbs hung from the ceiling; the shelves were cluttered with books and bottles and alchemical apparatus. But the room was smaller and somehow pleasanter—perhaps because it lacked memories, either of impatient old wizards or impetuous young knights.

Fand sat in a high-backed mahogany chair by the fire and watched while Teleri heated an infusion of willow-bark and valerian in a little clay pot on the hearth.

"It smells horrid." Fand wrinkled her nose when Teleri ladled the infusion into a bowl and handed it over. She took a tentative sip. "And tastes even worse."

Yet the potion seemed to do her good, for her face cleared as she sipped the scalding liquid, and she eagerly held her bowl out for a second dose.

"It is nasty, but quite effective," she admitted between sips. "Is willow-bark good for the eyes?"

Teleri studied her carefully. Fand was a beauty and knew it. She always dressed her lustrous dark hair with special care, wore exactly the right colors to complement her fair skin and deep blue eyes, and carried herself with the grace and dignity of a queen. Yet it seemed to Teleri that there was something about Fand now, a look of discouragement, of bone-deep weariness, that dimmed her beauty.

"Brother Gildas thought that your eyes were troubling you?"

"He told me not to strain them by sewing when the light is poor. But how else am I to keep amused during the winter? There is little else to do, so long as we're all kept indoors. But I do not think my trouble is in my eyes, nor in my head, either. I think—I think the problem is in my heart. Could you . . . could you read my palm for me?" she asked unexpectedly.

"Oh dear, now I've offended you," she said, when Teleri did not reply. "I suppose only tinkers and gypsies tell fortunes, and you were trained for a wizard."

"No, I can read your palm." Teleri knelt down beside the chair and took the other girl's smooth right hand in both of her own. "Though it depends on what you want me to look for."

"I want to know if I will ever marry," Fand said breathlessly. "And what sort—what sort of man it will be.

"Not that I haven't been asked," she went on, as Teleri examined her palm. "I don't mean to boast, but I have had many offers, and some of them from men I really liked. Only I had to turn them all down because . . . because my family expects me to make a brilliant marriage."

Teleri looked up. "And do you want to make . . . a brilliant marriage?"

"Yes . . . no." Fand blushed. "The truth is, I do want to marry and have children—what woman doesn't, unless she has a religious vocation?—but I would rather have a kind husband, one I could love, than one who was rich and powerful and cold. But my parents and my brothers are counting on me to mend their fortunes, because I'm the eldest daughter and accounted the beauty of the family.

"It's not—not the blessing that everyone seems to think," she added, very close to tears. "I did hope, for a time, that Fflergant . . . I *like* him, and my parents would be so pleased . . . but now he's lost interest and I don't think that he ever will ask. I begin to fear that I may have turned down the others to no purpose . . . and perhaps no one will ever ask me again. I am nineteen—nineteen and not even betrothed. My mother had three children by the time she was my age."

"But of course someone will ask you," Teleri said, with perfect certainty. "You were born to marry a rich and generous man, to bear strong children, and to be given beautiful things."

Fand wiped her eyes. "You can see all that in my hand?" she asked wonderingly.

"In your palm, yes, but not only there." Teleri released her hand. "It is written on your face, I can read it in your eyes . . . and one day, in the Solar, when you bent down to stir the fire, I saw the gleam of a golden ring on your finger and a jeweled coronet shining in your hair."

Fand was silent for a time, absorbing all this. "It must be splendid," she said at last, "splendid and terrible, to know everything that is going to happen."

"But I don't," Teleri protested, sitting back on her heels. "I can only see things sometimes—and then only things that are very close or absolutely certain."

"Very close or absolutely certain," Fand repeated radiantly. "And will he be a young man, this rich and generous husband of mine?"

But this time Teleri shook her head. "That is something I cannot foresee."

"It doesn't matter." Fand's smile lost none of its brilliance. "He will love me and give me beautiful things, and I will be grateful and learn to love him."

On a sudden impulse, she reached up and unfastened a jeweled necklace that she wore. "The stones are worth little . . . it is a poor payment for your kindness. But it is a pretty thing and would go well with your new gown," she said, pressing the necklace into Teleri's hand.

"But I've done nothing, really." Teleri was certain the necklace was more valuable than Fand was willing to admit.

"But you have," Fand insisted. "You've cured my headache

and my—my heartache as well. And I want to give you something in return.''

There was little holiday spirit in the Princess Diaspad's luxurious bedchamber.

''This,'' Calchas said, with an elaborate shiver, turning away from a diamond-paned casement, ''has been the coldest and dullest winter I can remember. Cooped up inside, day after day, with no sign that the weather will ever improve.''

Though the hour was long past noon, his mother was still in her loose white shift, curled up in the middle of her enormous curtained bed in a nest of pillows and sleeping furs, with her long auburn hair hanging in a tangled mass over her shoulders. Yet she had been awake and industriously occupied for hours. Two fat yellow candles burned in sconces on either side of her bed and Atlendor's Grimoire lay open in her lap. There were ink stains on her fingers and on the scattered pages of hastily scrawled writing that covered most of the bed.

''I was certain *you* would plan something diverting for the holidays,'' Calchas went on accusingly. ''A masked ball, a practical joke, a new style in sleeves or jeweled headdresses . . . something. But all you ever do is brood over Atlendor's wretched book and those pages you keep scribbling.''

Diaspad put aside the piece of paper she had been studying. ''Have I neglected you? Sit here beside Mother, and we will plan something to keep you amused. Something for the New Year . . . yes, we really ought to arrange some diversion for New Year's Day—such a great occasion for your young friends from Gwyngelli.''

Calchas perched on the edge of the bed. ''You are thinking of the Midwinter Knightings? Some nasty surprises for our gallant young heroes? Oh yes, that would be amusing.''

He picked up the paper she had just put aside, ran a casual eye over the writing, and was about to toss it aside when a sentence in the middle of the page caused him to sit up straighter and read it aloud. ''*The Uses of Sidhe-Stones. Of the Great Talisman Stone of the Kings of Celydonn.* Where did you come by this?''

''In Atlendor's wretched book, as you are pleased to call it. I deciphered these pages last night and I have been considering the implications all day. I must say, the book looks to be more valuable than I had hoped.

"Deciphering the Grimoire was simple, indeed, absurdly so, because I was already familiar with a similar cipher, one Glastyn sometimes used."

Calchas drew back, stared at her disbelievingly. "You are telling me that Glastyn taught *you* one of his secret ciphers?"

"By all the Gods that ever were—no!" The Princess smiled with lazy good humor, playing with a strand of her brilliant auburn hair. "I do not suppose that Glastyn used the cipher in his own secret books. It was something he taught Cynwas one summer on Aderyn, when my brother was ill and bored. It kept Cynwas amused, the two of them sending letters in cipher back and forth. I doubt Glastyn remembered where or under what circumstances he himself learned the cipher, or he would never have used it to entertain a fractious child. Cynwas taught it to me a year or two later, under similar circumstances.

"He was sometimes moved to these little acts of kindness," she added, a trace of bitterness in her voice, "when Ysgafn was in Walgan, his other friends were from court, and there was no one else for him to amuse himself with. But who would have guessed that his careless act of kindness would serve me so well now?"

"Who indeed?" Calchas smiled at the irony. "And you say the book contains spells we can turn to our advantage?"

One of Diaspad's leopards jumped up on the bed, stretching its long golden body between them. "The first part of the book was of no interest to me," said Diaspad, "dealing as it does with all manner of tedious warnings and prohibitions. But the final pages contain material on sidhe-stones, as you have seen, and the kinds of powers that Glastyn invested in the Clach Ghealach before he placed it in Cynwas's crown."

With a lazy hand, she stroked the great cat's spotted head. "I must say, I never suspected how dangerous it could be, working with the large stones, or why it was necessary for Cynwas to keep the gem locked away—not merely for safekeeping, as it turns out. Oh, I knew that sidhe-stones often possess the power to ward off hostile influences and that the power inherent in any stone can be augmented and increased as Glastyn was able to augment the powers of the Clach Ghealach. What I did not know was that other applications are possible, and that the power of the stone can be used to destroy as well as to defend."

Calchas sighed. "It is a pity you sent Dyffryn's sidhe-stone off to Rhianedd. But of course, you never guessed that it might prove useful."

"Had I the stone in my keeping now, I would have liked to put Atlendor's theories to the test, and see if I could arouse its latent powers," the Princess agreed. "Yet perhaps it is best that I work with a stone whose qualities have already been revealed, and see what I can do with that.

"I have always been particularly adept," she added smugly, "at adaptations and alterations—what Glastyn characterized as an ability to pervert almost any spell more creative minds could conceive, and turn it to something utterly destructive. Not meant for a compliment you say, but coming from Glastyn—who in general was inclined to disparage my abilities—I consider it praise of no mean order."

"But lacking Dyffryn's stone, what stone do you plan to use? You don't mean—?"

"Oh but I do." Diaspad yawned and stretched. "Why should I *not* make use of the stone that lies nearest to my hand? I shall learn to use the Clach Ghealach, master its powers and teach it to serve me instead of Cynwas, then—"

"—then make me King of Celydonn," Calchas crowed. "Destroy Cynwas with his own sidhe-stone and put me in his place. That is what you plan, isn't it?"

"I thought I might try something of the sort . . . yes," his mother replied sweetly.

Then Cynwas fab Anwas was crowned at Dinas Moren. And after the coronation, he called all the noblemen and sons of noblemen of his Realm together, proclaiming a new Order of Knighthood to be awarded by the King's gift alone.

"And the insignia of the Order of the Lion of St. March shall be a green baldric with the winged lion worked in gold thread," said the King. *"And no man may aspire to that honor by right of birth alone, but must prove himself worthy by acts of valor, courtesy, and charity. And no man of a noble line shall be judged unworthy because he lacks gold or land, so long as his heart be good and his deeds courageous."*

•When winter came, the court prepared for feasting and merrymaking. And every day of the twelve days of Christmas, Cynwas created his knights.

—*from Glastyn's* Chronicles of the Isle of Celydonn

4.

The Knight at His Vigil

Fflergant woke with a fierce pounding in his head and a dull resentment against whoever had awakened him. "It can't be time already," he groaned, burying his head under a pillow.

Someone laughed, and Tryffin (his voice muffled by the intervening pillow) said: "He's still asleep. That, or he's forgotten what day this is."

Memory came flooding back. Today was New Year's Eve, and at dawn preparations for the knighting ceremony on the morrow would begin. Fflergant tossed the pillow aside, sat bolt upright in bed—and promptly wished that he had not. He winced, put a hand to the back of his head. "Too much celebration last night. Why didn't someone stop me?"

The other boys all laughed heartlessly. "I should have liked to see anyone try!" said Gofan.

Fflergant looked around him. The tiny bedchamber was unusually crowded this morning. Tryffin, of course, occupied the next bed. Gofan perched at the foot, and Garanwyn, Kilraen, and young Nefyn were setting up a trestle table by the fire. "What time is it? The sun's not up, I hope?"

"An hour before sunrise. The younger lads will bring in your breakfast soon. You'll have plenty of time to eat before your fast begins at dawn," said Gofan.

Fflergant climbed out of bed and reached for his clothes. He grinned at his brother. "To think the day has finally come. I've often doubted that it would."

"You both have endless ceremonies and rituals to endure first," Kilraen reminded them. "To say nothing of your vigil tonight."

The door opened, letting in a blast of cold air from the antechamber and two pages carrying covered trays. Garanwyn crossed the room and lifted one of the lids. A savory aroma filled the bedchamber. "Beef, stewed tripe, and eggs. Do you think you can face it after last night?"

Fflergant and Tryffin both agreed to try. While they finished dressing, more trays arrived. By the time the two soon-to-be-initiated knights joined their friends at the table, everything was properly arranged. Fflergant noted with approval the spiced apples and pears-in-wine, the pickled herring, fresh bread and cheese, and mushrooms fried with bacon. He helped himself to everything, but soon discovered that his appetite was less than he had thought. A few bites more than sufficed.

He looked to the other end of the table, where Gofan was offering Tryffin a dish of saffroned eels. "I think not," Tryffin said, in a curiously stifled voice.

"Before God!" Kilraen burst out, glancing from one pale face to the other. "The pair of you look more like men anticipating hanging than two knights about to receive the accolade."

Fflergant and his brother exchanged a wry glance. "Well . . . perhaps I will try the eels after all," Tryffin said, grinning sheepishly as he held out his plate. Fflergant forced himself to swallow a few more bites.

After that, the meal proceeded merrily, with jests and songs and rousing tales of adventure to honor the occasion. And if the two young princes ate less and displayed little enjoyment of their food, the others said nothing about it. When everyone had eaten his fill, the younger boys cleared away the dishes, and Fflergant and Tryffin began anxiously to prepare for the ceremonies ahead.

Garanwyn lingered after the other boys had gone. "You take this . . . more seriously than I had expected."

Fflergant slipped a crimson and gold surcote over his head, reached for his belt. "This is a solemn occasion, as you ought to be aware. Just wait until your own time comes, if you doubt me."

Garanwyn sat down at the foot of Fflergant's unmade bed. "It *is* a solemn occasion. But before God, I never expected to hear either of you say so. I always thought—well, you know: You're Princes of Tir Gwyngelli, and your father might have knighted you both anytime he chose."

Tryffin sat down on the other rumpled bed, pulled on his long boots of soft scarlet leather, one after the other. "But he could not create us Knights of the Order of the Lion of St. March. And to be a knight of that particular order means a great deal—even to a Prince of Tir Gwyngelli. Or did you forget that our father and our uncle both played a part in founding that order?"

Fflergant reached for his own boots. "Perhaps he thinks that we came here to serve at meal times and clean out the stables just for a lark?"

This time, it was Garanwyn's turn to grin sheepishly. "You always behaved as though it were something of a lark. And teased me because I took everything so seriously."

Fflergant shook his head. "You misunderstood entirely. It was yourself we didn't like to see you take so seriously."

Garanwyn picked up a pillow and heaved it at him. Fflergant caught it and tossed it back. "Still," Garanwyn said soberly, "it is strange to think that I never guessed how much we felt and thought in common. Stranger still to find it out, just when . . ."

"Just when . . . what?"

Garanwyn shrugged. "Just when . . . you are both about to be knighted and everything is going to change. Oh, we have treated it all as a joke so far, but after tomorrow you will be knights and I will be your squire, and if you tell me to do a thing . . . why then I will have to do it."

"But we always tell you what to do," said Tryffin. "We always have. We're older than you."

"Yes, but I rarely *listen*," Garanwyn pointed out. "After tomorrow, I will have to."

Someone knocked on the door. While Garanwyn went to answer it, Fflergant and Tryffin picked up their cloaks. Fergos fab Neol and two other knights waited outside, ready to escort Tryffin and Fflergant to the Earl Marshall.

Fflergant fastened his cloak over one shoulder. With a sinking feeling at the pit of his stomach, he followed his brother out the door.

The rest of that day passed in a blur. Fflergant and Tryffin spent hours closeted with Manogan and their two sponsoring knights, Dianach and Scilti, in the Marshall's rooms in the South Tower. There, they were instructed in the duties and obligations they were about to assume, then quizzed on all the finer points.

To neither boy was any of this new. Yet Fflergant felt an odd detachment even as he recited the familiar phrases.

"What are the Virtues appropriate to a knight?"

"Courage, humility, generosity, loyalty. Be cruel to your enemies, kind to your friends, humble to the weak. . . ."

About noon, his stomach began to growl alarmingly. His mouth was dry and his throat scratchy after answering so many questions. But his fast was just beginning; nearly a whole day must pass before his next meal. He wished that he had forced himself to eat when he had the chance.

Fergos appeared briefly in the afternoon, carrying a silver goblet, which he offered first to Tryffin, then to Fflergant. The cup contained water, not wine, but Fflergant accepted it gratefully and took a long drink. Afterward, his stomach felt emptier than before, but the water had eased the ache in his throat.

At last the older knights were satisfied. "You have learned the precepts well," said the Marshall. "I cannot fault you on a single item." He embraced his nephews warmly and then sent them on to Brother Dewi.

In his cold little cell, the monk heard them confess, assigned appropriate penances, and granted absolution. Then he proceeded to lecture them much as their sponsors and the Marshall had done.

"Aim always to sustain the right and confound those who do wrong to young maidens, widows, and orphans. And love the poor always, and above all the Holy Mother Church. . . ."

Unfortunately, Brother Dewi's cell was located near the kitchens and the delightful aromas issuing therefrom served as a constant distraction. Fflergant found that he thought less about his duty to protect widows and orphans and more about the meals he and his brother had already missed.

Finally, at sunset, Brother Dewi allowed them to return to their own rooms, there to prepare for the vigil. Two wooden tubs filled with steaming water awaited them in their bedchamber. Fflergant threw off his clothes, climbed into the nearest tub, and sank gratefully down into the warm water.

While Fflergant and Tryffin bathed, Fergos reappeared, armed with a pair of shears and a long, wicked-looking razor. He rattled the scissors suggestively. "Who will be first?"

Fflergant climbed out of the tub, wrapped a towel around his middle, and sat down on a stool by the fire.

"About time someone trimmed your hair," said Fergos, setting to work on Fflergant's shaggy blond mop. "I'll wager you've neither of you been near a pair of shears since you came back from Gwyngelli. A pretty pair of barbarians you do make!"

Fflergant listened with only half his attention to the banter that followed. The old jests about blue paint and goatskin tunics, all the superstitious nonsense equating the Hillfolk and the Sidhe—he had heard it all before.

If I really did have fairy blood, he thought, *I would conjure up a feast. Fairy food has no substance, so they say, but even an insubstantial feast would be welcome just now. And if it be nothing but air and moonshine . . . why then, so much the better. I could eat my fill without violating custom and breaking my fast, and I could be knighted in the morning with a clear conscience.*

As soon as Fergos left, Garanwyn picked up a broom. He swept up the hair from the floor and tossed it into the fire. Meanwhile, Fflergant and Tryffin dressed for their vigil, donning robes of coarse black wool.

"They say Ceilyn mac Cuel wore sackcloth during his vigil," mused Fflergant. He picked up one of the robes and pulled it over his head. "And a hairshirt underneath."

Everyone looked at Gofan, who had been Ceilyn's squire. "I can't imagine who spins these remarkable tales."

"As I recall," said Kilraen, "I first heard the story from you."

Gofan had the grace to blush. "What a fatuous young fool I must have been, spreading a tale like that. For the love of God, don't let it go any further! Imagine what would happen if . . .

when Ceilyn comes back . . . if he learned I had started that one!''

Fflergant picked up the cord which was to serve him as a belt, and knotted it around his waist. He looked over at Tryffin, who had already donned the hooded cowl that completed the outfit, lending him a decidedly clerical appearance. ''We look like a pair of penitent monks.''

There was a knock at the door, and Garanwyn threw it open to admit Scilti and Dianach. The two knights entered the room and stood by the fire warming their hands.

''You are determined, then, to attempt this ordeal?'' Scilti asked. The question was a formality, and the physical ordeal that faced the two young initiates was no more than a long, cold, sleepless night—yet it served to remind them that such a night, spent in prayer and meditation, opening oneself to higher forces, could be perilous in ways beyond the physical.

As was proper, Fflergant thought for a moment before replying, ''I am so determined,'' and Tryffin's answer came after like an echo.

''So be it, then,'' said Dianach.

The other boys, grown suddenly sober, picked up their cloaks and pinned them on. Garanwyn wrapped the swords in a length of crimson velvet, while Gofan and Kilraen began to gather up Fflergant's and Tryffin's armor. Down in the Chapel of St. March, a bell tolled, marking the hour of Compline, calling the two young princes to their vigil. Fflergant looked to his brother, took a deep breath, and walked to the door.

Outside, the night was clear and frosty. They crossed the torchlit courtyard in a solemn procession, Fflergant and Tryffin with their heads bowed, their hands concealed within the wide sleeves of their black robes.

Just outside the chapel, two cloaked and hooded figures stepped out of the shadows. They lowered their hoods, revealing themselves as the King and the Earl Marshall.

Fflergant and Tryffin knelt on the icy porch to receive the King's blessing, but Cynwas, in one of his sentimental moods, bade them rise and embraced them one after the other. ''You are good lads,'' he said, with a catch in his voice. ''I regret, now, that this hour was so long delayed.''

The interior of the chapel was damp and drafty, and the candles on the altar flickered wildly with every gust of chilly air. Fflergant found the place assigned to him, at the back of the church slightly to the left of the altar, and knelt down on the flagstone floor to pray. He bowed his head, clasped his hands in front of him, but no prayer formed in his mind.

He wondered if Tryffin, kneeling about twenty feet to his right, experienced similar difficulty composing his mind for prayer. He could hear the younger boys moving about in the front of the chapel, the clatter of metal as Garanwyn and Kilraen arranged his armor, sword, and shield at one end of the altar, and Tryffin's gear at the other.

Instead of a prayer, a doubt came into his mind. *Am I worthy to be here? Have I the right—simply because I've spent the requisite amount of time currying horses and polishing armor, learning to handle a weapon, and to parrot all the fine phrases I ought to have taken to heart? Am I here merely because it had become an embarrassment to deny me the rank any longer?*

Ages passed, and Garanwyn and Kilraen completed their task. After a whispered conference, the three squires moved past Fflergant. The hinges on the door at the back of the chapel creaked once, Fflergant heard Dianach say something on the other side, then the door slammed shut. Abandoning even the pretense of prayer, Fflergant opened his eyes.

Up beside the altar, his armor gleamed dully and the jewels in the hilt of his sword winked in the flickering candlelight. Above and behind the altar, the painted Lion of St. March spread his great golden wings. Fflergant shifted uncomfortably in his place, tried to concentrate on a row of curly-headed apostles carved on the chancel arch. Even through the thickness of his monklike wool robe, the floor was punishingly cold and hard. He knew he should welcome the discomfort—it would help him to stay awake during the long hours ahead.

Not that he was sleepy. Light-headed, that was it, light-headed and, curiously, no longer hungry. His stomach was a hard knot of anticipation. He had never felt like this before: the rising sense of excitement coupled with an odd detachment. He had never supposed it was possible to feel both at the same time. *Exalted, that is how I feel. Though I would have laughed if anyone else suggested the word.*

He knew that he ought to pray, but his mind whirled with all the precepts he had absorbed earlier, and he could not concentrate.

Time was, a man had to prove himself in battle, distinguish himself by acts of uncommon virtue—but what have I ever done that didn't come all too easily?

Have I been generous to the poor? How could I be otherwise, who never lacked for anything in my life? Have I been coura- geous? Foolhardy is the better word, blundering around in the marsh that night, risking not only my life but Garanwyn's and Tryffin's as well. Have I been virtuous? Well, I never caused any woman harm that I knew of, but neither have I denied myself the satisfaction of my desires. The truth is, I've gone through life without committing any serious wrong, simply because no pressing temptation ever came my way.

The long hours went dragging by. Twice, Brother Dewi came into the church to replace the candles on the altar. Every eternity or so, a bell tolled, marking the hour. Fflergant's eyelids began to feel heavy, his eyes gritty. His legs ached with cold and cramp and his back grew stiffer and stiffer. Excitement dwindled, to be replaced by a leaden disappointment.

What did I expect? Visions—like Ceilyn mac Cuel at his vigil? A lot of bloody nonsense, that sort of thing, and I said as much to Garanwyn when he spoke of them. Visions . . . why, I can't even pray. Have I made light of all the important things for so long that I can't behave as I ought, even on the most important night of my life? God help me—I've no right to be here at all!

But it was too late now to refuse the honor, too late to back out gracefully now that his name had been proclaimed and the arrangements had already been made. That would be to disap- point everyone and to insult the judgment of Cynwas and the other knights after they had declared him worthy.

Yet if I am not worthy now, may I not strive to become so? Finally, he was able to form a heart-felt prayer. *Dear God, make me worthy. Teach me what I must know and make me what I must be. And if it be thy will, send me a sign to strengthen my faith, that I may labor to become in truth all that a good knight should be.*

But nothing happened. No sight, no sound, no revelation— and dawn remained an eternity away.

In the morning, their uncle and the Lord Constable came to escort Fflergant and his brother from the chapel.

In their bedchamber, a roaring fire awaited them and a light breakfast of cakes, ale, and venison. But Garanwyn insisted they each take a cup of lamb's wool before eating. "Drink this first. It will be easier on your stomachs after your fast, and you wouldn't want to get sick in all the excitement."

The mild sweet mixture of cider, ale, and frothy new milk went down easily, allowing Fflergant and Tryffin to do ample justice to the rest of the meal. While they ate, Garanwyn laid out another change of clothes. Then they dressed again and waited, impatiently, for the Earl Marshall's summons.

Now it came about at Christmastide—it was a long time ago—
that all the birds of the air came together to celebrate the Twelve
Days of Christmas. There were proud strutting peacocks and
dull little sparrows, throstles, magpies, and rooks, cardinals
and gay popinjays, gossipy ducks and mallards, noble hawks
and eagles . . . all came together to celebrate the birth of our
Savior, in the winter woods.

But on New Year's Day—and a fine bright, frosty morning it
was—some of the birds fell out, and this was the question in
dispute among them: Which of their number had performed the
greater service when Our Lord was upon the earth? As it was
impossible to agree, they chose the owl to judge the matter, because she was the wisest.

A cock with a red head and golden spurs presented his argument first. "I was the herald who spread the tidings on that first
Christmas morning. I cried the news through town and countryside. And when Our Lord was betrayed and denied, I crowed
three times to mark the sad occasion."

The owl deliberated for some time, but in the end she decided
to deny the cock's claim. "For," she said, "a messenger is neither to be blamed nor commended for the tidings he brings,
whether they be welcome or unwelcome."

Then came the gentle stork with her white feathers and long
yellow bill. "I left my young in the nest," said the stork, "and
flew to the stable in Bethlehem. There I found the infant in a
cold, mean bed of straw. I plucked the feathers from my breast
and made a downy bed for him to rest upon. For that reason, I
have been the patron of infants ever since."

The owl allowed that the stork had performed a great service,
but decided to hear the next argument before she gave judgment.

Next came the robin with his bright eyes and showy red breast.
"It was cold in the stable where the baby slept in his downy
bed," said the robin, "and only a meager, dim, smoldering fire
illuminated that place, dying for lack of fuel. I fanned the fire
with my wings until the flames roared up, and I remained there
all night fanning the blaze while the infant Jesus slept. But to

this day, the mark of the fire is still on me.'' And the robin displayed his red breast.

The owl admitted that the robin, too, had performed an exemplary service, but she decided to hear the next argument before she rendered judgment.

The nightingale was the last to present an argument. *''I sang for joy with the heavenly host,''* said the little brown nightingale. *''When the angels sang cradle songs to lull the newborn baby to sleep, so great was my delight in the occasion that I burst into song. And that was a miracle, for until that day I had no more voice than a crow has, but since that time my song has been one of the most beautiful in all the world.''* And the nightingale began to sing. Those who heard her were enchanted, and they all admitted that she really had a charming voice.

So the owl made her decision. *''Yours was the greater reward,''* she said to the nightingale, *''and that was the judgment of Our Father in Heaven. Therefore, as his judgments are unfailingly just and appropriate, yours must have been the greater service.''*

All the birds agreed with that pronouncement, and praised the owl for her wisdom.

—from an ancient Celydonian Christmas Carol, freely adapted

5.

The Carol of the Birds

It was a blindingly brilliant morning, the sunlight dazzling on drifted snow in the courtyard, on the shapely white marble statues in Sidonwy's garden. The Queen and her handmaidens came out of the Mermaid Tower, in their gay holiday finery, red, yellow, and green, and crossed the garden in a demure procession. The high wooden pattens they wore to keep their slippers dry and their trailing skirts and fur-trimmed cloaks from dragging in the snow, forced them to maintain a slow and careful pace.

At the end of the procession came Teleri, equally sedate, though she had no train to worry her, nor under her full blue skirts any satin slippers or wooden pattens to plague her. She wore practical boots of soft grey leather.

Outside the Chapel of St. March, the King and his household awaited the Queen's coming. His esquires and pages had bundled up in cloaks and bright woolen scarves, layer upon layer. Whenever they spoke, their breath came out in big, white, painful puffs.

As Sidonwy drew near, the King stepped out to meet her, offering her the support of a velvet-clad arm. They exchanged as amused glance.

"Do not hurry yourself, my love, on my account—I beg you," murmured Cynwas, saluting her on one cold, rosy cheek. "To see you in such health and spirits is all that I could ask!"

The Queen sketched a playful courtesy, as low as she dared, and they both burst out laughing.

They grew sober as they entered the chapel. With the assistance of her pages, Sidonwy removed her pattens, then she took the King's arm and, together, they ascended a flight of stairs to the gallery.

The King and Queen took seats directly behind the gilded railing. Sidonwy motioned to Teleri to stand beside her, in Ceilyn's old place, and Teleri readily complied, moving closer to the rail. From that vantage point, she could see everything that happened on the floor below.

After Mass was celebrated, a rustle of excitement passed through the chapel. The King and Queen left the gallery, and the Princess and Calchas moved from the back to take their seats. Pages brought two small thrones and placed them on the steps below the altar.

As Cynwas and Sidonwy seated themselves on the thrones, the Lord Constable stationed himself behind the Queen, and the Earl Marshall brought in Cynwas's unsheathed Sword of State and assumed a position beside the King. Then everyone waited expectantly.

The double doors from the courtyard swung open. Fflergant and Tryffin entered the chapel, all in crimson and cloth of gold, their father's colors. Flanked by their sponsoring knights, they moved down the aisle, and two boys carrying their embroidered banners followed behind. Garanwyn came at the end of the procession, bearing on a satin cushion the insignia of knighthood, two white belts, two pairs of gilded spurs, and the special badge of that most exalted order, the Order of the Lion of St. March: two baldrics of green silk, embroidered with gold thread.

As Fflergant and Tryffin drew near the thrones, the Marshall stepped down to meet them. "What do you desire of Cynwas the King?"

"We would be knighted by the King's own hand." They spoke in unison: Tryffin steadily, Fflergant with just the slightest tremor in his voice.

The King appeared to consider, though everyone knew he had already reached his decision. Finally, he nodded. "Let them approach."

The Marshall stepped aside. Dianach and Scilti helped their former squires to remove their heavy outer garments, then Fflergant and his brother, clad only in their long linen shirts and woolen hose, knelt down on the lowest step. The King spoke again. "Have the candidates proven themselves upon the field of honor?"

"They have," replied the Marshall.

"Have they shown themselves worthy by acts of courtesy, charity, and mercy?"

"They have."

"Are they godly men, sons of the Church, duly baptized and confirmed?"

"They are."

"Then," said Cynwas, "I am determined to create them Knights of the Order of the Lion of St. March."

Solemnly, Dianach and Scilti began to arm the candidates. At first, no one noticed anything amiss. A vambrace slipped out of Scilti's hand, falling on the marble steps with a loud clatter. A leather strap broke. The buckles on Fflergant's greaves proved recalcitrant, causing Dianach to spend long minutes fastening them on. Minor incidents, but on an occasion such as this even a minor mishap might be taken as an ill-omen. As incident followed incident, mishap followed mishap, the congregation began to stir uneasily.

Finally, the candidates were armed. The Earl Marshall handed the King's sword to one of the banner bearers. Manogan and Ysgafn knelt on either side of Fflergant, to ceremoniously fasten on his gilded spurs. This they accomplished without difficulty, then moved on to Tryffin.

But as Garanwyn offered the second pair of spurs to the Marshall, he somehow cut his fingers on one of the sharp rowels. Horrified, he watched the bright blood run down his hand and stain the cuff of his linen shirt.

This was an omen so obvious and unfortunate that no one

could ignore it. The young banner bearers shifted nervously. All the color drained out of Fflergant's face. Someone had the presence of mind to produce a handkerchief and wrap it around Garanwyn's hand, while the boy stood with a stiff back and a flushed face, the very picture of humiliation.

As for the stoical Tryffin, he clenched his jaw and stared steadily at the floor, all the time his uncle and the Constable were buckling on his spurs.

Up in the gallery, Teleri watched all this with growing unease. At the very least, she thought, someone had ill-wished Fflergant and his brother. She turned to look at the Princess and Calchas. Diaspad watched the ceremony impassively, her face perfectly controlled, but Calchas could not conceal his mounting glee.

Calchas, of course, was bound to take satisfaction in such a turn of events, whatever the cause. But Teleri suspected there was more at work than ill-wishes or bad luck. Casual mischief caused by the Princess, meant to spoil the day for Tryffin and Fflergant? Perhaps. But Teleri saw a larger purpose as well. This series of petty mishaps when discussed later, endlessly repeated and repeatedly magnified, would cause irreparable damage to the popularity the two young princes now enjoyed both at court and among the superstitious populace.

Down on the chapel floor, the Marshall and the Constable had resumed their former places. The King prepared to dub the candidates. "With whose sword will you be knighted?"

"With the sword of our uncle, Manogan fab Menai," Fflergant replied. This, too, had previously been decided. The Marshall's sword appeared from a place behind the thrones, and Manogan laid it carefully across the King's legs. Cynwas took the scabbard in both his hands, rose, and grasped the hilt. For a moment, the blade stuck in the scabbard, then Cywnas drew it halfway out. Those closest to him gasped. The Queen pressed a hand to her mouth, as though she were about to be ill. The blade was tarnished and crusted with dried blood.

A sheen of perspiration appeared on Cynwas's brow. He quickly resheathed the blade, handed it scabbard and all over to the Lord Constable, and took the other sword out of the banner bearer's hands. Yet for all that, everyone had seen the state of the Marshall's sword. A shudder passed through the crowd. Several people crossed themselves or made other, less pious signs against ill-luck.

Teleri knew what Glastyn would do if he stood in her place

right now. He would counter Diaspad's tricks with a spell of his own, an illusion so marvelous, so utterly enchanting that it would completely eclipse everything that had preceded it. Teleri sighed. What a pity that Glastyn was not there, what a pity that she was not competent to act in his place.

The King held out the unblemished Sword of State. Fflergant put his right hand upon the jeweled hilt, and spoke in a low, tremulous voice. "I, Fflergant Dywel Cynfelyn fab Maelgwyn fab Menai fab Maelwas fab Garan fab Maelgwyn fab Maelduin fab Pwyll, do faithfully swear fealty and service to the Crown and Kingdom of Celydonn, and especially to thee, Cynwas Cadwy Moren Cynwal, to be thy man in good faith and without deception, in all that I do and leave undone, in all that I say and leave unspoken, and give to thee my homage entire, swearing to defend thee against all manner of men who live and can die, from this day henceforth. So say I, Fflergant Dywel Cynfelyn, Prince of Gwyngelli."

"And I, for my part, do swear to be thy good Lord, rewarding thy service according to thy merits, and take thee and thy household and all men sworn to thee under my special and benevolent protection, from this day henceforth. So say I, Cynwas Cadwy Moren Cynwal."

Then the King offered the sword to Tryffin, who, pale but composed, took the hilt and spoke out clearly, "I, Tryffin Dyffryn Cynfarch . . ." and continued on steadily until two candles toppled off the altar and broke on the steps before him. He stammered and lost his place. When no one prompted him, he was forced to begin all over again.

Up in the gallery, Teleri watched, frustrated by her own inability. If Glastyn were there . . . if Glastyn were there . . . Suddenly, she was sick to death of that old refrain. Glastyn was *not* there, but he had chosen her to stand in his place.

She felt a momentary vertigo, balanced on the edge of her destiny. She was not Glastyn, was not an adept. At best she had mastered but two-thirds of the Three Parts of Wisdom—but was that not enough? Physician and Scholar, Wizard and White Witch . . . she stood on the boundary between the physical and mental worlds.

Suddenly, she *knew*. She knew she could devise something worthy of Glastyn himself, something peculiarly appropriate to the season, the occasion, and the participants, something utterly beguiling.

Teleri took a deep breath. Then she closed her eyes and *imagined* a miracle.

As Cynwas lifted his sword to bestow the accolade on Fflergant, the blade began to shimmer with a golden light. Once, twice, thrice, he touched Fflergant's broad shoulders with the flat of the blade, and every time the great sword rose and fell, a sweet melody, as of chiming silver bells, filled the air.

A murmur of surprise rippled through the congregation. Up in the gallery, the Princess Diaspad stiffened; Calchas's jaw dropped. The King contrived to keep his composure, and went on to dub Tryffin. The golden light continued to glow, and the silver bells chimed three more times. As he handed the sword back to Manogan, the King and his Earl Marshall exchanged a puzzled glance.

At the King's bidding, Fflergant and his brother rose to their feet. Ceremoniously, Cynwas fastened one of the green silk baldrics over Fflergant's shoulder. He embraced the newly dubbed knight warmly, then moved on to bestow the same honors on Tryffin. The Queen left her throne and moved down to the middle step, ready to play her part in the ceremony.

She took up Fflergant's sword and slipped one of the white belts through the frog at the back of the scabbard. As Sidonwy moved toward Fflergant to gird on his sword, the group before the altar began to change.

The King, the Queen, and the two young princes seemed to grow in stature and in beauty. Towering figures of light, they became, majestic and superhumanly fair. To some watching, it seemed that Cynwas and the others had taken on the form of angels. But others, remembering the legends that surrounded Maelgwyn of Gwyngelli and his sons, were certain they had been granted a vision of the Sidhe: two golden-haired knights of Faerie, and their liege lord and lady, the King and Queen of England, clad all in green and scarlet.

Elves or angels—like participants in some ancient hierophantic ritual, they continued through the ceremony. "Wear this in token of your valor, and be you a good knight!" admonished the Queen, in accents of overpowering sweetness.

The Lord Constable, looking small, colorless, and insignificant in the presence of such majesty, took up Tryffin's sword and handed it to the Queen. As she fastened the swordbelt around Tryffin's hips, the very chapel began to change.

Stone pillars threw out leafy branches; walls, windows, roof, marble arches, and all faded away—no church of stone surrounded the stunned congregation, but a sunlit snowy pinewood, a chapel of living green. In the branches overhead, hundreds of birds perched: peacocks, cardinals, and bluejays, robins, magpies, and throstles, and a hundred other species, preening their vivid plumage and singing ancient hymns of joy. As one man, the congregation released a sigh of wonder and contentment.

Only for a moment could Teleri hold the illusion. It faded more rapidly than it had appeared, leaving behind nothing but a breath of pine and fresh air, and a few brilliant fluttering feathers that dissolved before they touched the floor.

At the end of the ceremony, Fflergant and Tryffin—diminished in size if not in radiance—left the chapel in a daze. An aura of supernatural heroism remained an almost palpable presence around them.

By that time, the Princess Diaspad had already abandoned her place in the gallery, descended the stairs in unseemly haste, and retired to her bedchamber to sulk.

Up in her bedchamber, the Princess paced the floor for hours, nostrils flaring, chest heaving, her anger unappeased. Calchas perched at the foot of her bed, silently watching her restless movements. Finally, he had to speak.

"Well, but you know . . . no one could expect Glastyn to turn up after such a long absence, just in time to spoil our plans."

Diaspad came to a sudden stop, turned her green-eyed glare upon her son. *"Glastyn?"* she asked, in a voice that might have shattered glass. "You think it was Glastyn who interfered with my plans?"

Calchas nodded his head. "W-wasn't it? But I thought . . . It was exactly like—"

Diaspad ground her teeth audibly. "It was *exactly* like something Glastyn might have done. Oh, it was a little childish at the beginning, the glowing sword and the silver bells, so cheap and obvious, but after that, it was worthy of Glastyn himself.

"The clever use of the superstitions concerning the Gwyngellach and the Sidhe . . . and then to include the King and the Queen—especially Sidonwy, who, at least in the eyes of the common-folk, can do no possible wrong—yes, that was a master touch! Nevertheless, who could it have been except the girl, and right under my very nose! Had she not taken me entirely by surprise, it would have been the worse for her.''

Calchas cleared his throat. ''The girl? I take it you mean . . . ?''

The Princess threw herself down in the silver chair by the fireplace, where an aromatic fire of cedar and spicewood blazed on the hearth. ''The little apprentice. Yes, I am certain we have her to thank for this morning's entertainment,'' said the Princess. Calchas slipped off the bed and sat down on the tygerskin rug at her feet.

A door opened and Prescelli came into the room, looking pale and discontented, carrying a pile of clean bed linens. She deposited her burden in a chest by the windows, then moved around the room, tidying as she went.

''You need not tell me,'' the Princess said to Calchas, ''that I underestimated the girl. I admit that I was wrong about her, that I never imagined she could conjure up a vision so strong, and true, and moving. But perhaps she is not so clever as she thinks.''

Slowly, the old, sweet, confident smile spread across Diaspad's face. ''She was foolish to reveal her powers to me, and over such a petty matter. She'll not find another opportunity to spoil my plans. Before I put any of my grander schemes into effect, I shall make certain to deal with Teleri ni Pendaren first!''

''I want to be there,'' Prescelli put in unexpectedly. ''I want to help you when you . . . do whatever it is that you plan to do to her.''

''You?'' Diaspad raised one painted eyebrow. ''What have my plans to do with you?''

Prescelli clasped and unclasped her hands. ''Your plans for Teleri mean a great deal to me. She has everything her own way now, everything. New clothes and new friends, a place in the Queen's household—*his* place in Sidonwy's confidence. For all the Queen says that *she* sent him away, I know it was something that Teleri did to him. And I won't stand by and watch calmly while she usurps his place.''

The Princess continued to smile. ''Ceilyn's place . . . Yes, I see. And your indignation has nothing to do with the fact that she also stands where you would like to be? Ceilyn's was not the only place left vacant in the Queen's household.''

Prescelli flushed. ''It's true,'' she admitted defiantly. ''I enjoyed more prestige as the Queen's handmaiden than I do as your drudge! Supposing I am jealous? All the more reason for me to help you bring her down.''

"But I don't mean merely to *bring her down*, as you put it," Diaspad explained with exaggerated patience. "I mean to put her out of my way entirely. I mean to destroy her utterly."

Prescelli hesitated. Then she took a deep breath. "Then let me do it for you. I promise I won't flinch. I will strike the blow, administer the draft—whatever is required."

"Know, then," said the wizard Glastyn, *"that there is Unity in all things, an animating spirit that permeates both the corporeal and earthy and the subtle and invisible, making them one and the same. Therefore, it is no great thing to take water from the air, or air from the fire, or extract fire from the earth."*

The little girl considered his words long and carefully. "By what methods," she asked at last, *"does the Alchemist accomplish these things?"*

"The airy substance and the earthy, once divided, display a great attraction one to the other," said the wizard. *"Which, brought together in the proper season, will unite. All this may be accomplished through two effective virtues: Quicksilver and Sulphur."*

6.

Footprints in the Snow

On Twelfth Night, the King proclaimed a three-day tourney to commence on St. Valentine's Day. The castle began to buzz with activity and excitement. The first tournament to be held at Caer Cadwy in over two years—and only five weeks to prepare for it! Everyone accepted the challenge with wild enthusiasm.

Such a rubbing of armor, repairing of harness, and grooming of horses as followed! Middle-aged warriors who had not drawn steel in years took out their swords and polished them, and the younger men plagued the castle metalsmiths and armorers with so many commissions it seemed unlikely they would all be filled within so short a space of time.

For a solid week, the practice yard rang with the clash of steel, the lists resounded with the jingle of chainmail against plate, the thunder of hooves, and the thwack of a blunted lance meeting a quintain full force. When heavy snows drove everyone indoors, some of the keener spirits set up a practice hall in the cellar beneath the armory.

The ladies, too, had their preparations to make: banners and surcotes to appliqué and embroider for brothers, husbands, and sweethearts; favors to devise; new gowns to be stitched and old ones to refurbish. In a sudden surge of ambition, the Queen and her handmaidens vowed to provide all the pages with new livery emblazoned with the royal sea-lion badge (a fantastical hybrid combining the distinctive features of the King's winged lion and Sidonwy's heraldic mermaid) in green velvet.

And everyone said that the grand old days, the days of chivalry and adventure, were come again. Were not the King and Queen one in heart and mind, as they had not been in all the years since Glastyn disappeared? Had not two promising young knights been dubbed among wonders and portents of even greater things to come? And if a new Court Wizard had come to replace the old—standing not at the King's side, but at the Queen's—that did not cast doubt on the validity of anything they had witnessed. Quite the contrary. It was merely further proof that the proper order of things was now restored.

Teleri, too, took inspiration from the stirring events that marked the Midwinter Knightings—the more so because she knew how it had all come about. *She* had taken charge, had stepped in to fill Glastyn's shoes and—amazingly—had not been found wanting. Power had moved in her. And it had all seemed so right, so easy and natural, that she could only wonder now why she had hesitated for so many years to claim her power and take her rightful place.

She started to move more of Glastyn's books and apparatus into her new rooms in the Mermaid Tower. Before long, her stillroom was as cluttered and disorganized as the laboratory had ever been. She spent the better part of a week restoring order. Then, no longer satisfied merely to study the arts magical, she set about acquiring the practical experience she needed.

Night after night, she denied herself rest, staying up past midnight, burning incense, drawing magic figures in chalk upon the floor, or devising elaborate alchemical constructions of glass, exploring the uses and the possibilities of her powers, becoming in fact the sorceress she was by education.

But Teleri brought more from the Wizard's Tower than books and pentacles and green glass bottles. The old tabby cat— always, before, Glastyn's cat and not Teleri's—surprised the young sorceress by following her into her new rooms, inspecting the premises, and returning a day later with two blind kittens, tiger-yellow and silver-grey. She carried each one in by the scruff of the neck and deposited it on the hearth. When it became obvious that the tabby and her kittens had come to stay, Teleri brought them a basket lined with soft rags, and there they took up residence.

Within a few days, the kittens opened their eyes. Soon, they began to explore their new surroundings. They hunted in all the odd corners and cupboards in the stillroom and in Teleri's adjoining bedchamber. They stalked shadows, pounced on dustballs, and left their tiny footprints in the ashes on the hearth.

Teleri christened them Sulphur and Mercury, proper names for an Alchemist's cats. She allowed them to follow her around the stillroom, to curl up in her lap when she studied, or to perch, one on each shoulder, the better to observe her experiments.

She was absorbed in one such experiment—creating a miniature thunderstorm inside a glass vessel—late one evening, when a hesitant tapping at the stillroom door broke her concentration. The tiny thunderstorm lost form; drops of water condensed on the sides of the alembic.

Annoyed by the interruption, Teleri considered ignoring the summons altogether. Whoever had come calling at this unseemly hour could just as well come again at a more reasonable time. But Mercury leapt from her shoulder to the table to the floor, and bumped up impatiently against Teleri's legs.

"Oh, very well." She followed the grey kitten across the room. "I suppose I will have no peace until I satisfy your curiosity." Teleri threw open the door, and found Garanwyn and his little sister, Gwenlliant, waiting on the other side.

Not very graciously, she invited them in.

"I beg your pardon. I know it is late," said Garanwyn. "We can come again another time, if you like."

Teleri softened considerably; they both looked so lost, and frightened, and hesitant to approach her. "Come in, sit down, and tell me how I can help you."

They took their seats by the fire: Garanwyn on a stool, Gwenlliant on the hearth rug at his feet. Teleri brought the high-backed chair for herself.

The boy took a deep breath. "My sister and I have reason to believe that someone has been tampering with her mind."

Startled, Teleri looked at the child. Gwenlliant blushed and nodded her head.

"I believe," Garanwyn said slowly, "that we can trust you.

So I might as well begin by telling you, in case it makes any difference, that Gwenlliant sometimes sees things that other people don't see, and hears things that other people don't hear.''

Teleri nodded. ''I knew that.''

''You knew that?'' Garanwyn was taken aback. Until now, he had supposed that Gwenlliant's abilities had been successfully kept secret. But then it occurred to him that it was Teleri's business to know these things.

''I also know,'' Teleri said, ''that gifted as your sister is, yet untrained in the uses of that gift, Gwenlliant is susceptible to certain influences, and weak, where a trained gift would be strong, in resisting them.''

Garanwyn nodded. ''Yes, I understand all that. It is a gift—though I used to believe otherwise—and she has always been susceptible, as you say.''

He hesitated. ''This evening after supper, Gwenlliant came to me and she told me that certain—certain *kinds* of thoughts keep coming into her mind, entirely unbidden, and try as she might to put them aside, she simply cannot banish them.

''Well, I know that children do, sometimes, have nasty little minds,'' he admitted frankly. ''But these—these daydreams of Gwenlliant's go far beyond that.''

Gwenlliant blushed even pinker and hid her face in her hands. ''They are shocking and wicked and—and actually perverse,'' Garanwyn went on.

''And I take it that Gwenlliant . . . was equally shocked by these daydreams?''

Garanwyn nodded emphatically. ''Shocked and disgusted and absolutely terrified. She said—she said she felt as though someone had laid dirty hands on her mind.

''I will admit,'' said Garanwyn, ''that my first thought was to go to one of the Brothers for an exorcism. But then I thought: She goes to Mass practically every day, and takes Communion without the least resistance or ill-effect. So I don't believe she is possessed by demons—it must be something else.''

Teleri gazed at the miserable little figure hunched up on her hearth rug. There was no doubt that the child had been violated—as cruelly and wickedly used as if the assault had been a physical one. But like Garanwyn, Teleri suspected some human agency. ''I think you must be right. Someone is tampering with Gwenlliant's mind. But who would want to do such a thing to your sister? Have you any idea?''

Garanwyn hesitated again. "Well, it must be someone within the walls of Caer Cadwy—because the Clach Ghealach wards us from all outside influences, doesn't it? And I believe I do know someone with the knowledge and the inclination to do this vile thing. Only . . . I dare not accuse him openly.

"There was an incident last winter—of a different nature but equally nasty in its way. Calchas fab Corfil tried to lure Gwenlliant into Black Magic, but Fflergant and Tryffin and I found out and prevented him." Garanwyn rose abruptly and began to pace the floor. "Calchas said then that Gwenlliant was the witch and he completely innocent, drawn in against his will. We didn't believe him, of course, but others might . . . others might, and then . . ."

Teleri nodded. "Yes, however strongly you may suspect Calchas, it would not do to make any accusations you cannot prove or drag your sister's name through the mud. This is a matter we should deal with privately. I have reasons of my own to believe what you say, but others might not be inclined to do so.

"Then, too," she added thoughtfully, "just because it *could* be Calchas, we should not assume that it *is*."

"But who else could possibly want to torment Gwenlliant in—in that particular way?" Garanwyn asked. "She's just—just a little girl." Garanwyn looked sick at the thought that someone unknown might have designs on his sister.

"Tormenting your sister may not be the object," said Teleri, rising and walking over to the shelves. "I believe Gwenlliant has fallen under the influence of a sort of love charm, but another lady, perhaps older, may be the intended victim, and Gwenlliant affected quite by accident because she is so vulnerable. Those who use these charms refuse to consider the *violation* involved, but there are few men wicked enough to use one on a child."

Teleri began to rummage through the crowded shelves. "But however it comes about, I would counsel you to protect Gwenlliant, rather than seek to prove anything against Calchas or to retaliate."

Garanwyn began to look hopeful. "Protect her . . . yes. And you know how to shield her from future intrusions?"

"Oh yes, there are many ways," said Teleri. "I have a charm here, somewhere, that may serve the purpose.

"But truly," she added in a low voice, so that Gwenlliant should not hear her, "any sort of charm or trinket should be regarded as only a temporary solution. Such things are easily lost or misplaced. It would be better if Gwenlliant learned to protect herself. No, I do not mean that she should take up magic as a serious study, but I do think she would benefit from some instruction in the uses and misuses of her gift. There are disciplines suitable to a child her age, which I learned when Glastyn first brought me here, and I would willingly teach them to Gwenlliant. That is, if you would not object."

"I do not object," Garanwyn replied, without hesitation. "In fact, that would make everything much easier. I have been thinking, just lately, that I might not always be on hand to protect Gwenlliant when she needed it. And I think I could—I could follow my heart with a clear conscience, if I knew Gwenlliant had the benefit of your instruction.

"I don't know why I never thought of it before," he added. "If Gwenlliant's wild talents are unacceptable, why then of course she must study wizardry."

Teleri smiled. "The name of Wizard hardly insures respectability or acceptance—not when one is young and a female and only partially trained. There will always be those who are ready to accuse any woman with talent of witchcraft. Yet Gwenlliant is well-liked; she has friends in high places who will always think the best of her, if they can. I believe that is another gift of hers—a royal one, inherited from her princely ancestors—to be loved and protected by others, all the days of her life."

Teleri found what she was looking for: a small wooden casket. She opened the box and took out a silver disk, inscribed with cabalistic symbols, dangling from a thin chain.

"Yes," said Garanwyn. "I had noticed that about her before, though I didn't know how to name it. And yet . . ." He drew closer, lowered his voice, ". . . that particular gift is not infallible, you know. Calchas—if it *is* Calchas—Calchas does not love Gwenlliant or wish to protect her."

Teleri thought about that. "I am hardly expert in matters of love, being new to the emotion myself," she said, gazing wistfully at the pale-haired little girl. "But I have read histories, ancient sagas, poetry . . . and it seems to me that love is a powerful motivation, but not one that invariably motivates men toward good. I think, perhaps, that Calchas does love Gwenlliant, in his own way and as far as he is able. And that could be just as dangerous as if he hated her."

Garanwyn shuddered. "But surely there is more to love than a desire for possession."

"Yes, there must be. When love is strong, the product of a healthy mind and heart," Teleri agreed. "But as for Calchas: Speaking as a physician I would say that Calchas is diseased in the mind and sick at heart, and this ugly, twisted, grasping kind of love is all that he can feel."

At Candlemas, the holly and mistletoe, the wreaths of dry crumbling pine and fragrant laurel, all came down. The last day of the Christmas season passed with few celebrations to mark it.

Teleri helped the other young women to take down the greenery in the Solar, and cast it on the fire. Then the girls kissed each other in the spirit of the departing season, and retired early to bed. All but Teleri, who remained by one of the large fireplaces, breathing the sweet smoke of the burning bay, watching the pine boughs snap and crackle and explode.

Pictures in the fire . . . There had been a time when the dancing flames had been as good as any storybook. Knights and ladies, magicians and monsters, all had played out their histories on Teleri's hearth. But now, when she gazed into the heart of the fire, all she could see were the bright dark eyes of forest creatures . . . foxes, squirrels, and badgers . . . rabbits, deer, and hedgehogs . . . watching her warily.

She turned away from the fireplace, climbed the long staircase to her own rooms. She was weary; her eyes were too dry and heavy for study. She put down a bowl of cream for the kittens, brushed out her hair, and crawled into bed. Yet it was not possible to change the habit of weeks. Her mind remained restlessly wide awake for hours, though her body cried out for sleep. When she finally dozed off, she dreamed the whole night long.

She dreamed she walked through the snow, following a trail of bloody footprints. *A beggar has passed this way,* she thought. *A beggar . . . or a holy man doing penance, walking barefoot in the snow.* She hurried to catch up with him, but it was not easy running through the high white drifts. Soon, she was out of breath, and her limbs numb and leaden with the cold.

The footprints led her to a copse of trees: green holly and laurel and bare, twisted oaks. Under an oak tree sat a hunched figure in dirty rags, an ancient beggar with a long white beard covering his breast. Yet as she drew nearer, the beggar rose to his feet, and she saw that he was not an old man, as she had first supposed, but young and strong and straight.

A bend in the path between the trees obscured her view for a moment, and when she reached the oak tree the beggar was gone. There were no signs of him anywhere to be seen, only the line of footprints, blood-tinged as before.

Out in the snowy fields again, the wind began to rise, a wind that called to her with many voices, baying and howling like a pack of wolves. Suddenly, the tracks changed. No longer footprints, they were now the clearly marked pawprints of some large predator. Frightened, Teleri turned back, but the howling followed after her.

She knew then what quarry the pack was hunting.

The wolf ran at an effortless, mile-eating pace. Every now and then, he paused, to sniff at a tree or bush, to taste and test the frosty air. Then he set off again at the same easy gait, across the snowy fields.

Late in the morning, he discovered the tracks of a small horse or pony. The scent was fresh, the trail strongly marked. The wolf's stomach rumbled; he had not tasted meat in two days. He followed the trail, quickened his pace as the scent grew stronger.

The tracks led him up a gentle incline, then up a steep wooded slope, along a broad smooth path meandering through the trees. At the top of the hill, the trees thinned. The wolf stood on the crest, a breeze ruffling his shaggy grey fur.

He spotted his quarry at the bottom of the incline: a small, nervous pony, and an even smaller human female bundled up in cloaks and scarves. The pony had caught wind of him; she whickered and shied in distress. The little human slid out of the saddle and moved to the pony's head, trying futilely to calm her.

The wolf crouched low, considering how and when to attack. But something attracted the girl's attention. She looked up and spotted him waiting at the top of the hill. But instead of re-mounting or running, she tied the pony to a bush and started up the incline.

His hackles rose. . . . Then the wind changed, bringing her scent, oddly familiar. Something twisted inside him, and a moment later the wolf was gone. In his place sat a ragged young man who crouched in the snow, shivering, not with the cold but some strong emotion.

• • •

By the time Teleri reached him, Ceilyn had regained some measure of control.

"You!" he said indignantly. "What in the name of God are *you* doing here?"

Teleri drew back. "I thought you wanted me to come. I thought I heard you calling me last night."

Ceilyn shook his head. "Calling you? No, I've better sense than that, even if you have not." Her image was distorted in his eyes; even now, after so many transformations, he needed time to adjust to his altered perceptions. "Wolves roam these parts, in case you didn't know it. And some of them, I should imagine, are considerably less reluctant, this time of year, to taste human flesh."

"I know it," she said, kneeling in the snow beside him.

Gradually, his vision adjusted. With a shock, he took in her blue wool cloak, the scarf of furs wrapped around her neck. Her hood, thrown back, displayed a lining of silky white rabbit skins, her fine ash-blond hair had been braided and dressed in a new way, and she wore dangling earrings of gold and tiny glittering stones. She looked like all the other young women he had known at court—and nothing at all like Teleri.

A terrible suspicion took hold of him. "Where did you get those clothes? Holy Mother of God! Who gave them to you?"

"They came from the Queen. I didn't *steal* them, Ceilyn," she protested, misunderstanding him entirely.

"Steal them? No, of course not. I never thought—" But he could hardly tell her what he had thought. Already, he felt ashamed for thinking it.

"The Queen?" He frowned, failing to make sense of that.

"I have joined the Queen's household," she said. "I am Sidonwy's physician now. Other things have changed as well . . . so many things. And Fflergant and Tryffin were knighted on New Year's Day."

His face cleared. "It was about time that Cynwas came to his senses. I am glad to hear it. Though it may complicate things for me, if I ever go back. Fflergant and his brother fancy they have a quarrel with me, one they wouldn't be slow to press, now they are free to challenge me."

Teleri's eyes filled with tears. "I hoped you would come back with me today."

Ceilyn scowled. "Go back? Why should I? I'm not needed, am I?" He rose awkwardly to his feet, offered Teleri a hand up.

Her hand was cold to his touch, and she seemed strangely reluctant to relinquish her grip.

"Not needed, but sorely missed," she said. "I sometimes think that you are Glastyn's true successor, not I. People always speak of you the same way they used to speak of him—not a day goes by but your name comes up. I know that hardly anyone valued you when you were there, but I—they all feel differently since you left."

She put her hands inside her cloak to warm them. "There is to be a tournament in honor of St. Valentine. I don't know how it started but there is a story circulating through the castle that you will be back in time to fight in the tourney."

Ceilyn ground his teeth. "I can guess who started that story and I am tempted to go back just to settle with young Gofan. He always was too eager to spread talk about me, though I warned him time and again to guard his tongue."

The hard look in his eyes softened. "Ah well, wishful thinking, I expect. Gofan ought to be knighted this spring, but that can't happen if there is no one to sponsor him, and he can hardly attach himself to another knight until I`release him." Ceilyn frowned again. "But what of you? I thought people might blame you for my disappearance."

Teleri shook her head, wrapped her cloak more closely around her. "The Queen tells everyone that she sent you off on some mysterious errand."

Ceilyn passed a grimy hand through his tangled hair. "I suppose she did at that. She told me to do anything that was necessary to make peace with myself."

"And haven't you made peace with yourself?" Teleri asked wistfully. "Aren't you ready to come home yet?"

"No," he said wearily. "I have found peace . . . but I fear I would lose it again if I ever returned to Caer Cadwy. It is much easier being a wolf than it is a man . . . living by instinct without useless regrets. It is a physically demanding life, but blessedly uncomplicated.

"The truth is," he concluded, "I don't know when, or even if, I will ever be ready to go back."

7.

An Assault on the Castle of Love

Teleri stood in the middle of the laboratory, looking around
her. The room had a forlorn air, so many of the books, so much
of the equipment missing. She felt a little like a thief, sneaking
into the Wizard's Tower in Glastyn's absence and taking all his
things. Yet Glastyn was not coming back and everything in the
tower belonged to Teleri—she had finally accepted the truth of
that, and was learning to accept other, equally unpleasant truths
as well.

She began to gather together the volumes she had come for,
the last of the magic books and herbals. The other books: ge-
nealogies, gardening books, tomes of folk-lore, poetry, and history . . . they would all have to stay where they were. The shelves
in her new quarters would not hold so much as a single volume
more, after she added her present load.

She left the Wizard's Tower, locking the laboratory door and
the one at the bottom of the steps behind her. There was a

strange finality in the sound the key made turning in the lock. Then she scurried across the courtyard, keeping mostly to the shadows, hoping to reach her own rooms without meeting anyone.

For the price of Teleri's newfound respectability was her cherished privacy. A dozen times a day, the castle folk approached her, seeking her services as a physician or some charm or spell against the myriad evils the flesh is heir to. These were trying times, as everyone agreed, and what better protection could anyone ask than a trinket or a few scribbled words on a piece of parchment, straight from the hands of the Queen's new Wizard?

Teleri entered the Mermaid Tower, hurried down a short corridor, and climbed a twisting back stair, where tritons, mermaids, and dolphins carved in dark walnut formed the balustrade. She was about to congratulate herself on the success of her maneuvers, when a movement on the landing above, just outside her apartments, dashed her hopes.

Teleri sighed. She would do her duty, listen patiently, and offer what help she could. Then she would go into her own rooms and lock out the world, at least for the night. By the time she reached the landing, she had assumed an expression of sympathetic interest.

Her visitor moved into a circle of torchlight beside her door. He was a burly fellow with black hair and huge hands: one of the castle craftsmen, a blacksmith. He muttered an apology for coming so late.

"But it's for my wife's sake I've come. She's very near her time. If you would find a moment to step around and take a look at her, we would be that grateful."

"Your wife . . . she is not well?" Teleri's face mirrored her sudden concern. Over the years, she had helped to deliver many babies, but the care of pregnant women was the province of midwives, capable women who only called in a physician if the mother became ill or some serious complication developed during delivery.

The smith looked down at his feet, as if to apologize for bothering her with so trivial a matter. "As well as might be. But she had a terrible hard time when the last one was born. This time, the midwife thought a doctor ought to look at her beforehand, just to be certain that all is well. I was for asking Brother Gildas, but she's taken it into her head to see you. Says that a woman, even a young maid like yourself, understands more about child-birth than any man, and he a celibate monk.''

Teleri suppressed a smile, reflecting that it would be difficult to find a woman anywhere in Celydonn who had less experience of the feminine mysteries. And yet, unexpectedly, she felt a warm stirring of sympathy for the mother-to-be.

"I will come tomorrow, early. Or, if the pains should begin tonight, send for me at once.''

The blacksmith thanked her and withdrew. Teleri shifted her burden of books, opened the door, and stepped into the still-room.

In a chair by the fire, his arms folded across his chest, sat Ceilyn mac Cuel, with a kitten perched on either shoulder, and the old tabby curled at his feet. Teleri took a step backward, and the magic books and herbals slipped from her suddenly slack-ened grip and fell to the floor with a crash. Startled, the kittens jumped down and scuttled out of the room. The tabby rose slowly with a look of pure annoyance, and followed the kittens out of the room at a more leisurely pace.

"C-Ceilyn,'' Teleri said weakly. She stooped to retrieve the scattered volumes, but Ceilyn left his seat and took the books out of her hand. "Allow me.''

Numbly, she watched him gather the books into a pile. She saw that he had washed, trimmed his hair, and exchanged his dirty rags for clean garments of green wool and a pair of parti-colored hose. Superficially, he looked much the same, leaner and tougher perhaps, but the old Ceilyn, fastidious and well-mannered. Yet there was a predatory quality to his movements, a wildness in his glance, that was a little frightening.

"Have—have you seen the Queen? Does she know you are here?''

Ceilyn added a last book to the stack, an herbal bound in green leather. "How else should I have known where to find you?'' He straightened up. "Where did you want these?''

"Put them down . . . anywhere.'' Teleri made a vague gesture and Ceilyn deposited the volumes with a thud on the nearest table.

"I must say,'' he said harshly, "that you hardly seem pleased to see me.''

"You startled me, that is all.'' Remembering his early reluc-tance to join the wolves, his fear that he might somehow lose himself, she realized that the Ceilyn she knew might be lost indeed, somewhere out there in the snowy fields. She was uncertain what she ought to feel toward this dangerous young stranger who had returned to Caer Cadwy in his place.

"You did say, yesterday, that you weren't planning to come back," she said. "What made you change your mind?" She sat down on the three-legged stool.

Ceilyn took the chair again, crossed his arms, and regarded her with a bright, hostile gaze. "Can't you guess? It was for the honor of carrying your favor into battle that I returned. Why else?"

Teleri turned pink, uncertain whether he was mocking her. "I can hardly believe that you returned for my sake—not when you speak so, and glare at me as though you hated me."

The expression in his eyes softened. "I'm sorry. It isn't you, not really. I just find it all more difficult than I had expected." He glanced around the room. "So much has changed. You did warn me, but somehow I wasn't prepared. I still expected to find you in the Wizard's Tower, exactly as before. It is disconcerting to see you and all the familiar things in these new surroundings."

He leaned back in the chair, suddenly weary. "As for those things that have remained the same . . . the sounds and the smells, the people and the confusion . . . God knows, those things used to irritate me, but now—now I feel as if every nerve in my body was an open wound." He shuddered. "I can't believe that I actually lived in this place."

"Then why did you come back?" she asked again softly.

Ceilyn shook his head. "My capacity for self-punishment is apparently endless. And seeing you reminded me of all the things I had tried to forget. I came . . . simply because I could no longer stay away."

Early the next morning, Ceilyn walked down to the stables to visit Tegillus and see how the chestnut gelding had fared during his absence. Tegillus looked sleek and well-cared-for, but Ceilyn made a careful inspection anyway, while a nervous Gofan stood outside the stall, waiting for him to pass judgment.

"He looks fit enough," the young knight pronounced at last, patting a chestnut flank. "Has he been exercised?"

"Every day that the weather was fine," his squire assured him. "And I took him down to the lists, two or three times last week, and put him through his paces."

Almost, Ceilyn smiled. "That would account, no doubt, for the fact that my return surprised practically no one," he said dryly. "But what gave *you* the idea I would be back in time for the tourney?"

Gofan shrugged. "The first tournament in two long years—I couldn't imagine any circumstance that could keep you away."

This time, Ceilyn did smile. But then, thinking he had allowed the boy quite as much familiarity as was good for him, he added quellingly, "Let us hope you didn't teach him any bad habits while you were about it."

He patted the chestnut one last time, and moved on to the next stall to have a word with Garanwyn, who was grooming a fine grey gelding. "Is he yours?"

Garanwyn beamed proudly. "Since Christmas. Fflergant and Tryffin *said* it was necessary to keep up appearances after they were knighted, but you know, it was typical of their generosity."

Ceilyn nodded noncommittally, and left the stable. Outside, the sun was shining, the day was brisk and breezy. He passed a stableboy crossing the yard, leading a sidling black mare. Catching wind of Ceilyn, the mare rolled her eyes and shied violently. Without thinking, Ceilyn reached out to take her by the bridle and he spoke to her in her own language. *Peace, Fleetfoot. I mean you no harm.* The black mare grew calm under his touch, then meekly allowed the boy to lead her into the stable.

"That was amazing," said a voice behind Ceilyn. He turned to see who had spoken. Fergos fab Neol grinned at him. "Truly remarkable."

"Remarkable? Any groom or stableboy worth his salt knows how to steady a nervous horse," said Ceilyn, though the truth was, he had surprised himself. He suddenly remembered that Teleri's cats, after a little initial reluctance to approach him, had also become amazingly friendly after he touched them.

"Yes," Fergos was saying, "but until today, I'd never have reckoned *you* had that knack. That is—you always did well with your own faithful charger, but as for other men's horses . . . Where *were* you these last few months? And what were you doing, besides learning to handle horses?"

"I spent most of the time traveling from one place to another," Ceilyn replied smoothly. "I didn't stay anywhere for long. But yes, I did spend a great deal of time in the company of four-footed beasts."

Together, the two knights moved in the direction of the armory. "Little more than a week away, the tournament," said Fergos, as they passed through the door into the great echoing chamber lined with racks and shelves of weapons and armor. "Are you as fit as you look?"

"I am in excellent condition, I thank you," said Ceilyn. After nine weeks living hard in the wilderness, he could hardly be otherwise. "But I am bound to be out of practice."

They armed, each taking a turn acting as squire to help the other. Ceilyn was gratified to see that Gofan had not neglected his armor. The plate shone brightly and his chainmail showed evidence of a recent scouring in a barrel of sand. When the last buckle was fastened, the two knights picked up their blunted practice swords and unpainted wooden shields, and walked down to the practice yard.

As Ceilyn entered the yard, a sudden silence fell. He knew that everyone was curious to know where he had been and what he had been doing these last weeks, but unlike Fergos they lacked the courage to ask. That was just as well, Ceilyn reflected. He did not intend to answer any questions.

Out of practice Ceilyn might be, but after a quick warm-up at the wooden pell he joined the melee and dispatched his first three opponents with ease. His next opponent, Fergos, offered more of a challenge—the two had practiced together often in the past, and each knew the other's moves. After a lengthy and spirited exchange, even Fergos gave way before the fury of Ceilyn's onslaught, conceding defeat out of sheer exhaustion.

"Before God, Ceilyn mac Cuel," he panted, leaning on his sword for support, "don't you ever grow tired?"

"I do," said Ceilyn, taking off his helm. "But I try not to let it affect my fighting."

Fergos snorted, a sound somewhat muffled by his helmet. "We all know that you love nothing so much as aching muscles, but that is not what I meant. It is your energy that amazes me."

Ceilyn removed his mail coif and the padded hood beneath. After the exercise, his hair was damp and curly. "I don't like to lose. I can't bear any sort of failure," he said. "That lends me considerable force."

Fergos snorted again. "Much you know about defeat, since you never do lose." He slung his shield over his shoulder and moved toward the sidelines to watch the next melee.

Ceilyn followed him across the yard. At first, he did not heed the murmur that greeted his approach. But then one of the boys tittered. That was too much—Ceilyn spun around and wilted the miscreant with a single scorching glance. Then he looked in the direction the others were looking and understood what the commotion was about.

A gaudy figure in a threadbare crimson cloak perched on an upper rail of the fence that encircled the practice yard. She waved when she saw Ceilyn looking her way.

He groaned inwardly. If there was anything he dreaded, it was airing his private affairs in public. Nevertheless, he could hardly be so discourteous as to ignore her, not with half the squires and pages in the castle looking on—impudent young beggars, the whole lot of them, and all too ready to follow a bad example. He sheathed his sword, leaned his shield up against a wall, and walked to the fence.

"Good morning, Prescelli. What brings you here?"

Prescelli brushed a limp strand of dark hair out of her face. "You might have saved me the trouble. You were gone two months, but you didn't bother to pay me a visit when you returned."

Ceilyn sighed, hoping she had not come down there to make a scene. "I've been back less than a day, as you probably know. And you and I were hardly on terms of intimacy when I left."

Prescelli climbed down from the fence. Under the red cloak, she wore a low-cut gown of faded orange and crimson harlequin silk, a garment too light and flimsy for a cool day like this. A rip in one seam revealed the soft white flesh beneath. Trust Prescelli to come down to the yard, half-dressed and reeking of perfume, simply to embarrass him in front of the squires.

"And were you on excellent terms with Teleri when you left?" she inquired archly. "Yet you ran to *her* like a hound called to heel, the moment you arrived."

Ceilyn stiffened. "Pardon me for saying so, but that is no concern of yours. I think I told you before: Teleri is one subject I prefer not to discuss—certainly not with you."

Prescelli smiled sweetly. "And did you like what you found when you came back? Were you pleased to see her so changed? All tarted up, your innocent little Teleri, and no better than the rest of us."

He did not like to discuss Teleri with Prescelli—but somehow she always goaded him into it. "I saw nothing improper in the way she was dressed," he said coldly. "Her gown was a little brighter than the ones she used to wear, but perfectly modest and appropriate to her new position.''

''And I suppose you never wondered where she came by so many lovely things,'' Prescelli prodded him. ''When a poor, unattached female suddenly acquires new clothes and new jewels . . . but no, of course not—such suspicions would be beneath you.''

He *had* wondered, just for a moment, the day Teleri came looking for him, but he was not about to admit that to Prescelli. He felt himself blushing. ''The gowns were gifts from the Queen. The earrings and other trinkets were lent her by the other girls.''

Prescelli moved closer, put her hand up to touch his face. Her musky perfume enveloped him, and he was intensely aware of the voluptuous body under the thin silk. In spite of himself, he felt a warmth in his loins, a stirring of the old attraction between them.

''And the necklace—was that a gift from the Queen? Sidonwy is generous with her favorites, as we all know, but a gift of that sort . . . ?''

Ceilyn scowled and brushed her hand away. The origin of the necklace did trouble him. He did not think the stones were valuable, yet he could not imagine that Teleri would buy anything so showy for herself. And he knew Sidonwy well enough to know what sort of gifts she was inclined to bestow.

He had no intention, however, of allowing Prescelli to see that she had scored a hit. ''Speculation is idle and vulgar as well. I have better use for my time, and should hope you have as well.''

He turned on his heel and left her; though she made no attempt to follow him, her words stayed with him all morning and the image of her mocking smile continued to taunt him. It lent considerable power to his sword arm, but contributed nothing to his peace of mind.

Three days passed before Ceilyn was able to speak to Teleri alone. During his absence, supplies of candles, soap, and firewood had run low in the Mermaid Tower, and elsewhere: Silver had gone unpolished, wine had turned to vinegar, and pages had grown slovenly and careless. As Ceilyn labored to restore order and seemliness, he realized it might take him weeks, even months, to bring everything back up to the standard that had existed before he left.

As for Teleri, she was busy, too, though the nature of her

activities filled Ceilyn with deep dismay. Usually, she could be found with the other young women, learning to embroider, or reading aloud from a book while the others were occupied with their spinning, their mending, or their harp lessons. The only remnants of her old, scholarly way of life that Ceilyn ever saw were her tarot cards and the endless horoscopes she cast for the other girls.

To make matters worse, whatever Teleri and the other maidens happened to be doing when Ceilyn entered a room, his appearance invariably caused them to giggle and nudge each other, as if sharing some joke at his expense. Well, he was used to such teasing from the other girls, but the thought that Teleri . . . Though she never, as far as he knew, joined in the laughter, just to form a part of the group was betrayal enough.

By the third day he was determined to speak to her, so when Teleri left the Solar that evening, Ceilyn quickly made his excuses to the Queen, followed Teleri out, and hurried to catch up with her before she reached the stairs.

Hearing his footsteps, she turned and waited for him at the foot of the staircase. Unreasonably, he was annoyed by her ready acceptance of his company, wondering if she allowed *other* men to meet with her privately. As they climbed the stairs, her perfume tickled his nostrils, reminding him, unpleasantly, of Prescelli's musk and orris root.

"I was watching you this evening," he said. His voice came out sounding harsher than he intended.

"Yes," she answered quietly. "I saw you. And I wondered what I had done to make you scowl so ferociously."

"You wondered?" Ceilyn laughed a bitter little laugh. "Yet *I* wonder that it was not perfectly plain. Dressing up and drenching yourself in scent . . . reading palms and casting horoscopes for the amusement of a pack of idle, foolish girls . . . Is that why you spent nine years studying to be a wizard? Surely Glastyn intended that you direct your efforts toward better things."

She stopped on the first landing, gazing up at him with pain and bewilderment in her eyes. "But . . . isn't that what you wanted me to do all along? To find a place at court, to make myself useful in little ways so that people would learn to trust me and come to me when something important occurs? I thought—I thought you would be pleased."

It was *exactly* what he had advised her to do, and he knew perfectly well that he *ought* to be pleased. But he was not pleased and so did not like to be reminded that the idea was originally his.

"If I ever did give you such an improper piece of advice—" he began. But then the injustice of what he was about to say struck him, and he was unable to continue. Instead, he said the first thing that came into his mind. "That necklace you wear—who gave it to you?"

Teleri's hand went to her throat. "Fand gave it to me because I—but no, I suppose you would not approve of that either. Perhaps I should have not accepted it. I did wonder, but she said it was not costly, and indeed, she wore it quite carelessly for a fortnight herself . . . into town and out riding . . ."

Ceilyn leaned against a newel post carved in the form of a scowling trident-bearing merman. If Fand had flaunted the necklace for a fortnight, he could be certain that Prescelli had noticed, and had known all along where the necklace had come from. The absurdity of his own suspicions overwhelmed him now: that Teleri, with her horror of intimacy, should encourage the pretensions of any man by accepting his gifts! Yet knowing he had allowed one girl to make a fool of him did not improve his temper in dealing with the other.

"If I had known that you cared for that sort of thing," he said coldly, "I would have given you all the jewels you could possibly want."

Far from taking offense at this lordly assumption that he, and he alone, had the right to give her gifts, Teleri only looked mortified. "I see that I ought not to have accepted it. I will return the necklace tomorrow and beg Fand's pardon.

"I am glad that you are here to advise me now, Ceilyn," she added in a low voice, "for I admit that I am often puzzled as to what I may or may not do, and you always know exactly what is right."

But that was too much, and Ceilyn was heartily ashamed of himself. "No, no, wear the necklace if it pleases you. Of course you must not return it; that would be to insult Fand. It was just—just that seeing you enjoyed wearing it, I wished the necklace had come from me," he blurted out.

At last she understood him. "But . . . did you think I valued the necklace above your friendship?" she asked. "Oh Ceilyn, that w-wasn't very kind." She started up the steps again, but he caught her by the hand to stop her.

"No . . . wait. Let me explain."

"There is nothing for you to explain." Teleri blinked back tears. "I understand you very well. You accused me once, not—not without justice on that occasion, of being cold and incapable of any emotion. Now, it seems, I am calculating and mercenary as well."

"You are none of those things and I had no right to speak as though you were," he said, wishing he had torn his tongue out before he ever mentioned Fand's wretched necklace. "It is my temper, my wicked temper. You should know I don't mean half I say when the black mood is on me."

She was crying now, the tears sliding down her cheeks. "And who is to blame if you are unhappy and in a vile temper?" she whispered. "I ought never to have gone looking for you; you were better where you were. But I was selfish, thinking only of how much I missed you, how much I wanted you to come back."

He caught his breath. "Why didn't you tell me that you wanted me to come back? You told me that everyone else missed me . . . that there was going to be a tournament . . . but if I had known that *you* missed me—before God!—I would have been happy to return."

"Truly?" Teleri tried, ineffectually, to wipe away the tears with the back of her hand, and Ceilyn pulled a handkerchief out of his sleeve and offered it to her. "Please don't lie to me out of gallantry, or some misguided notion of chivalry."

"I swear to you, it is God's own truth. You know that I love you, I never made any secret of that," he said. "And all last year, I was such a romantic fool!" He shook his head in simple amazement at his own folly. "I wanted to go on quests for you, and bring you all the fabulous jewels of legend—and you wouldn't take anything from me, not even my homage when I offered it. You went about like a peasant lass, winter and summer, with holes in your shoes, and I—I would have dressed you in silks and velvets had you given me the chance.

"Then I went away, and when I came back . . . you had new friends, friends you allowed to give you all the things you never permitted me to offer. Do you wonder that I am jealous?"

"But they did it all for your sake," she said tremulously. "All to please you, to make me a suitable—they are *your* friends, whatever you may think, Ceilyn, not mine. And everyone thinks—" She stopped, turned her face away, so he would not see the sudden hot color.

Suddenly, it all made sense to him; he understood what all the giggling and whispering had been about. He took her face in both his hands and turned her to face him. "What does everyone think?" he asked gently. "Did those foolish girls imagine that we were secretly betrothed?"

"No one ever said, so I could never deny it," she said miserably. "But it was plain from all the hints, all the little favors they did for me, that they all thought something of the sort. And though I knew it wasn't true, what could I do when they were all so kind, so eager to be of service? I admit it was all very pleasant, after I grew accustomed to it, and when I thought about you at all . . . how could I have known that you wouldn't approve? You *ought* to be pleased," she added, growing a little indignant. "You weren't satisfied with me the way I was, you made that plain on more than one occasion."

"But I am pleased . . . now that I understand," he said. And he *was* happy, as happy as a man can be who feels he has been a brute and a bully and hurt the only woman he ever truly loved. He took off his cloak and folded it, and draped it over the steps. Then he pulled Teleri down to sit beside him.

"But as for the gifts and the other favors you received under the assumption that you and I were to marry," he went on, taking her hand in both of his, "it seems to me the only honorable thing you can do is make me even happier than I am right now, and consent to be my wife."

"You are mocking me," she said, on the verge of tears again. "I wish you would not, though perhaps I deserve it."

"Neither mocking you nor proposing out of some *misguided notion of chivalry*." He raised her hand to his lips and kissed it lightly. "Come, we've established this much long since: that I love you and that merely seducing you was never my intention." She trembled but did not try to draw her hand away. "What follows? Of course I want to marry you."

"But you can't," she insisted. "You were absolutely right: They are nothing but silly, sentimental girls, who have been encouraged all their lives to think of nothing but marriage. But only consider how unsuitable it would be. What would your father say if you married a—a sorceress? What would the rest of your family say if you married a dowerless girl?"

"My father can say anything he likes to say—I'll not be there to hear it, thank God. And there is nothing he can actually do, for I am of age and not dependent on him in any way," Ceilyn said firmly. "Nor can he disinherit me, for I *am* the eldest son, no matter how unsatisfactory he may find me. More to the point, Sidonwy—who does maintain me—seems to have encouraged this scheme to make you over into a suitable bride. She said, once, that she would rather see me happy than well-married. As for my mother and her people . . . well, they are Gwyngellach and regard these matters with admirable common sense. They would say—and I would agree with them—that a virtuous woman is her own dowry.''

He turned her hand over and kissed the palm. Under his fingers he felt her pulse flutter like a wild bird. He had just enough presence of mind—but only just—to prevent himself from crushing her in his arms and covering her face with kisses—a procedure that would certainly have sent her into a blind panic.

''When you think about it,'' he went on, ''whom could I marry if not you? Do you think I want to spend the rest of my life hiding my true nature from the woman who shares my bed? You are the perfect and the only bride for me.'' He kissed her palm again, was gratified to feel the rapid beat of the blood under her skin. Yet still he controlled himself, keeping his tone light and friendly, rather than passionate.

''Still,'' he added, suddenly realizing how selfish he sounded. ''You shouldn't think about that, not—not if you don't care for the idea yourself.''

Teleri shook her head, and smiled through her tears. ''I hardly know what I want. I never seriously thought I would marry anyone. I do love you, Ceilyn, but I wonder if that is enough.''

At the words *I love you*, Ceilyn smiled. She had not known he could smile like that: all the bitterness and the self-doubt erased in an instant.

He slid an arm around her waist. ''Think of it now. Take as long as you like. I can wait quite patiently, now that I know how you feel.'' Very carefully, to avoid alarming her, he tilted up her chin and kissed her, softly, on the mouth.

It was not their first kiss, but the first in which she had actively participated, and though it was a little awkward, Ceilyn thought it was entirely satisfactory.

And what is the nature of these men we call knights? In battle, they are strong, full of energy, bold and without fear. In love, they are fiery, fair-spoken, swift to defend the objects of their affections, men of passion yet temperate and loyal. On the field of honor, they put skill above brute strength, endurance above the weakness of the flesh, and honor above victory. Indeed, they are admirable men in every respect, and if they should err sometimes on the side of zeal, that is entirely pardonable.

> —*from the diary of one*
> *Anguish of Eyrie, Knight of the Order*
> *of St. Sianne and St. Gall (Rhianedd)*

8.

On the Field of Honor

In the final days before the tourney, folk came from Treledig and the surrounding villages to aid in the preparations: carpenters to build pavilions and viewing stands down by the lists, cloth merchants to drape these with rich fabrics; assistant bakers, brewers, and cooks to help provide the feasts that would follow the contests of arms, and jugglers, wrestlers, sword-dancers, and tight-rope walkers to provide entertainment. They set up a village of tents and other make-shift dwellings in the lower courtyard.

St. Valentine's dawned clear and cold—a perfect day for a tourney. But long before sunrise the castle was alive with activity, as knights, squires, and pages made last-minute preparations by torchlight in the pre-dawn gloom.

By first light, a dozen wagons stood loaded and ready to take armor and weapons down to the lists. As the camp in the courtyard began to show signs of life, the squires repaired to the stables to give their master's warhorses a final meticulous grooming before leading them down the road to the tourney site. The warriors themselves, too keyed up to feel much appetite, but conscious that food was necessary to lend them strength in the contest ahead, sat down to a light breakfast, served by pages in new holiday livery, in the Hall.

Soon after, the ladies rose and began to dress. In their little bedchambers above the Queen's apartments, Sidonwy's hand-maidens combed out their long hair and donned their most festive gowns, eagerly speculating as to which man would emerge victorious by the second day. The man whom the marshalls judged the winner would gain not only the fabulous heart-shaped ruby that Cynwas offered as a prize, but also the privilege of crowning his lady as Queen of Love and Beauty.

Fflergant and Tryffin were both prime favorites. "They are both so strong. And what could be the meaning of the wonders we witnessed on the day they were knighted, if not that one or both of them will distinguish himself at the tournament?" Finola asked, as she fastened the fifty golden buttons that adorned her undersleeves.

But the more practical damsels spoke up in favor of age and experience: "someone like Fergos or Ceilyn," venerable figures at the ages of twenty-two and twenty-one respectively. That the prize might fall to one of the senior knights—a man like Branach, Dianach, Scilti, or Ysgafn, heroes to previous generations of women—the young ladies did not even consider.

"If love of a maiden provides any inspiration—and I am sure we none of us doubt that it does—then Ceilyn will certainly win," said Fand, as she deftly plaited ribbons into her long dark hair. "Quite the blissful young lover, these last few days, and I must say it has done wonders for his temper. But love quite aside, I am convinced it cannot be *bad* luck to carry the favor of a maiden sorceress."

Megwen, who was lacing up the back of Gwenlliant's blue velvet gown, frowned. "You don't think . . . you don't suppose that she could use her powers to insure his victory?"

"I certainly meant nothing of the sort!" exclaimed Fand. "As though Ceilyn mac Cuel needed anyone's help to win his fights—or wasn't too proud to accept any help that was offered!" She stopped braiding her hair, struck by a sudden unpleasant thought. "I do hope no such notion has occurred to Ceilyn. Only think how disappointing it would be, after all our efforts, if he didn't sue for her favor for fear someone would accuse him of an unfair advantage. We must all take a vow that Megwen's foolish idea goes no farther than this room."

"Even if Teleri *could* do something like that, I am sure she would never think of it," volunteered Gwenlliant. "All wizards care about is maintaining and restoring the . . . the natural order of things."

"Just what does she teach you during those private lessons of yours?" Finola asked, smoothing the skirt of her wine-red silk. The girls were wild with curiosity, imagining all sorts of exciting transformations and manifestations.

"She teaches me to keep my mind quiet, to build a wall around my thoughts," said Gwenlliant, lifting her skirts to inspect the pretty shoes of red leather lined with miniver that became her tiny feet so well.

The other girls exchanged a disappointed glance. "That is all? But what is the use of that?"

"It will be very useful, after I learn to do it well," said Gwenlliant, adding, with a blush that none of the others noticed, "in case I lose my talisman and anyone tries to get into my mind without leave."

Everyone shuddered. "What a terrible notion," said Finola. "But things like that just don't happen at Caer Cadwy!"

After hurried prayers in the Queen's private chapel, the young women went down to the garden, where a painted caravan waited to convey them to the tournament. When the Queen arrived with her pages, Cynwas himself handed her up into the wagon.

Mounting his splendid white charger, the King preceded them down the road, and the Lord Constable accompanied him on a high-stepping grey. But Manogan fab Menai had been down on the field for hours; as Marshall, it was his duty—along with his knights-marshall and other deputies, and the heralds and their pursuivants—to organize the event.

Arriving at the site, Sidonwy and her young ladies abandoned their colorful conveyance and ascended a short flight of steps to the largest and most luxuriously appointed of the viewing stands. A green silk sunshade covering the center section of the stand served as the Royal Pavilion. The girls took seats on the long benches to either side of the thrones, directly behind the banner-draped railing, which offered the best view possible of the action on the field.

A fanfare of trumpets set the ladies into a flutter of excitement: The most romantic event of the day was close at hand. The contenders came out of their pavilions on the field, mounted their chargers, and rode past the crowded viewing stands, each man searching for the face of the one lady who would serve as his inspiration in the upcoming contest, by bestowing on him some personal token to carry as a favor.

The younger men all moved toward the Royal Pavilion, to sue for the favors of the Queen's handmaidens. Much good-natured jostling and shoving followed, for the youths were eager and their mounts restive in all the excitement.

A momentary unpleasantness occurred when Ceilyn's Tegillus danced past Fflergant's great red-gold charger. Seeing who hindered him, Fflergant bristled. "You can no longer claim precedence over me, Ceilyn mac Cuel. Move aside and let me pass."

"I don't forget it, my Lord Prince," Ceilyn murmured, uncharacteristically agreeable as he obligingly backed his horse to make room for his young kinsman.

But Fflergant was not so easily appeased. He lingered by the viewing stands after he had obtained a silken scarf from Fand, and waited while Ceilyn sued for and was granted one of Teleri's cherry-colored hair ribbons. When Ceilyn rode back toward his own pavilion, the big, red-gold palomino moved in to block his way.

"There is still the matter of the bones between us," snarled Fflergant. "When Tryffin and I were wearing gold spurs, you said, that would be soon enough to answer our questions."

Ceilyn reined in to avoid a collision. "You are mistaken if you think I promised you any explanation," he said evenly. "Now unless there is something else you wish to discuss, allow me to pass."

Fflergant gave way with no good grace. His charger sidestepped, shaking his cream-colored mane impatiently. "We will see if you are so close-mouthed after I have bested you on the field."

Ceilyn sighed. He had expected some such encounter, either with Fflergant or his brother, but he wished he had been able to avoid it. "You intend to challenge me?"

"I do," said Fflergant.

"Why then," Ceilyn said as he rode past, "I suggest you put on your armor and make your challenge properly."

Ceilyn dismounted outside his green and gold pavilion, and handed Tegillus over to Gofan. The chestnut gelding already wore the customary light body armor of boiled leather under his colorful trappings; now it was time for Gofan to buckle on the steel chamfron, crinet, and peytral which would protect the chestnut's head, neck, and breast.

Inside the pavilion, Gofan's younger brother, Nefyn—recently promoted from page to squire—waited to assist Ceilyn.

"Where is my shield?" the young knight asked.

Nefyn produced a newly painted shield. Ceilyn spent a moment inspecting it. With the King's permission he had abandoned his father's device, the white stag and cross, for his ancestral arms: a golden wolf's head on a green field, differenced with an orle of golden holly leaves and red berries. The change had occasioned some speculation, but Ceilyn could not regret his decision. To bear the ancient device of his clan felt somehow more honest, and even though he was not so foolhardy as to announce his true nature openly, he had finished lying to himself.

"Hang this up outside, then come back and help me to arm," he told Nefyn.

Meanwhile, in a scarlet silk pavilion on the other side of the lists, Tryffin and Garanwyn helped Fflergant to put on his armor.

"I still think I should be the one to challenge him," said Tryffin, as he passed Fflergant his chainmail byrnie. "He is bound to rouse your temper again. You will need a cool head to defeat Ceilyn, and I wonder if you are capable of maintaining one."

Fflergant scowled. "I won the toss. You agreed to abide by that." He stopped talking while he slipped the shirt of mail over his head and arms, began again when his head emerged through the neck hole. "You needn't fear—I will be as cool and calculating as you could wish."

The byrnie covered him from shoulder to waist, from his neck to his knees. He girded it with a wide leather belt around his waist, pulled a little of the slack up and over the belt, to distribute the weight. "I intend to *win* this encounter."

Garanwyn handed him his coat of plates, silently stood by while Tryffin buckled his brother into his body armor. Garanwyn did not understand the enmity that existed between his two friends and his cousin Ceilyn, but he was in a poor position to take sides. So he held his tongue and did his duty—and kept his thoughts strictly to himself.

With only young Nefyn to assist him, Ceilyn was still strapping on his leg harness when a resounding thud, as a lance struck the shield outside his pavilion, heralded his first challenge.

"That will be Fflergant," he said, as he fastened the last buckle and straightened up. "Unless someone has forestalled him."

Outside, he found Fflergant waiting for him, mounted and fully armored, except for the barrel-shaped jousting helm which he held balanced on the high front of his saddle.

"You have secured this end of the field and found a marshall to officiate?" Ceilyn asked.

Fflergant nodded. "Then I won't keep you waiting long," said Ceilyn.

Ceilyn fastened on his helmet, climbed into the saddle, and took the lance and shield his squire handed up to him.

"Don't go easy on him. Knock him out of the saddle on the first charge," Gofan advised.

Ceilyn was too surprised to scold the boy for his impertinence. "I thought Fflergant was a friend of yours."

The youth from Gorwynnion grinned and shrugged. "He is. But you know these southerners . . . they think chivalry was their own invention. It does them no harm when one of *us* shows them otherwise."

Back at his pavilion, Fflergant put on his helm, adjusted the strapping on his shield, and braced his lance.

Finally prepared, the two knights faced each other across the field: Ceilyn in green and gold with Teleri's red ribbon secured to his crest; Fflergant equally colorful in scarlet with dragons worked in gold thread. They waited for the presiding marshall to give the signal.

The knight-marshall dropped his baton, the two armored figures dug in their heels, and the great warhorses bounded into action. A little ponderous at first, the horses picked up speed as they went, reaching a full gallop before they came to the center of the field.

There was a tremendous crash as both lances found their marks, a moment of recoil, then the horses recovered and galloped on. Both lances had splintered with the impact but neither knight had lost his seat. Up in the stands, the crowd roared their approval.

At a more sedate pace, Ceilyn and Fflergant each returned to his own side of the field. Fflergant reined in, handed his lance down to Tryffin, and waited impatiently for Garanwyn to bring him a fresh one.

"I suppose he thinks he is being magnanimous," Fflergant said between clenched teeth. "He didn't even aim for my helm."

"Neither did you aim for the helm," Tryffin reminded him.

"I needed to reckon his speed, before I tried anything so risky. I will aim for his helm this time." He took the lance Garanwyn handed him and turned his horse for the next charge.

At the marshall's signal, there was another blinding rush, another mighty crash, another roar from the crowd. Ceilyn's lance met Fflergant's shield dead center, but the other lance hit the helmet too high and glanced off. Fflergant slipped sideways in his saddle, made a desperate effort, and managed to catch hold of the saddle horn with one hand. Though he lost his lance, he successfully regained his seat.

He returned to his own side of the field, breathless and chastened.

"Aim for the shield again this time," Tryffin said. "You can't afford not to take the surer stroke."

"I meant to miss him," said Fflergant, with as much dignity as he could muster. "It came to me at the last moment that if I knocked him unconscious or broke his neck, he would be in no condition to answer my questions. I need to best him on foot, get him down without actually cutting his damned throat, and force him to tell me what he knows."

"Ceilyn will guess what you intend. He won't let it come to foot combat if he can prevent it. You can be certain he means to unhorse you this time," said Tryffin. "Strike hard and sure, so that Ceilyn goes down as well."

"I will—and keep my own seat, too," said Fflergant, as he turned his horse for the final encounter.

The marshall's baton fell for a third time. The horses lunged into a gallop. There was a tremendous shock, sending both horses back onto their haunches, rearing and beating the air while their riders struggled to maintain their seats. Miraculously, nobody fell, and the horses were able to regain their footing. The crowd cheered even more enthusiastically than before.

Tryffin met his brother in front of the red pavilion; he reached up to relieve him of his lance and shield. Fflergant dismounted, holding his left arm against his side, as though he had sustained some injury.

"Strained, but not dislocated. I can still carry a shield—or swing a sword if I have to." He took off his helm, accepted the flask of water that Garanwyn offered him, and took several swallows. Wiping the perspiration off his forehead, he turned and glared at Ceilyn, who was accepting the ministrations of his young Gorwynnach cousins on the other side of the lists.

"These damned northerners." Fflergant continued to scowl at the three slender, brown-haired figures and entirely forgot Garanwyn's presence. "They don't look like they are made of much, but they are as hard as iron."

"As hard as oak," said Garanwyn, speaking up for the first time. "They say the Gorwynnach are made of oak. You would do well to remember it, though perhaps they *don't* look like much!"

Fflergant eyed him indignantly. "Whose man are you—mine or Ceilyn's?"

"Yours," said Garanwyn. "That is why I warn you. Don't underestimate Ceilyn. He is as strong as you are and agile into the bargain."

. . . and wearing the armor the hermit had given to him, Branach fought in the tournament at Regann, and no man knew him. At length, he was challenged by Dianach, his brother, and because he did not wish anyone to know his name, Branach accepted.

The two men fought all that day and into the evening, but neither could best the other. The next day it was just the same: They jousted with sharp spears, they drew their swords and fought on foot, but neither gained the mastery.

On the third day of the tournament, the contest continued, until Dianach struck his opponent such a mighty blow that the visor of his helmet was damaged and the face of the knight was revealed. Then Dianach knew him.

"Your pardon, my dear brother—I did not know you. Take my sword and armor, for you are the victor," said Dianach.

"No, no, the victory was yours. Take my sword and armor," said Branach.

When Cynwas the King perceived that there was some dispute between the warriors, he went out on the field to speak with them.

"Lord, here is my brother Branach, who has defeated me, but he will not claim my sword and armor, which he has won fairly," said Dianach.

"But it is Dianach who has defeated me," said Branach, "and he will not take my sword."

The King looked from one to the other, and with a great effort he concealed his amusement. "Do you, both of you, yield your swords to me," he said. "Then neither of you will have defeated the other."

—*from Glastyn's* Chronicles of the Isle of Celydonn

9.

A Question of Chivalry

After three passes on horseback, neither had scored a decisive victory, so Ceilyn and Fflergant now faced armed combat on foot.

Up in the viewing stands, the spectators watched them prepare. Though other fights were taking place on other parts of the field, word had spread of a quarrel between Fflergant and Ceilyn, thereby lending interest to their contest. At the Queen's suggestion, the King commanded that the fight take place directly in front of the Royal Pavilion.

As soon as they had put on additional armor and exchanged their heavy barrel-shaped jousting helms for the lighter crested helmets used in foot combat, the two young knights took their positions before the thrones. The marshall inspected their armor and their blunted tourney weapons, then asked if they were ready to proceed. They both signaled their agreement, and waited for a sign from the King: Ceilyn, calmly, with his sword crossed in front of his shield, while Fflergant impatiently moved his blade in small circles at his side.

At the King's signal, the marshall dropped his baton. Fflergant began to pace a wide circle, Ceilyn to turn slowly at the center, each trying to gain the advantage of position. Suddenly, Fflergant moved in. There was a brief flurry of blows, all of which Ceilyn easily blocked with his shield or parried with his sword. Fflergant moved back.

More circling, an occasional feint, then Ceilyn launched into a furious attack, pushing Fflergant back with the relentless force of his blows. Though hard-pressed, Fflergant was still comparatively fresh; he turned every blow aside until Ceilyn stepped back.

They circled as before, each awaiting the perfect moment to attack. Then both took the offensive, moving in at the same time. Shields locked and a fierce struggle followed, as each tried to shove the other back and gain enough space to strike effectively. The knight-marshall called a hold.

While the combatants caught their breath, their squires rushed in to check their armor for loose or broken straps. Finding all in order, the boys withdrew.

In the next engagement, Ceilyn took the offensive from the beginning, and this time he made every swing and thrust count, striking again and again, never making the same combination twice. But every blow landed on plate. By the time the marshall called another hold, Fflergant was bruised and considerably less confident than before, but otherwise undamaged.

In the next round, Ceilyn forced Fflergant steadily back toward the sidelines, finally causing the spectators to scramble for safety and the marshall to intervene. During the hold that followed, Fflergant discovered that a strap on one of his vambraces had broken: With the marshall's permission, he went back to his pavilion for a quick repair.

He arrived at the scarlet pavilion feeling frustrated and obscurely insulted. "This is pointless," he said, holding out his arm while Tryffin unbuckled the remaining straps on his vambrace. "The only way to win at this sport would be to batter him into submission or tire him out. But I've barely touched him, and as for Ceilyn growing tired . . . ! But if we changed to edged steel—then it is just possible I might win."

Tryffin's jaw dropped, and he stared at Fflergant as at one who has lost his wits. Tourney combat with edged steel had been the accepted practice in more violent times, but that dangerous sport, while never banned, had been virtually abandoned.

"No, I am not mad," said Fflergant. "I have thought it all out, and—"

"When?" Tryffin snorted. "When did you think? Out there on the field?"

"I thought it over carefully," Fflergant insisted. "If we fight with edged steel, I need only get in one good blow to gain the advantage. Once he starts to bleed, Ceilyn will tire as quickly as any man. I tell you, there is no other way I can possibly win."

Garanwyn appeared just as Tryffin unbuckled the last strap. "Repair this—take your time and do it properly," said Tryffin.

Once the younger boy was out of earshot, he said: "Even if that were true, you seem to have forgotten—you challenged Ceilyn, so the choice of weapons is his."

"I can't *choose* to fight with edged steel," Fflergant admitted, "but I can make the suggestion in such a way that Ceilyn won't dare to refuse."

"He will refuse if he has half the sense I think he has," said Tryffin. Lowering his voice, to be certain that no one overheard him, he added, "For the love of God, let the matter rest. It's not worth your life or Ceilyn's to make him talk."

Fflergant removed his helmet. "We agreed it was a point of honor to discover what Ceilyn knows about the bones. We *lied* for him—or at least . . . we did conceal Ceilyn's presence down at the tomb. In all good conscience, we need to be certain that we did the right thing.

"But quite aside from the damnable bones," he went on,

"there is everything that Ceilyn has ever said or done. I have endured his insults and his damned condescension as long as I can—and I will earn Ceilyn's respect today, if I die for it."

"As you very well might," said Tryffin. "Will you only think: Though neither of you may intend to do the other serious harm, accidents can happen, especially if you allow your temper to get the better of you. Men *have* died in these combats. . . . Ah well, why do I say anything," he sighed. "Ceilyn will refuse to fight you with edged steel, and there will be an end to it."

"Then you will find me a pen, paper, and ink, and a page to carry the message?"

Tryffin shrugged his shoulders. "The sooner this nonsense is settled, the better."

While Tryffin went off in search of the necessary writing implements, Fflergant sat down on a camp stool and mentally composed his message. Garanwyn came back with the repaired vambrace and fastened it on, then went inside the pavilion, still unaware of what Fflergant intended. He remained in the pavilion after Tryffin returned, so he did not see Fflergant tear the sheet of paper in half and write his message to Ceilyn. Tryffin stood by, silent and disapproving.

As Fflergant dispatched the page, a herald announced the next combat to take place on another part of the field.

"God save us," said Tryffin, on hearing his name called. "I promised my first passage of arms to Scilti, but I didn't think I would be called until after you and Ceilyn were finished. I will have to go and arm up now."

He had already arranged to arm in his uncle's pavilion, with the assistance of Manogan's squires. The Earl Marshall expected to be too busy to fight any challenges that first day.

"For God's sake," said Tryffin—though he was still convinced that common sense would prevail and Ceilyn would refuse Fflergant's suggestion—"don't do anything foolish while I am gone."

Garanwyn chose that moment to emerge from the pavilion, and Tryffin fixed him with a stern glare. "And don't *you* let him do anything foolish, either!"

On the other side of the lists, Ceilyn read Fflergant's message. "Jesu give me patience!" he said, when he had finished.

The tone of Fflergant's letter was so insulting that just for a moment Ceilyn wished that he was free to accept the suggestion and write back to his kinsman in a similar vein. Unfortunately, he could not do either. Constructed as he was, combat with edged steel gave him too much advantage, a secret advantage he could not honorably exploit. Therefore, he must keep his temper and try to pacify Fflergant.

"I will need a pen and ink . . . and see that the boy who delivered this waits for my reply," Ceilyn told Nefyn. Once pen and ink had been produced, he sat down on a stool to write his reply on the back of Fflergant's letter.

"Take this," he said to the page, "and deliver it directly into Fflergant's hands."

Fflergant read Ceilyn's reply through twice, then a third time aloud. "He says he is *sorry* I have chosen to resolve our quarrel on the field. *'I regret I cannot satisfy you, as I regret we cannot be friends, but I accept these things as I must, since you are determined to have them so.'* Perhaps he thinks this is conciliating? *'Nevertheless,'* he goes on to say, *'for the love I bear you because of the blood we both share, I would prefer not to engage in such perilous sport.'* From any other man, that would be virtually an admission of cowardice, but from Ceilyn mac Cuel . . . insufferably condescending! I will send him such a reply as will boil his blood. He won't refuse me a second time."

"But what is this about?" asked the bewildered Garanwyn.

Fflergant did not deign to reply. He picked up the second piece of paper, and using his shield for a writing desk, scribbled a second hasty message to Ceilyn. Only after he had dispatched the page, did he turn to Garanwyn.

"Bring me my sword—no, not that one. Ceilyn and I will be fighting our next bout with edged steel."

For a full minute, Garanwyn was rendered speechless. "Surely," he said at last, "this is your idea of a jest."

"It is not a jest," said Fflergant, rising to his feet.

"But this is insane . . . indecent. . . . Ceilyn is a kinsman of ours. That ought to mean more to you than it does to me."

"I will thank you," Fflergant said haughtily, "not to preach to me about proper family feeling, for you know nothing at all about it, and I will not stand for it."

Garanwyn required another moment before he was calm enough to reply. "Does Tryffin know what you intend?"

"He does."

"And makes no effort to convince you of your folly?"

Fflergant hesitated. "He has agreed to leave the matter entirely to my own judgment."

Garanwyn gasped. "Holy Mother of God! You can tell me that, bare-faced, when I heard Tryffin myself—"

"Do you accuse me of lying?" Fflergant clenched and unclenched his fists.

"That goes without saying," Garanwyn said nastily. The implication that he, a northerner, knew nothing about family loyalty rankled. "You people have no respect for the truth at all, everyone knows that—none of you except Tryffin, who has no choice."

Fflergant was uncomfortably aware that they had attracted the attention of the occupants of the pavilions on either side. He lowered his voice. "I asked you to bring me my sword."

"No," said Garanwyn. "You will have to fetch it yourself, or send a page. If you are determined to do this thing against all sense and decency, it will have to be without my assistance."

By now, Fflergant was in a white-hot rage. From the beginning, this challenge had not gone as he intended. He felt that Ceilyn had made a fool of him, in his first passage of arms as a belted knight, and that Ceilyn's letter added insult to injury. If anything was needed to complete his humiliation, it was only this: that his squire should refuse an order.

"I will remind you who you are and to whom you are speaking," said Fflergant, dangerously quiet. "And I ask you again— will you bring my sword?"

"No," said Garanwyn, folding his arms and shaking his head, making his refusal clear, if it was not already, to everyone within sight of him.

Goaded past bearing, Fflergant slapped Garanwyn, hard, across the face.

"I ask you a final time . . ." Fflergant's voice began to shake. "Will you bring me my sword?"

Garanwyn's face was pale, except where Fflergant's hand had left a red mark. "Yes," he said quietly. "I will bring your sword. And I hope to God that Ceilyn does not spare you, but gives you the beating you deserve!"

By this time, everyone in the Royal Pavilion was asking what had occasioned such a long delay between rounds, but they all fell silent when Gofan appeared and begged Teleri for a few words in private.

"It is Ceilyn who wishes to speak with you," he told her. "He wonders if you would step down to his pavilion?"

"Is there something amiss?" She had been uneasy all day without knowing why.

"I don't know, but I think there must be," said Gofan. "Messages have been flying to and fro across the field, and now Ceilyn has sent Nefyn for edged steel. Will you come?"

"I will," said Teleri. "Only give me a moment to ask leave of the Queen."

When Teleri arrived at the green and gold pavilion, Ceilyn waved his squires away and told her the contents of Fflergant's original message.

"You refused him, of course," said Teleri.

"I did. I sent back as soft a reply as I possibly could, but this is how he wrote me afterward." He passed her Fflergant's most recent message.

Teleri caught her breath as she read it. "I am afraid he must be in a terrible rage or he would not have said any of these things. I am convinced he cannot mean them."

"It is likely he doesn't mean half of them. Nevertheless," Ceilyn said grimly, "it seems young Fflergant needs to be taught a sharp lesson and has selected me to teach it. As the thing is not to be avoided, I sent for you. In the event that he should contrive to cut me a little, I would like you on hand to bind up my wounds."

"Yes, of course. But Ceilyn, there is something I need to tell you. Ever since—"

"It will have to wait until later," he interrupted her. He picked up his shield and helm. "I have delayed long enough. If I keep Fflergant waiting any longer, he will be justified in calling me a coward."

When the heralds announced that combat would continue with edged steel, the Queen gave a low cry of protest.

"Surely you will forbid this," she said, placing a pleading hand on the King's arm.

"On what grounds should I forbid it?" asked Cynwas.

"On what grounds? But my dear Lord . . . if you do not wish to see the thing go forth, that must be reason enough," said Sidonwy.

"I have never interfered in these matters of honor. And if

there is some quarrel between them, then it were better they settled it here before us all, where physicians are present and a priest to give the last rites if necessary.

"It is not so many years," he added, "since I took the field in similar contests, and you once watched these sports, and enjoyed them, too. How is this different?"

The Queen shook her head. "I do not know. Perhaps I am growing old. Perhaps it takes age to see the terrible vulnerability of youth. For it seems to me now that the two of them are perilously young to risk their lives in this unnecessary fashion."

The delay had not improved Fflergant's temper. He strode out into the center of the field, swinging his sword, eager to get on with it. At the marshall's signal, he took the offensive, launching a furious attack that momentarily took Ceilyn by surprise.

But Ceilyn quickly recovered. He blocked, stepped to Fflergant's shield side, and slid past him, circling his own sword for a backhand blow to Fflergant's helm. His sword hit the side of the helmet and glanced off. At the same time, Fflergant feinted, then thrust low, only to be stopped by Ceilyn's shield. His sword scored a deep mark across the painted field.

By Ceilyn's pavilion, Teleri watched the action. At that level, the battle was terrifyingly real, not at all the ritualized combat it appeared from the stands. With every ringing blow, Teleri cringed, expecting the worst.

Fflergant closed again. He hit the edge of Ceilyn's shield with the flat of his own, pushing it aside and leaving Ceilyn's upraised upper arm exposed where it was unprotected by plate. Fflergant swung, connecting with the base of his blade and shearing through the mail rings. The blade hit deep. Ceilyn staggered back.

Recovering in time to block Fflergant's next blow, Ceilyn lunged to the right, gaining a moment while Fflergant turned to face him. In that moment, he tossed aside his shield and switched his sword to his right hand, bringing it up just in time to parry Fflergant's next stroke.

Then, moving so swiftly that Fflergant never afterward understood exactly what had happened, Ceilyn swung again, cut under Fflergant's sword, struck downward, and connected with Fflergant's shoulder in the gap between rerebrace and body armor.

Suddenly, it seemed there was blood everywhere: on both swords, dripping from Ceilyn's wounded arm, staining Fflergant's scarlet surcote a deep crimson. The marshall called a hold. Garanwyn and Gofan raced to the center of the field to offer their assistance.

Refusing Gofan's and the marshall's offers of support, Ceilyn returned to his pavilion.

"There is linen for bandages in the armor chest," he said, as he collapsed on a stool. Gofan helped him to remove his helmet. "Only a scratch," Ceilyn insisted, though blood stained his mail and his green surcote all down one side.

Gofan started to unstrap the rerebrace. "Leave that," said Ceilyn. "Go to Fflergant's pavilion and find out if he was badly hurt."

"Nefyn can go," said Gofan. "My place is with you."

"Your place is to go where I tell you to go and do what I tell you to do," Ceilyn said sharply. "I am in the hands of a physician and you are not needed here. Tell Nefyn to . . . to . . ." Ceilyn searched his mind for some excuse to rid himself of the younger lad as well.

"Tell Nefyn that I left a basket of salves and ointments in the Royal Pavilion," Teleri supplied for him. "Tell him to run and fetch them."

She unbuckled the rerebrace and removed it; Ceilyn lifted his arm so that she could inspect the wound. "How deep was this, really?"

"It glanced off the bone," he said. "Has the bleeding stopped? I thought so. I wonder if my bones knit as quickly as my flesh?"

"As well that you haven't put it to the test, this time." Her voice shook and Ceilyn looked at her with sudden concern.

"You are as white as a ghost. Not of fear for me, surely."

"Partly on your account," said Teleri. "We know you are unlikely to bleed to death under ordinary circumstances, but a single fatal blow might kill you as readily as any man."

"Yes," said Ceilyn, "I know. And believe me, I haven't taken any foolish risks. I tell you this, I had no idea he was so fast and strong. He has improved considerably."

"His speed and his strength did not trouble you before he suggested you fight with edged steel." Teleri wrapped a strip of linen around the rapidly closing wound, lest those who had seen blood flow wonder at Ceilyn's miraculous recovery. "Afterward, you seemed to hold back."

"I do know how it feels to kill a man. Perhaps that hinders

me. But Fflergant, being ignorant, goes in reckless of the consequences," said Ceilyn. "Nevertheless, he is an excellent fighter, and if he were not such a young hot-head, he would be better still.

"But you said you were only partly concerned on my account. What else has frightened you?"

"I have sensed . . . something." Teleri made a vague gesture. "Sometimes I think these premonitions are more of a curse than a blessing, they can be so erratic and unclear. I would disregard this one, were it not for one thing: The Princess Diaspad is not here at the tourney.

"I suppose you would have noticed, had you not been so busy," she continued, "for everyone is talking about it. Calchas is here, along with Prescelli and some of the dwarfs, but the Princess stayed in her rooms this morning, pleading some indisposition. Well, I would not expect that she would send for *me*, even on her deathbed, but neither did she call in Brother Gildas. And if she is not *very* ill, then it is odd, don't you think—"

"—that the Princess would forgo a spectacle . . . or a bloodletting. Yes, it is odd," said Ceilyn. "And more than a little disquieting, to think of her up at the castle, virtually alone, and free to do exactly as she pleases, with no one to observe her."

"Not entirely unobserved," said Teleri. "I did not wish to stay behind, because if something should happen, I would want to be at the Queen's side. But I took such measures as I could, on such short notice.

"There is a man, a blacksmith, whose wife and little daughter I was able to save during a difficult delivery. He and his son are watching outside the Princess's rooms, and the boy will come to me if she so much as steps outside."

Ceilyn looked at her admiringly. "But that was very cleverly contrived on your part. Glastyn could not have done better. You are beginning to fill his place admirably."

Teleri shook her head. "I do not know if the smith and his boy are subtle enough to avoid the Princess's attention. And if something should arise, Ceilyn, it is you I will need at my side, alive and whole and not confined to your room by some supposed injury."

At that moment, Gofan returned with news of Fflergant. "Brother Gildas is with him. A minor wound—his mail took most of the force of your blow," the boy said breathlessly. It was evident he had run both ways. "The blood was deceptive."

"It often is," said Ceilyn, rising to his feet. "You can see that I am not badly injured either." He indicated his own neatly bandaged arm. "Is Fflergant satisfied, or does he wish to continue?"

Gofan said that he did.

"Then I suppose we will have to play this farce through to the end." Ceilyn turned to Teleri, kissed her lightly on the top of the head. "But I will bear in mind what you have said, and take no unnecessary risks."

In a thoughtful mood, Ceilyn put on his helm and walked out on the field. Perhaps, he mused, there were more important things at stake here than his pride or Fflergant's. And now that he came to think about it, he realized that Fflergant was justified in demanding some explanation of his actions on the night the bones had disappeared. It was unfortunate for both of them that all his questions were questions Ceilyn could not answer.

Like everyone else, Ceilyn had wanted to see Fflergant and his brother do well at their maiden tournament. Perhaps even more than anyone else, for Ceilyn had spent many long hours training his young kinsmen—it was just *because* he had been so exacting and persistent that he had orginally won their enmity.

Ceilyn wished he had gone easier on Fflergant in the earlier rounds, allowed him to show to better advantage. Remembering his own first tournament, Ceilyn thought it a pity that Fflergant would not cherish equally pleasant memories of his.

Forced by their injuries to fight off-handed without their shields, Fflergant and Ceilyn circled warily, each looking for a clear opening. Then Fflergant closed, cutting at Ceilyn's helm. Ceilyn blocked, aimed low, and swung past Fflergant's leg as the younger knight leapt back to avoid the blow.

They circled again. Fflergant feinted, but Ceilyn refused to take the bait. Frustrated, Fflergant moved in, launching a pressing attack. And Ceilyn gave ground, moving slowly backward, completely on the defensive. Convinced that he had the upper hand, Fflergant pressed harder, harder. . . . Suddenly, the quillons of their swords caught and locked.

They struggled, each straining to shove the other's blade aside. Then Ceilyn's sword flew through the air and landed in the dirt.

Without thinking, Fflergant stepped back and waited for his opponent to retrieve his weapon.

"Very noble." The sarcasm in Ceilyn's voice was unmistakable. "But this is not a practice bout. You must strike me or spare me, one or the other."

It was the same tone he had always used to reprove Fflergant for errors during practice. Flustered by his mistake, Fflergant obeyed. He raised his sword, put the point on Ceilyn's breast-plate, and spoke the ritual words. "Yield, or die."

"Naturally, I yield."

"And the explanation you owe me?"

"I owe you no explanation," said Ceilyn. "If that is a condition, I withdraw my submission. Cut my throat, if that is your intention."

Totally nonplussed, Fflergant stared at the slight, stubborn figure in front of him. It had never occurred to him that Ceilyn would refuse to speak, once he had lost the fight.

"I can't cut your throat. Damn it, you know that!" Fflergant protested. "Not so long as you are weaponless."

Ceilyn removed his helm. "Well then, you seem to have a problem. I have no intention of picking up that sword and accepting any victory that might follow as a gift of your courtesy. If you plan to murder me, you will have to do it in cold blood. In your place . . . I think I would just accept victory gracefully and declare honor satisfied," he offered helpfully.

Fflergant ground his teeth. "Coward."

"You've already called me that—and other unflattering names as well. For which reason, I have wasted the better part of the morning offering my body for you to cut into pieces. Well then, you won't find a better opportunity than you have right now, and all without blemish to your honor. What do you want to do?"

Fflergant sighed. He might not know when he was over-matched, but he had sense enough to know when he was beaten. "I will withdraw my condition, if you will submit."

"With the greatest of pleasure," said Ceilyn, dropping grace-fully to one knee. "I yield yet again."

Fflergant watched him rise and leave the field, torn between amusement and outrage. It came to him that Ceilyn was like some force of nature—there was simply no way of getting around him.

Up in the viewing stands, the men shouted and the ladies waved their scarves and handkerchiefs. Fflergant was halfway across the field before he realized what all the cheering meant.

Though he had not forced Ceilyn to speak, he had won his very first passage of arms. He had distinguished himself at his maiden tournament by defeating the hitherto unbeatable Ceilyn mac Cuel.

Finarfon lived happily for many years in his father's house, and he never thought once in all that time of the woman he had loved and left behind in the Land of Youth. When his father died, Finarfon became war-chief in his place. The fame of Finarfon spread throughout the land. Yet though many men offered him their daughters, Finarfon made no woman his wife, and it was always his sister, Nuala, who greeted his guests and poured wine for the war-band when they sat down to eat at his table.

One frosty morning, Finarfon put on his golden cloak and his chaplet of gold. Mounting the white steed that had come with him from the Land of Youth, he went out riding. He passed a place where a flock of blackbirds were feasting on red berries in the snow, and Finarfon fell to thinking of the woman he had loved.

"The wings of those blackbirds are no blacker or more glossy than the hair of the woman I love, nor are those berries redder than her lips," said Finarfon. "Though the sun shines brightly on that patch of snow, yet it is not whiter than the flesh of the Princess who dwells in the Land of the Ever Young."

And as he thought of her, a desire to see the woman entered into Finarfon.

—*from* The Book of the White Cockerel

10.

The Feast of St. Valentine

"I confess to God—if it had been any man but Ceilyn, I would suspect that he *gave* me that fight," said Fflergant.

The tournament was over for the day, and the participants had returned to the castle to wash up and dress for the feast that evening. Both Fflergant and his brother had acquitted themselves well, and had every reason to be pleased with their prowess, but Fflergant's mind was still on his unexpected and ultimately unsatisfactory victory over Ceilyn.

Tryffin led the way down a narrow winding alley between buildings that led from the inner courtyard to their tiny suite of rooms. "Not likely that Ceilyn would encourage you to get above yourself by allowing you to win a fight you ought to have lost."

Fflergant ground his teeth. "The next time I have my sword at Ceilyn's throat, I may not be so damned soft-hearted."

He opened a door set into a low archway decorated with crumbling figures of badgers and squirrels cut into the stone in high relief. He and Tryffin passed into the little room that served both as antechamber to their own bedroom and as Garanwyn's sleeping quarters. A driftwood fire blazed on the hearth. But the room was not as tidy as Fflergant had come to expect. Most of Garanwyn's clothes and all his small possessions were piled on his bed or stacked on the floor—everything but the travel gear Garanwyn himself wore and the things he was busy packing into a small wooden chest or had already stuffed into a large bag.

"Before God!" exclaimed Fflergant. "Just exactly what are you doing?"

Garanwyn looked up from his packing. "I am leaving Caer Cadwy tonight. I'm sorry . . . I did mean to say good-bye, but I started in packing and entirely forgot. Well, I would have told you before I left, because I am afraid I shall have to borrow some money. I'll need a mule to carry some of these things."

Fflergant stared at him, utterly conscience-stricken. "You are angry and insulted—and who can blame you? You did provoke me, but I ought never to have struck you."

Garanwyn shook his head. "You were within your rights." The truth was, he had forgotten the incident until Fflergant reminded him. He had been angry at the time, of course, but once his anger and humiliation had faded he readily forgave Fflergant, regarding his actions as perfectly right and natural under the circumstances.

Rhianeddi born and bred, he could hardly do otherwise. Though few among the Rhianeddi nobility stooped to actual cruelty in dealing with their servants and their young attendants, they did not tolerate impertinence or disobedience, and any squire acting as Garanwyn had done could expect a slap or a cuff as a sign of his master's displeasure. Garanwyn also believed that his *own* actions had been entirely justified—but that had nothing to do with it. He had done what his conscience dictated, and Fflergant had responded as a man in his position must, and if the result was a slap in the face and some temporarily wounded feelings on both sides . . . well, that was simply the way of the world.

But Fflergant and Tryffin were Gwyngellach, and saw things differently. Their people did not beat or bully those who served them. To do so, they believed, diminished both man and master.

Fflergant was deeply ashamed of his own behavior. "I ought not to have asked you to act against your better judgment. I apologize, and I hope you will forgive me."

"There is nothing to forgive. Don't give the matter another thought," Garanwyn insisted. He closed the chest and locked it, put the key in a pouch on his belt. "As God is my witness, my leaving Caer Cadwy has nothing to do with you. Or . . . well, it does, but only indirectly. As I stood there watching you and Ceilyn trying to hack pieces out of one another, I finally realized how violent and distasteful it all was.

"Tryffin asked me, once, how I felt about the Korred and their blood sacrifices," Garanwyn continued. "At the time, I thought the same as he did—a wicked, heathen practice. But don't you see? We shed more blood in a year here at Caer Cadwy, in the name of one sport or another, than the marshdwellers do in a decade to please their gods. That's not even mentioning the bear-baiting and the cockfights down in the town, or the witches and pagans that are burned in the north. But I don't want any part of the blood or the burnings, and I finally realized: I don't want to be knighted. I guess . . ." He sat down on the edge of the bed. "I guess I never stopped to think, before, whether the life I had planned was what I really wanted, or simply what was expected of me."

A gust of cold air reminded Fflergant that he had left the door standing open. He closed it and leaned against the doorframe, his arms folded across his chest. He searched for the right words to say, words that would convince Garanwyn that he understood his feelings perfectly, at the same time that he urged him to reconsider his decision.

"A crisis of faith—that's natural enough for a lad your age. I went through one myself, the year I came to Caer Cadwy. It will pass, I promise you, and everything you always believed will begin to make sense again. But even if, after considerably more thought, you decided you did not want to continue on here . . . that would be no reason to pack up your things on the spur of the moment and start out for Cadir Cynfarch—at this time of year, for God's sake, and sure to be bad weather ahead, and worse as you travel north—have you thought what kind of journey that would be?''

Tryffin moved toward the fireplace, stripped off his gloves, and held his hands out over the blaze. ''But Garanwyn isn't going to Rhianedd,'' he said over his shoulder. ''He is going to Teirwaedd Morfa.''

''Yes,'' the boy admitted. ''I will use the Lady's gift to find the marshdwellers and beg permission to live with them. And there is no use trying to talk me out of this, because it was not a sudden or hasty decision. I have been thinking and preparing for this day ever since we came back from the marsh. What happened today just helped me to finally make up my mind.''

''But do you really believe you could be happy living among the Korred—happier than you are here, with your friends and kinsmen around you?'' Fflergant asked incredulously.

Garanwyn shook his head. ''I can't be certain. But I do know that I can't be truly happy living any place where Tiffaine is not. I will try life in the marsh for a time, but if I find I don't belong there—and if Tiffaine is willing to go with me—then we will search the world for a place where a Christian and a pagan can live together happily. It may be there is no such place, but—''

''I believe there is such a place,'' said Tryffin. ''Even in Tir Gwyngelli it won't be easy, but I think you could make a good life for yourselves there. And I know your grandfather would be delighted to welcome you and Arfondwy both to Dinas Dallben.''

Garanwyn nodded solemnly. ''Yes, I thought of that, too. So you see, this may not be good-bye after all, we may all meet again someday in Tir Gwyngelli.''

Fflergant looked helplessly from his brother to Garanwyn, marveling that the usually practical Tryffin could actually be in favor of this insane plan. Then he shrugged, shook his head, and gave in. One madman in the family, that he could deal with, but two—and one of them the customary voice of sweet reason—that was too much for him.

''I have made such provision for Gwenlliant as I could,'' said Garanwyn. ''Teleri will teach her everything she needs to know: to master her powers and not be afraid of what she is. If I stayed, I would only stand in her way. I know in my heart that Gwenlliant is perfect just the way God made her, but there is a part of me that just can't accept her gifts. It is better if I go. And of course, I know that the two of you will always look after her the same as I would . . . only you'll not condemn her for what she has to do, what she *must* be.

"I said good-bye to her—she thinks that I am leaving tomorrow morning and I am afraid I allowed her to believe that I was coming back, because . . . well, what was the use of saying otherwise, when I don't know what sort of reception I will meet with in the marsh?"

Garanwyn pulled on his riding gloves, picked up his baggage, and moved toward the door. "But I will need the money I mentioned, for the mule and for other things. You can divide up everything I leave behind—it may be worth something to you. I suppose I ought to have asked before . . . ," he added sheepishly, ". . . will you release me from the oath I swore, the day I became your squire?"

Fflergant sighed. "What use is your oath if your heart isn't in it?" He put a hand on each of Garanwyn's shoulders, gave him the ritual kiss on the forehead, and Tryffin repeated the gesture. "I release you of all oaths and bindings. Go freely and live happily."

A short time later, down by the stables, Garanwyn and his kinsmen made their final farewells, embracing heartily in the sentimental Gwyngellach fashion. "I still think you have lost your senses," said Fflergant, pummeling the boy affectionately. "Leaving at this hour—how far do you think you will get by dark?"

"I'll only go as far as Treledig. I will buy the mule, find a place to spend the night, and then start at first light. Leaving Caer Cadwy is the hard part, and that won't get easier if I delay."

"If you should change your mind," said Tryffin, "for God's sake, don't let pride stand in your way. You can be sure of a welcome back here."

"I know that," said Garanwyn. "Perhaps that is what gives me the courage to go. But I don't think that I *will* change my mind, and I don't think I will ever come back."

In the corridor outside Gwenlliant's bedchamber, Calchas stepped out of the shadows. Taking the little girl by surprise, he grabbed her roughly by one arm.

"Come with me," he hissed in her ear, as the child cried out and struggled to be free. "I have a surprise for you, something very pleasant. But you have to stop that, and come with me at once.''

Gwenlliant continued to resist him. "You are hurting me, Calchas. Do let go of me. My brother says I am not even to talk to you.''

Calchas only tightened his grip and pulled her closer. His hands were clammy and his breath on her face was hot and wine-laden. "Your brother is a fool. He doesn't know . . . doesn't know. . . . Come with me now, and I'll—'' He whispered something in her ear that made Gwenlliant's eyes widen in shock. "Oh come, now, don't play the innocent with me. I know *all* your daydreams.'' He grabbed her by the hair and gave her a long wet kiss, full on the mouth. "There, you see. It's very pleasant when you decide to be nice to me.''

"If you don't let me be, I will scream. Yes, I will.'' Gwenlliant increased her struggles to be free. "I will tell my brother *and* my cousins what you just said to me.''

Calchas sneered. "Oh yes, tell them anything you please. They won't be able to touch me.''

But then his tone changed, became softer and more coaxing. "You have to come with me now . . . you'll be sorry if you don't. You may not believe me, but I only want to spare you pain.''

He started to drag her down the corridor, toward the back stairs. A gleam of silver around Gwenlliant's neck caught his attention. "What is that you are wearing?''

He tugged the chain and pulled the talisman up through the neck of her dress. "Ah God! That is why you resist my love charm!'' His eyes narrowed. "I daresay someone thinks they have been very, very clever, thwarting me this way. But not so clever as they imagine!'' He pushed her away with a vicious shove. The fine chain broke and the silver disk fell to the floor.

"I would have saved you. I would have taken you away . . . away to a place where nothing could harm you. Just remember that,'' he said, "when all Hell breaks loose, and it is too late then for anyone to help you.''

In her bedchamber on the floor above, Teleri was changing into a new gown of red velvet with a wide neckline trimmed with soft grey miniver. When someone knocked at the stillroom door, she hastily buttoned up her sleeves, crossed the outer room, and opened the door. Ceilyn waited on the other side, dressed for the feast in his best parti-colored green and gold.

As he crossed the threshold, Ceilyn bent to kiss her on the cheek. Teleri blushed, suddenly conscious, because of the way he looked at her, that the gown was cut very low across the shoulders.

"If you have come to escort me to the Hall, it must be later than I thought."

"The Queen sent me. I am not to attend the feast at all, unless you examine my wound and pronounce me fit. She gave me a stern lecture about the danger of fever after an injury."

"I think I would like to take a look," said Teleri. "I am curious to see just how quickly you heal under ordinary circumstances."

Ceilyn obligingly took off his belt, his swordbelt, and his doublet, and rolled up the sleeve of his shirt. Teleri unwrapped the bandage and examined his arm with interest. The skin was smooth and healthy-looking; the only remaining evidence of injury was a long pink scar. "Will this be gone by morning?" she asked.

"Undoubtedly. And I'll credit your skill as a physician, if anyone asks later."

She touched his right side, the place where Derry mac Forgoll had wounded him five months before.

"That one was bad," he admitted. "And there is still a pale white scar beneath the ribs. I suspect I will have that one always, thanks to the poisonous influence of Morc's silver brooch."

"Perhaps not," said Teleri, as she began to wrap a clean linen bandage around Ceilyn's arm. "You knew that you were seriously injured, that you might even die. I think it was that more than any injury or the effect of the silver that made the scar."

"I don't understand," he said.

"The ability to change your shape is a thing of bone, blood, and flesh. But there are patterns here"—she left off bandaging him for a moment and touched him lightly on the forehead—"that you unconsciously follow in changing your shape or in healing yourself when you are hurt. There is one pattern for the form you wear now, and another for the wolf. It is true that one or both of those patterns was slightly altered, or you would not be scarred after five months, but if you could repair the pattern, then your body would heal also."

Ceilyn frowned thoughtfully. "You mean . . . if I believed myself whole again, I would be?"

"I think so, yes."

"Well," he said, "I think I prefer it this way. It might be convenient, someday, to have one scar to show to people who wonder why I haven't any."

But the implications of what she said troubled him, and he continued to think them over as he donned his doublet and belted it.

"Those patterns you spoke of . . . in my mind. I suppose I was born with them, both the wolf and the man. You don't think—you don't think there might be more of them?"

"Possibly," she said. "But buried so deeply, I don't believe you need worry about them. Unless the time came when it was *necessary* for you to become something else."

He thought of All Hallows Eve, when he had spent an hour down in the meadow watching the Princess perform her pagan rites. To escape her notice, he had disguised himself as a bush of the holly for which he was named. Illusion—or reality? He had believed it illusion at the time, illusion created with Teleri's help, but now he was not so certain.

"God help me," he said, "I had trouble enough accepting the wolf inside me."

Teleri started toward her bedchamber, meaning to fetch her cloak, but Ceilyn reached out to detain her. "There was another reason I wanted to talk to you before the feast."

He took something out of a pouch he wore on his belt, and slipped it onto her wrist: a golden bracelet, slender and graceful, set with milky white sidhe-stones. "I hope you will accept this and wear it for my sake, though perhaps it isn't so pretty as the necklace Fand gave you."

She looked at the bracelet, torn between pleasure at the gift and a conviction that she ought not to accept it. "But this is far older and more valuable. An heirloom of your family? Ceilyn, I don't think—"

"I was told to give it to the lady of my choice—and who would that be, if not you? If you are not ready to accept it as a pledge between us, take it as a token of friendship, and don't deny me the pleasure of seeing you wear it."

On those terms, she could hardly refuse. And the bracelet was beautiful, perfect in its form and symmetry. "Thank you," she said softly.

And then something reached inside her mind and violently wrenched some part of her away. Everything suddenly went black.

Ceilyn caught her as she fell and carried her over to a chair. "What happened? Are you all right?" he asked, as soon as she opened her eyes.

Gradually, she became aware of him bending solicitously over her. But she was still dizzy and disorientated—and empty inside, as if something fundamental to the stability of her world had been suddenly and inexplicably torn away.

She took a long breath. "There is something terribly, terribly wrong. I felt something *move*, as if the very foundations of the castle were shaken. Ceilyn, run quickly and see if all is well with the King and Queen."

"And leave you, when you are so obviously unwell?" he protested. "*I* didn't feel a thing."

"Truly," she said shakily. "I really think you should go." But when he continued to hover over her: "If you must do something for me, pour me a cup of wine before you leave."

Ceilyn moved quickly to obey her. On a table by her bedchamber door stood two wooden cups and a stout green bottle. Without thinking, Ceilyn tasted the wine he poured into one of the cups, as was his habit when serving the Queen. The wine was a particularly potent vintage flavored with ginger. He handed the cup to Teleri and knelt on the floor at her feet.

"Are you quite certain I can do nothing for you?"

She managed a pale imitation of a smile. "You can reassure me that all is well with the King and Queen."

The aftertaste of the ginger wine still tingled. As Ceilyn started to his feet, his stomach contracted violently and his heart gave a mighty leap in his chest, then seemed to stop altogether. He staggered and fell to his knees again.

Teleri stopped with the cup at her lips. "Ceilyn, what is it?"

"Poison," he gasped. "I've been poisoned." His hands were cold and clammy, his heartbeat irregular. His mouth and tongue were numb. He reached to steady himself against the chair, and his eyes widened as he saw the cup in her hand. "Don't drink, for God's sake. The poison might be in the ginger wine."

She put the cup down on the floor. "Ginger . . . not elderflower wine?"

He sat back on his heels, still struggling for breath. Gradually, his heartbeat steadied, the pain in his midsection eased. "Jesus

. . . oh sweet Jesus . . . you nearly took poison from my hands. All those years, I've been testing Sidonwy's wine . . . and I didn't stop to wonder why the ginger was so strong.''

With an effort, he rose to his feet. Teleri would have risen, too, but he waved her back. "I am better now. The seizure has passed."

Another wave of dizziness came over her, forcing her to obey him and sit back in her chair. "How much did you drink?"

"Only a sip—just a taste, though as God is my witness I never suspected—"

"You mustn't blame yourself," she said. "You have taken poison apparently meant for me—not the other way around."

But then she began to realize what that meant. "Oh Ceilyn . . . if someone wants me out of the way, badly enough to poison me—"

"Something is afoot," said Ceilyn. "Something the Princess does not want you to interfere in. I'll go downstairs and look for the Queen."

"I will come with you," Teleri said, trying again to rise from her chair.

But Ceilyn pushed her gently back. "You were taken worse than I was. And you haven't my . . . resiliency. You stay right here until you get your strength back. God knows, you may need it later."

Down by the stable, the Princess Diaspad waited, mounted and dressed for travel. A hood drawn low over her forehead only partly obscured her face: What could be seen was pale and uncharacteristically grim. Lashed to the horn of her saddle was an oddly shaped bundle wrapped in black velvet, which the Princess touched every now and then, as if to reassure herself that it was really there.

Most of her household had gone ahead with the wagons and the caravan, but Diaspad and her dwarf guardsmen lingered by the stables, waiting for Calachas to arrive. All the dwarfs were mounted on bandy-legged steeds, all save the smallest and most misshapen dwarf of the troop, who stood with reins in hand trying to calm Calchas's fidgeting black stallion. Two ponies were tied up by the stable: a pretty little dapple grey and an ugly but sturdy dun.

"Where have you been?" Diaspad hissed, when Calchas finally appeared. "What delayed you? You very nearly spoiled everything."

The boy shrugged. "I had business of my own to attend to." He snatched the reins from the dwarf and swung up into the saddle.

His mother urged her mare between Calchas and the gate. "Business . . . yes. And would your business concern that pony you ordered saddled?"

Calchas shook the lank dark hair out of his face. His eyes widened, as if in surprise, as he gazed at the dainty grey. "That pony? I ordered nothing of the sort." He glared at the smallest dwarf. "If that ugly little freak says otherwise, he lies."

The Princess moved out of his way. With Calchas in the lead, they rode out the gate. But as they proceeded down the road, the Princess caught up with him.

"Later on, Dear Boy, we will discuss the matter at length," she said. "And perhaps you can tell me then just exactly how you knew *which* dwarf it was that saddled Gwenlliant ni Cyndrywyn's pony."

"And so," said the King, "your experiments have been successful and the power of the sidhe-stone is even greater than before."

Cynwas and his two friends, Manogan and Ysgafn, had joined Glastyn in his little study at Dinas Moren. Shelves lined the walls, but not enough of them to contain all the wizard's books, which spilled over to a long table, both of the chairs, and a large portion of the floor. Like the King, Glastyn was eager to move into larger and more comfortable quarters on the big island.

"Entirely successful," said the wizard. "All that remains is to place the stone in the crown, and then you may move the court to Caer Cadwy as soon as you wish."

Cynwas looked gratified. "I do not like to be so isolated, as I must be, here on Aderyn. It will please me to be back at the heart of things."

"You will be at the heart of things—and yet, thanks to the warding properties of the stone, as isolated from the dangers that beset the common-folk as if you had remained at Dinas Moren."

Someone knocked on the study door, and the wizard turned to smile at the young Earl Marshall. "That will be the Virgin. Remembering what you said about their scarcity at court, I sent to Castell Aderyn on the other side of the island."

Glastyn opened the door, and a servant came in, leading a child by the hand. She was a pale little creature with long, flyaway hair.

"But this is a child . . . an infant," protested Manogan.

"You did say that any female who had seen more than three or four summers must be suspect," the wizard reminded him.

Manogan scowled darkly. "That was a jest—and a poor one. You do ill to turn it against me at this child's expense."

Glastyn dismissed the servant, picked up the little girl, and placed her on a high stool. "There is no danger in the procedure, I assure you. She shall place the Clach Ghealach in the crown, and take no harm in doing so.

"And I did not intend to turn your jest against you, my soft-hearted Gwyngellach friend. I merely took your words for an omen. This is Pendaren's daughter, Teleri, and she is just three years old."

11.

A Night in Bedlam

When Ceilyn returned to the stillroom, he found Teleri sitting on a high stool by the long table where she had set up her stills and other alchemical apparatus. Apparently recovered after her mysterious seizure, she held up a flask containing a pale golden liquid, and peered into it as though she expected it to contain the answers to all her questions.

Ceilyn cleared his throat to gain her attention. "The King and Queen are both well and no one has seen anything odd," he said. "Or rather . . . no one but me. It is probably my imagination: I find myself starting at shadows, thinking I see something out of the corner of my eye—but when I look, there is nothing there."

Teleri put down the flask. Ceilyn sat down beside her, on another, shorter stool. "But there has been one unpleasant incident. I am not certain if it means anything. When I saw the Queen, Gwenlliant was there, weeping and hysterical. The only sense that anyone could make of what she said was that Calchas made her an indecent proposal. But I see this comes as no surprise to you."

Teleri shook her head. "Not a surprise, no. Though Garanwyn and I both hoped . . . She wasn't harmed in any way, was she?"

"Apparently not. They sent for her brother, but for some reason he was not in the castle. Tryffin and Fflergant were with her when I left. In a fine rage, the pair of them. It seems this was not the first time Calchas has run afoul of them with his attentions to Gwenlliant." He clenched his fists. "If there is anything left of Calchas after they are finished with him, I would like an opportunity to deal with him myself."

"Then you haven't seen Calchas . . . or his mother . . . anywhere about the castle?" Teleri asked.

"No, but I spoke with your friend the blacksmith. Though you only asked him to watch while you were down at the tourney, he and his son have taken it in turns all evening. There's been a good deal of activity coming and going from Diaspad's rooms, but *she* hasn't ventured out since morning.

"But what have you been doing here?" Ceilyn asked. "Is that the wine?"

"I've been testing it. No, I didn't drink any. That would have been one way of learning, and not so dangerous as you might think, but Glastyn taught me to use many different methods for detecting poisons."

"And you discovered?"

"The wine is laced with aconite," said Teleri. "Enough in that one cup to kill ten or twelve men. But there were smaller amounts of other poisons as well: belladonna, hellebore, and digitalis."

"A powerful dose for one small female!" Ceilyn exclaimed.

"Perhaps not. I have a high immunity to most poisons. All those I just named are used medicinally in their proper dosage, and Alchemists use poisons like arsenic in their work. Dealing with so many dangerous substances—and especially when I first came here as a child—it was inevitable that accidents would happen. So Glastyn saw to it that I acquired natural or magical immunities to practically every poison you could name. When I was younger, he used to feed me sugarplums laced with arsenic and . . . Well, I see you don't approve, but it may have saved my life on more than one occasion."

Teleri took up the flask again. "It might require a full cup of this wine to kill me, though much less would suffice for the strongest man in the castle. So you see, our would-be poisoner was not prodigal. In fact, were I in her place, I might be tempted to make it even stronger, just to be certain it would do its task. And I would never have included the digitalis: Foxglove is the antidote for aconite poisoning, though it acts more slowly and would be of little use against so lethal a dose."

She put the flask down on the table. "But the use of aconite troubles me. It makes me wonder if the poison weren't meant for you instead—and then to wonder: Who could possibly know enough to try and poison you with wolfsbane?"

Ceilyn frowned. "But the poisoned wine was left here for you."

"Or left for the two of us to share. Everyone knows that you come here often," said Teleri. "And anyone who has observed your habits might also expect you to pour and take the first dose.''

Ceilyn considered that. ''It seems a slip-shod way to proceed. You might have been alone when you drank the wine. Or shared the wine with practically anyone in the castle.''

Teleri sighed. She took the stopper out of a tiny blue glass phial, and poured a few grains of coarse white powder into the palm of her hand. ''That is the way of poison—it often goes astray. It is a reckless weapon.''

''A coward's weapon,'' Ceilyn said sternly. ''What is that you are doing?''

Teleri dropped the white powder into the flask. ''This is alicorn—ground unicorn's horn. It will neutralize the poison, allowing me to dispose of the wine safely. I wonder how long it sat there on that table. It might have been there since yesterday morning, or only for a few hours. This room should be warded like the laboratory—I was careless not to have seen to it earlier.''

''Then we don't know if the Princess hoped to be rid of you earlier,'' said Ceilyn. ''Or whether she planned this little surprise to take place this evening. So we can't guess when—''

''Something *has* happened, already. I know I am sometimes vague and uncertain when it comes to possibilities, but when it comes to things that have already happened, my prophetic gifts are rather more reliable. I know that something momentous has already occurred, I just don't know what it was. And I dread that discovery.''

''Then what,'' said Ceilyn, ''ought we to do in the meantime?''

Teleri shook her head. ''I don't know. I suppose we might as well go down to the feast. That is the only way we can both keep a close eye on the King and the Queen.''

''You are certain this threatens one or both of them?''

''No,'' said Teleri. ''But surely as long as the question remains open, we ought to assume that it does.''

Fflergant and Tryffin arrived late for the feast, looking so grim and determined that Ceilyn knew at once they had been balked of their prey.

Seated by Teleri at one of the long tables, Ceilyn had a clear view of the dais. The Princess Diaspad's place at the King's right hand remained empty. Word had circulated that she still suffered from the same mysterious ailment that had kept her away from the tournament.

Ceilyn had not expected Calchas would show his face after the incident with Gwenlliant, but he searched the crowd in vain for any glimpse of Prescelli, and he wondered uneasily why it was that none of Diaspad's dwarfs and woodwoses were seated among the other servants at the two lower tables.

At his side, Teleri remained quiet and watchful, eating and drinking little, though everything on the plate she and Ceilyn shared, or in their cup, had come from a common platter or flagon. Ceilyn was not hungry either—his narrow escape earlier had hardly stimulated his appetite. But the young knight had waited a long time for a night such as this, a night when he could sit by Teleri's side as her acknowledged champion. He was determined to make the most of the opportunity, to keep up the pretense of enjoyment in the hope that pretense might become reality.

"I beg your pardon. I was listening to the wind," Teleri said, when he finally succeeded in gaining her attention.

He put down the wine cup. "The wind? Even I can't hear the wind over all this clamor."

"Nevertheless," she said. "The wind is rising."

Ceilyn listened, straining to sense what she sensed, but it was impossible to hear anything outside over the noise in the Hall. Yet there was something, an undercurrent beneath the clatter of eating implements, the music, and the babble of voices: a faint rustle, as of tiny clawed feet running the length of the table. Once, he felt something brush against his foot, but when he lifted the cloth to look, he saw nothing there.

"You feel it, too," Teleri said softly.

"I don't know," he said, looking toward the dais. "I don't know what I feel."

The King and the Queen had entered into a spirited conversation; the Marshall and the Constable spoke together in muted tones; did any of them feel anything amiss? Farther down the High Table, Fflergant was flirting with Fand, smiling and whispering something in her ear. Tryffin's expression was, as usual, unreadable, but he glanced over his shoulder and around the room, as if he, too, sensed something out of the ordinary.

The heavy doors from the courtyard burst open and a cold wind swept through the Hall. An armored man appeared on the threshold, stumbled across the room toward the dais, and fell to his knees on the steps. A green surcote emblazoned with a silver crown, worn over his armor, marked him as one of Cynwas's treasury guards. Ceilyn saw his lips move, but the wind, rising to an ear-shattering howl, drowned out his words.

At Ceilyn's side, Teleri stiffened and clutched his arm. "It is gone—Diaspad has taken the crown and the sidhe-stone. I felt it leave the castle, felt it and never knew what I felt. Oh Ceilyn, I have failed Glastyn's trust. It was my task, above all others, to guard the Clach Ghealach."

Before he could answer her, she was off the bench and running toward the door. After a moment of startled inaction, Ceilyn followed. She was too swift for him, and ran out of the Hall before he could catch her.

The inner courtyard swarmed with dark shapes, a confused mass of things that crawled and things that hopped, things that flapped overhead with a rustle of dry wings. All the dark chaotic forces that had besieged Caer Cadwy over the years, all the creatures inimical to man that had tried to find a way in and been repelled by the Clach Ghealach, had assaulted the castle in force.

Heedless of any consequences to himself, Ceilyn pushed through the dark throng and followed Teleri through gates and courtyards to the Wizard's Tower. Again and again, something caught at his ankles or his shins, or fastened in his hair, but each time Ceilyn shook it off and continued on with single-minded determination. At last he reached the tower. Slamming the door behind him, he leapt up the stairs after Teleri. He caught up with her on the first landing.

"What are you going to do?" he demanded.

"I must learn where she is taking it. There is a link between the stone and me, Glastyn must have forged it all those years ago, and I can trace that link and find the stone and crown wherever she takes them."

Ceilyn gripped her arm. "But not—not without leaving yourself vulnerable to these things that are attacking the castle."

"There will be some danger," she admitted. "But the laboratory is warded, and the wards offer some protection."

"If the wards *hold*," he said. "But will they hold, now the Clach Ghealach is not here to support them? Can they protect you against such an onslaught as this?"

"That is a risk I will take." Teleri twisted out of his grasp. "You must guard the door for me. Nothing can pass the threshold so long as you are there and alive to forbid it. You are armed with cold iron and your own magic as well. Surely you can hold the door until morning!''

He reached out to catch her again, but again she was too quick for him. She ran up the stairs and into the laboratory, slamming the door behind her. He heard a bolt fall into place and a key turn in the lock.

While Teleri lit candles and drew pentagrams on the floor in the Wizard's Tower, chaos reigned down in the Hall. Women and children shrieked in terror, men reached for their weapons, servants ran about in confusion. The wind tore banners off walls, toppled candlesticks and wine goblets, and extinguished torches. The fire in the great fireplace flickered and nearly died, then roared into new life, burning with an uncanny green flame.

In the eerie half light, the air was filled with swirling phantoms, as all the ghosts laid by Glastyn's spells returned to haunt the living. Grim-faced warriors with gaping wounds materialized and stumped through the crowded room, carrying their severed limbs with them. A procession of ghostly women came in at the door, with the blood of childbirth still on their loins; a crowd of pale infants and wasted children followed in their wake, holding out their spindly arms as if in supplication.

Sidonwy and her women wept, torn between pity and horror. The King rose from his throne, drew his sword, and brandished it. Then madness and delusion seized him and his men.

The older knights, forgetting the passage of twenty years, rushed out of the Hall, intent on pursuing the adventures which had last occupied them two decades before.

Fergos and a group of younger men, knights and guardsmen and squires, organized an expedition against Gandwy of Perfudd—the Warlock Lord, dead for more than a century.

And Fflergant and Tryffin, almost simultaneously, fell victim to a compelling certainty that the Dragon of Ildathach had come back to life and was ravaging the northern countryside. They, too, rushed out of the Hall. Stopping at their rooms only long enough to garb and arm themselves like barbaric Gwyngellach warriors of old, they rode out through the Main Gate, determined to slay the monster.

By morning, every man who could lift a weapon or mount a horse had deserted the castle on Brynn Caer Cadwy—every man but Ceilyn mac Cuel.

• • •

Ceilyn drew his sword and took up a defensive position in front of the laboratory door. He knew when Teleri began her magical search, because the winds lashed the tower with increased fury as she drew the worst part of the attack in her direction.

He did not hear the door at the foot of the steps burst open, but he felt the wind sucked up the tower and he saw the torches flicker in their cressets. A terrible racket surrounded him, like the screeching of a thousand cats at a Tagharim, and a dark tide swept up the steps, a mass of misshapen creatures that threw themselves against him in a frenzy, or beat against the wooden door.

Goblins and bogles pinched and bruised him with crooked fingers. Grotesque, dwarfish square-foots ripped at him with piglike tusks. Water leapers, horrible hybrid things with goggling toads' eyes and bat-winged snake bodies, flew at his head and shoulders. Ceilyn struck at them with his sword, slashing and cutting to left and right, but as swiftly as he slew them, worse things came to replace them.

A shapeless brollochan attacked him, and a galleybeggar, carrying its own head under one skeletal arm, cast itself at Ceilyn shrieking and laughing with insane glee. Wraithlike apparitions laid cold hands on him, sucking the warmth out of his body. At the touch of his sword, many of the night things simply disappeared; others dragged themselves away, dribbling noisome fluids.

The door gave way behind him, but Ceilyn remained at his post, remembering that nothing could pass the threshold so long as he was alive to forbid it. "You cannot enter," he defied them. But as the hours passed he grew steadily weaker. He wondered how he could possibly continue to fight until morning.

When Ceilyn was too tired to swing his sword any longer, he slipped into wolf-shape and fought with his great tearing teeth. As a wolf, his endurance was greater and his jaws powerful enough to crack and splinter bone. Yet still they came, hour after hour, ripping and wounding him, infecting him with subtle poisons. Pookahs and yell-hounds, great shaggy creatures, demoneyed . . . the hideous nucklavee from out of the sea, the muscles of his skinless body glistening with blood . . . giant armless fachens, stumping up the stairs on their single legs, snapping at him with gaping jaws.

At last, just when it seemed that he could fight no longer, the tide began to ebb. The forces besieging the tower retreated; the wind and the howling died. Ceilyn knew then that dawn could not be far off.

In the sudden eerie silence, he thought he heard a new sound, faint and distant—the light dissonant tinkling of many small bells. Somehow, that sound was far from reassuring.

As Ceilyn listened apprehensively, the last of the creatures slipped away. The chiming bells grew louder. Ceilyn shifted back into man-shape, took up his sword, and gripped it defensively.

"It is in the Underworld, in the Valley of Lamentation," said Mael-Duir, "that you will find my daughter's heart."

But if the giant's words dismayed him, the lad gave no sign. "I have tamed the falcon of Oenafwyn, which no man had ever captured. Nine time ninety heroes tried, but all of them failed. I lived seven days under the sea, herding Dylan's cattle, and forty days at Caer Sidi, serving as page-boy to the White Witch. I have sworn brotherhood with Bleiddwn, the grey wolf. I have traveled far and suffered much in order to bring you the Twelve Treasures of the Isle of Celydonn.

"All these tasks you gave me, and I performed them every one. I never turned back; nor shall I turn back now," said the youth. "I will go into the Underworld, even into the Valley of Lamentation, and when I return I shall bring with me your daughter's heart."

"Listen, then," said Mael-Duir, "and I shall tell you how you will know when you find what you seek. By these signs you shall know: by an appletree flowering out of season, by the fire that does not burn, by the white doe, and the green snake, and by holly, whin, and oak. But if you do not recognize the signs when you see them, my daughter will never be yours."

—*from* The Black Book of Tregalen

12.

Lord of Holly and of Oak

Heavy footsteps approached the tower and climbed the stairs. The chiming of bells drew nearer.

Around a curve in the stairwell came a creature out of legend: Twelve feet tall and proportionately broad, it wore the form of an ancient king, noble of mien, magnificently bearded, and splendidly robed. And all about him was fair, seemly, and majestic, save for one thing: The King and all his garments glowed a ghastly unnatural green.

Ceilyn took a step backward, moving closer to the doorframe. "You cannot enter," he protested wearily. "I forbid you to enter."

The creature continued to climb the stairs. On his head, he wore a crown of oakleaves, across his chest an embroidered baldric heavy with the chiming bells. In one huge green hand he carried a bough of holly, in the other an enormous battle-axe. As he approached he grew in size, swelling until it seemed impossible that the stairwell, even the tower, could contain him. With a roar he lifted his axe.

The battle-axe came down with a mighty rush. Ceilyn flung up his sword to ward off the blow, but the heavier weapon came down with shattering force, shivering the steel blade into a thousand glittering fragments and driving the young knight to his knees.

Ceilyn waited, helpless and weaponless, for the next blow. He was determined to make a good end, since that was all that was left to him. But nothing happened. The grim King did not strike again. And Ceilyn looked up, puzzled, to see what stayed his hand.

The apparition loomed over him, regarding him with blood-red eyes. When he spoke, his great booming voice seemed to arise out of the stones of the castle, out of the depths of the earth.

"Which one?" the Green King demanded. "I claim my ancient right to a life, given or taken. Which one shall it be?"

Ceilyn was too weary to resist, too weary to protest, almost too weary to answer. Yet he knew that Teleri must live to restore the sidhe-stone to the King.

"Let it be mine, then," he whispered, and waited for the axe to descend.

But an uncanny smile spread over the green face. "The offering is acceptable. But I have a better use for your life, Ceilyn mac Cuel, than to extinguish it. It is enough, for now, that you have offered."

"Who are you?" Ceilyn asked. "How do you know me?"

The creature laughed, a deep hollow laugh. "My name is the same as yours: Celin I am called, or Cuileann in the north. I am the Holly King, he of the glas-tann, Lord of the Wild Things. How is it that *you* do not know *me*?"

And suddenly he was gone. Ceilyn stared at the spot where the Holly King had stood, as dazed as a sleepwalker waking suddenly from his dream. For a moment, he believed he *had* been dreaming—until he moved his sword arm and found it stiff and numb, his sword surprisingly light. The blade was broken, about a foot from the hilt. He would have wept, but he was too weary for tears.

As the first pale light of morning came in through the arrow-slots in the tower wall, Ceilyn collapsed at the top of the stairs and passed beyond conscious thought.

He woke, stiff and cramped, minutes or hours later. He rose painfully to his feet, dismayed by the silence on the other side of the half-open laboratory door. Pushing the door aside, he staggered into the room.

Teleri lay, dead or unconscious, in a forlorn little heap of scarlet in the middle of the floor. An odor of incense lingered on the air, and the smell of burnt wax. As Ceilyn crossed the floor, something crunched under his feet. Looking down, he saw that Teleri was surrounded by splinters of ice or glass. A bronze tripod stood above her, and the glittering shards fanned out around it. Ceilyn's heart beat faster as he realized what had happened: Teleri's crystal ball had shattered into a thousand needle-sharp pieces.

He went down on one knee to see if she still lived. She lay on her side, with her knees drawn up and one arm across her face, as if to protect it from the flying crystal shards. Dreading what he might find, he lifted her arm.

By some miracle—or some spell of her own—her face was unmarked. At Ceilyn's touch, she groaned and opened her eyes.

"Dear Heart," he said hoarsely, "are you hurt? . . . Can you speak to me?"

"I don't . . . I don't think I was hurt."

"Thank God," he said, as he helped her to sit up. "Thank God you were spared."

She looked around her, at the remains of her shattered crystal, at the chalk symbols on the floor, and the candles arranged in a circle around her. "What happened here?"

"Don't you remember?"

She frowned, straining to recall. "Last night . . . I searched . . . Yes, I remember. The sidhe-stone is gone. I failed Glastyn's trust."

"But did you discover where the Princess has taken it?" he asked.

Teleri closed her eyes, concentrated for a moment. "The crown is moving north . . . and east. I can feel it moving farther and farther away."

She stood up, pale and tremulous in her bright scarlet gown. The brilliant color emphasized her waxy skin and the dark circles under her eyes. "It was difficult at first, when I didn't know where or how to begin to search. But once I touched the stone with my mind, I could strengthen the link. I believe I will always know where she takes it now."

Teleri passed a weary hand over her forehead. "There was something else . . . a name. Caer Wydr. When I touched the stone, I also touched Diaspad's mind for a moment. She and the crown are heading for Caer Wydr."

"Caer Wydr." Ceilyn spoke just above a whisper. "Of all the ill-omened names!" For Caer Wydr, the legendary Castle of Glass, was known in songs and stories as the kind of perilous place where every sort of supernatural adventure was likely to overtake the visitor—and few who entered in were ever known to depart.

Even to find the place, if it really existed, presented a challenge, for the location of the castle had been variously described as on land, under the earth, among the stars, or beneath the sea.

"But who knows the way to Caer Wydr?" Ceilyn wondered aloud. "Certainly not I."

"Nor I," said Teleri. "But it seems that the Princess does know. And if she takes the Clach Ghealach there, then I must follow."

As Ceilyn and Teleri left the Wizard's Tower and crossed the courtyard, the castle was ominously quiet. "It must be well past Tierce." Ceilyn scowled up at the sun. "And this place is like a tomb. Where is everyone?"

He thought he heard voices in the lower courtyard, so they headed for the Gamelyon Gate. Passing through the gate, they spotted a knot of nervous, red-eyed women—laundresses and scrub maids, and a few of the craftsmen's wives—gathered together by the well.

At the sight of Ceilyn, several women cried out. They surged around him, begging for word of their husbands, the King, the guards. . . . Had he seen them? . . . Were the others coming back?

"I am sorry," said Ceilyn. "I spent the night in the Wizard's

Tower battling goblins. I know nothing about your husbands. You must tell me what happened.''

They all began to speak at once; Ceilyn had difficulty sorting out all their stories. There had been encounters with ghosts, several women reported visions and other odd experiences—but it seemed that the worst part of the attack had been centered, as Ceilyn had guessed, on the Wizard's Tower. What concerned the women was the behavior of their men. The King and his knights and squires had begun it, arming up and running off in search of adventure, and the guardsmen had followed close behind. But then the madness spread. Blacksmiths, wheelwrights, and stablehands raided the armory, claiming the few remaining edged weapons and taking the blunted practice blades down to the smithy to sharpen them. The cook and his assistants provided their own weapons: butcher's knives and cleavers. Even the monks succumbed. The King's elderly confessor struggled into a suit of rusty armor the other men did not consider taking, and Brother Gildas, that gentle solemn man, had hitched up his robes, snatched a sword from one of the squires, and run out the gate brandishing the weapon wildly.

''Are there *no* men to defend this place?'' Ceilyn asked.

''No one but yourself, Lord,'' replied a stout laundress.

''No men and no wards,'' said Teleri, ''now that the Clach Ghealach is gone. But I can attend to that much before we go.''

Ceilyn stared at her. ''Go? And leave the Queen and the other women to fend here for themselves? Run off to storm Caer Wydr—or wherever she actually takes the stone—just the two of us? We have to wait until some of the men come back, take as many with us as are willing to—''

''We can't wait,'' Teleri interrupted him. ''Or I can't, anyway. You must do as your duty dictates, but mine requires that I follow the Princess as swiftly as I can. You do not know—the sidhe-stone harms us not only by its absence; there are also ways she can use the stone. And I have to recover the crown, before the Princess realizes the full potential of what she has stolen.''

Ceilyn took her aside, spoke low so that the other women should not hear him. ''If you go, of course I go with you. But will you only think . . . what could we do, once we caught up with the Princess? There are a dozen or more armed men in her household—good fighters, too, even if they are less than four feet tall—to say nothing of the woodwoses and the giant. The odds against regaining the crown—''

"It is a desperate enterprise, yes, but more perilous the longer we wait. We have more chance of success if we follow her swiftly, than if we waited and arrived at Caer Wydr at the head of an army," Teleri insisted.

"But tell me this," she added softly. "If I were to stay behind . . . were the task given to you alone . . . would you hesitate to take it on, no matter what the odds?"

Ceilyn shook his head. "You know I would run right off, eager to play the hero. But that doesn't mean that I would be wise in doing so—or that I am foolish now, to try and protect you."

Teleri flushed. "I don't ask for your protection. I do ask for your help because . . . because I don't think either of us could succeed on our own. But the task was appointed to me, and I must perform it to the best of my ability and according to my own judgment."

"Yes," Ceilyn agreed reluctantly. "The task is yours; I suppose I ought to respect that. But before we go running off, we ought to at least make certain that the Queen and the other ladies have survived the terrors of the night."

They found Sidonwy and her handmaidens in the Solar, huddled in a tense little group, their chairs drawn up before one of the fireplaces. Ceilyn went down on one knee beside the Queen and kissed her hand. "Thank God you are well."

"Oh Ceilyn," Sidonwy said tremulously. "They are all gone, even the boys. The King has led such a quiet life for so many years . . . what will become of him, going off in search of adventure now?

"Both my pages, too," she added mournfully, "and young Nefyn. A month ago he was one of them, dressed in silk with pretty ringlets like a maiden. . . . I had scarcely adjusted to the sight of him in man's dress, and now he goes off carrying a sword . . . !"

Ceilyn soothed her as best he could. "I hear that the Marshall and the Constable followed the King when he left the castle. Those three survived many notable adventures together—not just by strength and fortitude, but by wit and courage . . . qualities they still possess.

"As for Nefyn and your pages," he went on lightly, "those young rascals are tougher and wilier than you might think. Have they not survived years of training at my hands? I am a hard taskmaster, as you know, and boys who are soft do not last long in this household.''

The Queen achieved a pale smile; several other faces brightened as well. ''You are quite right. The King and his old comrades were great men. No''—she stiffened her spine—''they *are* great men, as great as they ever were. And as for the boys . . . they will have their adventures and return in a day or two none the worse.''

But Teleri had noticed that one face was missing from the group by the fire. ''Where is Gwenlliant?'' she asked, and the young women exchanged stricken glances, the Queen's smile faded.

''Come with me,'' Sidonwy said softly as she rose from her chair. ''I will show you where Gwenlliant lies.''

The Queen led Teleri out of the room and up the back stairs, and Ceilyn and the young ladies followed. ''She was distraught last night, too upset to attend the feast, so we put her to bed with an old serving woman to watch her,'' said Sidonwy. ''I wonder now if that was wise. But what could I have done for her, even had I kept her by me?''

She paused outside the bedchamber Gwenlliant shared with two other girls. ''Apparently, she was asleep when—when everything began to happen. But she woke with a cry, the woman says, and then fell back.'' Sidonwy opened the door.

The child lay on her own bed with a cloth of gold brocade covering her from her breast to her feet and her pale hair fanned out around her. Candles burned on a table beside the bed.

''She is *dead*?''

Sidonwy and the girls nodded mournfully.

Teleri walked to the bed and pulled back the gold brocade. Someone had dressed Gwenlliant in her best gown, had lovingly brushed her hair and composed her limbs. It seemed impossible that the girls could have performed those services without detecting any remaining spark of life. Yet Teleri could not believe that the child was dead. Looking over her shoulder, she saw Ceilyn shake his head, as though he, too, lacked any sense that he stood in the presence of death.

Teleri touched Gwenlliant's hands and face, felt for a pulse at her wrists and throat, put an ear to her chest. The little girl was cold, and Teleri could detect no heartbeat. Yet the rigor of death had not set in. The young sorceress lifted Gwenlliant's arms, one after the other, and flexed them at elbows and wrists.

"Bring me a mirror," said Teleri.

Fand brought her a tiny hand mirror in a gilded frame, and Teleri held the cold surface to Gwenlliant's lips. A faint mist formed on the glass.

"She lives. I do not think she has suffered any bodily injury, but her mind . . ." Teleri looked up again. "Who removed the chain from her neck? Was she wearing the talisman when you found her?"

"She was not," said Fand, taking up something off the table. "I found this in the corridor this morning, after . . . after we dressed her."

Teleri took the silver disk. "Without this, she was too vulnerable to the psychic barrage of last night's events. Thrown back on her own resources, she took this way of preserving her sanity."

The young women exchanged hopeful glances. "And can you call her back?" the Queen asked.

"No," Teleri admitted regretfully. "But she may wake of her own accord, in a day or a week or a month, when she feels it is safe to do so. In the meantime, do not attempt to disturb her. To wake her now might break her mind."

"But she will die if she does not eat or drink for a month," Sidonwy protested.

"I do not think so," Teleri said, pulling the golden brocade back up to cover Gwenlliant. "Her body requires very little while she remains as we see her. She will not begin to waste away for many months. We must hope that Ceilyn and I can recover the crown before that happens. With the sidhe-stone in the castle again, Gwenlliant may choose to return. But even if we should fail, even if she never wakes on her own . . . which would you choose for her: death or madness?"

While Ceilyn gathered provisions and made other preparations for travel, Teleri was also very busy.

"I cannot ward the entire castle," she said, laying a large iron-bound volume on the long table in her stillroom. As the Queen and her young ladies looked on, Teleri gathered candles and incense, a bottle of water drawn from a holy well, and put them on the table.

"To ward the entire place would take longer than I dare delay.

But I can create a wall of protection around the Mermaid Tower and the Keep. The women and children who have kinsmen in the town must go there before nightfall, but the rest can move into the Keep . . . at least until the men begin to return.''

"You cannot tell us when that may be?" Sidonwy asked.

"No," said Teleri. "But I see no reason why they should not return eventually."

"Well then, we shall have to fend for ourselves until that time," said the Queen, smiling gallantly. "I daresay we are capable of doing that—women do, in times of war or crisis."

"Truly," Fand said staunchly. "We will do very well. We have enjoyed a soft life here at Caer Cadwy, but I daresay we are just as capable as our less favored sisters. Or if we aren't . . . Well, we can just *learn* to be, that is all."

Megwen and some of the other girls looked as though they doubted that, but Finola loyally (if unenthusiastically) agreed with her older sister.

"I will need an assistant," Teleri said, looking directly at Fand. "Someone to hold the book while I read off the spells."

Fand put on her bravest and brightest smile. "Of course," she said. "I will do whatever you say."

When Ceilyn returned to the Solar, an amazing sight greeted him. By the larger of the two fireplaces, a serving woman stood roasting several small fowl on a spit, and on the other hearth, soup bubbled merrily in an iron pot. Alternately stirring the soup and peeling turnips was a scrappy little scullion, some six or seven years old, who looked decidedly out of place in his elegant surroundings.

The Queen came to greet Ceilyn. "We regard ourselves as under siege here," she explained brightly, "and we are adapting to life under those conditions."

Ceilyn smiled faintly. It was as well, he thought, that she was determined to make a kind of game of it, but he wondered how long she and the other ladies could continue to make light of their situation. He did not think it would take many days subsisting on meals prepared by laundry women, scrub maids, and scullery boys to try their patience past bearing. He only hoped that the cooks would return before that happened—and before smoke and cooking odors spoiled the tapestries and the red velvet curtains.

A long table and several benches occupied the center of the

chamber. Fand and Megwen were laying out the cups and silver plates.

"Well," Fand sniffed, catching Ceilyn staring, "I suppose you think we cannot set a table as well as any boy?"

"I believe that women do perform that task in less exalted households," he replied mildly, and wisely refrained from advising her on the care and cleaning of the royal plate. He turned back to the Queen. "Have you seen Teleri?"

"She said something about the Princess Diaspad's bedchamber," said Sidonwy. "But surely you do not plan to leave us so soon?" she asked, seeing that he had changed into his riding leathers.

"If we hope to travel far before nightfall, we cannot delay much longer," said Ceilyn. "But I am going down to Treledig now, to buy a sword."

For the first time, Sidonwy noticed that the scabbard he wore at his side was empty. "But where is *your* sword?"

The hot color rose in Ceilyn's face. He believed the loss of his sword was entirely his own fault. Had he not dishonored and desecrated the blade on All Hallows Eve? Little wonder, then, that the sword had failed him. "The blade was broken."

Sidonwy's face mirrored her sympathy. "Oh Ceilyn, that was an excellent blade—and your grandfather's gift, too!" But then she brightened. "And yet . . . perhaps the loss is not so great. Come with me."

With a mysterious smile, she led him into a small adjoining chamber. She threw open an oak chest and lifted out a long slender object wrapped in silk.

"As you can see, I have another blade for you," she said triumphantly. "One that was fated to be yours from the day it was forged."

Stripped of its silken windings, the sword proved to be a beautifully tempered blade with a golden hilt. A pattern of oakleaves and holly had been worked on the quillons and the pommel, and etched into the blade. Ceilyn tested the sword for weight and balance. It was perfect in every respect.

"You will remember that I promised you a sword when you were knighted," said Sidonwy. "This would have been that sword. The finest swordsmith in Camboglanna made it—Glastyn recommended him and promised that the result would be something extraordinary. But when the other blade arrived from Gwyngelli, the sword your grandfather had been saving for you since the day you were born . . . what could I do but bury my disappointment, and allow Meredydd fab Maelwas the pleasure of presenting you with your first sword?''

Sidonwy laughed ruefully at the memory. ''I will admit that I spoke quite sharply to Glastyn, believing, I suppose, that he ought to have known the other sword was coming. As perhaps he did,'' she added, ''and divined also that the day would come when you would need another sword.

''I kept this sword,'' she went on, ''intending to give it to Garanwyn when he was knighted, or to one of your younger brothers. But you can see by the design: The sword could never really have belonged to anyone but you.''

''I scarcely know how to thank you,'' Ceilyn said, around a sudden constriction in his throat. ''It is a gift worthy of your generosity, and that is the highest praise I know.''

He slipped the sword into the scabbard at his side. Then, impulsively, he bent forward and kissed her on either cheek—a kinsman's affectionate salute, not the respectful homage he usually paid her. Then he blushed at his own boldness.

But Sidonwy laughed, delighted at the success of her gift, and returned the kisses.

''And shall you name the sword?'' she asked. ''Surely a blade that comes to you under such interesting circumstances ought to be named?''

Ceilyn furrowed his brow thoughtfully. Many of the older knights had named their swords in memory of their exploits. Some of the younger men had named their swords, too—usually in jest—but those names tended to be frivolous. He thought it would be pretentious on his part to give the Queen's gift a worthy name while he and the blade remained untested.

''I will see what name the blade earns,'' he decided at last. And Sidonwy nodded her approval.

Teleri stood on the threshold between the antechamber and Diaspad's bedchamber. Neither room showed signs of a hasty departure. Quite the contrary: mattresses, rugs, bedcoverings, tapestries, furniture, and all had been removed—even the candles and torches out of the wall sconces. Not a scrap of parchment or a dropped scarf or ribbon remained to show that the rooms had been occupied so recently as the day before.

That explained all the activity the blacksmith had reported yesterday. Yet how had the larger pieces of furniture been removed? Teleri decided that the Princess's servants had taken advantage of all the confusion before the tournament to carry out the bed, the tables, and the chairs unnoticed.

"And no one suspected a thing, least of all me,". she said aloud.

Yet it hardly seemed possible that *nothing* had been dropped or missed or forgotten. So Teleri made a thorough search of the Princess's bedchamber, the antechamber, and the smaller rooms occupied by Calchas and the servants. The Clach Ghealach would lead her to the Princess and the crown, but Teleri hoped to find something that would give her some insight into Diaspad's plans.

Unfortunately, the Princess had anticipated her. Fearing that the poisoned wine would not find its intended victim, or perhaps that another wizard would be employed in Teleri's place, Diaspad had taken special care to insure that nothing was left behind, not anything imprinted with the personality of anyone in her household, which could be used to trace their movements. Teleri smiled at the irony: For all her trouble, the Princess still carried with her the one object that must invariably draw Teleri after her, as surely as a lodestone draws iron.

Teleri searched through the ashes in the fireplaces, on top of mantelpieces, in corners and nooks—discovering only a stale crust of bread in one of the dwarfs' bedchambers, and, in a corner of the antechamber, a little pot containing a greasy substance.

The bread was useless, yielding nothing to her probing but a strong impression of the minds of the mice who had nibbled it earlier. The little pot, Teleri put down hastily as soon as she opened it. From the symbol on the stopper and the appearance of the contents she guessed that it contained Hecate Ointment, an unholy concoction used by witches when they wanted to levitate themselves. Teleri knew what ingredients went into the ointment—the fat of unbaptized infants was one of them—and she had no desire to scry either the pot or its contents.

She shuddered at the thought of the Princess smearing the stuff over her skin. The ointment was expensive and hard to come by—that such a thing could be carelessly left behind . . . Suddenly remembering the digitalis in the wine, Teleri wondered if someone in Diaspad's household—for malice or self-interest or some other unknown motive—might be actively working to thwart the Princess's schemes.

One thing the Hecate Ointment did explain, and that was how the Princess had left her bedchamber without being seen by Teleri's spies. She had simply left by the window, undeterred by the four-story drop.

Teleri turned away, and started toward the door. But she paused on the threshold and looked back. After a moment of hesitation, she went back in, picked up the ointment, and stoppered the pot.

She certainly had no intention of ever using the Hecate Ointment—even handling the pot made her feel soiled—but perhaps there might come a time when she would regret leaving it behind.

*. . . but if you would know the way to the place where the Sun
and the Moon meet, you have only to look around you. The
answer is everywhere and for all men to see, for it is written on
the earth, but only the Wise Man knows what he sees. Again, I
say to you: If you wish to come to the Castle of Glass, if you
would know the way to the Lair of the Green Lion, the road is
clearly marked, and it begins at your very feet.*

—*from* The Testimony of the Philosophers

13.

Written on the Earth

Ceilyn and Teleri met down by the stables. For the journey,
Teleri had changed into an old grey gown and cloak, and braided
her hair into a single plait. Seeing her in that familiar guise,
Ceilyn felt an echo of remembered pain. She too closely resem-
bled the old untouchable Teleri, the woman he wanted but could
never have.

Along with Tegillus, Teleri's shaggy grey pony was saddled
and waiting, and Ceilyn had borrowed a third horse, a sturdy
sorrel, to carry the baggage.

"At least half the horses are gone," he told Teleri. "It is a
mercy that ours were left behind."

Teleri stroked the pony's soft grey muzzle. "But who will look
after those that remain? Are *all* the grooms and stableboys
gone?"

"I found two old, old men who didn't go off with the others,"
said Ceilyn. "One of them used to be a groom. With the help
of his nephews and great-nephews down in Treledig, he thinks
he can manage until the other men return."

They mounted and rode out the Main Gate, followed the road
down the hill and across the meadows. After about an hour, they
came to a crossroads, where Teleri dismounted and bent over to
examine the ground. Ceilyn did the same.

So early in the year, the ground was still soft and moist, marked with many impressions of hooves and wagon wheels. Some of them looked fresh.

"It is difficult to tell on a road as well-traveled as this one," Ceilyn said, "but it does appear that a large party of horses and wagons came this way, today or late yesterday, and took the East Road."

But Teleri shook her head. "There are tracks leading north as well . . . horses and at least one heavy wagon," she said, pointing. "I *know* the Princess is heading north. What puzzles me is why she would want to divide her party and send most of her people along the eastern road."

Ceilyn gazed down the road. "Not to gain speed . . . not if she has taken a large wagon with her. The second group could lay a false trail for whoever followed. If the stone were not drawing you north, which trail would you follow? The road to Gwyngelli and Mochdreff, I'll wager, the road that leads directly to Caer Ysgithr."

Teleri nodded. "She does not expect to be followed at once, for she knows that the King and his men are all scattered. But eventually they must come to their senses, and then they will begin to think: The crown and the sidhe-stone were stolen, the Princess was absent from the tournament and the feast, she has always desired to see Calchas on the throne of Celydonn—they cannot fail to guess that she was the thief, and they will guess also, less accurately, that she has taken it to her own stronghold at Caer Ysgithr. Diaspad planned for this, and sent most of her people to Caer Ysgithr to keep Cynwas and his men occupied when they finally arrive. In the meantime, she has taken one or more of the wagons—the caravan most likely, for we know that she likes her comforts—and is proceeding north at a leisurely pace. She can always turn east later. There are other roads to Mochdreff, though this is the most frequently traveled."

"And you believe it was some spell cast by the Princess that sent the King and his men off?" Ceilyn sounded doubtful. "That it wasn't just the result of the general madness?"

Teleri climbed back into the saddle and took up the reins. "No," she said, "it was much too convenient for the Princess, to have come about by accident."

They followed the North Road for about an hour. Then Teleri reined in.

"Look," she said, indicating a spot about a dozen feet from

the road, where stones had been arranged in a ring, and evidence of a great bonfire still remained. "If I am not mistaken, this is the place where she stopped to cast her spell."

Ceilyn gazed uneasily at the ring of stones, the circle of blackened earth inside it. A whiff of smoke lingered on the air, and something else, decidedly less wholesome. The fine hairs on the back of his neck stood up, and a strong aversion rose up inside him.

But Teleri had already dismounted. Leading Kelpie by the reins, she moved toward the stones. Ceilyn stayed in the saddle, but he urged Tegillus and the packhorse after her.

Teleri picked up a stick off the ground, poked tentatively at the ashes. "Balefire," she said, looking over her shoulder at Ceilyn's approach. "She burned something here—you can see the bones."

Teleri mounted and took up the reins. "You never told me before that you and the sidhe-stone were linked," Ceilyn said. "Or was that supposed to remain a secret?"

"Not a secret," she said. "At least . . . not anything I meant to keep from you. I always knew that Glastyn expected me to keep the Clach Ghealach safe, but I was never certain why he had assigned that task to me, or how I was supposed to go about it. Only when I felt the sidhe-stone leave the castle—when I knew what had happened to it and understood what I felt—that was when I realized the truth.

"Though perhaps I should have suspected long ago," she added, as she led the way back to the road. "I was the one who placed the sidhe-stone in Cynwas's crown, you know."

"No, I did not know," said Ceilyn. "And you told me that Glastyn did not choose you for his apprentice until you were old enough to read. The stone and the crown were joined together long before that—everyone knows that much."

"Yes, long before that," Teleri agreed. "I am not certain how much I remember, how much Glastyn told me later. He worked with the stone, increasing its power a hundredfold—and it was a mighty talisman before that. The final task was to place the stone in the crown, and for some reason a child was needed. There were few other children on Aderyn, and I was the right age. Certainly, Glastyn did not show any interest in me after that, not until a long time later. Until today, I thought it was a coincidence that he took me for his apprentice so many years after."

Ceilyn shrugged. "A coincidence . . . perhaps. But we both know that Glastyn's *coincidences* were seldom the result of mere happenstance."

They followed the North Road for many days. That was an easy, well-traveled road that took them through fields and farmlands, then through a deep cut in the hills, between the roots of great oak trees that grew on either side of the gorge, and brought them in good time to the valley on the other side. Ceilyn remembered Ystrad Pangur as a pleasant, populous region, but the valley had changed since he last passed that way, six years before. Many of the farms were deserted, their buildings burned or fallen into ruins. The villages looked poorer and shabbier than Ceilyn remembered them.

The weather continued warm and clear, and the earth, mistaking the thaw for a change of season, began to quicken. Tiny green buds appeared on grey branches; grass and clover sprang up in the fields. But Ceilyn found this new growth ominous. "False spring. In a week or two there may be a hard frost and everything will die. Then what will be left to grow in the proper season?"

At the inns and public houses where he and Teleri stopped to spend the nights, Ceilyn heard troubling tales. Again and again, innkeepers and kindly strangers warned against venturing out too early or too late: "There are bad men abroad, and worse things, things that are *not* men though they may resemble them."

"Such tales are common enough in the north," Ceilyn whispered to Teleri after one such warning. "But here in Camboglanna, in the King's own demesnes?"

In spite of these warnings—or even, partly, because of them—Ceilyn was enjoying himself. He and Teleri were off on a quest together, a dangerous quest with the possibility of robbers and monsters along the way, the Princess Diaspad as a worthy adversary, and a fabulous jewel to be won at the end. It was everything he had hoped for, everything he had ever wanted, back in the old days spinning fancies of knights and quests and virtuous maidens—and better, because instead of the impossibly beautiful and impossibly perfect lady he had once imagined, here was his own Teleri, warm and human and accessible, entirely his for the first time since he had known her, with no books or studies to distract her, no duties to call him away. He almost wished there *would* be robbers, bad men he could kill without compunction, and watch the dawning respect in Teleri's eyes.

Ceilyn was happy—much happier than he had ever expected or deserved to be—and so, of course, he was suspicious. In his experience, happiness never lasted long, and it had always to be paid for. For himself, he would gladly pay the price, whether it be blood, pain, or heartache, but the price was his to pay and not Teleri's. So he savored each moment they spent together with an almost painful intensity, his happiness made sweeter and more poignant by the premonition—no, the *certainty*—he felt of impending loss, and for Teleri's sake he curbed his more reckless impulses.

Teleri was eager to press on in the hope of overtaking the Princess, but she usually agreed when Ceilyn suggested they seek shelter long before nightfall. "She cannot travel quickly in that great slow caravan. Surely we are gaining on her."

Yet when trouble did come, it came in broad daylight, as Teleri and Ceilyn forded a shallow stream. Armed men appeared out of the scrubby growth on the far bank, and attacked, almost before Ceilyn had time to draw his sword. While four of the bandits engaged Ceilyn, two others circled around and splashed through the stream toward the packhorse and Teleri.

Ceilyn had dropped the lead rein when he drew his sword, and the sorrel, panicking, shied, reared, and might have bolted, had not one of the bandits caught her by the bridle. The other made a grab for Teleri.

Kelpie displayed surprising mettle, standing her ground, but Teleri froze in the saddle, too terrified to resist. Rough hands pulled her off the grey pony and into knee-deep water. She felt a blade of cold steel pressed up against her throat, and a hard arm encircling her waist.

"That's right, Sweetheart." The robber's breath was hot in her ear. "You be good now, and perhaps I won't kill you afterward."

His mind opened to her and Teleri gasped, flinching from the ugliness and the urgency of his desire. Instinctively, she defended herself in the only way that she knew.

The bandit cried out in sudden agony; the knife fell from his hand. The arm around Teleri's waist loosened, and the man fell to his knees in the water, gasping and fighting for breath. As Teleri watched in fascinated horror, he floundered for a minute, desperately struggling to keep his head above water, then slipped below the surface.

A sound warned Teleri of the other man's approach. She whirled around. He had dropped the sorrel's reins and moved toward Teleri with one hand held out before him in a ritual gesture meant to repel evil, but in the other hand he held a long knife.

"Witch," he hissed, and Teleri, shaking her head, backed away.

The long knife went up. But the look on the robber's face changed rapidly from one of triumph to shock and terror as the blade turned in his hand and began to move slowly but irresistibly toward his own breast.

Meanwhile, Ceilyn was hard-pressed, fighting men who were armed with spears, broadswords, and cudgels. Reckoning him the more dangerous prey, but eager to gain his fine horse and bright new sword, the other four bandits moved toward him in a ragged line, intending to surround and attack him all at once.

They had not reckoned on the instant responses of a trained warhorse. At Ceilyn's command, Tegillus charged toward the man on the right, trampling him under iron-shod hooves. The others gave way for a moment; before they could re-form their line and redirect their attack, Ceilyn had guided the chestnut around in a circle, gaining a better position. He swung an overhand cut at the nearest man. Failing to block the blow, the robber died swiftly and bloodily.

Then Ceilyn closed with the other two men, riding in between them. He blocked a sword blow on one side and narrowly avoided a thrust from a spear on the other. An instant later, Ceilyn's sword cut through the ash shaft of the spear, leaving the startled bandit holding what was now only a six-foot quarterstaff. The man turned and fled.

The remaining robber managed to parry two sword strokes, but the third blow, aimed at the head, turned in mid-strike to take him in the side instead. He fell, mortally wounded, and Tegillus walked over him.

In the sudden silence, Ceilyn looked around him. His opponents were all dead except for the man who had run away. Teleri knelt on the stream bank beside the body of one of her attackers. The young knight dismounted, went down on his knees beside

Teleri. White and shaken, she bent over the body she had pulled out of the water, and was frantically trying to resuscitate it.

"Are you all right?" Ceilyn asked. Teleri nodded. He tried to take her in his arms, but she pushed him away.

"Don't," she said, trembling violently, whether because she was soaked to the skin or in reaction to all that had occurred, Ceilyn could not tell. "Don't touch me. You don't know what I have done."

Ceilyn looked down at the dead man. There was that in his face, a look of pain and horror, that made the knight look away almost immediately. "What have you done? Killed a man who would have killed you . . . or worse."

"I stopped his heart," Teleri whispered. "I squeezed until it stopped beating. . . . I felt it burst inside him. I *stopped* it, but I can't make it start again."

Ceilyn stared at her. "For God's sake—why would you want to? You bring him back to life, I'll just have to slit his throat." He indicated the body of her second attacker, where it lay face down in the shallows. "What happened to that one?"

Teleri sat back, wringing her hands. "I turned his own knife against him—made him dis-disembowel himself. Don't you *see*?— I killed them both with magic. How am *I* any better than the Princess Diaspad, with her spells and her bottles of poisoned wine?"

Ceilyn shook his head. "The Princess tried to kill you by stealth and deception, but this was a fair fight."

"You felt differently about these things on the night Morc and Derry died," she said.

He rose to his feet, offered Teleri a hand up. "I suppose I did. Perhaps I am wiser now than I was then."

Teleri accepted his hand, but once she was on her feet she flinched away from further contact. Ceilyn felt disappointed. He was excited and elated after the battle, and wanted Teleri to feel the same. With a sense of ill-use, he helped her to pull all the bodies out of the stream.

"Past helping, every one of them," Ceilyn said, as they hauled the last corpse onto the embankment. "Don't even bother to try."

"Past helping," Teleri agreed mournfully. The body at her feet had been all but decapitated by Ceilyn's sword. "It is easier to kill than to heal."

Ceilyn stared down at the body. "This man looks familiar. And that one over there. I have seen them both before, though

I don't remem—they were in the public room at the inn last night! They must have left at sunrise in order to get here first and wait in ambush. The innkeeper was probably in this with them, asking where we were headed and then talking to that man over there. He acted like he knew them, too."

"The innkeeper felt honest to me," said Teleri. "And he could know these men without knowing what they intended. In difficult times, men *change*, and who knows what his neighbor may become tomorrow?"

Ceilyn continued to frown down at the body. "Yes," he acknowledged at last. "It is plain that the folk in these parts have fallen on hard times. It was a good harvest last year, for those who had seed to plant and land to sow it in, but for those who had already lost everything in the bad years before. . . ?" He shrugged. "Perhaps we can absolve the innkeeper. A few years past, this man and his cohorts might have been as respectable as they appeared to be back at the inn. But you have no cause to feel any guilt for killing them. Adversity doesn't *make* people bad, it only tests them."

"Yes," Teleri said softly. "But those of us who haven't been tested in that particular way are ill-qualified to judge those who have."

The packhorse had bolted during the fight, but Teleri refused to search for her until after the bodies were buried.

Ceilyn stared at her disbelievingly. "It will take hours to bury all these bodies—and why should we? In the north, we hang thieves at a crossroads and leave them there to rot."

"Dead bodies breed contagion," said Teleri. "Or would you like to be responsible for bringing down a plague on the nearest village? And this isn't a crossroads. These men died violently and the corpses may walk in three days' time, if we don't weight them down with earth."

Ceilyn reached a swift decision. "We will bury the bodies," he said.

That took the entire afternoon. Without any spade to dig a grave, they had to gather stones from the stream bed and erect a cairn. When that was done, Ceilyn hunted up some branches and tied them together to form a rough cross.

Catching Teleri looking at him, he scowled ferociously. "Since we have taken the trouble to bury the bodies, we might as well give some thought to their souls."

"Yes," Teleri said quietly. "It was a kindly thought."

• • •

They spent another hour trailing the sorrel packhorse. When they finally found her—miles off their road—Ceilyn lured her back with his newfound powers of communication with four-footed beasts.

"I think we should avoid inns and guesthouses after this," Ceilyn said, as they resumed their journey. "Even if the folk who run them are honest, there is no vouching for the other guests. We must present an overwhelming temptation to thieves: only the two of us, and you a woman. And even though we don't carry much gold, there are the three horses and all our gear to be gained. A wonder we didn't run into trouble sooner, as trusting as we were.

"I don't see how we can avoid chance encounters," he added grimly. "But at least we can deny those who would rob us the opportunity to lay their plans in advance."

Teleri agreed, and they planned to stop at a cottage or a farm and beg shelter for the night. But the land around them was wild and deserted. By nightfall, they had no choice but to set up camp.

"I will build a fire, one that will burn all night on very little fuel," said Teleri. "And I will weave a circle of protection around our campsite, one that will keep both man and beast at a distance."

While Ceilyn unsaddled and fed the horses, Teleri collected sticks from the low bushes that grew near camp. Some of these she used to build her fire, but the rest she laid carefully, end to end, in a circle around the camp. She chanted softly under her breath as she did so. Busy with the horses, Ceilyn caught only an occasional word, but there was something in her tone, in the rhythms of the chant, that he found soothing, a quality that suggests peace, and security, and comfort. Images and impressions came, unbidden, into his mind: rainy evenings spent basking in the glow of a fire, the touch of his mother's hand. Home . . . Teleri's song seemed to say . . . home, and safety, and love.

But when Teleri straightened up, the illusion was shattered. Ceilyn was back in the wilds of northern Camboglanna, and only the dim glow of Teleri's fire held back the menace of the deepening twilight.

Stepping back to survey her handiwork, Teleri caught Ceilyn watching her. "Well, test it for yourself," she said, amused by his puzzled expression. "You can't see it, but the barrier is there."

Ceilyn walked to the edge of the circle, put out a hand at chest height . . . and encountered a wall. He ran his hands over it, unable to believe what he felt there. He had expected something different: either something solid, like the invisible gate that kept visitors out of Glastyn's garden, or something entirely insubstantial, like the forces running along a ley line. This felt more like the hurdles of woven willow branches that farmers used as fences, or covered with mud and whitewash to make their wattle and daub cottages.

"How high does this extend?"

"It is twelve feet high," said Teleri, "and if there were more grass, I could make a thatched roof as well. As it is, it won't keep the elements out, but it will protect us from practically everything else—until morning, when the first rays of sunlight dissolve the wall."

They cooked their dinner and rested well that night, their sleep undisturbed by man or beast. In the morning, they packed up and continued their journey.

At mid-morning it began to drizzle; by afternoon the rain had become a downpour, forcing them to seek more substantial shelter than Teleri's circle of protection could offer them. They were in the hills by then, on the far side of Ystrad Pangur. There were no villages in the Pangur Hills, no farms or cottages along the path, but they found an abandoned sheepcote, a high-fenced enclosure with a windbreak at one end: two wooden walls and a thatched roof.

They contrived a third wall by hanging up their cloaks, and tied up the horses at the open end of this improvised shelter. When Teleri lit a tiny fire, the sheepcote became warm, even cozy. But Ceilyn was disturbed, as he had not been the night before, by Teleri's proximity.

Somehow, that had not bothered him when they slept under the sky, but under a roof the intimacy of their present sleeping arrangements made him uncomfortable. He lay awake most of the night, listening to Teleri's breathing, acutely conscious of the fact that she slept on the ground beside him, not more than a foot away.

He thought of all the old stories he had heard, tales of iron-willed knights and virtuous maidens, going off on quest together with never a thought for the impropriety of the arrangement, the inevitable temptation. And he, like all the other credulous fools who listened to those fantastic tales, had never entertained the slightest *doubt* that such heroic virtue was possible.

He drifted off to sleep a little before sunrise, and woke an hour or two later with a pounding head and a grudge against the world.

But the morning was bright and breezy, and Ceilyn's mood improved as the day passed. They left the hills, and the road turned east, toward the River Arfondwy and Perfudd. They made good progress that day and the days following, and Ceilyn began to hope that they might soon overtake the Princess.

On the fourth day, they reached the river and the Perfuddi border. The road ended abruptly at the river; the bridge was gone. Only a few timbers remained to show where the great arched span of wood and stone had been.

"I expect it is very deep, but the current is not so *very* swift," said Teleri. "I think the horses can swim across, don't you?"

Ceilyn did not think so. The river ran several feet below the high-water mark on the banks, but the recent thaw had swelled the waters with snowmelt from the Coblynau Hills and sped the current to the point where crossing seemed risky. "Surely there must be a wider spot where we can ford more safely."

"If there were a ford within twenty miles of here, the road would turn that way and the bridge would never have been built," said Teleri.

Ceilyn still hesitated. "Tegillus is a strong swimmer and the sorrel looks capable of making it across. But your little Kelpie—"

"—is island-bred and swims like a fish," Teleri assured him. "I can swim also. If you and the larger horses can make it across, you need not fear for Kelpie or me."

Before Ceilyn could say another word, she urged the grey pony down the embankment and into the water, leaving Ceilyn no choice but to bring the packhorse and follow her.

The water was shockingly cold. But Tegillus and the sorrel swam gallantly, and Ceilyn soon discovered that Teleri had not exaggerated Kelpie's abilities. The grey pony did not swim like any fish that Ceilyn had ever seen—she reminded him of a seal, cleaving a smooth path through the foaming water, as though it were her native element. The girl and the pony arrived safely on the far bank and watched while Tegillus and the packhorse wallowed through the water.

In the middle of the river, the current tugged a heavy bundle containing Ceilyn's armor off the sorrel's back, and Ceilyn watched his plate sink below the flood. Cursing the mischance, he dismounted on the embankment.

Declining Teleri's offer to accompany him, he stripped off his heavy outer garments and plunged back into the river. He was a strong swimmer, and soon arrived at the spot where he had seen the bundle sink, in spite of the river's efforts to pull him farther south. But it seemed he had misjudged the spot after all; though he dove and dove again, he could not find what he sought. Finally, chilled to the bone and exhausted by his battle with the current, he had to admit defeat and swim back to shore.

Teleri had built a fire. Ceilyn threw himself down on the ground, as close to the flames as he dared. "God help me—I don't know how I could be so far wrong. And the bundle was too heavy to be swept away." He folded his arms over his knees and rested his head on them. Then a sudden notion came to him and he looked up at Teleri hopefully. "Perhaps you could guide me from the shore. If you concentrated on all that iron, surely you could sense something?"

Teleri shook her head. "In the midst of running water? That would be impossible." She dropped his green wool cloak over his shoulders.

Ceilyn pulled the cloak more closely around him, and reluctantly abandoned his plate as lost. "At least I still have my mail byrnie, and my sword and shield. I suppose I should be thankful for that."

The road took them north again, back through civilized country. But the land was bleak; little grew there but grass, gorse, and heather. Even the sky was a hard, uncompromising blue. The Perfuddi raised sheep and goats, and only by great diligence and hardship could they scratch any other living out of the soil.

Like their neighbors and sometimes allies, the Mochdreffi, the Perfuddi harbored a general grudge: against their fellow men and against Nature herself, regarding the world as a hostile place, peopled by witches, demons, and malicious elemental spirits. For that reason, they painted and carved elaborate hex symbols on their houses, barns, and stables, to repel evil influences and forbid their enemies to enter. The Perfuddi even carved their strange knotwork devices into the earth itself, sketching them on broad barren downs and chalky hillsides.

"Since the road to Caer Wydr leads through Perfudd, it is

little wonder the Princess brought the caravan with her,'' said Teleri, as she and Ceilyn rode past a lonely sheepherder's cottage. It was a ramshackle building, badly in need of repair, but the hex symbols above the doors and windows had all been freshly painted. ''It would be difficult for her to find any place where she could rest for the night.''

Ceilyn raised a skeptical eyebrow. ''You really think those heathen symbols would keep her out? She passes in and out of the chapels at Caer Cadwy just as she pleases, for all you might think the holy things kept there would make it impossible.''

''A church is not constructed with an eye toward keeping the likes of the Princess Diaspad out—the cross and the holy vessels are kept at the altar, not put up over the doors and windows,'' said Teleri. ''I would imagine that she *does* experience discomfort when the wine and the bread come around, just as she would if she tried to cross the threshold of that cottage, but I doubt she would be harmed by it.

''If she could be exorcised with church bells or holy water, as St. Teilo destroyed the witch in that old tale,'' Teleri added, ''we might have defeated her long ago. But I was thinking of the poverty of these people. I doubt the Princess would find the accommodations in these parts much to her liking.''

In the morning, a hard frost lay on the ground; by afternoon, the snow was falling in big, wet, sloppy flakes. ''Snow on the first day of March,'' Ceilyn muttered under his breath. ''I feared as much . . . and what could be a worse omen for the growing season ahead?''

Teleri looked at him in surprise. ''You've developed a fine concern for matters that ought to be the province of farmers and herdsmen. You never used to spare a thought for harvests and things. Why should you care about them now?''

Ceilyn shook his head; he did not entirely understand it himself. ''It just seems—it seems as though I feel a kinship with those who live close to the earth.''

At sunset, they arrived at a tiny, typically run-down farm, and convinced the farmer to allow them to spend the night in his stable. While Ceilyn looked after the horses, Teleri hauled the saddlebags and the bedrolls up the ladder to the hayloft. By the time Ceilyn joined her there, she had changed into a dry grey gown and sat brushing her fine silvery hair by lantern light. She looked very fragile, pale and heartbreakingly vulnerable. Ceilyn felt all the old pain and longing well up inside him.

He knelt in the sweet, dusty-smelling straw beside her, touched her face softly. "I think I should sleep down below with the horses."

Her eyes widened in surprise. "But why?"

Ceilyn released a long, heart-felt sigh, torn between exasperation and amusement. "Because, my poor sweet innocent child—"

"I am not *that* innocent," she said. "I only meant . . . I trust you."

He took her left hand out of her lap, and dropped a light kiss on the open palm. "And so you may trust me. But that trust places something of a burden on me. Because it is not so easy to be with you so much and spend the whole time . . . being so damnably trustworthy."

Her face clouded. "I never meant to cause you pain," she said. "But Ceilyn, we can't afford to be distracted now, not with such a task before us."

"I know that," he said.

She put down the hairbrush. "If it were not for that . . . there would be no need for us to sleep apart."

Ceilyn felt a lump rising in his throat. He knew that she meant that, that it was not like All Hallows Eve when she had thoughtlessly promised him anything he might want. But he doubted that even now she really understood.

He lifted a strand of fair hair, wrapped it around his fingers. "So long as things remain unsettled between us, I think it would be a mistake for us to share a bed. It would bind us together in ways you don't know about, ways you might regret. I don't think we should risk that, until you can tell me you are ready to be my wife."

Her eyes filled with tears. "I don't know that I could promise you that—even if it weren't for the task ahead of us. But the thought of returning to Caer Cadwy and living apart . . . I don't know which frightens me more: being your wife, or *not* being your wife."

Ceilyn sighed, smiled, and shook his head. "Well then," he said, "until you are able to decide that question, I will feel much better sharing quarters with the horses."

In those days, there was a monster living at the bottom of Loch bel Dragon. Some say it was an afanc, a cold serpent: part snake, part beaver, and part crocodile. But others called it the Dragon of Ildathach, after the great city on the shores of the lake, and that was how Loch bel Dragon acquired its name.

Whatever the creature was, it ate but seldom; when it did feed, it could devour a herd of horses or an entire village in a single day. The people who lived near the lake, in Draighen and in Perfudd, began to appease the dragon by bringing it horses (not the pick of their herds, you may be sure), offering them up four times a year: on May Day and Lammas, at Samhain and Candlemas. The creature devoured the horses, and left the people and their herds alone.

But Gandwy of Perfudd wanted to tame the monster. He brought it only the finest pure black mares to feed upon. Some say they were not natural mares at all, but the twelve beautiful dark-haired daughters of Guaire, who had scorned Gandwy's love and been changed into horses for revenge.

Mares or maidens, the dragon feasted with a good appetite. And when the serpent had fed, Gandwy sat by the water, and he called in a voice as sweet as birdsong. The dragon came up out of the loch, and did all the Warlock's bidding.

—*from* The Book of Dun Fiorenn

14.

An Uneasy Alliance

A half day's journey to the north, a wild white blizzard raged. Driven to seek shelter in a shabby little inn, the Princess Diaspad claimed the single drafty bedchamber for herself, leaving the rest of her damp, miserable, and contentious party—numbering sixteen—to camp together in the common room. There was barely enough space for them all to lay out their bedding, and the dwarfs quarreled vigorously over a warm place by the fire.

But more than the weather and poor accommodations plagued Diaspad's expedition: Two horses had gone lame, and the gaudy scarlet caravan had lost a wheel and been left behind.

"This whole scheme was ill-considered and unfortunate from the very beginning," Prescelli muttered to herself, as she negotiated the narrow staircase carrying a tray bearing the remains of the Princess's supper. "And what use is the crown or the marvelous Clach Ghealach against wind or snow or the mishaps of travel?"

"You could always go back." Calchas appeared at the foot of the stairs, backlit by the fire in the common room. Prescelli started violently and almost dropped the tray. She had not expected her words to carry over the racket made by the dwarfs.

"You could go back to Caer Cadwy," Calchas persisted. "I feel certain they would all be delighted to see you. They will be wanting to know, for instance, just who it was that put poison in Teleri ni Pendaren's wine. And who had a better motive than you? Why don't you go back and tell them all about it?"

Prescelli swept past him, and deposited the tray of dishes on the long battered table that ran the length of the room. "What need to go back? Do you imagine that Cynwas fab Anwas and his famous knights won't be coming after us—later if not sooner? And Glastyn . . . this ought to bring him out of hiding. To say nothing of the Old Ones, who seem to take such an interest in your mother's affairs. Quite a little gathering we ought to be playing host to, by the time we reach wherever it is we are going."

Calchas only laughed. "But none of them know where we are going, not any more than you do. Even if I told you, you wouldn't believe me."

Prescelli sniffed. "You and your mother think you are very clever. But none of her other schemes have succeeded, not entirely, and I don't think this one will either. She has forgotten something, failed to take something into account, and that mistake will catch up with her sometime.

"And I want to be there," said Prescelli, "when your precious mother realizes that she has overstepped herself at last."

Twenty miles distant, Ceilyn slept fitfully, tossing and turning on a pile of prickly straw. He dreamed of Teleri's castle of ice, that illusory refuge she had once described to him, the place where she went when she wanted to be alone. He knew that the castle was not real, was no more than an imaginary construct, yet the crystalline walls seemed remarkably solid. He wandered down long corridors, lost in a maze of white halls and chambers and long echoing staircases, until the first light of morning came in through a chink in the stable wall and woke him.

When Teleri came down from the loft, they shared a cold breakfast of bread, cheese, and fruit. They fed and watered the horses, saddled and led them out of the stable. The sky was overcast when they mounted up and rode away from the farm, but the clouds parted before noon, and a soft breeze sprang up. The day became warm and pleasant.

But Ceilyn's vision of the castle of ice continued to haunt him, along with another image that was disturbingly similar: Caer Wydr, the legendary Castle of Glass, where they were presumably heading. Castle of ice . . . castle of glass . . . again and again the question echoed in his mind: If the two places really were one and the same, he and Teleri might enter in easily, but at what cost would he be able to bring her back out again?

At the next crossroads, they altered their course as the pull of the stone drew them eastward again. The landscape continued to be flat, rocky, and barren, growing bleaker, if such a thing were possible, as they traveled east.

The weather was unreliable, even for Celydonn: sunshine and warm breezes one day, a clattering shower of hail the next, a blizzard that scoured the moorlands for two days, followed by another warm spell. Not surprisingly, they met few travelers along the road. But those they did meet, peddlers and tinkers and strolling entertainers, Ceilyn regarded warily, on his guard since the encounter with bandits in Ystrad Pangur.

Yet one warm morning, chancing to meet a ragged figure hobbling along the road, Ceilyn's better nature overcame him, and he could not resist the impulse to ride back and offer assistance.

A lame beggar with a bandage around his leg and a short wooden crutch under his arm—Ceilyn knew it might be a ruse, such deceits being common among thieves and sturdy beggars. It was possible, even likely, that the man was no more lame than Ceilyn was himself. But the young knight had taken a vow to succor the sick, the crippled, and the destitute. It was simply not in his nature to pass the beggar by.

"Are you in any need—is there anything I can do for you?"

Ceilyn reined up, and looked down on the man with a mixture of pity and suspicion written plain on his face.

The beggar looked up at him, leaning on his crutch. Ceilyn saw that he was not an old man, and he looked remarkably well fed for all his rags. Except for the limp and the bandaged leg, he looked perfectly hale. He was a tall man with a golden beard and eyes a particularly piercing shade of blue. Rhianeddi, Ceilyn thought, even before the man spoke.

"A drink of water would be welcome—this road being a dusty one."

Ceilyn unfastened and handed down a waterskin, though not without a glance back over his shoulder first, to make certain that all was well with Teleri. She had stopped farther along the road, and started back to see what delayed him.

The beggar drank, restoppered the waterskin, and passed it up to Ceilyn. "Perhaps there is something I can do for you, to repay your kind favor."

Ceilyn did not think so. The apparently innocent offer only served to increase his suspicion. But the man continued on.

"This road, now . . . the way you are traveling, it leads to a crossroads not half a mile from this place where we stand. If you plan to turn north, you might think again, for the left-hand turning leads through dangerous territory. If I had known two days ago what I have learned since, I would never have attempted to travel that road myself."

"And yet," said Ceilyn, "you seem to have survived the journey, though you were lame and on foot. Why shouldn't we do as well on horseback?"

The beggar shrugged. "Ah well—who is to say that your luck will be as good? It is true that I met with no misfortune along that road, but the stories I heard as I traveled would strike terror into your heart, so they would, did I but tell you the half of them."

Ceilyn scowled, convinced now that the man had been sent to entrap them, to send him and Teleri down the wrong road and into the arms of confederates who were waiting to rob them. And yet . . . the ruse was such an obvious one.

"It's not easily done, to strike terror into my heart," Ceilyn said. "Just what were those stories you heard along the road?"

Teleri reined up beside Ceilyn, and the beggar told his story, addressing her as much as Ceilyn: "Tales of monsters and demons. Common enough in these times, I know. Aye, we're all accustomed to tales of strange creatures that walk by night, but on that road the monsters have blue skin and appear in broad daylight."

Ceilyn raised a skeptical eyebrow. He was the last man to discount tales of nightwalking horrors, but this was utterly fantastic. "Monsters that walk boldly under the sun? I think someone has taken advantage of your credulity, considering that your accent betrays you as a stranger in these parts as surely as mine betrays me."

"Maybe so, maybe so. It is true that not everyone told me the same story. There was one man, now, who said they were not monsters at all, but two young heathen giants out for a ride, all decked out in blue paint. Fair-haired giants, fierce in their golden armor and scarlet cloaks, riding their great ruddy-gold stallions, like something out of an old tale," said the beggar. "Or so I was told, for I never laid eyes on the creatures myself."

Ceilyn and Teleri exchanged a startled glance, for the picture the beggar conjured up was a vivid one, and not so unfamiliar a portrait either.

Big blond men in scarlet cloaks, loaded down with the heavy golden jewelry the Gwyngellach loved to wear: arm-guards and pectorals and gorgets, which might be mistaken for light armor. Indeed, the ancient Gwyngellach had worn them as such, scorning to ride into battle with any protection beyond an ostentatious display of wealth and the woad they used to dye their skin and lend an appearance of horrible ferocity.

With an absent-minded thank-you to the beggar, Ceilyn turned Tegillus and continued down the road, with Teleri and the pack-horse trotting behind him.

"I know what you are thinking," he said. "But I can think of more reliable allies that Fflergant and his brother, at least so long as they are both out for my blood."

"But we aren't likely to *encounter* any other possible allies," said Teleri. "If Tryffin and Fflergant are to be found by following the road north—"

"*If* they are still on that road, and *if* we could find them . . ." Ceilyn began, and then stopped. The truth was he could only regard them as intruders, an unwanted third and fourth party, when he and Teleri had been traveling so agreeably as a pair, but that was unimportant.

They took the left-hand turning, but they had traveled some distance before they heard a pounding of hooves farther down the road, and a sound, swelling as it drew nearer, like the wailing of all the banshees in Christendom or all the tormented souls in Hell.

"There are but two pairs of lungs capable of raising such a racket," said Ceilyn.

A cloud of dust rose up on the road before them and began to move their way. As it grew larger, it was possible to make out two fine red-gold chargers moving at the center of the cloud and two terrifying figures mounted upon them, red cloaks billowing in the wind of their passage.

The true Gwyngellach, the Hillfolk, were a tiny dark-haired race, who had once painted their skins and arrayed themselves in barbaric splendor in order to appear more formidable in battle. But Maelgwyn of Gwyngelli's big, golden half-blood sons were an impressive pair to begin with. With their faces painted in blue spirals and other intricate figures, their blond hair caught up in great horse tails to make them appear even taller than they were, with the sun shining on their gold jewelry and the swords they brandished overhead, Fflergant and Tryffin looked much more than formidable.

"Holy Mary Mother of God!" Ceilyn said, under his breath. "No wonder the people in these parts walk in terror for their lives!"

The road was wide, but Ceilyn and Teleri prudently urged their mounts over to the shoulder. The two terrible figures continued to approach, whooping and wailing and ululating their barbaric warcries. They drew abreast, then swooped on by without slackening their pace.

"It is the Princess's spell that has sent them both demented, I suppose," said Ceilyn, as the racket died down and horses and riders disappeared in the distance. "Not that Fflergant was any too stable at the best of times. Do you think you can restore them to sanity?"

"The spell ought to be wearing thin by now," said Teleri. "A familiar face or voice may be all that is needed, and no counterspell necessary. Though first we will have to catch up with them."

"Perhaps not," said Ceilyn. "I thought Tryffin recognized us as he rode by, and I believe I hear them returning."

A moment later, Teleri heard hoofbeats, too, and the cloud of dust reappeared. "You must speak to them as soon as they come close enough to hear you."

"I? You expect me to remove the spell?" said Ceilyn. "But surely that is for you to do. I wouldn't know what to say to them."

"You must address them in your usual manner, say something ordinary and natural," said Teleri. "It is the shock of the commonplace that will bring them out of the dream they have lived in for so many weeks."

Tryffin and Fflergant pelted toward them, at the same breakneck pace as before. Then they began to rein in. With no time to think what he would say, Ceilyn just said the first thing that came into his mind.

"As God is my witness, a pretty picture the two of you make. Riding about the countryside decked out in this fashion, just as though there weren't matters of deep importance you *ought* to be attending to. Have you no sense of fitness or responsibility at all?"

Fflergant glared at Ceilyn, momentarily speechless with indignation. He was a warrior in the full flower of his strength and manhood—it was not meet that anyone should address him in such a disrespectful manner.

"Speak you of great tasks to be performed? Yet even now the Dragon of Ildathach lays the countryside to waste. I shall slay the beast, I and my brother, and—"

"You poor deluded fools," Ceilyn said, shaking his head. "The Dragon of Ildathach has been dead these hundred and fifty years."

As soon as he heard that, Fflergant remembered that it was true. How on earth had he forgotten a thing like that? Yet he was not about to allow Ceilyn to think he had gotten the better of him. He gathered the rags of his dignity about him.

"I knew that," Fflergant began haughtily. "Everyone knows that. But—" A sudden disorientation assailed him, and he could say no more. The world turned upside down and inside out, and his thoughts shifted into a new pattern.

What *were* he and Tryffin doing, out here in the middle of nowhere, decked out in blue paint and gold jewelry, listening to Ceilyn mac Cuel berate them like a pair of erring squires caught neglecting their duties? It made no sense at all.

Explanations followed, explanations that Ceilyn and Teleri had to repeat again and again before Fflergant and Tryffin were able to grasp all the details. By that time, it was well past noon. At

Ceilyn's suggestion, they found a place to set up camp and prepare the afternoon meal, off the road and near a shallow stream. While Tryffin and Fflergant put aside their flamboyant trappings and went into the stream to wash off their warpaint, Teleri and Ceilyn built a fire and began to cook dinner.

Fflergant and his brother came back to camp pink and well-scrubbed. "An incredible coincidence that our paths should cross out here in the wilds of Perfudd," Fflergant said, sitting down by the fire.

"We did turn aside from our path in the hope of meeting you," Ceilyn said. "Though if it hadn't been for that lame Rhianeddi beggar, we would never have guessed you were anywhere within a hundred miles of here."

Fflergant and his brother exchanged a glance. "Rhianeddi . . . a tall man with a golden beard and a pronounced limp, was he?"

Ceilyn nodded. "You met him? But no, he said he never caught sight of you, though he heard tales all along the road. The man I met was a cripple with a bandaged leg. Though I did wonder," he added thoughtfully, "if he was really the beggar he appeared to be. In spite of his rags and his limp, he talked and carried himself like a nobleman."

"Then it was the same man," Tryffin insisted. "We met him . . . yesterday. Or was it the day before? He told us the dragon had been spotted, and directed us down this road. It had to be the same man, but he wasn't wearing rags when we met him. All in purple robes he was, leaning on a golden staff, and there were ravens flying overhead, and two perched on his shoulders. We took him for Cynfarch of the Ravens come back to life again.

"Though perhaps we imagined the ravens and the purple robes. Likely, he was only a beggar as you say."

Dinner was ready, and Teleri began to serve up stew in wooden bowls. "What I fail to understand," Ceilyn said, as they all sat down to eat, "is where you came by the blue paint and how you were able to apply the patterns so skillfully. I thought it was something of a lost art."

"We painted each other," said Tryffin. "In the Hidden Country, young boys like to play at being warriors and daub themselves with blue mud in imitation of our ancestors. But Fflergant and I weren't content just smearing ourselves with mud. We found an old man who had learned the patterns from his great-grandfather, and begged him to teach us how it was properly done. We used to paint each other and deck ourselves out, especially to startle our sisters and female cousins.''

''And kept a supply of blue paint on hand at Caer Cadwy, I suppose, due to a sentimental attachment,'' Ceilyn said sarcastically. ''Or was that to frighten the girls, too?''

''No, we were never much interested in frightening the girls at Caer Cadwy,'' Tryffin replied mildly. ''I seem to recall stopping at a dyer's hut after we left the castle, and demanding woad. Fortunate for us that he gave us something less permanent instead.''

Fflergant nodded emphatically. ''For myself, I wouldn't have cared to return to Caer Cadwy before the dye wore off; you can imagine the jests we would have to endure. We hear quite enough about blue paint and naked savages as it is, thank you very much.'' He glared at Ceilyn. ''And I will thank you, too, not to speak a word of this to anyone when we do return. Or the next time we meet on the tourney field things might end very differently.''

''Almost certainly they would,'' Ceilyn said agreeably. ''But I have no intention of embarrassing the pair of you—not any more than you have embarrassed yourselves already.''

Fflergant continued to glare at him. ''It seems we all made fools of ourselves—and only you were spared the indignity. Now, I wonder how that came about?''

''Ceilyn was preoccupied,'' Teleri volunteered. ''There is something you might remember, in case you have warning that someone is tampering with your mind, and you haven't a score of goblins on hand to conveniently distract you: You must concentrate as hard as you can on something else. It needn't be a spell—a song, or a bit of poetry, or a verse from the Bible will serve nearly as well, so long as you repeat it over and over and think of nothing else.''

''Is that what you taught Gwenlliant?'' Fflergant asked, before he thought.

''No . . . I tried to teach her a surer way,'' Teleri said softly. ''A method that worked all too well, it seems to me now. No one can touch Gwenlliant's mind—no one can touch or speak to her at all. She is quite beyond our reach. But if I had set her to reciting Bible verses instead . . . I do not think it would have been enough to save her.''

''No one blames you for what happened to Gwenlliant,'' said Fflergant. ''You did the best that you could for her. And with

Garanwyn . . . out of the castle, Tryffin and I were responsible for Gwenlliant.''

Tryffin nodded glumly. ''We failed that sweet child in her hour of need. If one of us had been with her to reassure her . . . perhaps she would not have felt the need to retreat so far into herself.''

Ceilyn looked up from his bowl of stew. ''Gwenlliant is *my* first cousin. If anyone was responsible for her, it was I. But that was another thing I have wondered about: Just where did Garanwyn go, that he wasn't at the feast that night? He was seen leaving the castle long before the panic started, but no one seems to know where he went or why.''

Fflergant looked to his brother, for the story was a long one and parts of it could not be told. Tryffin shook his head, almost imperceptibly. There had been no opportunity to devise a plausible explanation for Garanwyn's disappearance, a tale that would be true in its essentials while it skirted all the more awkward facts. Now it occurred to them both that the strange events which had followed Garanwyn's departure made everything much easier. They could pretend ignorance, and hope to be believed.

''We haven't the least idea,'' said Fflergant, bold-faced, because he was the one who could tell a lie. ''The fact is . . . we wondered if you might be able to tell us. Something or someone disappears, you're usually involved one way or the other.''

Ceilyn bristled up, but Teleri stepped in to avert a quarrel. ''The disappearance of the crown is what ought to concern us all now. Whatever questions the three of you might like to settle between you, I hope you can agree to set them aside until after the crown and the sidhe-stone have been recovered.

''We do hope you will come with us,'' she added earnestly. ''For the four of us to attempt to recover the crown—that is a desperate enterprise, but our chances of success are greater than if Ceilyn and I attempted it alone. You will come with us and lend us your aid?''

''We have a common cause and a common enemy. Fflergant and I will come with you gladly and lend what aid we can,'' said Tryffin. ''Truth to tell, you would find it difficult to leave us behind, now we know you can lead us to the Princess and the crown.''

''Not much chance we would leave all the opportunities for heroics to Ceilyn,'' Fflergant said. ''Though what the four of us can hope to accomplish against an entire garrison I don't know.

I wonder how many armed men the Princess keeps at Caer Ysgithr?''

"But we aren't going to Caer Ysgithr—we are going to Caer Wydr," said Teleri.

Fflergant and Tryffin stared at her, dumbstruck, for neither she nor Ceilyn had mentioned that name earlier.

"And what defenses the Princess can muster there—even before she masters the sidhe-stone and bends it to her will—I really do not know," Teleri continued. "But I think . . . I have an uncomfortable suspicion, that we would be much better off facing an army."

*Mabon followed the boar Ysgithrwyn the length of Mochdreff and
back again, all in seven days. But except for a single silver bris-
tle, Mabon and his men got nothing for their efforts.*
                                    —*from* The Oral Tradition of Tir Gwyngelli

15.

On the Borders of Hell

For a day and a half, Ceilyn and Teleri and their new allies
followed the road east, until the vast shadow of the Mochdreffi
Woods appeared on the far horizon, dark and foreboding.

"If the Princess continues to travel east, she will lead us right
into the woods," said Ceilyn. "And that is a road I would rather
not travel."

"But you were born and reared on the edge of a forest every
bit as deep and vast as the Mochdreffi Woods," said Teleri.
"Surely your woodcraft is sufficient to bring us through."

"The forests of Gorwynnion are not like these woods," he
said. "There are wild beasts there and wicked men—but the
trees, thank God, are just trees. They don't roam about from
place to place, or reach out and grab travelers with their
branches, or trip them up with their roots, as the trees do in the
Mochdreffi Woods.

"Though I will admit that travelers' tales are sometimes exaggerated," he added, "and perhaps the trees in the forests of
Mochdreff are no more active than they are elsewhere."

It became evident that they would not be putting those tales
to the test—at least not immediately—when the pull of the stone
began to draw Teleri north again.

"If it made any sense at all," said Fflergant, "I would say
we were headed for the Rhianeddi lowlands. But why would the
Princess go into Rhianedd, where she has no allies and even the
very soil will be hostile to her Mochdreffi entourage?"

"I believe she will lead us into Mochdreff eventually," said

Teleri. "If we continue to travel north we will skirt the woods, and if we go east after that, we will come into the disputed region around Loch Gorm. Few people live there, and if Caer Wydr is to be found anywhere on Ynys Celydonn, then northern Mochdreff is just such a remote location as I would expect."

Their course did turn east as soon as the shadow of the woods lay behind them. On the tenth day of March, they crossed from Perfudd into Mochdreff. No boundary marked that border, but everyone knew the moment when they passed onto Mochdreffi soil. It was a hard, tight, secretive land, and even the very air was cold and bitter-tasting.

"And yet . . . it is not as I expected it to be," Tryffin said to his brother. "I had thought to feel a sense of personal animosity emanating from this land of our ancient enemies. But all I sense is an undirected sort of challenge."

"Even the Mochdreffi feel that challenge," said Teleri, chancing to overhear him. "They win nothing from the land save by a fierce struggle. Yet Glastyn always said that in order to know the people it is first necessary to understand the nature of Mochdreff. That is an understanding no man has ever gained, except possibly the Mochdreffi themselves."

Instinctively, Fflergant reached for the little bag he wore on a leather thong around his neck, the packet of earth from Tir Gwyngelli. The land-loving Gwyngellach were wont to regard their native soil as a nurturing and fiercely protective mother. It had never occurred to Fflergant that other places might be entirely different, and that other men might live virtually orphaned in the land that gave them birth.

They passed few signs of human habitation. Twice, there were clusters of mean dwellings, once they spotted a barefoot youth tending a herd of surly-looking pigs.

When they made camp that night, they had difficulty gathering wood for a fire, the vegetation was so sparse and stunted. And even though the wood they found was dry, Fflergant and his brother could not make it ignite, though they took turns trying for almost an hour.

"This is a niggardly land," Fflergant exclaimed, putting his tinder box aside in disgust. "It gives you nothing . . . nothing!

"Hell must be like this," he said. "I've never quite believed in a Hell of eternal flames and damnation, but to spend eternity in a barren, heartless place like this—I tell you, the thought

ought to be enough to make a more hardened sinner than I am consider mending his ways.''

"Good," said Ceilyn. "I look forward to your future emendation."

"Let me see what I can do," Teleri volunteered, stepping forward before Fflergant had a chance to reply.

Even using magic, it was difficult to kindle a fire using Mochdreffi wood.

The next morning, Teleri began to sense a difference in the sidhe-stone. "It no longer moves away from us at the same rate we move toward it," she told Ceilyn. "I can feel the pull of the Clach Ghealach grow stronger with every mile we travel."

A short while later, she stiffened in the saddle, and drew in a sharp breath. "What is it?" Ceilyn asked, alarmed by her sudden change of color. "What happened just now?"

The others looked at her, too. "Something . . . something brushed against my mind," Teleri whispered. She flinched and put a hand to her head. "There it is again. I think the Princess is concentrating on the stone, trying to learn how to use it effectively, but whenever her mind touches the Clach Ghealach, it also touches me."

Her companions exchanged a worried glance. "Does she know you are alive, then? And that you have come for the crown?" Ceilyn asked.

Teleri shook her head. "Not yet. The contact was so light and tentative, she seemed puzzled, but not suspicious. Yes . . . she reached out again, just now, but this time I was able to evade her. She took me by surprise at first, but now I know what she is doing, I should be able to escape her notice."

Ceilyn frowned. "For how long? How long can you continue to evade her?''

Teleri sighed. "As long as I must. She cannot concentrate on the stone always, you know. She will grow tired, as surely as I will, and need to eat and rest."

Their first glimpse of Caer Wydr came as they stood in the shelter of a paltry grey wood, about a quarter of a mile distant. Neither the slender glittering towers of glass that Teleri, Fflergant, and Tryffin had expected, nor the castle of snow and ice that Ceilyn dreaded, Diaspad's fortress was a massive pile of stone, covered with a smooth black reflective substance.

"A vitrified hill fort, that is what this looks like. All but that great tower at the center—I've never seen anything to match that," said Fflergant. "But these places are usually in ruins. What force of man or nature could have melted those rocks, fused them, and turned everything into glass without toppling the ramparts or the tower?"

"Dragon fire, possibly," said Teleri. "One tremendous blast of heat that vitrified the entire structure almost instantly. If not that, I simply don't know."

But the riddle of Caer Wydr's origins concerned them less than the more pressing question: how they were going to get inside.

"We know that she didn't bring more than a handful of men with her," said Ceilyn. "A dozen . . . two dozen at most. But she may have garrisoned the fortress in advance. Impossible to tell from this distance if there is anyone walking those walls, but there must be some sort of a watch sufficient to turn us back—supposing there was any way for us to scale the walls in the first place."

While the young men discussed the fortification and possible means of entry, Teleri said little. But she took Ceilyn aside later, into the wood where the other two could not see or overhear them, and she showed him the little pot she had found in Diaspad's quarters back at Caer Cadwy.

"It is Hecate Ointment—that is the name used by witches. A very little, rubbed into the surface of the skin, confers the power of self-levitation. But if the witch strips and rubs her entire body with the ointment, they say it will transport her to any location she desires, even were the place a hundred miles distant. Used that way, it has certain drawbacks, for though she may travel far and swiftly, she cannot take anything with her and must arrive at her destination naked and defenseless."

From the look on Ceilyn's face, Teleri guessed that he had heard of the ointment before, and knew something of the ingredients that went into it. "It is not something I would think of using under ordinary circumstances," she went on, "but it may provide us with the only possible means of entry into Caer Wydr. If one of us, using the ointment, were to go into the fortress ahead of the others, and open the gate—"

"No," Ceilyn said emphatically. "Before God, I can hardly believe you would suggest anything so obscene. This stuff is filthy, poisonous, and unholy, and we would be no better than the Princess Diaspad if we stooped to such means. If we are capable of that, the Clach Ghealach is no safer in our hands than it is in hers.''

He reached to take the pot out of Teleri's hands, but she refused to relinquish it. ''The only decent thing to do is bury it,'' he insisted. ''Come, you know I am right. Not only to remove the temptation to use it, but out of respect for the poor little creatures whose bodies were defiled in order to make it.''

Reluctantly, Teleri yielded. ''Yes, I know you are right. But how are we to enter Caer Wydr without the use of magic?''

''I never said we shouldn't use magic, only that we shouldn't use the same tools the Princess Diaspad would. I think if we *are* meant to succeed here,'' he said, ''then we are also meant to do so by virtue of our own gifts, now that we are finally learning to use them.''

That evening, Ceilyn did not join the others around the fire. Leaving his sword and his knife behind him, he slipped away from camp, went deeper into the wood, and shifted into wolf-shape. Then, running swiftly and stealthily, keeping as much as possible to the cover of the scrubby brush that grew around the fort, he moved toward Caer Wydr.

A pale sliver of moon rode low in the sky. The ground was covered with dew already hardening into frost. In the colorless, shadowy world in which Ceilyn the wolf moved, the fortress on its low hill was a looming presence, darker than the surrounding darkness.

A narrow path led up the shallow incline to the main gate. Ceilyn spent a long time outside the gate, listening and sniffing the air. Only twice did he detect movement on the other side of the gate, and the scent of two different guardsmen.

Leaving the gate, he circled around the fort, continuing to listen and test the air. Once, he picked up a scent he did not recognize, a raw, faintly feline odor that made his hackles stand on end and a deep growl rise up in his throat. A big cat no, there were subtle undertones of something else, vaguely familiar . . . and a bitter metallic tang, like heated iron.

It was more than Ceilyn, in his present form, could long endure. Human curiosity warred briefly with instinctive aversion, but instinct won. He moved around to the back of the fort, opposite the main gate, where he discovered another, smaller gate, all but hidden by a tangle of leafless bushes.

Pleased with the success of his scouting expedition, he returned to the wood and to human form. He walked into camp, woke Teleri, and told her everything he had learned.

"Two dwarfs at the main gate—say, three at the most. I may have missed one man, but it is unlikely I missed more. There may or may not be someone patrolling the walls; I never caught sight, sound, or scent of anyone. But the walls are just as smooth as they look from a distance, and undoubtedly as slippery. Even with ropes and scaling ladders, which we lack, it would be difficult to mount them.

"I couldn't pick up a single scent at the back gate, not even a cold one, though they may keep it under observation from some other place. On the whole, it looks like she didn't expect to be followed, and decided not to attract undue attention locally by garrisoning the place in advance."

But about that other, more puzzling something he had detected, Ceilyn was not so sanguine. "I think she may be keeping some large animal inside. I've never smelled anything like it, either man or beast. But I didn't like it. Dragon fire, you said. You don't suppose . . . ?"

"That the Princess keeps a dragon as a watch dog? No, I do not," said Teleri. "If she had a real fire-breathing dragon to do her bidding, why bother with the crown or with her other schemes? The dragon that vitrified Caer Wydr may have lived a thousand years ago. And as for taming such a beast . . . even Gandwy of Perfudd never looked so high. The best he could do was a cold serpent—terrible enough, in its way, but nothing to rival a dragon.

"But Gandwy had other creatures at his command," she went on. "You know of the monsters he bred. Some of them survived his downfall, they say, and escaped to live and breed in dark places: Coill Dorcha, the mines in the Coblynau Hills, and the Mochdreffi Woods. It is possible that Diaspad has captured and tamed one such hybrid: a manticore, perhaps, or an opinicus or griffon."

Ceilyn took a long deep breath, exhaled it slowly. "How large and dangerous would such a monster be?"

Teleri shook her head. "I do not know. Smaller and less formidable than a dragon or a cold serpent, but not anything we would care to tangle with, I am certain of that."

"Then we will just have to hope that she keeps the creature—whatever it may be—caged or leashed," said Ceilyn. But Teleri thought he sounded more intrigued than worried.

• • •

In the morning, over a cold meal of bread and cheese and dried meat, Ceilyn told Tryffin and Fflergant all that he and Teleri had learned or surmised. Just how he had come by so much information he did not say, leaving them to assume that Teleri was the source, that she had divined the knowledge through her powers as a wizard, or had picked some of it up from the mind of the Princess during Diaspad's intermittent attempts to master the sidhe-stone.

"We have discussed the possibilities, too," said Tryffin. "You know that we are not far from the Rhianeddi border here. We have kinsmen up there. If we were to ride to Glynn Hyddwyn and bring back a troop of men, it wouldn't take more than a week, ten days at the most."

"We may not have a week to spare," said Teleri. "Once she knows how to use the Clach Ghealach offensively, it would take a great army to dislodge her from a position so secure as Caer Wydr. And even before that, she must have spies or other means of detecting the movements of anything so obvious as your troop of men. Then she would have time to marshall other defenses, defenses we know nothing about."

"Yet if we could find a way inside, just the four of us, we might take her by surprise, and succeed where a larger expedition would fail."

After much discussion, Tryffin and Fflergant finally agreed. "As you say, it is a desperate enterprise, but probably the only way. Very well, then, we enter the fort by stealth tonight, by way of the back gate," said Fflergant.

"At least the gate should present little difficulty," he added with a grin, "so long as we have a Wizard among us, so justly famed for her skill at opening doors and gates."

But Teleri shook her head. "I can unlock doors, but as for gates . . . they usually have bars or great iron bolts to keep them shut, and moving those aside may not be so easy as you seem to think."

For nine days, the lad wandered in the Valley of Lamentation, and neither man nor beast did he meet. On the ninth day, he came to an iron tower and a dark wood close by, and that was the Fortress of Night. There was a bird like an eagle, but greater than an eagle, with a brass beak and talons, perched upon the roof of the tower, and lions guarded the gate.

As he approached the fortress, the youth saw that the gate stood open. There was a fearful outcry and a great lamentation and a mighty roaring, as of a thousand caged beasts upon the other side. The lad was not daunted. He went in past the lions at the gate, and entered the Fortress of Night.

—from The Black Book of Tregalen

16.

In the Fortress of Night

By moonrise, preparations for the assault on Caer Wydr were well under way. Fflergant and Tryffin donned their light antique armor, with many a wistful thought for the full harness they had left behind in Camboglanna. Ceilyn slipped into his shirt of mail rings and strapped on the heater shield painted with his grandfather's arms.

Teleri stood just within the margin of the wood, staring at Diaspad's stronghold and steeling herself for the dangerous task ahead. By the last red light of sunset, the walls of the vitrified fortress glowed with a subtle fire.

In the last year, Teleri had done many dangerous things, but usually under pressure of circumstances. In time of crisis, in the face of a clear and present necessity, she had always found the courage to do what was needful. But the task she now faced called for another kind of courage: the courage to walk deliberately into peril without knowing precisely what form that peril would take. She wondered if she possessed that sort of courage.

She turned and walked back toward the camp. As she approached, Ceilyn came to meet her.

"There is one thing we must settle now," he said. "The rest of us are expendable—you are not. You are the one who must lead us to the crown. You may well be the only one who can challenge the Princess for control of the sidhe-stone. Your first duty, then, is to survive."

Teleri opened her mouth to protest, but Ceilyn headed her off. "No, you may not risk capture or death even to save the rest of us. If it comes to a fight with Diaspad's guards or whatever creature she is keeping there for a watch dog, you must utilize your talent for invisibility. Just disappear in the old way and don't do anything that might draw attention and shatter that invisibility. It may be hard for you to stand aside and watch me or Tryffin or Fflergant die, but that painful duty may well be yours, and you might just as well prepare yourself for it now."

Teleri nodded miserably, knowing he was right. "But if the rest of us should fall . . . if you are forced to defend yourself," he continued, "you might have need of this." He took the dirk out of his belt and offered it to her.

Teleri stared at the dagger. "What am I to do with that?"

"I have been thinking . . . the way you felt when you killed those bandits, you might not wish to defend yourself again in the same way."

"But I am a physician, a healer," Teleri protested. "I have no skill with weapons."

"As you are a physician, you will know where to strike," Ceilyn pointed out. "And I don't like to think that you could be taken, weaponless, by Calchas and the other men. They have nasty habits, the Mochdreffi."

Teleri's eyes widened in shock. "You are suggesting that I might want to turn this on myself?"

Ceilyn felt the heat rising in his face. "Women have chosen that course before. And if it should come to . . . the final extremity, I would like to think you had that choice."

Wordlessly, Teleri accepted the dirk and tucked it into her belt.

There was so much else, so many tender things, that he wanted to say to her. He stared at her helplessly, keenly aware of all the unfinished business between them, equally aware that this was not the time or place for them to settle anything.

All that he could do was lean forward and whisper in her ear. "I love you." Then they exchanged a brief, self-conscious kiss.

When the last ruddy light of sunset disappeared from the sky, they left the horses tied up at camp, divided, and crept through the darkness toward Caer Wydr: Ceilyn in the lead, then Teleri, Fflergant, and Tryffin. Moving silently from one place of cover to another, they circled around the fortress, and all arrived safely by the hidden back gate, breathless and elated at that first small success.

Teleri pushed the shrubbery aside to reveal the gate. Placing both hands flat on the timbers, she merged her consciousness with the wood until a clear picture formed in her mind: stout oak planks held in place by iron hinges, two bolts made of cold steel, and a heavy wooden beam securing the gate in place.

"It is worse than I feared. Two bolts *and* a wooden bar." She leaned forward and rested her forehead against the gate, closed her eyes and concentrated on moving the first bolt. Slowly, the steel cylinder slid back.

"Now the other," Teleri breathed, as she moved her hands lower on the gate. But the second bolt was rusted into place, and loosening and moving it left her weak and exhausted. She leaned against the gate, marshaling her strength for the yet more difficult task of lifting the wooden beam.

"I've been thinking now," said Tryffin, in his soft Gwyngellach lilt. "This wooden bar . . . unless it's considerably newer than the rest of the gate, it will be weathered, perhaps even rotten in places." Teleri nodded. "Would it be easier for you to move the beam aside . . . or find the weak places in the wood and splinter it?"

Teleri considered his suggestion. "The wood *is* old and there are many deep cracks running along the grain. And it is always easier to influence something in accordance with its own properties than to subvert the laws of nature. That is one of the first rules of Wizardry." She shot him a curious, inquisitory glance. "I had no idea you had a knowledge of the Art."

Tryffin shrugged. "You don't have to be a Wizard to know common sense."

Again, Teleri put her hands, palms flat, against the gate; again, she pressed her forehead against the wooden planks, this time concentrating on the bar on the other side. She merged her mind with the wood until she knew every change in texture, every knot, every place where the fibers of wood parted. Then she sent a shock through the beam, concentrating on all the weakest spots. With a loud crack, the wood splintered.

Everyone listened breathlessly, waiting for the alarm to be raised on the other side. When all remained quiet, Tryffin and his brother put their shoulders to the gate and threw their weight against it. The splintered beam gave way, and the gate creaked slowly open, leaving a gap about eighteen inches wide.

Teleri slipped through the opening; the others followed her, turning sideways to squeeze through, and with swords drawn and ready, stepped into the courtyard on the other side.

Ceilyn caught up with her and hissed in her ear: "Next time, I will go first. Don't you remember what I told you?"

"Yes," Teleri said, "I remember." The pull of the stone was so strong now that she had forgotten the danger for a moment.

She followed Ceilyn across the deserted courtyard and Fflergant and Tryffin fell in behind. On the far side of the yard, another gate, standing half open, gave way into a larger courtyard.

Flickering torches, spaced at twenty- or thirty-foot intervals around the walls, lit the inner yard. Where the torchlight was brightest, the glassy black walls cast back dim and wavery reflections.

Alerted by a sound behind him, Ceilyn called out a warning. Everyone whirled around to face the five dwarf guardsmen who appeared out of the shadows at the edge of the yard and charged toward them.

Teleri moved apart from her companions, sought the nearest patch of darkness, and melted into invisibility.

Three dwarfs closed with Fflergant and Tryffin, stabbing with shortswords and daggers. Forced to take the defensive against the close-in weapons of the dwarfs, Fflergant and his brother had to give ground.

The other two dwarfs ran toward Ceilyn, attacking him from either side. In spite of their small stature and awkwardly formed bodies, Diaspad's guards were tough, experienced fighters, but they could not counter Ceilyn's extraordinary speed and skill. One after the other, he cut them down.

Tryffin killed one of the other dwarfs, and when Ceilyn joined the fray, the remaining guards died swiftly.

No one had time to do more than draw breath before six more dwarfs ran through the gate. Better armed than the first wave, this second contingent wore helmets and knee-length mail hauberks; three carried swords and shields, three were armed with two-handed axes. Better organized this time, the dwarfs formed a line, shields in front and axes behind.

Fflergant and Tryffin snatched up two bronze-edged wooden round shields from the fallen dwarfs, and joined Ceilyn in the center of the yard. The three knights took up a defensive position, back to back. Diaspad's guards advanced slowly, shields steady and weapons ready to strike. They paused a few yards short, and then, at a word from one of their shieldmen, all rushed forward at once.

As Teleri watched from the shadows, the melee became a chaos of oddly matched moving figures. One of the dwarfs fell, blood pumping from a wound in his side. Fflergant's sword glanced off a helm, and the stunned dwarf staggered back and fell. As if to make up for their losses, the other guards pressed even harder than before.

Ceilyn thrust past the haft of an axe, impaling the dwarf behind it. Fflergant advanced, forcing his opponent to back away. Purely on the defensive now, the dwarf tried desperately to counter the heavy blows that rained down on his shield. Forgetting that he left himself open to attack from the rear, Fflergant continued to press him back.

As Teleri watched, the dwarf Fflergant had stunned earlier picked up his sword, lurched to his feet, and moved toward Fflergant's unprotected back. Heedless of Ceilyn's instructions, Teleri called out a warning, but her cry was lost in the clamor of battle.

But just as the dwarf drew back his arm for the fatal thrust, another stocky figure appeared unexpectedly out of the shadows and cut down Fflergant's would-be assassin with a blow from a two-handed axe. Then the newcomer joined the fray, fighting on the side of Ceilyn and his kinsmen.

The other dwarfs, enraged by this unexpected defection, fought even harder than before. And when his axe caught for a moment in the rim of a wooden shield, Fflergant's savior fell under a rain of furious blows. Yet he had accomplished this much: In their zeal to kill the traitor, two of the other dwarfs left themselves open. Fflergant and Tryffin, taking swift advantage, cut them both down.

The last dwarf, finding himself without allies, threw his axe wildly in Ceilyn's direction and ran toward the gate. Ceilyn dodged, stopped the flying axe with his shield, and took off after the dwarf. But the dwarf was through the gate before Ceilyn could catch him. The gate slammed shut, and a bar fell into place, just as Ceilyn threw his weight against the timbers.

Suddenly, the courtyard was very quiet. Teleri stepped out of hiding. She knelt down to examine the body of the dwarf who had saved Fflergant's life. She recognized him; it was Bron, Diaspad's principal dwarf. She unfastened his mail hauberk and put her hand inside, hoping to detect a heartbeat. As she started to draw her hand back, her fingers brushed against something.

She drew out a leather bag tied to a thong around the dwarf's neck. Fflergant and Tryffin cried out in astonishment and distress as Teleri opened the bag and poured a trickle of dry earth into the palm of her hand.

"Gwyngellach," Fflergant breathed. "He had to be. No Mochdreffi that I ever heard of developed a sentimental attachment to his native soil."

They all stared down at the body of the dark-eyed little man. As oddly proportioned as any of Diaspad's dwarfish retainers, at four and a half feet Bron had easily been the tallest of the lot. In Camboglanna or the north, his small stature made him an oddity, but in the Gwyngelli Hills, where the common run of man was considerably shorter, his size alone would have occasioned little comment.

"My God," said Fflergant. "Seeing him in the company of Diaspad's dwarfs, it never occurred to me that he was any different from the rest. But what was he doing serving the Princess all those years?"

"A spy," Ceilyn suggested with a frown. "*Does* your father keep spies in other great households?"

Fflergant and Tryffin did not know how to reply. It was difficult, even for them, to guess what Maelgwyn of Gwyngelli might or might not do.

Somewhere, far off, metal clanged against metal, like the door of a cell opening. Then there was a sound like a rush of mighty wings. Ceilyn stiffened. "There is that smell again."

The others caught it, too: a stench like a whole menagerie and a smithy combined. The thunder of wings grew louder, and everyone looked up.

Over the top of the wall it appeared, hung in the air for a moment with scarlet wings flapping, then descended in a rush.

It was a griffon: half eagle and half lion, bright crimson in the frosty moonlight. And it was huge, more than twice the size of a man, and it was armed with iron claws and a wicked curving beak. As Teleri watched it descend, she felt her heart beat fast with wonder and terror.

Screaming like a hawk, the monster touched earth, and began to circle around the bodies of the guards. While the others stood frozen in place, uncertain whether to attack or flee, Ceilyn moved toward the fabulous creature with a look of rapturous recognition on his face.

Fflergant and Tryffin would have rushed to Ceilyn's aid, but Teleri cried out to stop them. "No, this fight is Ceilyn's. Don't you see . . . he has waited for this all of his life. We mustn't interfere."

As the others watched breathlessly, Ceilyn moved toward the griffon, and the griffon leapt to meet him.

Avoiding the downward plunge of the beak, Ceilyn jumped to his left. He ducked under an outstretched wing and swung at the monster's breast. His blade sheared through the layered scarlet feathers, but the feathers absorbed most of the impact.

The monster turned and Ceilyn turned with it. Baiting like a hawk, it reared back on feline hindquarters and attacked with taloned fore-feet. Again and again, Ceilyn fended off the raking claws, the cruel iron beak. The air was full of crimson feathers, but Ceilyn's blade was growing dull.

Frustrated, Ceilyn tried another tactic. He stepped back, waited for the griffon to attack again. When the monster leapt, he leapt, too, throwing himself to the ground, rolling over, and bringing his sword up to score a shallow cut across one fur-covered flank. The griffon screeched, more in rage than in pain.

Ceilyn rolled again, narrowly avoiding the powerful, lashing tail. He sprang to his feet, ready for the next rush. The griffon was wary this time. Rearing up, supported by its beating wings, it moved forward until it towered over him. Then it lunged, jabbing with its beak and stabbing with its claws at the same time. Ceilyn dodged the beak, blocked the feet with his shield, but the impact drove him backward as the talons scored the painted face of his shield and splintered the laminated wood beneath.

Ceilyn fell to his knees. The griffon's claws caught in the iron banding on the rim of his shield, stuck there, and wrenched the shield off his arm. The heater flew through the air, and landed on the ground, far beyond Ceilyn's reach.

He scrambled to his feet, breathing heavily. The air was thick and nauseating with the animal stench, the smell of blood, and an odor like burning metal. He backed up, gripping his sword in both hands. But the griffon slipped past his guard, and one taloned foot came down on Ceilyn's shoulder, ripping through chain, padding, and flesh, scraping across his breastbone, and hooking around two ribs. Ceilyn hacked desperately at the scaly leg, struggled to free himself from the griffon's grip. As he pulled away, he felt the ribs crack, and something burningly sharp pierced his lung. In a daze of blood and pain, Ceilyn sank to the ground.

The griffon drew back, flapping its wings, then struck again, this time with the terrible curved beak. Ceilyn swung wildly and delivered a stunning blow to the monster's head. Before the griffon could recover, Ceilyn's blade descended once more, cleaving the thin birdlike skull.

The griffon staggered, knocked Ceilyn a dozen feet with a powerful sweep of a scarlet wing, and collapsed, wings still beating and lionlike tail lashing.

Teleri ran across the yard, threw herself to her knees on the ground beside Ceilyn. He lay in a dark pool of blood, and more blood continued to pump from the deep wound in his chest. From that she knew that his heart was still beating, though his skin was waxen and his breathing shallow or nonexistent.

She spoke his name again and again, but Ceilyn did not answer. And that frightened her, because she did not know to what extent his power to heal depended on a conscious will to live.

Behind her, she heard Fflergant speaking. ". . . God knows, a pity to leave him here . . . would have wanted it that way . . . the sidhe-stone more important than any one of us—"

"We are not going on without him." Teleri surprised herself with the steadiness of her voice, her absolute certainty that she was doing the right thing. She pulled Ceilyn's dagger out of her belt, ripped open the seam of her underdress near the hem, and began to tear off strips to make bandages. "He isn't dead, and we are not going to leave him behind."

"Not dead yet, perhaps, but for the love of God, just look at him," said Tryffin. "Not even breathing, and the shock if not the loss of blood—"

"He *is* breathing . . . he *must* breathe. And if you will help me to lift him, I can bind up his shoulder and stop the bleeding."

In spite of themselves, Fflergant and Tryffin were impressed by her determination. This was a side of Teleri that neither of them had suspected: the iron-willed wizard woman. Tryffin knelt down at Ceilyn's other side, and slipped an arm under his shoulder. The wounded knight moaned softly and opened his eyes.

Ceilyn struggled to breathe, but breathing was agony, one lung on fire, and every time he inhaled, the fire burned hotter.

Ceilyn. He could not see her, but Teleri's voice was urgent. *Ceilyn, try to imagine yourself whole. Call up the pattern in your mind. You have learned to shape yourself consciously from wolf to man—use that power now to heal yourself.*

He tried. He tried to picture himself whole and healthy, but pain kept interfering, making it nearly impossible for him to concentrate. But Teleri's voice continued—not outside him, he realized, but speaking inside his head. *I have stopped the bleeding, but you need to close the wound and make more blood.*

Slowly, Teleri's face came into focus, oddly intent. With great difficulty, he forced out the words. "No time . . . go on with the search. Leave me to—"

We go on together or not at all. You said we were not meant to succeed here except through the use of our own gifts. But I have a sense of our destiny here as well, and I say we can never succeed here unless we do so side by side.

There was a stubborn look on her face, an expression Ceilyn had seen there once before, that told him one thing at least: She was not going to take a step without him. And that being so, whether her assurance came of a true seeing or merely a desire to believe her own words, the success or failure of their quest depended on his ability to rise up and walk.

He tried again to picture himself whole and healthy. This time, he had better success. As the picture he created in his mind became clearer, the pain in his chest subsided and he was able to sit up.

"Can you stand?" Teleri asked him. Behind her, Fflergant and Tryffin both protested at once.

"I believe," said Ceilyn, "that I can stand up." With a considerable effort he staggered to his feet, and stood there, swaying, until Tryffin offered him the support of an arm. Teleri bent down and picked up his sword.

Fflergant was staring at him with the look of a man who has just seen the dead stand up and walk. Ceilyn could not see Tryffin's face, but imagined that he looked equally surprised. There would have to be explanations if and when they all walked out of Caer Wydr alive, and how he was going to explain what they had just witnessed, Ceilyn had no idea.

With Tryffin's help, he walked unsteadily, following Teleri and Fflergant across the yard and through a gateway, then up a short flight of smooth black steps to the foot of the great drystone tower. The double doors at the top of the stairs were decorated with strange symbols cut into the wooden panels.

"Not locked, but certainly warded," said Teleri. She knew that the Clach Ghealach was somewhere in the tower; she could feel its presence strongly. And she knew, also, that the Princess had renewed her efforts to master the stone.

"Iron may be of some use," she said. Lifting Ceilyn's sword, she placed the top of the blade upon the lintel above the doors. She spoke something under her breath. There was a flash of brilliant light and the doors swung slowly inward.

Teleri handed the sword back to Ceilyn, and led the way through the door and down a long corridor, dimly lit by rush-lights in rusty iron cressets along the walls. Declining Tryffin's further assistance, Ceilyn followed after her, using his sword as a prop. The top of the blade scraped against the rough stone floor of the passage. Tryffin and Fflergant walked to either side of Ceilyn, weapons drawn, alert for signs of another ambush.

But when a loose flagstone turned under Teleri's foot, it was Ceilyn with his keen ears who heard a grinding of gears and the rush of some heavy object descending. He leapt forward, knocking Teleri to the floor and falling on top of her, just as a solid iron gate fell from above and hit the flagstone floor behind them with a resounding crash.

*. . . and when Tomaltach and his men had been forty days upon
the sea, they came to an island. There was a silvery, sandy
beach, and a grove of fruit trees glowing with many jewel-like
colors. And under a tree stood a woman, like to no woman any
of them had ever seen: a purple cloak around her and a golden
circlet in her dark hair and a robe of thin silk next to her white
body.*

*Tintagel said, "This is a fair and fruitful land, and the woman
is beautiful and queenly, a fit bride for our leader. Let us go
ashore and woo her in Tomaltach's name." But Tomaltach would
not allow any man to go ashore until he had consulted with the
priest.*

*The priest came up from below the deck and stood at the prow
of the boat, gazing at the island. There he saw no silver beach,
no graceful fruit trees, but a harsh, barren, waterless land, and
a forest of sword blades, hard, sharp, and burning. No woman
it was who came down to the shore to meet them, but a rough,
hairy monster, with a body like a horse and the tusks of a wild
boar.*

*Then the priest said, "Take up your oars and row with all the
strength that is in you. For I tell you that this is an evil place,
and any man who lands here, were he only to set one foot upon
the shore, does so at the peril of his immortal soul."*

—from The Voyages of Tomaltach

17.

The Serpent's Invitation

Ceilyn rolled off of Teleri and painfully levered himself up
into a sitting position. He looked at the iron gate dividing them
from Fflergant and Tryffin, and he shuddered. "If one of us had
been standing there when it fell . . ."

The metal barrier began to vibrate with the blows of their
frustrated allies. But Teleri's concern was all for Ceilyn. His face

was drawn as if he were in pain, and a bright red stain had spread across his makeshift bandage.

"You have opened the wound in your shoulder. You are bleeding again."

"A little. But you were right, I can speed up the healing process if I concentrate. I will be able to go on again in another minute."

He propped his back against a wall, drew up his legs, and rested his head on his knees, calling up the pattern that would make him whole again. Teleri examined the gate, searching for some lever or mechanism that would raise it. Finding none, she tried to lift it herself, but her efforts, both physical and mental, were frustrated.

She sank wearily to the floor beside Ceilyn. "I cannot move it. I simply lack the strength." Tears of anger at her own helplessness filled her eyes. "There is a limit to what I can do. I cannot go on moving bolts and lifting spells and bars and gates all night long. The mind and the will grow weary, too."

Ceilyn lifted his head. "No one expects you to work one spell after another without growing tired. Rest for a moment, and then we will go on. Tryffin and Fflergant must find a way to lift the gate, or another way into the tower. But you and I must save some of our strength for the final confrontation with the Princess."

Teleri allowed herself to rest for a moment, but only for a moment. Then she rose slowly to her feet.

Ceilyn did not tell her that this time he had not been able to heal himself as efficiently as before. Whether he lacked the faith, or the energy, or the determination, he did not know. The bleeding had slowed but the wound was not entirely closed. He stood, sheathed his sword, and offered his right hand to Teleri.

Hands clasped, they moved down the corridor until they came to a place where two passages crossed. "We must find a stair leading to the floors above," said Teleri. "That is where we will find the sidhe-stone."

Ceilyn took a rushlight off the wall, and they chose the left-hand turning and followed a long passageway with doors deep-set into the walls on either side. They opened doors and explored passages until they found a long flight of stone steps. The steps were so narrow and so crumbled at the edges that Ceilyn, who led the way carrying the rushlight in one hand and leading Teleri with the other, had to climb sideways in order to maintain a safe footing.

At the top of the stairs there was another corridor, and more rooms, some of them so tiny they were scarcely more than niches in the thick stone walls. The doors and the ceilings were often so low that even Teleri had to duck her head in passing through them. Though the glassy outer walls looked deceptively smooth, it was now apparent that the whole pile was constructed of un-dressed drystone and great rugged beams of oak.

"Who built this place, do you know?" Ceilyn asked.

"Perhaps the same people who built the stone chapels and raised the standing stones. The walls . . . the walls do speak to me, but it was all so long ago. . . ." She paused and tilted her head, as if straining to hear something, then she shook her head and went on. "Tiny dark-eyed men and women used to live here—smaller than the Mochdreffi and the Hillfolk. They wor-shipped the Moon as a goddess, and the Sun as her consort."

They continued their search, passing through one empty chamber after another. Though the air was good, they never passed any windows; apparently, the tower was ventilated by an ingenious arrangement of shafts that brought in air from outside. Yet the sheer weight and bulk of stone on every side became oppressive after a while.

"I do not like this," Ceilyn said uneasily. "This place is much too empty, much too quiet. Surely she knows that we are here."

"She knows," said Teleri. "And she knows the Clach Ghea-lach drew me here. That is why she strives to master the stone, hoping to destroy me before I can challenge her face to face."

They turned a corner and found another narrow flight of stairs leading up into darkness. As they climbed, Ceilyn became aware of a rank, pervasive odor. His grip on Teleri's hand tightened. "I smell something unwholesome here."

At the top of the steps was a door. Ceilyn hesitated, strangely reluctant to open it. "There is something wrong . . . I sense something evil on the other side."

"The Clach Ghealach is on the other side, somewhere very near," said Teleri. "We must pass through this door in order to find it."

Still Ceilyn hesitated. Yet even if there were another way, another stair, another door, surely there would be traps and spells there as well. "If we must, then. But I will go first."

So saying, he opened the door and stepped across the threshold.

Ceilyn looked around him in surprise. This room was not what he had expected. It was a large sunny chamber with a polished wood floor and many diamond-paned windows, very like his mother's sitting room at Caer Celcynnon.

He turned back to speak to Teleri, but the door had closed behind him and she had not followed him in. Confused, he looked around him, more carefully than before. Tall arched windows graced one wall of the chamber; green velvet curtains were drawn aside to let in the late morning sunlight. On the opposite wall was a handsome wooden mantelpiece beautifully worked with vines and leaves and fruit as only the woodcarvers of Gorwynnion knew how to craft them. The room was not *like* the Solar at Caer Celcynnon, it *was*, and Ceilyn, inexplicably, had come home.

And there in a high-backed chair by the fireplace, surrounded by her handmaidens all industriously bent over their needlework, sat Merewyn herself. She looked up and, spotting Ceilyn, gave a cry of surprise and delight.

"My dear boy . . . what a marvelous surprise. To think that I never expected you." She crossed the room on flying feet, hugged him and kissed him and hugged him again, laughing and crying at the same time. "Six years . . . it has been six long years. And now you return—not the boy I remember at all, but so tall and straight, and strong . . . !"

Ceilyn could not answer her around the painful constriction in his throat. To come home again after so many years, and find her as sweet and loving and beautiful as ever . . .

She took him by the hand and led him to her own seat by the fire. The girls all looked up at his approach, but none of them were familiar to him. He was not surprised. The young women who had served his mother when he left Celcynnon would all be married by now, with households of their own to manage. Naturally, these were all new girls . . . all but one, a dark girl in shabby harlequin silks who sat spinning wool in a corner by herself.

"You must be tired after your journey," said Merewyn. "You must be hungry and thirsty. Bring us wine," she said to one maiden, and "Bring us bread," she said to another. Then she turned to the dark girl with the spindle. "Prescelli . . . bring fruit to refresh my son after his journey."

The girl stood up, and she *was* Prescelli, Prescelli with her too red mouth and her too tight gown, in his mother's Solar at Caer Celcynnon, where she had no right to be. Ceilyn felt a hot flush spread slowly across his face. If Merewyn knew, if she guessed what he and Prescelli had been to one another . . .

With a sly smile, Prescelli crossed the room and selected a glossy red apple from a bowl piled high with ripe fruit. As she moved toward Ceilyn, he saw that she had not changed since the last time he had seen her: the same sinuous walk, the same insinuating smile, the same gown of thin silk that clung to every curve of her body. She offered him the apple, but Ceilyn did not want to take it.

"You are afraid," she said, laughing in the old scornful way. "The truth is, you are just afraid." She reached up with her free hand and loosened the pins in her hair. The dark locks came tumbling down, over her bare white shoulders and full, scarlet-tipped breasts. Prescelli stood naked before him, and it was not an apple she offered him, but her own body instead.

She sat down on his lap. Crimson with shame and horror, Ceilyn tried to push her away from him, but her arms were twined around his neck and her fingers tangled in his hair. The whole situation was so unbelievable and obscene . . . it could not be happening to him . . . it was like a bad dream . . . yet, unlike a bad dream it was so solid, the evidence of his senses so utterly and undeniably convincing . . . the scent of Prescelli's musk and orris root, the salt taste of her mouth against his, the girls all giggling in the background. . . .

"Dear Heart, do not hesitate to refresh yourself," said Merewyn, gently reproving. "This is your father's house, and you may take whatever you need."

"I can't," Ceilyn said, and began to shake in every limb. For the worst of it was that he wanted Prescelli so much, the old lust rising up hot inside him. *But not in front of the others. Oh dear God, not in front of my mother!*

"Ceilyn." Merewyn was beginning to sound annoyed. "It is not like you to refuse a lady anything she might ask. Where are your manners? Take the girl and be done with it."

"I can't . . . I simply . . . can't." And everyone laughed at him, mocking his inadequacy.

Even Merewyn. Her gentle face changed, took on a look of

contempt that Ceilyn had never thought to see there. "Can't? Then it appears I was wrong. You left here a boy, but you return . . . considerably less than a man."

Humiliated and betrayed, Ceilyn wrapped his arms around Prescelli. But even as he did so, some part of him resisted, crying out against what he was doing. And the woman in his arms began to change: The white shoulders and white breasts remained the same, but below the waist, where the cleft between her legs should be, her trunk thickened, was covered with hard, glittering, jewel-like scales . . . she wasn't a woman at all, but a colossal green serpent.

With a cry of horror, Ceilyn tried to thrust the evil thing away from him, but the snake-woman coiled around the base of his chair, sinuous and hissing. Ceilyn frantically disentangled himself from her grip, leapt out of the chair, and ran for the nearest door.

As he ran, the room changed around him. Windows, fireplace, women, and all, everything shimmered and faded away. And when he reached the door, he found Teleri waiting there for him.

"Illusion," she said. "It was all an illusion."

Ceilyn looked around him, and saw that she spoke the truth. They stood beside a closed door in a dark, empty chamber with rough stone walls. It seemed he had dropped the rushlight somewhere along the way, but the room was lit by a circle of black candles standing in pools of their own congealed wax, arranged in the middle of the floor.

He leaned against the door, shaking as if he had just performed some mighty exertion.

"Nothing we saw here was real," said Teleri. This time he heard the tremor in her voice. Had she been there all along? Had she seen Prescelli? But no, he did not think so, for she returned his gaze, steady and unblushing, and that she could never have done. Yet something had frightened her. He wondered what other demons, beside his own personal devils, haunted that chamber.

"Nothing we saw here was real," Teleri repeated, as though she, too, needed reassurance. "Therefore, nothing we saw here could possibly harm us."

But Ceilyn was not so certain; he knew how close he had come to accepting the serpent's invitation. "There are other dangers than those that threaten the flesh," he said. "Our very souls may be in peril here."

Teleri reached for the door handle, but Ceilyn stopped her. "If the next room is as bad as this one . . . perhaps we can aid one another." He took her hand in his. "This time, we cross the threshold together."

The instant Ceilyn stepped through the door, Teleri was gone again. He stood in a cave, a stone chapel, like the cavern beneath Dinas Conn where he had served briefly as a page. These cavern-churches were to be found all over Ynys Celydonn, places where the pagan Celydonians had once practiced their rites, but since cleansed, consecrated, and rededicated to Christian worship.

A purple cloth richly embroidered with gold and silver threads covered the altar, and a thousand candles burned, arranged in a hundred niches carved into the living rock. Before the altar was a kind of platform, a slab of stone hollowed out to form a smooth, shallow basin, rather like a baptismal font, only much larger.

As Ceilyn moved toward the altar, he saw that the basin was filled with clear water. Below the surface, floating *in* the water but not *on* it, suspended in fluid between air and stone, was a sword with an intricately worked hilt and letters of gold set into the blade.

"Who takes up this sword shall be King hereafter," said a soft voice.

Startled, Ceilyn looked up. A figure in scarlet robes, hooded and cowled like a monk, had entered the chapel on silent feet and taken up a position to the left of the purple-draped altar. "Take the blade and claim your destiny."

Ceilyn's heart began to pound. His destiny—to become King of Celydonn? Without even willing it, he took a step toward the basin, reached out to take the hilt—and drew back suddenly as the water began to steam and tiny silver flames danced on the surface.

"The blade burns, and the hilt is red-hot to the touch," said a deep voice. Another figure, this one in robes of dark forest-green, had appeared to the right of the altar. "Who takes it up shall suffer pain almost past bearing."

"Not so," countered the first voice, tender and melodious, and very like the voice of the Princess Diaspad. And though he could not see her face, the drape of the scarlet robes revealed a woman's form beneath them. "In the hands of any common man, it would sear the flesh from off the bone. But you alone,

Ceilyn mac Cuel, may take the blade and wield it without suffering any lasting harm.''

The young knight caught his breath. Had not Teleri said it herself? The ancient gifts were kingly gifts. Had he been formed and created as he was for some purpose greater than he had ever imagined?

The flames in the basin began to die, and again Ceilyn reached out to take the sword—again drew back. The blade was not so bright as before. A black tarnish was spreading up the blade, and the water took on a scarlet tinge.

"Whose blood . . ." Ceilyn's voice sounded hoarse in his own ears." ". . . at the cost of whose blood could I be King?"

"Do not regard it," said the figure in red. "It is unfortunate when good men must die to promote the common good, but the weak must give way to the strong. Will not all men live better lives if the best and the strongest man rules them?"

But the deep voice, the voice of the figure in forest-green, answered him: "The blood of Cadifor and Llochafor . . . of Dyffryn, Manogan, Maelgwyn fab Menai and his sons . . . over the bodies of your kinsmen shall you mount the throne."

Ceilyn took a step backward. "I cannot take it, then."

"But it is essential," said the sweeter voice, "that a strong man sit on the throne. For the common good, Ceilyn, for the common good."

The young knight shook his head. "It is essential that strong men support the King. No man . . ." Ceilyn searched for the words he had never formulated into a coherent declaration before. ". . . no man in and of himself is strong enough to rule. But if he can draw good men to him, they can lend him their strength and their wisdom, lay down their lives for him, if need be, making him stronger than any one man can be."

"But such a king as you describe must be a man of vision," Diaspad's melodious voice answered him out of the scarlet hood. "A man of passion and purpose to draw them to him, inspire them, and unite them with a common goal."

Ceilyn looked toward the figure in green, expecting him to speak. But the green hood only nodded encouragingly.

Ceilyn thought hard. "Such a man need not be King to provide that inspiration. Who was the man of greater vision: Anwas or Glastyn? Glastyn was the man with a passion and a purpose, and that purpose changed the course of events, though it was Anwas and his son Cynwas after him who sat upon the throne."

He took another step back from the basin and the temptation the sword presented.

"Fool," said the figure in scarlet, and this time the voice was not nearly so sweet. "Fool and worse than fool, for others shall suffer for your folly."

But the figure in green threw back his head and laughed long and merrily. His robes no longer appeared to be the somber green of deep forest glades—now they were the bright new green of young leaves upon the bough—and though Ceilyn could not see the face, he thought he recognized the laugh. Then he looked again at the sword in the water, and Ceilyn recognized it, too: his old sword, the one the Holly King had shattered, but reforged, and adorned with letters of gold.

"It is true that the sword was once mine, but it is mine no longer. I have accepted a new weapon and a new destiny." Ceilyn looked reproachfully at the green-robed figure. "Why should I be tempted to take it up again?"

The green hood was lowered, and the face revealed was the crafty-wise face of the wizard Glastyn, and the red-eyed visage of the Holly King, and the ragged old man with the owl, and the fresh-faced young magician with the rings and the white doves—it was one face, and it was all these faces, and another one besides: Ceilyn's own face looking back at him.

"Not once shall you be tempted, nor twice, nor three times," said the Lord of Holly and Oak, "but nine times ninety and nine, and though you may think the temptation a small thing now, there may come a time when you find it harder to resist."

But Ceilyn shook his head. "I do not think so. It is true that I used to dream of glory, to long for a high destiny—but I never wanted to rule other men, only to rule myself."

This time it was the figure in red who laughed, a laugh so full of bitterness, and anger, and longing, that it chilled Ceilyn to the marrow of his bones. The red robes moved closer, and Ceilyn saw, for the first time, the face, pale and stern within the folds of scarlet cloth. When it spoke, it spoke in the low melodious tones of the Princess Diaspad, but the face was that of Ceilyn's father, Cuel mac Cadellin.

"You passed this test easily, but one test remains. We shall see if you are as strong to resist as you think." Cuel took him by the hand and led him toward the back of the chapel. Reluctantly, Ceilyn suffered him to do so.

• • •

But the moment Ceilyn reached the door, Teleri was there beside him, and the hand clasped in his was not his father's hard, dry one, but Teleri's hand, small, cold, and damp. He realized that he had been holding on to her all along.

And when he looked back, the chapel was gone. This chamber was exactly like the one before it: small, dark, and empty, save for the circle of candles glowing feebly in the center of the room.

"It seems we must face each test alone," Teleri said shakily. "Though we cross the room together, we cannot see or hear or feel each other until we reach the far side."

Ceilyn nodded grimly and opened the third door.

All in an instant, Ceilyn was transported to a green woodland. A crystalline stream bubbled and danced between the trees. Larks, blackbirds, and cuckoos sang in the sheltering wood. Some little distance from the place where Ceilyn stood, there was a hut with a thatched roof, shaded on one side by a rowan tree crowned with red berries. Nearby stood a branching hazel heavy with nuts.

Enchanted by the prospect, Ceilyn moved toward the hut. As he came nearer, he saw that ivy and honeysuckle had grown up around the door, and fat honey-bees hummed among the delicate white and gold blossoms. Four or five hens scratched in the bare earth by the door, and a red fox, a rabbit, and a striped badger shared a patch of golden sunlight, basking side by side, as friendly as brothers.

The animals greeted his approach with nothing more than a twitch of a whiskered nose, a lazy movement of a bushy red tail. This was just such a pleasant retreat as Ceilyn had often longed for: a peaceful woodland setting where a man might live and pray and meditate, at peace with God, with nature, and with himself.

Stooping to avoid the low lintel, he pushed the door aside and walked in. There were no windows, but a beam of pure sunlight came in through a hole in the roof, lighting the interior. The hut was simply furnished, with a stool, a low table, and a bed of pine boughs and green mosses in one corner of the room. On a shelf near the bed, a wooden plate, cup, and bowl were neatly stacked.

Yet there was a cloth of white linen on the table, and an open book, and a bowl of oil with a blackened wick floating on the surface. Someone had mounted a wooden crucifix, plainly but painstakingly carved, above the door. And on a peg on one wall,

Ceilyn saw a robe of some coarse brown stuff hanging, and a pair of sandals precisely placed, side by side, on the floor beneath. No simple woodcutter or huntsman lived here, then, but a holy hermit, who had renounced all worldly pleasures and retreated to the greenwood.

Ceilyn sat down on the stool. He wondered if the hermit might allow him to stay for a day or two. He leaned over to take a closer look at the open book. It was an illuminated missal, exquisitely decorated with tiny pictures along the margins and between the lines: a salmon in a pool, a deer in a thicket of strange flowering vines, a wolf and a squirrel mildly regarding each other. But the pictures were dim and faded . . . no, only obscured by a fine layer of dust, and dust lay on the tablecloth and clouded the surface of the oil in the lamp. It appeared that the hut had been deserted for many days.

Ceilyn did not think that the hermit had intended such a long absence—not when he left his book of devotions lying open on the table, not when he left that and his other possessions behind him. Death or some other misfortune had overtaken him, keeping him away longer than he had planned. It might well be that he was not coming back at all.

Ceilyn drew in a deep breath. *He* might take the hermit's place—why not? To dwell in this lovely spot, praying and reading, and meditating, living on berries and nuts and honey, making friends with the amiable beasts—he could not imagine a dwelling fashioned more perfectly to his taste, a life better suited to his personal inclinations.

"Here, I could find peace. Here I could live so far removed from sin and care that holiness would come quite naturally."

While he thought about it, he absently slipped off his battered mail, his blood-stained shirt, and his high leather boots, and replaced them with the brown robe and sandals. He found this new way of dressing light, airy, and entirely comfortable.

"Yes, I am suited to this life," he said, but even as he spoke the words a memory struggled to take shape in his mind, the memory of some important task he had taken on and then put aside, though the nature of that task eluded him.

"But if it was really important, how could I forget?" he asked himself. "The fact that I feel guilty and responsible is no indication at all, for I'm always tormenting myself over one minor transgression or the other. I have no sense of proportion, and I never did."

Already, he thought, he was beginning to put things in their proper perspective. "None of it mattered so much as I thought."

He sat down on the stool again, folded his arms across his chest, and looked out the door at the peaceful scene in the clearing. The fox yawned and rolled over on his back, exposing his furry white belly to the sun. The rabbit began to wash herself fastidiously, like a cat, licking her paws and running them over her long grey ears.

To live like the beasts, entirely in the present moment, he had lived that sort of blessedly uncomplicated life once, and had given it up. Why?

Because Teleri had come to him and reminded him of all the unfinished business he had left behind. As something kept trying to remind him now . . . Ceilyn shook his head, unable to remember.

"I was a fool to go back then—just as I would be a fool to go back now." But somehow, he was no longer certain. The more he thought about it, the less certain he became. "The choice was entirely mine . . . I was a man with a mind and a conscience to guide me, not mere instinct like a beast, and I chose to be a man and accept all the joys and sorrows of that condition."

And part of that condition—at least in his own case—was an overmastering sense of responsibility. "Even here. As long as I feel there is something I ought to be doing elsewhere—even if I cannot for the life of me remember what that something is, or why it should be so important—I could never be happy, even in so idyllic a setting as this."

Ceilyn stood up. He looked around him wistfully—he had a feeling that once he left this place he would never be able to return again. Yet there was a growing sense of urgency, a pressure to make his choice and be done with it, that warred with his desire to linger on the threshold between one course of action and another.

In the end, that urgency impelled him forward. He moved toward the door of the hut, and as he did so, the sunny woodland scene framed in the doorway shimmered and faded away.

Teleri waited for him in the dark by the door, pale and shaken by her own ordeals in Diaspad's chambers of illusion. Memory came flooding back, and Ceilyn realized how close he had come to abandoning both the quest and Teleri.

"By the rules of magic she cannot test us more than three

times," said Teleri. "Even the Princess Diaspad would not dare defy the Rule of Three. I do not know what dangers await us on the other side of this door, but I think they must be . . . more tangible and less personal."

"Whatever she conjures up to meet us after this, it can't be worse than what we have already faced: the peril we each carry with us."

And so saying, Ceilyn drew his sword out of its scabbard, threw open the last door, and stepped into the chamber beyond.

*Know then, the harshest and sternest law of magic: the Law of
Contagion. As like attracts like, so that which is worst in thought,
deed, and intention invariably attracts the same. Ill-deeds beget
ill-consequences, and just as a child in the body of his mother
contracts leprosy from a diseased womb by reason of location
and infection, though the seed be healthy, so our deeds may be
corrupted by our baser intentions, for what is engendered in the
mind also takes root in the physical world. Therefore, sow even
a small crop of greed, malice, or envy and no matter what other
seeds you cast forth, there shall come a woeful season when you
reap a bitter harvest.*

> —from a letter written
> by the Mage Atlendor
> to his pupils at Findias

18.

A Stench of Burning

For a moment, Ceilyn thought he had stepped into another
illusion, so unexpected was the sense of open space. He had
entered a vast round chamber with a vaulted ceiling. All around
the wall were doors and arches, giving the impression of a mul-
titude of corridors and passages converging on the vaulted chamber like the spokes of a great wheel.

He moved aside and Teleri stepped into the room. Torches set
at intervals between the doors and arches lit the perimeter of the
hall, but the low stepped platform at the center stood in a circle
of wan moonlight which came in through a round opening at the
top of the vault. Upon the dais stood the Princess, in a gown of
white silk and a silver girdle. Her head was thrown back, her
eyes were closed in concentration, and her copper-colored hair
hung loose to her waist. Utterly still, like a statue or a pillar of
ice, she stood poised with arms upraised, as if offering the crown

to the pale crescent moon shining through the aperture. In her hands, the silver circlet and crystal sidhe-stone glowed with an uncanny blue light.

Below the dais, in a semi-circle looking out, stood three armed dwarfs.

Ceilyn's hand tightened on the hilt of his sword. His shoulder throbbed painfully and he knew that his wound would open as soon as he began to swing his sword. But this was the last barrier between Teleri and the Princess and the sidhe-stone—if he could not clear the way for her, all their efforts so far, the slaughter of the griffon and of Diaspad's guards, would come to nothing.

The dwarfs moved his way; Ceilyn had to think fast and move even faster. Already weak from loss of blood, he knew that his one hope lay in a short, decisive encounter, one that would be over before his strength failed.

Gripping his sword in both hands, he charged the center of the dwarfs' line. At the last moment, he veered toward the guard on the left, knocking the dwarf's feet out from under him with a flying kick and swinging a slanting overhand cut at the man in the middle. The first dwarf went down, and the second, taken by surprised, was too slow to parry. Ceilyn's broadsword took him in the side of the neck, and the dwarf crumbled to the floor, mortally wounded.

But the third man was on Ceilyn before he had time to recover and block. The keen edge of the dwarf's shortsword cut through Ceilyn's mail byrnie and deep into the muscle at the back of his thigh. Before the shock wore off and his leg gave out, Ceilyn had parried the next stroke and swung again, a solid blow that landed with great impact on the dwarf's left side. The dwarf doubled over, staggered, and slipped in the other guard's blood. Dwarf and knight went down at the same time.

So Ceilyn was on his knees and doubly vulnerable without a shield, when the first dwarf scrambled to his feet and rushed at him with axe and shortsword. Ceilyn parried the sword but moved too slowly to avoid the axe; it grazed his left side just below the ribs. He could not block the next blow, and the axe was descending . . . falling toward Ceilyn's unprotected head . . . when a dagger came flying through the air and buried itself in the dwarf's throat.

Robbed of force and accuracy by the dwarf's suddenly slackened grip, the axe hit Ceilyn on the shoulder, glanced off, and clattered to the floor.

• • •

Up on the platform, a tremor passed through the still figure of the Princess. She opened her eyes and lowered the crown to breast height. She looked right past Ceilyn where he knelt, bloody and tattered, at the foot of the dais, past the fallen dwarf, and fastened her brilliant green gaze on Teleri.

Teleri stood with her arm still upraised from throwing Ceilyn's dirk, the spell of accuracy she had put on the dagger still on her lips. Diaspad's voice was low in that vast hollow chamber but it reached Teleri where she stood by the open door.

"So . . . it appears I underestimated you. I should have taken greater care in disposing of you. Next time, I shall be wiser in choosing my weapon."

Teleri lowered her arm, took two cautious steps toward the dais.

The Princess turned her gaze on Ceilyn, and he felt something cold and vicious touch his mind. "Kill her," said Diaspad.

Too weak to resist her compulsion, Ceilyn watched, horrified, as his hand reached out and pulled the dirk from the dwarf's throat. Blood ran down the blade and left a trail of dark drops across the moon-bleached floor.

"No!" Ceilyn had enough will left to force out that anguished protest, but he was helpless to control the hand that clutched the hilt of the dagger. His arm rose, aimed, and cast. . . .

After many attempts to raise the iron gate, Fflergant and Tryffin abandoned the effort. They took a torch off of the wall, and retraced their steps to the door where Teleri had counterspelled the wards. Outside, they followed the curving outer wall of the tower until they found another, smaller door. It was locked, but by throwing their weight against it repeatedly they broke the lock and opened the door.

The corridor on the other side led them to a series of tiny, interconnected rooms, and at last to the corridor on the far side of the iron gate. But by that time Teleri and Ceilyn had vanished, and it was impossible to determine which way they had gone. They could only go on to explore more rooms and passageways, in the hope they might meet them by some accident of good fortune.

At length they found the stairs, and climbed to the next floor. But that level was as mazelike and confusing as the floor below. "There may be signs or markings to guide the way, but I've not spotted them," Tryffin muttered to himself. "You ask me, this place was designed by a madman."

In mounting frustration, they wandered for what seemed like hours. "I think we've come this way before—impossible to tell. These rooms and passages are all so much alike," said Fflergant. "The truth is, I've lost all sense of direction."

Tryffin nodded glumly. "If we had any *sense* at all, we would have marked the way we came, scratched signs on all the doors we passed by or through—but it is a bit late to be thinking of that now. God help us—I hate feeling such a damned fool!"

He paused with his hand on the handle of a door. Unlike all the others he had tried previously, this door refused to open. "Locked or bolted. . . . It seems we have stumbled onto something after all," he said in a low voice.

Fflergant shrugged. "Oh aye . . . we've stumbled onto a locked door. For all the good that does us."

Tryffin gave him a disgusted look. "You have a mind of sorts . . . pity you never learned to use it. No one locks a door unless there is something he wishes to keep safe on the other side. And bars and bolts don't slide into place on their own. There may be somebody in there."

"Yes, I've puzzled that out in my own dim way," Fflergant retorted, more sharply than he had intended. "But how are we to open the lock or move the bolt aside . . . neither one of us being a Wizard? Or did you intend to break this door down—and announce our arrival to whoever it is on the other side?"

"We have seen that many of these rooms are connected," said Tryffin. "There may be another way in."

They passed through another doorway, so low that they had to bend over double to avoid the lintel, and into another series of tiny chambers, then into a short corridor. The next door that Tryffin tried refused to open, and the one after that. "I smell woodsmoke . . . cedar or spicewood," he whispered.

There was a tiny creaking sound, like the movement of hinges. Looking back down the corridor the way they had come, they saw the door they had first tried standing open to the width of two or three inches. A white face peered at them through the crack.

As quick as a cat, Tryffin leapt for the door. Too late—it slammed shut and there was a small sound like a key turning in a lock.

"Damn! If one of us had been a little quicker," Fflergant exclaimed.

Tryffin put a finger to his lips, and motioned his brother back down the corridor and into one of the rooms they had explored before. "I heard the door locked, but no bar falling into place. Perhaps there isn't one."

Fflergant started back toward the corridor. "No hope of entering unannounced now. The longer we wait to batter down the door, the longer the Princess—"

Tryffin put a restraining hand on Fflergant's arm. "I don't believe the Princess is in there with Calchas. Stop a moment and think. . . . If Diaspad and the sidhe-stone were in that room, then so would Teleri and Ceilyn be. The stone would have led them straight to it. No, Calchas is alone, but perhaps he can lead us to the Princess. We won't gain anything by battering down the door. The noise might alert the Princess, and it would certainly cause Calchas to take the back way out, if there is one. But if we keep quiet so that he doesn't know where we are, he won't go anywhere for fear if he bolts he will meet us again, and no locked door between us. Meanwhile, we devise a way in, one that doesn't give warning in advance."

Fflergant rolled his eyes. "You're so clever, you tell me—the walls are six feet thick at least and the doors solid oak. . . . What other way—?"

"There may be more than one key."

Fflergant nodded. "No doubt, and in the hands of the Princess Diaspad at that. All *we* need do is find her—which is what we have been trying to do all these hours—find her and ask her for the key, and persuade her somehow that she really ought to oblige—"

"Oh aye, she's likely to be carrying the key about with her, now isn't she?" Tryffin exploded. "Just the same way that Cynwas and Sidonwy are in the habit of carrying keys and opening doors for themselves. Will you just think back and remember who it was that generally performed that office for her back at Caer Cadwy!"

A memory of the Princess Diaspad formed in Fflergant's mind, Diaspad trailing majestically through the halls at Caer Cadwy with her retinue accompanying her: the hunchback Brangwengwen to carry her train, a pair of woodwoses as torch-bearers, and the dwarfish Bron scurrying on ahead with a ring of keys in his hand.

"You are right. Our late friend in the courtyard might aid us yet again," said Fflergant. "But how to find our way back there, and then back *here* through this damnable maze, before Calchas works up the courage to bolt?"

Tryffin pulled the dagger out of his belt. "Finding our way out may be difficult, but this time we'll make certain we know how to find our way back."

It took some time to find the stairs to the lower level, but after that their luck improved. They located the door to the courtyard almost immediately. Outside, they moved quickly and quietly down the steps and through the gate, into the yard where the bodies of the griffon and the guards still lay undisturbed.

Tryffin sheathed his dagger, handed the torch to Fflergant, and knelt down to search Bron's body. Just as they had hoped, there was a ring of keys on his belt.

Back inside the tower, they ran swiftly through rooms and corridors, propelled by a renewed sense of urgency. But when they found the short passageway leading to the door where they had seen Calchas, they stopped and drew their swords.

While Fflergant held the torch, Tryffin went through the keys, searching for the one most likely to fit the lock. "That one looks older than the rest," Fflergant hissed in his ear. "No, not the brass. The big black iron . . ."

Fflergant's voice trailed off and he and his brother stared at each other in sudden dismay. A thrill of superstitious horror snaked down Fflergant's spine. Tryffin had taken iron from a dead man and in doing so had violated one of his geasa.

For a long moment, neither of them spoke. The penalty for violating a geas was usually a sudden, violent death—either for the guilty party or for someone bound to him by blood. In all probability, one of them was doomed.

"Well then," Tryffin whispered at last, "I've done what I never should have done, and an ill-fate is on me—but it is too late to do anything about that now."

With the iron key in his hand, he approached the door. The key fit perfectly in the lock, and turned easily. Slowly, Tryffin pushed the door open.

The room on the other side was different from any chamber they had passed through previously. Rich carpets and the skins of exotic animals lay on the floor, tapestries hung on the walls, and a large pile of aromatic woods burned in a shallow pit in the center of the chamber. The ornate furnishings implied a living area, and a low archway leading to another room suggested a bedchamber beyond. A rattle of metal against wood and a low curse betrayed someone's movements in that other room.

"Calchas . . . we have him cornered now, the filthy little beast," whispered Fflergant.

Tryffin nodded wordlessly and stepped into the antechamber. Fflergant followed two paces behind. A pale and shaken Calchas appeared in the archway between the two rooms, holding a two-handed sword awkwardly before him.

"As God is my witness, it is almost pitiful," said Fflergant. "He hasn't the least idea how to handle a sword."

Two of the spotted furs lying beside the firepit yawned and stretched and rose gracefully to their feet. And Fflergant and his brother too late remembered Diaspad's golden leopards.

"Damn," said Tryffin, entertaining a brief, ignoble regret that *he* was no longer holding the torch.

Calchas hissed a command, and the leopards attacked. As the smaller cat leapt toward Fflergant, he was able to fend it off with the torch, whirling the flaming brand to make the fire burn hotter, and thrusting it into the leopard's face. Snarling, the spotted cat backed away.

But Tryffin barely had time to unsling the shield he carried on his back and slide his arm into the straps before the larger leopard was on him. He caught the big cat on his buckler, but the weight of the springing leopard bore him backward. He went down on one knee, with one hundred and forty pounds of caterwauling fury attached to his shield. Swinging a wide stroke, he managed to connect, but the leopard continued to scream in his face and rake at him with fore and hind feet. He swung once more, and landed a solid blow to the head. The leopard screamed again, and then went limp.

Ceilyn's aim was true, but Teleri was already moving. The dirk flew through the air and hit the floor several feet behind the place where Teleri had been standing.

As she ran toward the platform, she slammed up against an invisible barrier, a solid wall of mental force that sent her reeling back. Bruised and shaken, Teleri picked herself up off the floor.

"Little fool," said the Princess. "You are no match for me."

"We are perfectly matched," Teleri said softly, and realized that she spoke the truth. "We have both relied on illusion—I to appear less than I am, you to appear more—but illusion will not serve either of us now.''

Step by cautious step, Teleri moved forward, arms outstretched before her, until she encountered the barrier again. Under her hands, it felt as solid as stone, but by a concentrated effort of will she was able to make it melt and grow pliable, to part and move aside. . . . . There was a little resistance as the Princess put her own mind to bear on maintaining the wall, but not enough to hinder her.

In that moment, their minds were laid open to each other, and Diaspad recognized a trained will greater than her own. Panic surged through her, and by virtue of the bond between them, through Teleri as well, panic that changed to horror as the young sorceress realized what Diaspad intended.

''No! Don't! The stone will—'' But Teleri's cry of warning came too late. There was a sudden blinding flash, a sizzle, an odor of singed hair and scorching cloth, then the sickening stench of burning flesh.

When Teleri could see again, the dais was empty—empty save for the pitiful little pile of cracked bone and and smoking cloth that had once been the Princess Diaspad.

Teleri took a step forward, put a hand over her mouth, fighting back the bile that rose in her throat. Then she sat down on the bottom step and tried to convince herself that she was *not* going to vomit.

''Holy Mary Mother of God . . .'' That was Ceilyn, still kneeling bloody and dazed on the floor before the dais. ''Did *you* do that?''

Teleri swallowed, and shook her head. Then she rose unsteadily to her feet and forced herself to climb the steps, move aside the reeking pile of cloth and bone, and retrieve the crown.

''The Princess killed herself,'' she whispered. ''It was her own spell turned back on her by the sidhe-stone.''

Ceilyn opened his mouth as if to speak, but no sound came out. One hand was clamped to his side, and Teleri saw blood seeping between his fingers, blood that ran down his side and pooled on the floor. He swayed from side to side, as if the effort to hold himself more or less upright was becoming too great.

Brought out of her own daze by a sudden concern for Ceilyn, Teleri moved to help him. But just as she reached out to catch him, the young knight went limp and crumbled to the floor.

• • •

Fflergant's leopard crouched, ready to spring, but still held at bay by the threat of the flaming torch. Fflergant crouched, too, holding his sword low in front of him as he threw the torch full in the leopard's face. Maddened with pain, the spotted cat rushed forward—and impaled itself on the blade, spattering Fflergant with blood and wrenching the sword out of his hand.

Tryffin cried out a hoarse warning, and Fflergant looked up, just in time to dodge a clumsy swipe of Calchas's two-hander. The Mochdreffi youth swung again, but Fflergant avoided the blow and tripped Calchas up, all in one movement. The boy went sprawling, face down on an oriental carpet. The sword flew out of his hand, and landed at the edge of the firepit.

By the time Calchas regained his breath and rolled over on his back, Fflergant had pulled his own sword out of the dying leopard, and was waving thirty inches of bloody steel in his face.

"Where in this God-forsaken pile of stone can we find the Princess and Cynwas's crown?"

Calchas made a gurgling sound, deep in his throat, but vouchsafed no other reply.

Tryffin limped across the room. "You heard the question— where is your mother, and what is she up to?"

Calchas winced as Fflergant nudged him with the tip of the sword, just above his breastbone. "I don't know where she is— no, I swear to you—she doesn't tell me things anymore, she doesn't—she doesn't trust me, ever since—"

Fflergant prodded him again. "Since . . . ?"

"Since I tried to bring Gwenlliant with me, when we left Caer Cadwy. I was trying to save her, I swear to you. She is a taking little thing, and I . . . was fond of her."

Fflergant and his brother continued to gaze down on him with undisguised contempt. "Oh aye, we know about that," said Tryffin. "We know how you were fond of her. And we warned you what would happen if you ever laid hands on her again. But don't worry . . . we'll give you a chance to die like a man." He looked at Fflergant. "Let him get up now and give him back his sword. Then we'll try odds and evens to see who kills him."

Fflergant withdrew his sword, and Calchas staggered to his feet. Looking from one grim face to the other, the boy from Mochdreff panicked and began to babble. "You can't kill me . . . not an unarmed man. I won't pick up the sword, no I won't . . . and then you will have to spare me. You'd never touch me anyway, not if you knew. You're Gwyngellach, and kinslaying is the one unpardonable crime.''

Fflergant scowled at him. "Kinslaying, is it now? No kin of ours, you filthy Mochdreffi pig!''

"But I am,'' Calchas insisted. "We're first cousins. My mother and your uncle . . . you can't pretend you didn't know.''

"Everyone knows that affair ended years before you were born,'' said Fflergant.

"They broke it off, yes . . . but they met again, years later, when she was betrothed to my—to Corfil of Mochdreff. They slept together one last time, and I was conceived. But it never really ended, not for her,'' Calchas insisted passionately. "I have suffered for that every day of my life . . . all her rage and frustration because she couldn't have him. The sins of the fathers, that is what it was. My curse that she could never look at me without seeing *him*, but my salvation if you have the eyes to see the resemblance, too.''

Confused, Fflergant looked to his brother for advice. Tryffin continued to look at Calchas with such an expression on his face as his brother had never seen before. "The eyes and the hair . . . a superficial resemblance, maybe. But it was a long time ago. He may know something that we don't—though you'll notice family feeling didn't prevent him from trying to kill you. Ah well, who can say? Take his nasty little dagger and pick up his sword, and then we'll decide about killing him.''

Fflergant relieved Calchas of the dagger he carried in his belt, then turned toward the firepit to pick up the two-hander. At that same moment, Tryffin turned, as if in response to some sound or movement from the dying leopard. That was all the encouragement Calchas needed.

He slid a second, smaller dagger out of his sleeve and leapt at Fflergant. Tryffin's sword met him halfway; there was a sickening sound as the blade hit Calchas's midsection, and the boy fell to the floor, cut nearly in half by the force of the blow and his own impetus forward.

"Mother of God!'' Fflergant stared down, aghast, at the bloody corpse at his feet. Then he looked up at Tryffin. "You *tricked* him. We could neither of us kill a man who was unarmed and begging for mercy, so you tricked him into attacking me.''

"I swear before God, that was not what I intended,'' Tryffin protested. "I never meant to endanger you. I was certain he would go for me first; I was the one he hated the most.

"Ah God, he had to die," he insisted, as Fflergant continued to stare at him incredulously. "You heard what he said."

"But that was a lie. I admit I wondered for a moment. But no one could seriously believe—"

"It was the truth. I don't know how, but it was God's own truth. He wasn't lying when he said all that about the sins of the fathers. And he would have tried to use the same story back at Caer Cadwy, to save his miserable skin. It wouldn't have saved him, but Manogan would have been hurt by it . . . such a son as that, and all the world to know of his treason! We couldn't allow that to happen.

"Don't you see? Calchas had to die," Tryffin said. "And one of us had to be the one to kill him."

"I am weary," said King Anwas, *"for the years and my labors have robbed me of strength. Moreover, the Age of Wonders has passed, and my work is completed."*

"Not so," said Glastyn. *"Many things exist and will continue to exist which would amaze you if you knew of them. This world was old ere you or I came into it, yet Nature loses neither her delight nor her capacity for invention. Therefore, new marvels are born in each generation, and every age is an Age of Miracles for those who retain a sense of wonder."*

19.

The Passing of Griffons

Ceilyn woke in an unfamiliar bed, an enormous four-poster, in a great soft nest of feather mattresses, velvet pillows, and silky sleeping furs. The room was strange, too, a tiny square chamber with walls of undressed stone, windowless, except for some narrow arrowslots in one wall. Pale sunlight came in through the slots and lay in golden bands across the bed.

When he tried to sit up, a sudden dizziness overcame him. He lay back and closed his eyes until the dizzy spell passed. He tried to remember how he had come to be there.

He had a vague recollection of a long time lying on his back with his head in Teleri's lap, gazing up at the ceiling of the vaulted chamber. *"The others?"* he had asked, between waves of pain, and Teleri had replied, *"They must find us eventually. I cannot carry you to a better place myself, and I will not leave you."*

After that there was a period of darkness and pain and distant voices . . . and the next thing he remembered was waking up in this bed.

When he opened his eyes again, the first thing he saw was Teleri's face, pale and concerned. *"How do you feel? Is there any pain?"*

Ceilyn started to shake his head, thought better of it, and tried to speak instead. His voice came out stronger and clearer than he expected. "I feel as though I had been cut to pieces by Diaspad's dwarfs, then badly stitched together again."

Teleri sat down on the edge of the bed beside him, carefully, to avoid bumping or jolting him. There was a look of strain around her eyes and mouth, but she answered him lightly. "You *were* cut into little pieces by Diaspad's dwarfs—or the next thing to it. And I did sew up your wounds; they looked so bad and they weren't healing in the usual way. Perhaps now you are finally awake, you can speed the healing process."

Ceilyn frowned. "Just how long was I unconscious?"

"We brought you here just after sunrise, and the sun is setting now."

He began to understand why she looked so white and worn. "And you have been here all that time—watching at my bedside?"

"Yes, I knew you wouldn't want Fflergant or Tryffin to nurse you. They did help me to bring you here, but I tried my best to hide the full extent of your wounds. Still, there was no hiding the fact that you were badly hurt."

Ceilyn sighed. "I hate to be tied to this bed any longer than necessary, feigning weakness for their benefit. We have to take the crown and return to Caer Cadwy as quickly as possible."

"As to feigning weakness . . . you lost so much blood, it may take you longer than you think to recover," said Teleri. "Perhaps several days."

Ceilyn was determined to be well and out of bed long before that, but he was not inclined to argue the point. He closed his eyes again. "At least we know now how much damage I can sustain and still heal myself afterward."

"Truly," Teleri said softly, "your powers of healing are . . . miraculous. But you are not invincible, after all."

Ceilyn opened his eyes. "I never believed I was. I always knew I could be burned to death, or killed by a sword thrust— or a wooden stake—through my heart. I am vulnerable to silver and to other poisons. You need not fear I will begin to entertain any delusions of immortality.

"I wish to God I knew how much Fflergant and Tryffin have guessed by now," he added ruefully.

"When last I spoke with them, they seemed uncertain whether to ascribe the miracle they witnessed to *your* virtue or *my* powers as a wizard and physician," said Teleri. "But after watching you slay the griffon, sustain terrible injuries, yet rise up and walk again, they appear to feel they have seriously underestimated your heroic qualities in the past, and that some sort of an apology is due to you. I think, when you see them, you will find them both . . . meek, and exceedingly tractable. Fflergant, especially."

Ceilyn doubted that happy state of affairs would long continue; he felt certain a time would come when his kinsmen would demand some sort of an explanation. But the idea of Fflergant grown meek and eager to oblige him was irresistible. "That should be amusing, for as long as it lasts."

"Your turn," said Tryffin, as he handed the shovel to his brother. Careful of his wounded leg, he lowered himself to the ground, and watched while Fflergant tossed dirt into the grave.

Tryffin squinted at the sun riding high in the sky, then his gaze wandered to the black clouds piling up on the horizon. It was nearly noon; there would probably be rain before nightfall, and the carcass of the griffon had still to be buried.

Tryffin and Fflergant had buried the dwarfs the day before, the task made difficult by the lack of a spade, but mitigated by the fact that the earth was still moist after the last rain. Fflergant found a short-handled pitchfork in the stable, and they used it to loosen the earth, then they tossed out the dirt with an equally short-handled shovel, formerly used by the dwarfs to clean up after the horses.

Thirteen dwarfs shared a common grave, but they had buried Bron separately, and sprinkled earth from the bag he wore next to his heart into the open grave.

Today, they were burying Calchas—without any ceremony, for neither of them knew the Mochdreffi rite and in spite of Calchas's revelation, the Gwyngellach ceremony seemed inappropriate.

Diaspad's bones went into the same grave. Those bones had caused Tryffin and Fflergant considerable puzzlement. Blackened and cracked as the bones were, certain anomalies were still obvious: the curiously feline shape of the skull, the pointed teeth, and a strange lengthening of the spine that suggested a tail.

They had shown the bones to Teleri, hoping for an explanation. *"Not a natural deformity, I would think,"* said Teleri. *"But perhaps of long standing. It might explain why she chose to sur-*

round herself with so many other abnormalities. Some curse or contagion she contracted while experimenting with forbidden magics. . . . It would be as well," she had added unexpectedly, *"not to say anything about this to Ceilyn."*

With the Princess and Calchas buried, Tryffin said, "I have been thinking . . . I'm sick and tired of all this grave-digging. And it would take an immense hole to bury the griffon intact. Why shouldn't we burn the beast, and bury the bones afterward?"

Fflergant considered that. "I am tired of digging, too . . . but gathering enough dried branches to make a bonfire, and carrying them up from the wood below—even if we take one of the horses we'll be busy all afternoon. And that's supposing we can get the damned Mochdreffi wood to burn, once we build a pyre."

"We can break up the furniture in Calchas's bedchamber and take down a couple of doors. All seasoned wood, and it ought to burn fast and hot. We can use straw from the stable for kindling," said Tryffin.

"But we should speak to Ceilyn first," said Fflergant. "He might want to keep something: the skull or one of the feet, as a trophy. Or just to show everyone there really *was* a griffon."

When his kinsmen knocked at the door, Ceilyn was sitting up in bed, propped up by pillows and velvet cushions. He had taken advantage of Teleri's absence by climbing out of bed, wobbling across the room, digging through the gear which someone had conveniently brought in for him, and changing into a clean linen shirt and breeches.

At the prospect of company, Ceilyn tossed the pillows aside, and lay back on the bed, trying to look even weaker than he felt. "Come in," he said, in what he imagined was a suitable tone for an invalid.

The door opened and Tryffin and Fflergant came in, looking remarkably sober and respectful. At Ceilyn's invitation, they took seats: Fflergant on a stool, Tryffin at the foot of the bed. They told him of their plans for disposing of the griffon.

"I am sorry that all the unpleasant tasks fall to you, while I lie here useless," said Ceilyn.

The door opened halfway, and Teleri came quietly into the room.

"But as for disposing of the griffon's bones . . ." Ceilyn went on, ". . . it seems disrespectful, somehow, to take a trophy for people to gawk at. And yet . . . and yet, that might be all the griffon that anyone will ever see again.''

"No need to display it publicly, if that is what you mean," said Fflergant. "But keep something for future generations—a kind of heirloom to pass on to your children and grandchildren. Only think how *you* would feel if your grandfather had slain a griffon, and not kept anything to show you.''

In the end, they convinced him to keep the skull and some of the feathers.

"I would like some feathers, too," said Teleri. "And a piece of bone. To test them for magical and medicinal properties. That is . . . if you don't mind very much.''

After Fflergant and Tryffin had taken their leave, she sat down at the foot of the bed. "You are regretting now that you killed the griffon." It was more a statement than a question.

"I wish—I wish that it hadn't been necessary.''

"Not even a natural beast," said Teleri. "One of Gandwy's creations, a creature of artifice, an unnatural mingling of flesh and metal. It was worse than the little hybrid beast Failinas killed, and you called that an abomination.''

"Yes, I know. *Neither bird nor beast, fish nor serpent,*" he quoted. "But it was splendid—beautiful and terrifying both at once. Only . . . a thing like that could never breed. Perhaps it was the only one of its kind left in the whole world. The last griffon, and I killed it.

"I used to dream of slaying monsters," he went on. "And I used to fear that the days of adventures were all past. I longed for magic and mystery and fabulous beasts. But it never occurred to me before: If my wish came true, and I went out and killed all the dragons and griffons that there were, I would be destroying the very thing I longed for.

"I don't say," he added, "that I would like things to be as they were in the old days: monsters roaming about freely, terrorizing people and carrying maidens and little children off to be eaten. But it seems . . . it seems there ought to be some sort of middle ground between utter chaos and a world that is safe and colorless and dull, without even the *possibility* of peril, or wonder, or surprises.

"I don't know," he said, "that I want to live in a world without griffons.''

• • •

When Ceilyn woke the next morning, a wan grey light was coming in through the arrowslots and he could hear rain pounding on the walls outside. Though the hour might be anytime between sunrise and sunset, he suspected it was still early, or Teleri would have come in to light the candles.

He climbed out of bed, and was pleased to discover that he could stand without wobbling. He lit the candles and kindled a fire on the hearth. Except for a certain light-headedness, which he ascribed to hunger, he felt perfectly fit. Too well to lie in bed like an infant or an invalid and wait for Teleri to bring him his breakfast.

The bedchamber was on the fourth floor of the tower—the only floor (so Teleri had told him) with windows or arrowslots—and the room had belonged to the Princess. Teleri had removed Diaspad's clothes and her personal possessions, deeming them "improper furnishings for a sick room." All that remained were the big bed and an oak chest at the foot. In this, Teleri had stowed Ceilyn's armor and his clothes.

Opening the wooden chest, Ceilyn donned woolen hose and a long green cyclas, belted it, and pulled on his boots. The bedchamber door stood slightly ajar. Pushing it open, Ceilyn stood at the top of a long flight of stairs. Teleri's room, he knew, was at the bottom of the steps, several flights down.

He descended the stairs until he reached the ground floor. Teleri's door stood open, but he walked past it, drawn by a creaking sound farther down the corridor, the sound a rusty windlass makes in drawing up a heavy bucket of water.

The well-chamber was a small octagonal room with the well in the center. When Ceilyn entered the room, Teleri was just unfastening a large oaken bucket from the windlass.

Instead of one of her own grey gowns she wore black velvet, a dress much too large for her, which showed a distracting tendency to slip off her shoulders. The sight of Teleri in one of Diaspad's gowns troubled Ceilyn in more ways than one.

Despite her protests, he bent down to replace the hinged iron well-cover, and relieved Teleri of her bucket.

"You ought not to be out of bed," she insisted, lifting up her heavy velvet skirt to follow him out of the chamber. Ceilyn, half-turning, caught the flash of her little white feet under the folds of her skirt.

"Neither should you be wandering around this cold, drafty place in your bare feet," he said sternly.

Though he knew that Fflergant and Tryffin might be some-where about to see him, he could not resist putting down the bucket and sweeping Teleri up into his arms. "I will come back for the water," he said, as he carried her down the passageway.

"You are quite, quite mad," she said breathlessly, "and if you hurt yourself—"

"—I will have only myself to blame for refusing to act on the advice of my physician," he finished for her. He crossed her bedchamber in two strides and deposited her on the bed.

The room had been formerly occupied by one of the dwarfs—Bron, most likely—the furniture was small, the legs sawed off short. Which meant that everything was nearly the perfect size for Teleri. There was a bright red covering on the bed, and a blue fire blazing on the hearth.

Ceilyn went back for the bucket, brought it in, and set it down by the fire. Then he sat down on the bed beside Teleri.

She opened her mouth as if to scold him again, but Ceilyn spoke first. "Perhaps you can tell me whatever possessed you to imitate the Princess's taste in clothing."

Teleri flushed. "It wasn't a matter of choice . . . or taste. I had nothing else to wear. The things I wore the night we stormed the fortress were all stained with blood or torn up to make ban-dages. The rest had to be washed sometime. I am sorry if my attire offends you," she said, not sounding sorry at all.

Ceilyn was amused by this rare show of spirit. And now that he came to look at her, the effect of Diaspad's gown was unex-pected: She ought to have looked perfectly appalling, innocence masquerading as decadence, but the slashes and patches and elaborate dagging made her look rather like a little bird, her feathers all ruffled with anger, and the black velvet accented the dazzling fairness of her complexion.

Impulsively, he reached out and drew her to him, tangling his hands in her hair and covering her mouth with his. Always be-fore he had been so careful, afraid of hurting or alarming her—but perhaps he had been too cautious. Far from repulsing him, Teleri wrapped her arms around his neck and returned his kisses eagerly.

It was difficult to think with her mouth so warm and soft beneath his, her heart beating so wildly against his breast, but Ceilyn understood enough to realize it was time for a change of tactics. He drew her down on the bed beside him, kissing her eyes, her mouth, her neck. . . . In his eagerness, he knotted the ribbon that laced her bodice.

"Let me," she said. "I can—"

"No. I want to do it." The knot loosened and he slid his hand in between the velvet and her skin, cupping her breast. Teleri gave a little gasp of surprise at his touch, and they exchanged another breathless kiss. Then suddenly she became cold and still against him.

Ceilyn withdrew his hand. "I'm sorry," he said against her hair. "I didn't mean to frighten you."

"N-no," she said, "you didn't—it wasn't . . . I just remembered something I forgot to tell you, and after I remembered I didn't feel the same."

He propped himself up on one elbow, glared down at her in outraged surprise. "You remembered something you forgot to *say* to me? For the love of God—couldn't you think of it some other time?"

Teleri shook her head. "I'm sorry." She took a deep breath. "Prescelli is here at Caer Wydr."

Ceilyn closed his eyes. "How long have you known this?"

"I knew a woman had occupied the room next to this one—I thought it might be her. But I wasn't sure until last night, when Fflergant and Tryffin told me they saw and spoke to her. She is staying in the barracks where the dwarfs used to sleep, and she says—she claimed your protection and asked to speak with you privately."

He rolled off of her, lay back on the bed, staring miserably up at the ceiling. The news that Prescelli was at Caer Wydr came as a nasty jolt.

"I am sorry," Teleri repeated in a whisper. "It was an awkward time for me to remember to tell you this."

Ceilyn laughed mirthlessly. "The situation goes far, far beyond awkward. Almost certainly she knew something, played some small part in the Princess's schemes, but just how guilty she is would be difficult to determine.

"I suppose . . . oh Sweet Jesus Christ, I suppose we ought to take her back to Camboglanna and bring her to trial."

"It is for you to decide," Teleri said softly. "We discussed the matter, your cousins and I, and we all thought that you should decide whether to take her with us or leave her here."

Ceilyn glared at the ceiling. Why should *he* be the one to decide? Why not Fflergant or Tryffin? They had *found* Prescelli, why couldn't they decide what to do with her? Or Teleri . . . the quest for the crown was her quest, after all; they had agreed on that at the beginning.

"Dear God," he said. "The crown. What have you done with it—is it safe?"

"Yes," said Teleri. "I put it away where Prescelli could never find it."

But she did not tell him where the crown was hidden, an omission which Ceilyn did not fail to notice. Feeling hurt as well as frustrated, he sat up, and swung his legs over the side of the bed.

Teleri sat up beside him. "You can't see her now. She knows you were badly hurt. And you said, once, that she knows too much about you. If she saw how fast you had recovered, she might put it together with all the rest, and guess . . . more than it would be safe for her to know."

Ceilyn ground his teeth. "Yes, yes, you are right of course. But just how long do you expect me to continue this farce?"

"I know you believe you are quite recovered," Teleri said, busy relacing her gown, and so unable to look at him. "But you might learn otherwise if you attempted to travel so soon. And I am not satisfied that Tryffin can travel yet. His leg isn't healing as it ought. Cat scratches are prone to infection, and a scratch from a leopard, being so much deeper, could be dangerous. As long as we remain here for his sake, I see no harm in pretending we stay for your sake also."

Ceilyn left the bed, began to pace restlessly around the tiny bedchamber. "I keep thinking of Sidonwy and the other women at Caer Cadwy, waiting for us to return with the crown. The longer we stay here, the longer they lack protection."

"The other men may be returning home now," said Teleri. "The spell had already worn thin when we met Fflergant and Tryffin. Once the men begin to return, the Queen and the others will not lack for protection."

"But they will *all* lack the protection only the Clach Ghealach can offer," Ceilyn persisted. "And every day we waste here . . ."

Teleri sighed. "My time is not being wasted." She left the bed, picked up a book with a cover of worn blue leather that she had left lying open on a little table by the fire. "I have been looking through some of Diaspad's things—no, don't look at me that way, Ceilyn. Not all of the Princess's things are tainted. I have no idea how she came by this book, but it was written in

Atlendor's own hand and cipher. Only think of it . . . Atlendor was Glastyn's master, and he lived for more than a hundred years. How wise he must have been, how many wonderful things he must have learned. And it may all be written in this book, for you can see by the ink and the increasing unsteadiness of his hand that he wrote in this volume over a long span of years.''

Ceilyn stopped pacing and stood, legs spread apart, with his back to the fire. "If the book contains all Atlendor's accumulated wisdom, I wonder that the Princess did not profit by it.''

"But no one could profit by anything Atlendor wrote in this book, unless she was familiar with the cipher he used," said Teleri. "And even knowing the cipher, as I do, it is a laborious task translating the book. The early part seems to contain only simple spells and elementary principles of magic, but I plan to translate the entire volume lest I miss something of importance in the first pages.''

Ceilyn had an uneasy feeling there was a lesson in patience in all of this, meant for his benefit.

"As we are speaking of magic . . . there is one thing I do not understand. You said the Clach Ghealach turned her own spell back on the Princess. Why didn't your spell rebound when you killed the dwarf?''

Teleri put down the book. "It was your knife that killed the dwarf, not my spell. I put my spell on the knife, to make it fly more accurately.''

Ceilyn thought that over, then he nodded. "Yes, I see. Your spell did not harm the knife any more than her attempt to control my actions did me any actual harm. Neither spell was sufficiently . . . aggressive to activate the sidhe-stone. But even if your spell had come back to you . . . the dwarf would have died just the same. Very clever.''

"I am afraid I didn't think it out so far as that," said Teleri. "But I have lived all these years in proximity to the sidhe-stone, so I am always careful of the kind of spells I use. The Princess had not developed that same habit of caution, and so she died. She acted without thinking and tried to destroy me with the most devastating spell she knew. She died before she had time to realize her mistake. I would not say that either of us was particularly clever, but *she* was arrogant as well as foolish, and that is why she died and I am still alive.''

Ceilyn shrugged. "If you are alive and she is dead, that must make you the superior sorceress.''

"Perhaps." Teleri did not sound convinced. "But the distinction is not an enviable one. I never admired her, and now I don't even know why I feared her. She had a certain . . . presence which I found intimidating, but she was never really that formidable. It was all just a pretense."

*Then Amren and his men waged battle on Goreu, and Goreu
was slain and all his lands and goods were taken. Nynve, the
daughter of Goreu, came out to greet the victor, and seeing that
Amren was a goodly man, she smiled on him, using such arts as
a woman practices on a man. Love for the daughter of Goreu
entered into him, and Amren desired to make her his wife.*

*Now the woman was not a good woman, and she hated the
man who had killed her father. But she thought of the gold neck-
laces and the other fine things he could give her, and also the
position that would be hers as the wife of the strongest man in
the land. And so she consented to marry him. When Amren took
Nynve into his bed, he took a viper to his breast.*

—*from* The Black Book of Tregalen

20.

A Viper at the Breast

Ceilyn dutifully kept to his room for the next two days. Teleri
brought him his meals, as well as herbal concoctions and bitter-
tasting healing drafts, morning and evening. He took his medicine without protest, though once he was moved to point out:
"It is Tryffin you ought to be dosing, if his leg is as bad as you
say. *I* feel perfectly well."

"I have not neglected Tryffin," said Teleri. "He has had his
share of medicines, and poultices made of cobweb. His leg is
better, but he continues to be morose and listless. I think there
is something preying on his mind."

But Teleri's visits did not come often enough to suit Ceilyn.
And her manner when she did come was vague and distant. He
knew she was spending most of each day poring over Atlendor's
book, a task which absorbed not only her time but most of her
attention. Yet he could not help but wonder if her manner was
partly assumed, in order to keep him at a distance.

He had time to think, in those restless days, to consider the adventure up to that point and to contemplate his own actions. He was troubled by the things he had seen and felt during Diaspad's magical "tests." His vision of the stone chapel was particularly disturbing.

A new weapon and a new destiny. The words had been his, they had entered his mind unbidden, but he had thought he knew what they meant at the time. Now he was not so certain. The Holly King had shattered his old blade, accepted Ceilyn's offered life—*not* as a sacrifice—and then another sword with the Holly King's own mark upon it, had been provided. That much Ceilyn understood.

But who *was* the Holly King? Was it Glastyn? One of the ancient powers Teleri had once described to him, *"who walked abroad of old in form and manner like to men and women"*? And what sort of bargain had Ceilyn made, all unknowing, with the master of the Wild Magic?

But when Ceilyn abandoned these puzzling, metaphysical speculations, another problem, more pressing and personal, demanded to be faced. He needed to see and talk with Prescelli. But how to find her? He had no idea where, in that vast pile of stone, Diaspad's dwarf guardsmen had been quartered, and he felt uncomfortable broaching the subject to Teleri.

He spent the third day alternately pacing the floor and staring listlessly out through the arrowslots, down at the muddy courtyard below. Fflergant and Tryffin could tell him where to find Prescelli. He had watched the two of them earlier, going in and out of a low building, presumably the stable.

When Teleri appeared again, he told her he wanted to visit the horses. "I would like to see Tegillus and the sorrel—make certain Tryffin and his brother are looking after them properly." That was not a lie, neither was it the whole truth.

Teleri looked him over, frowning. "I do not think—" she began.

"We will be leaving in another day or two. What better way to discover if I am fit than to allow me a little exercise around the castle. And it won't make much sense to the others if I am bedridden one day, and able to travel the next."

She considered that carefully. "Perhaps you are right. Very well. Just let me fetch my cloak, and I will take you down to the stable."

She disappeared before he had time to protest. He needed her to guide him down to the courtyard, but he did not want her to accompany him to the stables, lest she linger there and learn his real purpose. Still, he could hardly refuse her company now she had offered it. He put on his own cloak and followed her down the stairs.

She emerged from her bedchamber a few minutes later, wrapped in layers of grey wool and carrying a lighted torch. She led him down the passage, through the octagonal well-chamber, and a whole series of tiny, interconnected rooms. She walked quickly and confidently, as though the way was now familiar to her.

"It was all very confusing at first, but there is a kind of plan to all the rooms and corridors," she said, as if guessing his thoughts. "The numbers three, nine, and twenty-seven evidently had some significance for the builders. Once you learn that, it is comparatively easy to find your way around."

She led him to the door by which they had originally entered. Outside, the rain had slowed to a drizzle, but the mud in the courtyard was ankle deep. Wading toward the stable, Ceilyn realized that it would have been impossible, even if Teleri had been willing to travel, to take the horses out in such filthy weather.

Inside the stable, lanterns hung at intervals all along one wall. Every stall was occupied. Besides Tegillus, Kelpie, the sorrel packhorse, and the two red-gold chargers belonging to Fflergant and Tryffin, there were all the horses and ponies which had belonged to the Princess and her party. It was obvious that Fflergant and Tryffin were spending much of their time in the stable; Tegillus and all the other horses looked sleek and well-cared-for.

Fflergant was grooming the big chestnut, and Ceilyn could see Tryffin at work in a stall at the end of the row. He turned around to speak to Teleri, but she had slipped away without a word.

Ceilyn looked around him, counting the horses in all the stalls. "We will have to set some of them loose, unless we plan to herd horses all the way back to Camboglanna."

Tryffin came out of the stall, where he had been currying Bron's piebald pony. As he limped down the aisle, Ceilyn was surprised by the change a few days had wrought in his big blond cousin. Tryffin looked not ill, precisely, but somehow diminished, brought down to size—duller and more ordinary.

"We thought you might want to look them over before we

decided which ones to take and which ones to loose," said Tryffin. "The draft horses might prove useful, if we decided to take one of the wagons with us."

Ceilyn walked down the aisle, stopped outside the big box stall where Calchas's black stallion moved restively. "This is a magnificent beast. A pity to let him go. I have a mind to take him along."

Fflergant snorted. "Oh yes, he is very pretty to look at—but he is also one of the meanest bastards this side of Purgatory. True, that is largely the result of Calchas's mishandling, but it would take a better horseman than you or I to undo the damage now."

"Do you think so?" Ceilyn could not resist opening the door to the stall and walking inside.

"God Almighty—you are taking your life into your hands. Come out before he—" Fflergant stopped and stared in amazement as the black stallion dipped his head and nuzzled Ceilyn affectionately.

"He seems perfectly gentle to me," said Ceilyn. "Though it might be different if I tried to mount him."

Fflergant continued to stare at him. "Just when did *you* acquire the ability to handle wild horses?"

Ceilyn shrugged. "I don't know. I used to be a bit afraid of horses—they can sense that you know—but I've since learned to be at ease among them." He stroked the black's broad forehead. "What did Calchas call him—do either of you remember?"

"Twrch," said Tryffin. In the Old Tongue, the word had signified a wild boar.

"No wonder he is savage then, trying to live up to a name like that." Ceilyn continued to gentle the stallion with his hands and his mind. "Perhaps that was Calchas's intention—some men admire a dangerous horse. I will rename him, and see what happens."

He left the stall and fastened the gate behind him. "I need to know where the barracks are, the place where Prescelli is staying. No, don't bother to come with me. Just tell me how I can find it."

The barracks where the dwarfs had lived was a long low room. Thirteen beds stood in two rows of six and seven each. The beds were long and narrow, evidently made for taller men, but the legs had been sawn off short. Prescelli was not there, but a fire blazed on the hearth at the far end of the room, indicating that she would soon be back.

Ceilyn moved toward the fire, drew up a bench which had suffered the same treatment as the beds, and sat down to wait. He had not been waiting long when Prescelli came in, wrapped in a long brown cloak with the hood drawn up over her dark hair. She started at the sight of him.

"They told me you were badly hurt. I would—I would have come to see you, but they gave me to understand that I would not be welcome."

She removed the cloak, tossed it down on one of the beds, and moved toward the fire. "You appear to be quite recovered now."

"Yes, I am nearly recovered." Ceilyn rose politely. "It is possible they exaggerated the extent of my injuries."

Prescelli surprised him by throwing her arms around his neck and burying her face in the folds of his cloak. Ceilyn wrapped his arms around her and held her tightly. It felt good to hold a woman who was warm and eager in his arms—especially after Teleri's coldness these last few days. But he could not let his feelings cloud his judgment.

He held her for a moment before putting his hands on her shoulders and gently moving her away. "You are in serious trouble."

Prescelli released her hold on him. "Yes," she said meekly. "I know that I am." She sat down on the bench, folding her hands in her lap, like a child who is about to be reprimanded. "And you have come here to tell me my fate—that is right, isn't it?"

"Hardly that," said Ceilyn. "Your fate is not in my hands. But I have come to tell you that we are taking you back to Caer Cadwy with us, to answer for your crimes."

"Yes, I see," said Prescelli, in a small voice. "And just what are my crimes? What do you imagine I have done?"

"You poisoned Teleri's wine. No, please don't try to look innocent. I know very well that the Princess would never make the mistake of mixing foxglove with aconite, but I can easily believe that you, in your eagerness to harm Teleri, would make just such an error."

"Yes, I did want to hurt Teleri," Prescelli admitted. "I did want to hurt her, but when the time came I found I didn't quite have the heart to *kill* her. So I put in foxglove as an antidote for the wolfsbane, and only poured half the mixture into the wine bottle. I knew a dose like that would not be enough to kill Teleri. But if I had refused the Princess—and some more trustworthy servant had been given the task—your little Teleri would be dead."

"Teleri did not drink the wine—I did," said Ceilyn. "Only a sip, but I very nearly died. There was enough aconite in that one cup, Teleri said, to kill ten or twelve men."

"Then she lied to you," said Prescelli. "Or the Princess lied to me, which is much more likely. She had a way of guessing what I would do, sometimes before I knew it myself, and manipulating me accordingly. I suppose she knew I might lose my nerve and only pour in half the phial, so she doubled or tripled the dose."

"Perhaps," said Ceilyn. Knowing Prescelli and knowing the Princess, her story was at least plausible. "But that hardly excuses you—or relieves you of your larger culpability in helping the Princess to steal the crown."

"But I didn't," Prescelli protested. "I did nothing to help her. I never knew precisely what was afoot until we were out of the castle and halfway across Camboglanna. You can't believe she confided the whole of her plan to *me*. I think she only brought me along with her, the better to keep an eye on me.

"And Ceilyn," she said softly, piteously, "I don't—I don't want to die. My life is not worth much, I know, but it is precious to me. Please don't hand me over to be executed."

"It won't come to that," said Ceilyn. "God knows, Cynwas is not a vengeful man. And the Queen will plead on your behalf."

"But it *will* come to that—it must. It wasn't just the crown, it was what it represents. Even if Cynwas were inclined to be merciful, his council would convince him that someone will have to suffer, an example will have to be made, and I am the only one alive to serve as a scapegoat. Oh, I don't doubt my death would be swift and painless: Cynwas would grant me that much to salve his conscience. But I don't want to die—not for the sake of mere expediency."

"Hardly a matter of mere expediency, with—as you remind me—the King's authority, his ability to keep peace and order within the realm, at stake." Ceilyn tried to sound stern, but the thought of Prescelli's death troubled him. "You could die in a worse cause."

"But I don't want to die in *any* cause," said Prescelli. "I am not the sort of person who dies for causes."

"No, you are not," said Ceilyn. He sat down on the bench beside her. "You want me to let you go. You want me to pretend you were never here. But that would make me as guilty as you, guilty of complicity if not of any act against the crown—"

"I don't want you to let me go," said Prescelli. "There is no place where I can go, no way that I could keep myself—except, perhaps, as a common whore. I *want* to go back to Caer Cadwy. I will come willingly—and relieve you of the embarrassment of taking me back as a bound prisoner—but in return, you must promise to stand as my champion when I come to trial."

Ceilyn ran a hand through his hair. He had seen this coming from the beginning, but he still did not know how to make her understand why he could not help her.

"Prescelli," he said, as gently as he could. "You only ask this because you don't believe that God intervenes in these matters. I do. And believing that, I do not see how I could possibly win. Better to plead your case yourself than demand a trial by combat and put your fate in the hands of a champion who has no heart for the task of defending you.

"Even if I did believe that the strongest man would win, regardless of guilt or innocence, I could never consent to circumvent justice in that way."

"But you would not be circumventing justice," Prescelli insisted. "I may not be innocent, but I am not guilty of all the things they will accuse me of. I don't deserve to die. The King and his council may feel they have to condemn me for—for reasons of their own. But will you stand by and allow them to do it, after—after all there has been between us?"

Ceilyn wanted to say that he could—but, unfortunately, he knew better. They might talk forever about the right or the wrong of it, but he knew full well that when the time came he would not stand by and make no attempt to save her. To sacrifice *himself* for a principle, that was something he knew how to do, but he lacked the kind of courage it takes to sacrifice another. Not for him the moral certainty that allowed his father to send witches and heretics to the stake and watch impassively while the flame consumed them. He was simply too soft.

"No," he said at last, "I can't do that—more is the pity. I will champion you, but only if and when it becomes evident that you are about to be punished more severely than you deserve.

And only then if you agree to . . . to retire from the world, to enter a convent and take the vows. Is that understood?''

Prescelli nodded her head.

''As for accepting your parole . . .'' Ceilyn knew that would be more convenient for everyone. It would be awkward and embarrassing to bind Prescelli, and he was reasonably certain that Teleri and the others would take no pleasure in humbling her to that extent. ''. . . that holds only so long as you behave yourself. If you cause any trouble along the way, not only will you arrive at Caer Cadwy as my captive, but our other agreement will be broken as well. I will hand you over to the King's justice, and not move a hand to save you. Is that, also, understood?''

''I promise to behave.''

But Ceilyn shook his head. ''I am not interested in any promise from you. I know exactly how long your best intentions are likely to last. I just want you to understand the consequences if you misbehave. Your own self-interest will rule you better than any promise to me.''

Prescelli heaved a great sigh. ''I don't always act according to my own best interest. Certainly, I never did where you were concerned. But it will serve in the present instance. I will be so well-behaved that you will scarcely know me.''

''You had better,'' said Ceilyn. ''For both our sakes.''

Teleri listened quietly while Ceilyn told her of his conversation with Prescelli. She stood in the bedchamber that had once belonged to the Princess Diaspad, with her head down and her hands folded in front of her, and heard him all the way to the end without once interrupting him.

''She is coming back with us—not precisely as a prisoner, but she has agreed not to cause any trouble along the way,'' he concluded.

Teleri looked up. ''And you trust her to keep her word? You believe she will be able to resist the temptation that the proximity of the crown and the sidhe-stone must inevitably present to her?''

Ceilyn shook his head. ''The Clach Ghealach means nothing to Prescelli. Her ambitions do not extend nearly so high. If she did make mischief—and I do not think she will—it would more likely be something petty and malicious, aimed at me or you.''

''You think you know her very well,'' Teleri said softly.

"Yes," said Ceilyn. "I know all her virtues, such as they are, and every one of her faults."

Teleri looked down at the floor again. "And yet you were attracted to her once."

"Prescelli is small-minded and lives entirely in the moment," Ceilyn admitted. "But she experiences that moment with great intensity. Yes, I did find that attractive, at one time."

"And you do not think that the sympathy which exists between the two of you on that account is clouding your judgment?" Teleri asked.

"No, I don't." Ceilyn was beginning to feel exasperated. "If you thought it might, why did you leave the decision in my hands?"

"Whether to take her prisoner or to let her go—that was the choice as the rest of us saw it. No one thought you would choose a third course. We thought . . . I was certain you would decide to let her go."

"In fact, you left the decision to me only because you believed you already knew what I would choose to do." Ceilyn began to pace the floor. "And that the most cowardly and dishonest course of all."

"Not cowardly and dishonest," Teleri protested. "I expected you to be merciful and . . . reasonable."

Ceilyn stopped, folded his arms, and glared at her. "Whereas now you think I am being totally *un*reasonable? Blinded by my past attraction to Prescelli and willing to risk the success of the quest merely to please the woman who was once my mistress. That is what you think, isn't it?"

Teleri shook her head. "No, no, I never thought that. I just don't understand why it is you can't leave Prescelli here, let her go free to find her own way, back home to Ynys Carreg or wherever she wants to go."

"She can't go home—do you think they would stand between her and the King's wrath? They care nothing for her on Ynys Carreg. But perhaps I *do* owe her something for the sake of the past. Not for her sexual favors, but because she was warm and kind and understanding at a time when I needed warmth and understanding more than anything."

He had not meant a reproach to Teleri in that, but she took it as such. He could read the hurt in her eyes.

"Yes, I see," she said in a small voice.

"No, I do not think that you do see. My feelings for Prescelli are not at issue here—my judgment is." He began to move restlessly around the room again. "And I think you might trust me to do what is right—I think I deserve that much from you."

"I *do* trust you to do what you *think* is right," Teleri said. "But as for trusting your judgment—how can I, when it runs counter to my own? And I do know that when a woman is involved there is just no way of predicting what you will do in response to the dictates of some misguided notion of chivalry."

Ceilyn drew in his breath sharply. "Misguided notion of chivalry! I must say, that is very good coming from you! *You've* never taken advantage of that particular failing of mine, now have you?"

"Yes, I have," she admitted. "I know that I have, and we both had cause to regret it afterward. Which is exactly the reason I have to be careful now."

"As God is my witness!" he said. "This is so unfair!"

"I *know* that it's unfair," said Teleri, very close to tears. "But I cannot help that. I mustn't think what is best for you or for me right now. I have to think what is best for the safety of the crown and the kingdom."

He clenched his fists. "So now I am supposed to go back to Prescelli and tell her that my promises to her mean nothing. That my word—"

"Of course you must do no such thing. I am not asking you to break your word. But if you would talk to Prescelli again and convince her to change her mind about accompanying us . . . then we would be relieved of the responsibility of taking her along, and you would not be foresworn."

"No," said Ceilyn. "I cannot do that. I do truly believe that it would be utterly base to abandon her here."

"And if it was a choice between abandoning Prescelli and parting company with the rest of us?" Teleri asked.

"I do not think," Ceilyn said stiffly, "that you would force me to make that choice."

"No," Teleri admitted with a sigh. "I would not. Very well then, Prescelli may travel with us under whatever conditions you have offered her.

"I still think we would all be better off it we left her behind—you most of all," Teleri added earnestly. "But as you seem to think you are somehow honor-bound to champion her . . . why then, there is nothing more to be said."

The nature of a viper is that it is venomous; so, too, are spiders, scorpions, toads, lizards, and dragons. Though every creature is perfect according to its own nature, being fashioned in accordance with one perfect and settled arrangement of the Creator, yet many of them are, at the same time, healthy and venomous. They are healthy, because every creature is made wholesome in relation to itself. But they are venomous, because in relation to other creatures they are pure poison. And even though spiders, lizards, toads, and scorpions are innocent of intent, either for good or evil, yet their venom is just as deadly. Therefore, a wise man shuns that which is noxious, knowing the harm it will do him.

— *Atlendor, in a letter on "The Doctrine of Poisons"*

21.

The Nature of Scorpions

The next day dawned cold, grey, and muddy, but a sharp wind rose shortly after sunrise, ripping the clouds to shreds and sending the tattered fragments flying south. When Ceilyn went down to Teleri's bedchamber, he found her packing for the journey back to Camboglanna.

"So you have decided that we leave today?" he asked, standing stiff and resentful in the low doorway. He was as eager as she to depart, but he still smarted from some of the things she had said, and the fact that she had made up her mind without consulting him did not sit well.

"We can't be certain how long the weather will hold," said Teleri. She gathered up several items and dropped them into a large woolen sack: a battered iron pot, a mortar and pestle, a box which Ceilyn knew contained pouches of dried herbs and flasks of medicine. She picked up Atlendor's book, wrapped it in a cloth, and put it into the bag. "If we wait another day or two for the roads to improve, another storm may blow in. You won't rest and neither will Tryffin, so I see no reason for further delay."

She took up a round hand mirror with a carved ivory frame and a pair of silver combs, put them into a velvet bag, and deposited them in the larger sack with the medicines and the book. Ceilyn raised an eyebrow. All his earlier misgivings about Teleri borrowing Diaspad's gowns and aping Diaspad's ways returned.

Then his gaze fell on a wooden coffer that sat in the middle of Teleri's narrow bed. Ceilyn eyed the box curiously, for among the things Teleri had failed to discuss with him was her plan for carrying the crown safely back to Caer Cadwy. A slender iron chain encircled the wooden chest and a large brass lock secured the chain.

"An awkward burden for you to carry all the way back to Camboglanna," he said. "Or did you plan to hide the chest among the other baggage?"

Teleri hesitated before answering him. "I think it best that we entrust the chest to Fflergant or Tryffin. You will have enough to occupy you, between Prescelli and Calchas's stallion. And I— I would not like to be encumbered should any difficulty arise."

Ceilyn was hurt and did not try to hide it. It was one thing for her to assume sole responsibility for the safety of the crown, it was quite another for her to turn that responsibility over to anyone other than him. It was obvious to Ceilyn, in that moment, that Teleri no longer trusted him.

"Yes," he said coldly. "It wouldn't do to give the crown into irresponsible hands."

Teleri flushed painfully. "I didn't mean to imply . . . It is just that I depend on you, Ceilyn, for so much already. If we were to meet with outlaws again or any other danger, I would not want you encumbered either. Tryffin and Fflergant are of some use—God knows, they *look* formidable enough—but if there should be real trouble, why then it is you I depend on to help me bring us through."

Ceilyn continued to frown at her. It was true that he could hardly carry the chest and effectively wield a weapon, true also that the proximity of a silver crown and an iron chain might hamper the use of his other abilities. But if that was Teleri's concern, why had she not said so in the first place?

Teleri looked up at him pleadingly. "Ceilyn, I really do not want to quarrel with you. Especially not about this, because the crown . . .''

"Yes," he said impatiently, when she showed no sign of continuing.

She shook her head. "It really does not matter which of us actually carries the crown. Not so long as I am linked to the sidhe-stone. It is not as though it could be lost or mislaid." She 9put a hand on his arm. "I really do not want to quarrel with you," she repeated wistfully.

Ceilyn continued to glare at her. "No," he finally admitted grudgingly. "I don't want to quarrel with you either."

While Teleri gathered together food and other supplies from the store the Princess had brought to Mochdreff with her, Ceilyn went down to the stable to help his cousins with the horses. By noon, every horse and every pony had been fed and watered, those chosen to be released had been driven out the front gate, and those remaining—including Twrch the black stallion, Prescelli's dun mare, and two sturdy draft horses—were variously saddled, laden with baggage, or hitched to a light wagon the travelers had decided to take with them, and tied up outside the stable.

By the time that Teleri brought down the wooden chest and handed it over to Tryffin, Ceilyn's temper had cooled. He followed her as she moved toward the grey pony, and waited while she tied her bag of medicines to the saddle, intending to offer her a hand when she mounted—not so much as an apology, but at least as a gesture of reconciliation.

But Prescelli chose that moment to appear. Wrapped in her brown cloak, she crossed the yard with a haughty smile but a hesitant step, as though she could not make up her mind whether to efface herself and avoid a snubbing, or brazen it out.

Her mare, a bony, long-legged dun, had been tied up at a post some distance from the other horses, but nearer to the place where Tryffin and Fflergant stood talking than to Ceilyn and Teleri. Prescelli untied the reins, slipped them over the mare's head, and then stood looking around her expectantly, as if waiting for one of the men to assist her.

Fflergant and his brother ignored her, standing with their heads close together, speaking in low, earnest tones. Ceilyn could hear enough of their conversation to tell they were really absorbed, not just shamming for Prescelli's benefit, but her ears were not so sharp. Imagining an intentional discourtesy, the girl turned pink with mortification.

Ceilyn sighed. He left Teleri's side and walked over to help Prescelli into the saddle. By the time he came back again, Teleri had already mounted the grey pony and gathered up the reins.

"For the love of God," Fflergant said to his brother, as they rode out the front gate, "you are just poisoning yourself with guilt. I admit I was shocked at the time, did not understand why it was you who killed him, but we were all a bit mad that night, after so much excitement, so much bloodshed. You were probably in another battle fury and didn't know what you were doing."

"I won't say I was in my right mind, but neither had I lost my wits," Tryffin said wearily. They had discussed all this before. "I knew exactly what I was doing and how I would feel about it afterward. Or thought that I did. I knew there would be a burden of guilt and shame which I imagined I was capable of bearing. If that burden is greater than I had anticipated . . . why then it is still no more than I deserve."

"But Calchas wasn't worth it, neither the guilt nor the shame," Fflergant protested. "He wasn't worth much, when all is said and done."

"Maybe he was not," said Tryffin. "But how long did I take to weigh his life in the balance and reach that same conclusion? *I* judged him, *I* condemned him, *I* executed him, and all as though the matter was not worth a second thought. God help me—the sheer *arrogance* of that appalls me!"

Fflergant shrugged. "Well, perhaps you did make a hasty judgment. Not surprising under the circumstances. For the love of God, we both imagined ourselves as good as dead—and if Calchas hadn't died, one or both of us surely would have. Another time, you'll practice mercy and discretion, remembering—"

"God of Heaven!" Tryffin exclaimed. "There isn't going to *be* a next time, not for Calchas fab Corfil. How does *he* benefit if I have learned my lesson and practice 'mercy and discretion' the rest of my life?" He stared at his brother with something akin to hostility in his gaze. "You don't see it, do you? Well, how could you? I have killed a man, and that act is irrevocable, there is no possibility of doing it over again or doing it differently." He passed a hand over his eyes. "That is what causes the sick feeling inside, the helplessness and frustration, far, far worse than any guilt or shame. Because no matter how many questions I may have now, there is just no undoing the thing that I have done.''

The roads were poor and progress was slow; the horses tired quickly ploughing through the mud and had to be rested frequently. The long grey shadows of evening overtook Teleri and her companions while they were still a long way from any habitation where they might stop and ask shelter for the night. But they could sleep in the wagon, and though the brush grew sparsely around their chosen campsite, there looked to be enough to fill their needs for one night.

While the men tended the horses, Teleri and Prescelli gathered heather to serve as mattresses, and foraged for firewood.

''But don't expect me to prepare supper,'' said Prescelli with a sniff, as Teleri kindled the few dry branches they had been able to find, ''for I know nothing at all about it. I was handmaiden to the Princess Diaspad—not a kitchen drudge!''

''Truly,'' Teleri said under her breath, ''no one would ask you for meat or drink—not after that concoction you so thoughtfully prepared for me on St. Valentine's Day!''

With Tryffin's help, Teleri started supper, while Ceilyn and Fflergant rearranged the baggage in the wagon and erected a kind of tent inside to keep out the weather. Then, when everyone sat down by the fire to eat, Teleri picked up the sack containing the medicines and Atlendor's book, and wandered out into the gathering darkness.

After a few minutes, Ceilyn put down his wooden plate and followed her. He found her out beyond the place where the horses were tethered, kneeling on the muddy ground, heedless of any damage to her gown. Teleri had drawn the little bronze knife out of her belt, and by the last fading light of sunset, was scratching figures in the damp earth.

Ceilyn stared at the circle Teleri had already drawn encompassing the campsite. ''This is different from the circle you wove before. The twigs and branches—''

''—are no longer necessary,'' said Teleri. ''We have the sidhe-stone now, and it is more powerful than any spell I might make without it. All that is needed here is to establish a boundary, and the stone will ward all within those bounds. Really, the circle is not essential; my mind is linked to the Clach Ghealach and what I define as the boundary within my mind, that much will the stone's power encompass—within reasonable limits. The circle is here to help me visualize what I want to protect."

Ceilyn moved down to her level, squatting on his heels. "Back at Caer Cadwy, you told me we had to wrest the stone from the Princess before she mastered it, because once that happened she would be able to use the Clach Ghealach offensively. I don't understand how that could possibly be, since the powers of the sidhe-stone are purely protective."

Teleri shook her head. "The properties of sidhe-stones are largely misunderstood. I, myself, know less about them than I probably should, because Glastyn would not say much about them. I hope to learn more from Atlendor's book.

"But this much I do know: Sidhe-stones are well-adapted for use as wards because their properties are essentially passive, that is, they reflect or absorb power, they do not engender it. Glastyn had keyed the stone to serve as a ward, so when the Princess sought to destroy me, the stone cast her spell *back* at her, and she was destroyed instead. But if she had been linked to the stone, she might have channeled the spell *through* the stone, and not only increased the power of the spell but directed its effects precisely where she wanted them."

Ceilyn frowned, not understanding. "Increased its power—how? You said that a sidhe-stone absorbs and reflects."

Teleri cleaned the mud off her bronze knife by wiping it on her skirt. "It is hard for me to explain it, since some things are best understood if you don't try to describe them too closely. But it is something like this: There is a—a place within the sidhe-stone that is like a circle of mirrors, each reflecting back the images the others give it. If one were to make use of this property of the sidhe-stone by rekeying it, the mirrors could reflect the spell again and again—in theory infinitely, if the stone and the spellcaster were strong enough to bear it—and with each reflection the spell would become stronger."

Teleri slipped the knife back into her belt. "If Diaspad had been able to use the Clach Ghealach in that way, she would not have tried to kill me by creating a ball of fire—no such effort would have been necessary, for a tiny bit of heat, no more than would be needed to light a candle, channeled through the sidhe-stone and augmented by it, would be just as devastating."

Ceilyn shifted his position uneasily. "But you have the sidhe-stone now, and you *are* linked to it. Does that mean you could . . . ?"

"Yes," Teleri said quietly, "it does mean that I could. Does that make me a monster in your eyes? But you have known for some time that I can kill a man with little more than a touch. Is this so very different?''

Kneeling there on the ground beside him, she looked deceptively small and frail—incapable of harming anyone, much less of burning a man to ashes with a few chanted words. "No," he said slowly, "I suppose not. But it is just beginning to dawn on me how dangerous you have become.''

The next two days were grey and drizzly—not so wet as to make travel impossible, only damp and miserable and discouraging. But late on the second afternoon, when they crossed into Perfudd, everyone heaved a sigh of relief, as if some heaviness or oppression native to the Mochdreffi air had suddenly lifted.

Ceilyn rode with Prescelli a little apart from the rest of the party, guiding Twrch on a leading rein along behind him. Now he handed the rein over to Prescelli, and attempted to maneuver Tegillus into position beside Teleri. Somehow—Ceilyn was not sure how it happened—Fflergant was there before him, riding along at Teleri's side, leading the sorrel pack horse, just as though he had not been riding at the head of the party only a moment before. And when Ceilyn tried to move around to her other side, Tryffin interposed the wagon in between.

An oppression of another sort settled over Ceilyn. Ever since leaving the Castle of Glass, it seemed, the others had methodically excluded him from Teleri's company. When they were riding or even when they were all sitting around the campfire, Ceilyn rarely found an opportunity to get close to Teleri. When he did, Fflergant or Tryffin would suddenly materialize, to ask him a question and draw him away, seeking his advice with a flattering deference which Ceilyn found highly suspicious. And when they all started up again in the mornings, Ceilyn was always just a few seconds too late to lift Teleri up into the grey pony's saddle.

He could not be certain that the whole thing was planned, or if it was, to what extent Teleri was a willing partner in the arrangement. Certainly, few words passed between her and the brothers from Gwyngelli, and no significant words or gestures that Ceilyn could see. Yet the pattern of exclusion was there, and Ceilyn could not help feeling hurt by it.

To make matters worse, the black stallion became more and more difficult to manage, snorting and side-stepping and struggling against the bit. Ceilyn could not understand it. Back at Caer Wydr, he had been able to soothe and subdue the stallion, but now his efforts to communicate with Twrch failed.

They camped that evening in the ruins of an ancient watchtower. They had a roof over their heads and the floor was dry, and they could enjoy the benefits of a blazing fire.

"Do you know," said Fflergant, holding his hands out over the dancing golden flames. "I never considered Perfudd a hospitable sort of place, but after a fortnight in Mochdreff—"

"—after a visit to Hell, Purgatory is bound to have its attractions," his brother finished for him. Though Tryffin smiled, the smile did not reach his eyes, which remained hard, bright, and wary.

Looking at him, Ceilyn suddenly realized what it was that ailed him. Tryffin had lost confidence in himself, and that had undermined his faith in everyone and everything. It was a malaise that Ceilyn knew all too well.

Teleri said nothing to anyone. She took the knobbly woolen bag that accompanied her everywhere—as though, Ceilyn thought, anyone was likely to tamper with a musty old volume that no one but Teleri was able to read—and she sat down by the fire, wedged in between Fflergant and a bulky pile of baggage, again frustrating Ceilyn's hopes of speaking to her privately. He sat down on the other side of the fire, folded his arms over his chest, and regarded the others with hot, resentful eyes.

After supper, sounds of agitation among the horses drew Ceilyn out of the tower. Overhead, the clouds had thinned, allowing a little pale, watery moonlight to shine through. Twrch stamped restlessly, tossing his head; his dark coat was flecked with white foam. Ceilyn put a hand on the stallion's bridle, spoke to him mind to mind, in the way he had learned to communicate with four-footed beasts. The stallion refused to be calmed, sending back a sense of angry frustration.

Heat throbbed through the stallion. Mind-linked as they were, Ceilyn felt an answering heat rising in his loins. One or more of the mares had come into season, and that was what agitated Twrch.

"Ceilyn."

The young knight started; even with his keen ears, he had not detected Teleri's approach. She stood only a few feet away, looking pale and insubstantial in the moonlight, with some of the old fey quality about her, reminding Ceilyn, poignantly, of past pain, past disappointments. His hand tightened on the bridle.

Teleri indicated the shivering black stallion. "You have some idea of renaming him, as I recall. Have you decided what you are going to call him?"

"I thought of naming him Duir, after the fairy steed that Pefyn brought back with him from the Lake Country," said Ceilyn. "He was a steadfast friend and a valiant companion, according to the tales. I believe Twrch has similar good qualities, if someone took the time to encourage them."

But Ceilyn was no longer certain he would have that time. The mares were not his to dispose of, and if Twrch became unmanageable, Ceilyn would face a painful choice: either to release the stallion, or sell him in one of the towns they passed through.

"And your sword . . . you were going to name that, too."

"I have named it Griffon." Ceilyn made an impatient movement of his hand. "But I do not think you came out here to talk about Twrch or my sword."

Teleri took a tentative step in his direction. "No. I came because—because whenever we do talk, we seem to be skirting the real issue between us. It's not really who carries the crown back to Camboglanna, or whether we bring Prescelli with us. The real question is . . . whether or not we care for one another."

"Yes," Ceilyn said. "I suppose that is the question. It seems that our feelings have grown so strong that they color everything we say and do."

Teleri hesitated, then began again. "We agreed that the quest was the most important thing, that we ought not to allow our feelings for one another to distract us. But we *have* allowed ourselves to be distracted. So perhaps it would be better if we settled the matter between us once and for all. Then we would be free to think of other things."

Ceilyn felt a knot tightening in his stomach. "And so . . . ?"

Teleri's voice began to tremble. "And so . . . when we arrive at Caer Cadwy . . . if you still want to marry me, I would like to be wed as soon as possible."

Ceilyn heard himself laugh derisively. "This is supposed to be a bribe, meant to insure my continued loyalty, isn't it?"

She made a tiny painful sound. "No," she said faintly, "no, of course not. How can you think that?"

"Perhaps," he said, "because it sounds so much like another

proposition you made me, last All Hallows Eve, when you were also eager to insure my cooperation."

Teleri's face went white. "I only wanted you to know that our—our present disagreement need not change anything between us. That none of it makes any difference to me."

Ceilyn stared at her, measuringly, for a long time before he replied. "But perhaps . . . perhaps it makes a great deal of difference to me."

Turning on his heel, he went back into the ruined tower. He did not join the others by the fire, but found a dark, quiet corner to himself, and sat down on the cold flagstone floor. The enormity of what he had just done began to sink in.

He closed his eyes, tried to convince himself that he was not going to be sick, not going to disgrace himself. But the memory of Teleri's shocked white face rose up before him, and the pain clawing his stomach gripped even harder.

There was a rustle of cloth. When Ceilyn opened his eyes, Prescelli was standing beside him. He glared up at her. "If you have come here to gloat . . ."

Prescelli knelt down on the floor next to him, reached out as if to touch him, then thought better of it and withdrew her hand. "You look terrible . . . like a man walking about with an open wound. I thought there might be something I could do for you." She licked her lips, took a deep breath. "I take it—I take it you and Teleri have quarreled?"

"Quarreled?" Ceilyn laughed mirthlessly. "Dear God, if it were only that! But how do you quarrel with someone who never loses her temper and hardly ever fights back. No . . . she just stands there quietly and allows me to say every stupid, cruel, and hurtful thing that comes into my head, and by the time I finally come to my senses it is too late—because I have already said far too much, and there is no way on earth I can unsay any of it."

Prescelli raised a skeptical eyebrow. "I had no idea Teleri had such an angelic temper. But if she has . . . why then you needn't worry. She is certain to forgive you."

Ceilyn leaned back against the cold stone wall. "Forgive me? Yes, most likely she will, for she never carries a grudge. But I need more than Teleri's forgiveness now. I need to convince her that I didn't mean anything that I said. And doing that," he said hollowly, "doing *that* may require a good deal more than just begging her pardon."

• • •

The next morning, it was harder than ever to get near Teleri; she seemed to fade away whenever Ceilyn approached her. But he persisted until finally he caught up with her, while she was saddling Kelpie.

"Can I help?" he asked, coming up behind her. He tried to make the question sound casual and friendly, but his voice shook despite his best efforts to keep it steady.

"No thanks," said Teleri, in a small breathless voice. "I can manage by myself."

He put his hand on top of hers, but she made a little shrinking movement, and he drew back again. "I want—I want to apologize for last night. The way I spoke was inexcusable, but I—"

"No," she interrupted him. "I am glad you were so—so honest with me. I have been afraid all along that you wouldn't be able to tell me if you—if you changed your mind. I thought you might think there was no honorable way to withdraw your offer of marriage. You have relieved me of that fear, and I—I am grateful."

"But I haven't changed my mind," he protested. "Before God! You ought to know me better by now, my vile temper and my wicked, reckless tongue. The things I say when the black mood is on me . . ." His voice faded out; he suddenly realized what he should have known long before.

"God help me," he said softly, "all the time when you seemed so unsure about your own feelings, it was *my* feelings you doubted." Teleri nodded wordlessly and tightened the cinch on her saddle.

"All these months," he said incredulously. "It took me all these months to convince you that I really wanted you, and I spoiled it all with a few thoughtless words! But I swear to God, it is you that I love and no other woman upon this earth."

Teleri shook her head, blinking back tears.

"If my word isn't enough to convince you . . . perhaps there is some way I can show you," he pleaded. "Only tell me what I must do in order to convince you."

"But I don't think there is anything you *can* do," she whispered. And throwing her arms around Kelpie's neck, she buried her face in the pony's rough grey mane and began to cry.

The Wizard's Garden at Caer Cadwy was a riot of greenery, ranging from the pale silver- and grey-greens of chamomile and catnip to the dark glossy green of wild rose. Teleri knelt amidst the spiky catnip, cutting out the old woody growth in order to make room for the new, and Ceilyn watched her work.

"There is a mountain," said Teleri, "somewhere . . . very far away. At the top of the highest peak stands a castle of ice. The walls of the castle are high and the peaks of the mountain so sheer, from a distance they look so sharp you could cut yourself on them."

Ceilyn shuddered, for the picture she conjured up was not a pleasant one. "It sounds a terrible place."

"Oh no," said Teleri. "The castle is very beautiful, very peaceful. The walls are transparent and I can see for a thousand miles in every direction. But the chasm on the other side . . . that frightens me. Once, I stood on the very edge of the abyss, looking down and down. . . . "

She saw that her words had shaken him. "It is nothing to worry about," she said softly. "It is only a game I sometimes play."

22.

The Castle at the Edge of the World

A light rain fell all morning, steadily and depressingly. Everyone smelled of damp woolen cloaks and wet leather. Ceilyn watched Teleri ride on ahead of him, with her hood drawn well forward concealing most of her face, a forlorn little figure in grey, curiously isolated though Tryffin and Fflergant rode to either side of her.

He cursed himself for a fool. If he had doubted Teleri's love before, her pain now was all the proof he needed.

In the afternoon, the clouds split and the rain came down in sheets. Ceilyn urged Tegillus forward until he drew abreast of Fflergant. "If this keeps up, we will have to stop and ask shelter at the first farm we pass. The horses can't keep on in weather like this." Fflergant nodded his agreement.

The rain continued to beat down and the wind began to rise, whipping their cloaks around them. Ceilyn spotted a group of weatherbeaten buildings huddled together, about a quarter of a mile from the road. Signaling the others to follow him, Ceilyn set off across the moor.

The farm consisted of a run-down cottage, an enclosure full of damp, unhappy-looking sheep, and an empty stable. The farmer was a sullen man, as weatherbeaten as his farm, but he offered them the stable for the duration of the storm.

While the men looked after the horses, Teleri and Prescelli climbed up a rickety ladder to the loft and changed into dry clothes. When she climbed down again, Teleri arranged the few sticks of dry wood the farmer had provided as firewood, and tried to kindle a fire. But the spell eluded her, and concentrate as she might, she could not make the sticks ignite. In the end, she was forced to make use of flint and steel.

"I have almost forgotten what a real fire feels like," she said to Tryffin. "It is hard for me to even picture it in my mind."

"But we had a fine fire just last night."

Teleri drew her cloak more closely around her. "Was it only last night? It feels like at least a year."

Two long nights and a long restless day they camped in the stable. Tempers frayed under those cramped conditions and the enforced intimacy. By the time the weather cleared, everyone had abandoned even the appearance of civility, and conversation was reduced to short, clipped sentences.

When Ceilyn led Twrch out into the grey morning light, he saw that the black stallion was limping. How the black had lamed himself Ceilyn could not tell, but a careful inspection revealed that the right hock was hot and swollen.

Ceilyn went back into the stable to ask for Teleri's advice, though he was embarrassed to beg even so simple a favor. When he spoke to her, Teleri did not answer for such a long time, Ceilyn was certain she was going to refuse even to look at the leg. Then she picked up the bag containing her medicines, and followed him silently out of the stable. She spent so long a time over the job that Ceilyn began to fear there was something seriously wrong.

"Can you treat him?"

Teleri blinked her eyes. She seemed to return from a long distance away. "Treat him? Yes. But have we linen for a bandage?"

"I have a clean shirt we can use," said Ceilyn.

She nodded, opened her sack, and took out the box of medicines and the other odds and ends that it contained, laying them out on the ground. Ceilyn went back inside, dug through his own gear until he found the shirt. Taking out his knife, he cut and tore the linen into strips. When he returned to the farmyard, Teleri had arranged all the bags and bottles of medicines neatly before her, and was surveying the collection with a vague air of bewilderment. She started when Ceilyn spoke to her.

"Is there anything more you need?"

Teleri shook her head. She opened a flask, soaked a strip of linen in something that smelled like horse liniment, and proceeded to bandage the injured hock. Ceilyn held the stallion's head and soothed him with low, wordless sounds.

But Ceilyn's mind was not on Twrch. He was remembering, with painful clarity, that time only a few weeks past when he and Teleri had been on their own, out on the road, sharing the excitement of a grand adventure. The memory brought no comfort—it only served to sharpen his present misery, now that the adventure had gone sour.

He tried desperately to think of something he could say, something that would make things . . . if not right, at least more comfortable between them. But her manner was so odd and distracted that casual conversation was obviously impossible, and the words of love and remorse he really wanted to say froze in his throat.

"It is as well no one is riding him," Teleri said, as she secured the last strip of linen. "But it would be better if he carried nothing at all . . . not even his saddle."

She began to gather her things together, and Ceilyn—eager to be of service, if only in so small a way—picked up the velvet bag containing the mirror and the silver combs, and reached for the iron pot. A sharp protest from Teleri stopped him. "No . . . don't. I can see to those things myself."

Puzzled and hurt, Ceilyn put the bag down.

• • •

Several fine days followed, cool but clear. The roads improved and the travelers made good progress. But the black stallion—now named Duir—continued to be a problem. Though his injured leg improved, his disposition did not. He nipped at the other horses, and laid back his ears when anyone but Ceilyn came near him. At night, his restless movements outside the wagon kept everyone awake.

In the brisk, bright weather, other travelers began to appear on the road: mostly respectable merchants and tradesmen, but there were others, battered-looking, hard-faced men, with a hungry look that reminded Ceilyn of the robbers in Ystrad Pangur.

On the watch for trouble, Ceilyn eyed with suspicion every solitary footsore itinerant beggar they met along the road, scrutinized the faces of every band of travelers they passed. More than that, he extended his senses of sight and sound and scent outward to their very limits, as if in that way he might pick up some whiff, some rumor of peril. Perhaps that was why he failed to notice the more immediate problem which grew worse every day, right in the midst of his own party.

While the weather held, they slept every night in the wagon, for Ceilyn's earlier distrust of innkeepers now extended to the farmers and herdsmen in their isolated little cottages.

One evening after supper, Fflergant asked Ceilyn for a few words in private. They left the others by the campfire, and went around to the other side of the wagon, where no one could overhear them.

"Perhaps you won't thank me for interfering . . . God knows, I have hesitated to say anything for fear of offending," said Fflergant, leaning against the wagon box. "But it has come to the point where it is painful to watch, and I can't in conscience keep silent any longer. You are the only one who has any hope of helping her, for she looks right through the rest of us as though we were not there."

Ceilyn frowned at him, frankly puzzled. "I haven't the least idea what you are talking about."

Fflergant looked at him with pitying tolerance. "I thought you hadn't noticed. Well, I was a long time noticing myself, what with you sulking . . . and Tryffin walking about with all the guilt of the world on his shoulders . . . while all *she* did was grow small and grey and silent—more so, I swear, than she ever was before. And when I reached out to help her down from the saddle tonight, her hand was as cold as ice.''

Ceilyn continued to stare at him, uncomprehending. ''Are you trying to tell me that Teleri is . . . ill?''

''Ill? Yes, though whether that would be the cause or the effect I couldn't say.'' Fflergant shook his head. ''There is something seriously amiss. At first, I thought she was only lonely and unhappy over her quarrel with you, but now . . .'' He lowered his voice, though there was no one near to overhear, ''. . . the *fire* dies down whenever she approaches it.''

Without a word, Ceilyn went back around the wagon. Teleri sat alone, cross-legged on the ground, some distance from the campfire. She did not move or otherwise react when he knelt down beside her, took one of her hands, and brushed it with his lips. The hand was cold and lifeless.

''Dear Heart,'' Ceilyn said softly. ''What have you done with your riding gloves?''

She did not answer, so he asked the question again, this time louder. Teleri frowned and made a vague gesture with her free hand. ''I don't remember. Perhaps I lost them.''

Ceilyn pulled his own leather gloves out of his belt. ''Take mine, then, and come closer to the fire. You will take a chill, sitting here in the cold.''

She accepted the gloves, but made no move to pull them on, holding them loosely and carelessly in her hand. ''Thank you. But I am quite comfortable as I am.''

Ceilyn felt a sick, sinking sensation. How could she *not* notice the cold, when her skin was exactly like ice? ''Come closer to the fire,'' he repeated, ''to please me, if not yourself.''

But Teleri did not seem to hear him, and as many times as he asked her, she gave him no further response. Finally, frustrated, he took off his cloak and wrapped it around her.

All the next day, with mounting frustration, Ceilyn watched Teleri closely. What ailed her . . . what he could possibly do to help her . . . what would become of her if he could not . . . to none of these questions was he able to find a satisfactory answer.

This much he did learn—and that he found scarcely reassuring: When he was near Teleri, he often caught Prescelli watching him with a look of unmistakable amusement. Yet the sight of the two of them together ought to cause Prescelli pain rather than pleasure.

Could Prescelli be somehow responsible for Teleri's condition? Ceilyn thought not. Any feeble attempts at witchcraft of which Prescelli might be capable would pose no threat to an accomplished sorceress like Teleri. But Prescelli *knew* something, of that much he was certain, and Ceilyn needed to know what that something was.

Late that night, when all the others were sound asleep, Ceilyn shook Prescelli awake. "I want to speak to you," he hissed in her ear. "Come outside with me, so that we do not disturb the others."

Prescelli sat up and pulled her blankets up to her chin. "It's the middle of the night and freezing cold! Whatever you want, it can wait until—"

"It can't wait and you *will* come. Or do you think I would hesitate to drag you out of here by force?"

Though it was too dark for Prescelli to see his face, his tone was enough to convince her. "I will go outside with you," she said.

The moon was in its second quarter waxing near to full. Ceilyn helped Prescelli to climb down from the wagon, then led her away from the camp, beyond the place where the horses were tethered, to the edge of Teleri's circle of protection.

Prescelli hung back at the boundary. "I don't see any reason to go so far. We can talk just as well here."

Ceilyn took her roughly by the arm and pulled her over the line. "There is nothing out here that frightens *me*, and nothing more dangerous to *you* than I am at this moment."

A dozen yards from the boundary he finally released her. Prescelli rubbed her bruised arm and stared at him reproachfully.

"Teleri is ill . . . perhaps even dying," he said. "But not of any natural disease. I have seen you watching her, and I think you know what ails her."

Prescelli tossed her head. "Perhaps. Yes, perhaps I do know something. But what would be the use of anything I might say? You would never believe me anyway."

"Possibly not," he said. "But why don't you try me and see?"

"Because if I do tell you and you don't believe—"

Ceilyn took her by the arm again. "If you don't tell me something—and that immediately, so I know you've not taken time to invent something—if you don't answer me just as quickly as you

can, the consequences then, I promise you, won't be pleasant!''
He gave her a little shake to emphasize his threat.

Prescelli came to a swift decision. "It is the sidhe-stone, the
Clach Ghealach, that has made Teleri ill. Oh yes, you can frown
at me all you like, but I am telling you the truth. I heard the
Princess and Calchas discuss the properties of the stone many
times, and it is all right there in that musty old volume Teleri
carries around with her. All you have to do—but no, you can't
read it, can you? You will just have to take my word for it.''

He glared at her. "Very well then, enlighten me. What did
the Princess learn about the Clach Ghealach—what could she
possibly have learned—that Teleri did not already know?''

"That prolonged contact with a stone of that size and potency
can be dangerous. The Princess knew something of sidhe-stones
before, but she didn't know *that* until she read it in Atlendor's
book. And even then she didn't really understand it, until she
began to suffer symptoms very like Teleri's. Then, of course,
she took steps to counter the influence of the stone.''

Ceilyn tightened his grip. "None of this makes any sense.
Teleri has been linked to the sidhe-stone for most of her life,
and it never affected her before. Why should it harm her now?''

"No effect on her?'' Prescelli smiled contemptuously. "I
wonder that you can say so, who have suffered from her coldness
so many times. The influence of the Clach Ghealach is lunar—
passive. It sucks the power out of things. In Teleri's case, it is
drawing out her life force. It had the same effect on the Princess—being a woman, you see, and therefore doubly vulnerable,
for the moon is the female principle and like calls to like. But
even for a man, prolonged or frequent physical contact can be
unwholesome. *That* is why Glastyn told Cynwas to keep the
wretched thing locked away.

"But Teleri always was a drab, passive little thing, cold emo-
tionally if not physically. I think that her link with the Clach
Ghealach was partly responsible for that. That may have been
part of what Glastyn intended. Not that Glastyn and the stone
were entirely to blame,'' Prescelli added maliciously. "He probably chose Teleri for his apprentice in the first place, because
she had a natural aptitude for perpetual virginity.''

Ceilyn continued to glare at her. Though he was inclined to
distrust her, much that she said matched what Teleri had told
him about the nature of sidhe-stones, as well as her admission

that she did not know all she should about the power of the stones.

"But you mentioned prolonged or frequent contact, as though Teleri were somehow *touching* the stone. Which she is not—not in any way that she hasn't been touching it all along. She keeps it locked up in that wooden chest and she hardly ever goes near it. If the stone really did present a danger to anyone, it would have to be Fflergant or Tryffin, not Teleri."

Prescelli's smile changed from malicious to scornful. "From which anyone with half a wit might easily guess that the crown and the sidhe-stone are not in the wooden chest at all. Did you see Teleri put it there? Did she ever *say* the crown was in the wooden box?"

Ceilyn's grip on her arm relaxed. "I don't remember that she ever did. But it is obvious, isn't it? The box is the safest place, the only safe place, and if the crown is not there—then where would it be?"

"Rather too obvious, when you think about it. All chained up in that little box, a virtual invitation to thieves, a proclamation that here it is, the only thing of value we are carrying with us. You would think Teleri would carry it concealed, and that any protection she put on it would be subtler in nature. Yet at the same time she takes such ostentatious precautions to keep the thing safe, she never goes near the treasure herself.

"I would guess that the box is empty, or else it contains rocks or something else of no value to give it the proper weight," said Prescelli. "And the crown is elsewhere . . . somewhere that Teleri can touch it a dozen times a day, if she wants to."

As plausible as all this sounded, Ceilyn still doubted her. "That would be in the sack with the medicines and other things she always carries with her. But it isn't there. I have seen everything that sack contains: bottles and flasks, an old iron pot, some trinkets that used to belong to the Princess, and Atlendor's book. The book is the reason she guards the sack so carefully. She is afraid of losing—" He stopped, shook his head, appalled by his own stupidity. "You are right. I wondered often enough myself: why guard the Grimoire which no one but she knows how to decipher? And all the time, she hardly seems to spare a second thought for the safety of the Crown of Celydonn."

He scowled at Prescelli. "But if the crown *is* in the bag with the other things—why hasn't anyone seen it? She has opened the bag a dozen times and—" Then the answer came to him, and it was so obvious that he marveled he had not guessed it before. "She has disguised it. She put a *seeming* on the crown."

"Very good," said Prescelli. "I am glad to see you are capable of some rational thought where Teleri is concerned."

But Ceilyn ignored her, staring out across the moonlit moor, trying to work the whole thing out in his mind. "Dear God," he said at last. "I was offended because she had entrusted the crown to Fflergant and Tryffin . . . and now it appears that she has been watching over it herself all this time."

"She has been *deceiving* you all this time," Prescelli reminded him. "She didn't trust you and she kept you in ignorance."

Ceilyn let out a long slow breath. "No, I think she did try to tell me, once or twice. Or start to, anyway. But I was so damned certain I had been slighted, I made it difficult for her to confide in me. It must be the ivory hand mirror. I wondered about that . . . that and the silver combs."

But Prescelli shook her head. "Too valuable and therefore too tempting. I daresay the whole elaborate pretense was designed as much for my benefit as for any chance-met thieves along the road. Ironic, isn't it, that I was the only person she was unable to fool for long? Of course, she didn't know that the stone would make her ill, or that her symptoms would start me thinking. She brought the mirror and the combs just in case I should yield to the temptation to steal *something*, and she disguised the crown as something no one would want to steal."

"The iron pot," said Ceilyn. "It would weigh about as much as the crown, and none of us would notice any difference if we chanced to pick it up." He smiled grimly. "All this time, Fflergant and Tryffin have been guarding a box full of worthless stones, and Teleri has been carrying Cynwas's crown of state around in the form of a battered pot!" His smile faded. "Now all I need to do is convince her to turn the wretched thing over to me. Very unlikely, as things are now. And the more so if I credit my sudden knowledge of the properties of sidhe-stones to *your* sage advice!"

He ground his teeth audibly. "Which no doubt explains your willingness to tell me these things. You don't believe there is any way I can get the crown from Teleri."

Prescelli smiled brightly. "Truly. She won't give you the crown willingly. You have only to see how she guards it to realize the obsession is growing on her. The Princess was the same way. I believe she would have cut out Calchas's heart had he so much as offered to touch the crown. And if you try to take it by stealth or by force—I wonder how many ways Teleri knows to kill a man?''

''And you don't think I would be willing to take that risk?'' Ceilyn asked her.

''Oh yes, if you thought it would do any good,'' said Prescelli. ''Sacrifice yourself to save Teleri—yes, that would be just like you. But not knowing it would do her no good, not knowing that once she had finished killing you all she had to do was step over your corpse to pick up the crown again.''

''But you said that the Princess was similarly affected, and found some way to counter this . . . lunar influence.''

''Did I say that?'' Prescelli failed to sound as innocent as she would have liked. ''Well, perhaps I did. And why shouldn't I tell you—you'll not find that knowledge any more useful than anything else I told you.

''She countered the lunar influence, which is female, by union with the solar, or masculine, principle. Can you guess how she did that? I think you can. You northerners have such prurient ideas of what magic is all about, and sometimes you are even right. It was the marriage of the sun and the moon, the mating of sulphur and mercury. The Princess Diaspad restored the balance by sleeping with her dwarf guardsmen. Such nasty, misshapen little creatures, as they were, too. But rather than relinquish the crown to anyone else's keeping, she conquered her revulsion and invited the little freaks—a different one each night, so they wouldn't get inflated ideas—into her bed. I can assure you they did not spend the whole night sleeping.'' Prescelli smiled as Ceilyn's eyes widened in shock. ''Have you ever heard cats mating? It sounded exactly like that.''

''I don't believe you,'' said Ceilyn. ''Or at least . . . if the Princess behaved as you say, it was some perversion of her own and had nothing to do with the sidhe-stone or Teleri. You've made the whole thing up, created this elaborate story just to bring Teleri down to your own level.''

''It would be convenient for you to think so,'' said Prescelli. ''Because if I am telling the truth . . . Teleri is doomed. You know as well as I do: You haven't a chance in Hell of luring Teleri into bed with you, not as things are now!''

And the lad traveled through the Realms of Fire and Ice, bearing with him, in a little crystal box, the heart of the giant's daughter. In the Realm of Fire, the flames burned him black, and great was his anguish. Nor did his suffering diminish in the Realm of Ice, for there, too, he was burned, but with a cold fire which did not consume him. When his pain and grief became too great to bear, he took the maiden's heart out of the box and put it inside his tunic next to his skin, and there he could feel it beating against his breast.

—from THE BLACK BOOK OF TREGALEN

23.

In the Realms of Fire and Ice

In the morning, Teleri spoke to no one. While the others broke their fast, she climbed out of the wagon and wandered over to the place where Kelpie was tethered. By the time that Ceilyn joined her, she had saddled the grey pony, untied the reins, and was just swinging up into the saddle.

Ceilyn caught hold of Kelpie's bridle as Teleri rode by. "Don't be so impatient to be off. The rest of us won't be much longer, and this is dangerous country for you to travel on your own."

Teleri let the reins fall, but she did not dismount. Uncertain what she might do next, Ceilyn remained at the pony's head, talking of the weather . . . the road . . . anything that might catch and hold Teleri's attention, while his cousins and Prescelli broke camp, hitched up the draft horses, and saddled the riding horses. Teleri listened with a puzzled, abstracted air, as though she were trying to understand what he told her, but was failing to make some connection.

When Ceilyn finally gave the pony her head, Teleri took up the reins and started off, with never a backward glance to see if the others followed her.

• • •

They rode due south with a cold wind at their backs. That was broken country, land that grew rougher and more irregular with every mile they traveled south—a land too hard for farming, so the inhabitants raised sheep and goats and occasionally swine. The roads were rocky and rutted. Had they turned west earlier, toward the river and Camboglanna, instead of traveling the length of Perfudd, they would have followed a broader, easier road. But that was the road to Ystrad Pangur, and Ceilyn had no wish to enter that nest of robbers again.

In the afternoon, when the others stopped to eat, Teleri remained in the saddle, the leather reins in one hand, clutching with her other hand the woolen sack which was tied to the saddle horn. Ceilyn came up beside her. When he made as if to untie the bag, her grip tightened and a spark of determination came into her eyes. "No," she said quietly, and that was the first word she had spoken in two days.

Though she would not let him take the sack, she did permit Ceilyn to help her down from the saddle, and lead her over to the knoll where the others sat on the thin, dry, Perfuddi grass, eating a cold dinner of fruit, cheese, and dried meat. Teleri would not eat, for all of Ceilyn's coaxing, but she did swallow a mouthful of water when he handed her the waterskin.

In desperation, Ceilyn turned to Fflergant and Tryffin. Taking them aside, he told them all he had learned from Prescelli. "I don't know what I ought to do—I don't even know what I ought to believe," he concluded miserably.

Tryffin and Fflergant exchanged a glance, as though they could hardly believe he was asking *them* for advice. Well, Ceilyn thought, that was not to be wondered at; he was not in the habit of seeking advice. But he needed help now, and was not too proud to ask for it.

"God knows, if we knew any better than you, we would tell you, Cousin," Fflergant said, with a warmth that surprised Ceilyn.

But then he wondered why he should feel surprised. They were his kinsmen, after all—and everyone knew what store the Gwyngellach set by kinship—and he and they had been to Hell and halfway back again, a proceeding that was bound to strengthen the bond between them. The wonder was that he had not noticed when they had become his friends as well as his kinsmen.

"Just how much of what we do and say do you suppose she notices?" said Fflergant.

Ceilyn shook his head. "It is difficult even to guess. She is . . . removed, somehow. With us, and yet not with us, and retreating further every day."

"You think she has retreated to a place inside herself, as Gwenlliant did?" asked Tryffin.

"No," Ceilyn said slowly. "No, this is different. You've not seen Gwenlliant, so it would be difficult to explain. This is akin to something Teleri used to do, when there were people or situations she wished to avoid. She just went . . . elsewhere. There was one place of retreat in particular which she described to me. Her castle of ice, she called it. And she said something else, something that made me think there might be a danger, a danger that she might someday be unable to return.

"Then you don't think it is the sidhe-stone affecting her after all?" said Fflergant.

"I do think it is the sidhe-stone," said Ceilyn. "I think the Clach Ghealach and Teleri's castle of ice are one and the same."

After dinner, when the others mounted up, Teleri mounted also. She took up the reins but made no move to urge the grey pony forward.

With a sinking heart, Ceilyn dismounted. He helped Teleri out of the saddle, led her over to Tegillus, and put her up on the big chestnut gelding. She allowed all this, neither willing nor unwilling, just passive and obedient like a small child, but when Ceilyn tried to take the sack containing the crown from her, she pulled it back with surprising strength. Rather than risk alienating her further, Ceilyn let her have her way.

He swung up behind her, put his arms around Teleri's waist, and drew her under his cloak. He still did not know how far he could trust what Prescelli had told him, but surely this much contact would do Teleri no harm, and might possibly do her some good by countering the "lunar influence" of the Clach Ghealach.

Prescelli rode up on her sway-backed dun mare. "You will have to do better than that," she said.

Ceilyn's arms around Teleri tightened and his face grew warm. "I cannot speak to her . . . cannot communicate with her in any way. How does a man make love to a woman who scarcely even knows he is there?"

"Very easily, I should think," said Prescelli, with a bright malicious smile. "No need to talk to her, to coax her into bed with you. She just follows wherever you lead her. I daresay you could do with her exactly as you like, so long as you don't try to take the sidhe-stone from her."

Ceilyn glared at her, utterly outraged. "What you are suggesting, in fact, is little better than rape," he said, in a cold tight voice.

"I suppose that it would be," Prescelli admitted. "Well, that does present you with an interesting dilemma, doesn't it? Ravish her in order to save her life . . . or behave like a man of honor and watch her die."

"I don't *know* that Teleri is in danger of dying," Ceilyn protested, though the stillness of the slight body he held in his arms argued that Teleri *was* in danger. "And I certainly have no good reason to believe that what you suggest would do her more good than harm. Where Teleri is concerned, why *should* I trust you?"

"As you say," said Prescelli sweetly. "Why should you believe anything I tell you?"

Toward evening, dark, angry clouds began to pile up on the eastern horizon. The wind tasted of rain. Faced by the prospect of a storm before morning, Ceilyn allowed Tryffin and Fflergant to overcome his mistrust of strangers, and agreed to seek shelter from one of the grim Perfuddi herdsmen.

Again they shared quarters with the horses, not in a stable this time, but in a long, low thatched hut. Chickens and guinea fowl roosted in the rafters, piles of dirty straw lay scattered on the packed earth floor, and there was a distinct aroma of goats.

But Teleri curled up on a pile of straw, with the sack containing the crown clutched in her arms, and immediately fell asleep. Leaving her in Tryffin's care, Ceilyn went outside to search for wood and brush to make a fire.

In the gathering twilight, the landscape looked bare and sullen. The soil was thin in that part of Perfudd; grass and occasional low shrugs grew there, but no trees. For lack of anything better, Ceilyn gathered some dried gorse he found rooted on a rocky hillside.

Walking back to the hut, the hex symbol mounted over the door caught his eyes, reminding him that last night he and his companions had camped outdoors without the benefit of Teleri's circle of protection. Nothing had disturbed them. Somehow, he did not think it was the proximity of the sidhe-stone that had kept the night things at bay. Once again, he wondered what kind of bargain he had made with the Holly King.

"You can't burn that," Prescelli protested, when he entered the hut, his arms full of his gleanings. "It is bad luck to carry whin into a house, and even worse if you put it on the fire."

"This is not a house. In better days, it was obviously a goat shed," said Ceilyn, dropping the dried stems on the floor and clearing a space to build his fire.

"A house . . . a shed . . . a barn . . . a cave . . . any sort of dwelling at all," Prescelli insisted. "It is bad luck."

Ceilyn took out flint and steel. "We will have to chance it."

When the fire was blazing nicely, Ceilyn stood up and unfastened the brooch that held his cloak. He spread the cloak, fur lining uppermost, on a pile of straw near the fire. Then he carried Teleri over. The flames flickered and lost color, changing from yellow to a wan blue.

Prescelli sniffed. "Is that why you are willing to bring ill-fortune down on the rest of us? But it won't do her any good, you know. She can draw all the heat out of your fire and it still will not save her. *Animal* heat is what she needs."

Ceilyn lowered Teleri to the cloak. She stirred in her sleep but did not wake. He touched her face, her hands—at first they were cold, but her flesh warmed under his. If Prescelli spoke the truth . . .

He looked up to see Prescelli watching him intently. He knew that the more she teased him to do the thing, the more convinced he ought to be that Teleri would only be harmed by it. And yet, he was uncertain how far her malice extended.

"I wish to God I knew your motives," he said softly. "I cannot believe that you wish to save Teleri, nor that you care to spare me pain. But I can't quite believe, either, that you would be so wicked as to suggest . . . what you have suggested . . . merely to make sport of a dying girl."

"But I do want to save her," said Prescelli. "And you needn't trouble yourself over my motives, for they are purely selfish. If she dies, you will blame me—that is inevitable, whatever I say or do—but if she lives—"

"If she lives, I am going to marry her," said Ceilyn.

"I don't think so," said Prescelli. "I don't believe she will have you. I think she will break your heart, having no heart of her own, and then you will come to me for comfort."

Ceilyn was more confused than ever. "What if I told you," he said, watching her expression very carefully, "that Teleri had already consented to marry me?"

Prescelli raised a skeptical eyebrow. "I would say you do not have the look of a man who was happily betrothed," she said cooly.

The storm struck just after dark, with surprising ferocity. Long after his companions had fallen asleep, Ceilyn lay awake listening to the shrieking winds and the lashing rain. If the elements were at war outside the low building of thatch and mud, Ceilyn was at war within himself.

Had Prescelli told him the truth? The more he worried at that question, the less likely he seemed to find the answer. Prescelli did have her odd moments of compassion, as Ceilyn had reason to know. And if she were moved by Teleri's pitiable condition, it would be like Prescelli to hide her concern behind a mask of mockery and self-interest.

But say that her motives were exactly as she claimed, say that Prescelli was convinced that Teleri dead was a more formidable rival than she was living . . . but no, the Prescelli he knew was more likely to believe that an obstacle removed was one she need no longer worry about.

Ceilyn moved restlessly, unable to find a comfortable position and fall asleep. Say then that Prescelli intended Teleri only harm—how might she try to accomplish that? By offering Ceilyn a false cure, one that would degrade him and Teleri both—or knowing that Ceilyn would mistrust her, by telling him the true cure, believing that to be the surest way to keep him and Teleri apart?

Even supposing Prescelli *was* telling the truth . . . that Teleri could be saved in that and no other way—*"little better than rape,"* he had said, and that was not too harsh a judgment. To take Teleri as she was would be like molesting a child. But . . . his honor or Teleri's life? No, that was putting it selfishly. He would sacrifice more than honor if he could only be certain. . . .

The night wore on. Ceilyn tossed and turned, aroused by Teleri's nearness and her helplessness, yet ashamed that he could desire her under those conditions. The real question was how she would feel afterward, once she was herself again. Would she blame him? Would she hate him? Or would she, understanding the necessity that drove him . . . dear God, what had that to do with anything, whether she forgave him or not? How would she feel about *herself* afterward? Would she feel soiled? Would she feel shamed? Would she think her life had been bought at too dear a price, and that she was better, much better off dead?

And yet again . . . he remembered Teleri kneeling in a circle of lantern light, that night in the hayloft, saying, *"If it were not for the quest, there would be no need for us to sleep apart."* She had wanted him then, he was certain of that, and later, at Caer Wydr, when they had come so close to making love. . . .

He burned with desire and grew cold with shame, and all the time the aching heaviness was almost unbearable.

To lie with Teleri, to touch her, to feel her move beneath him . . . but no, she would not respond at all. She would just be as cold and still as she had been in his arms all day. But even so . . . to hold her, to make her entirely his own, and give her in return not his love only but her own life back as well.

He threw off the blankets that encumbered him, crept over to the place where Teleri lay. The fire had nearly burned out, was nothing more than a few bright sparks among the ashes. But that was enough for him to see by.

He lifted the blankets and the cloaks he had piled on Teleri earlier. She lay on her back, with her hair coming loose from its braid, a silver shimmer against the dark lining of the cloak. One arm covered her eyes, the other cradled the bag containing the crown. He thought that her loose-fitting gown would be no real obstacle.

He bent and kissed her, softly at first, then more insistently, willing her to grow warm, to awake and welcome him. Her mouth was as sweet and cold as honey wine, but that was no matter—he had heat enough for both of them.

Yet just as he was moving to lie down on top of her, a noise, a tiny rustle of movement from one of the other sleepers, reminded him that he and Teleri were not alone; it would be impossible for him to make love to her without the others hearing and knowing what he did. As if what he meant to do were not indecent enough—the thought of doing it while the others listened, and wondered, and drew the inevitable conclusion, filled him with such shame that he could not continue.

Ceilyn went back to his own bed. But sleep was impossible. As the long stormy night dragged on, he asked himself again and again: Was it a sense of honor and decency that had restrained him . . . or something more contemptible?

• • •

The storm passed on before morning and Ceilyn fell into a fitful doze that lasted until Fflergant rose and opened the door, letting in the pale golden light of morning.

Despite all the noise the others made making breakfast, Teleri slept on, rousing only when Ceilyn shook her gently and spoke in her ear. She opened her eyes and sat up, but she would not eat and she drank only a sip or two of water. Then she drew up her knees, put her arms around them, and lowered her head with a weary little sigh. Her hair fell over her face in such a way, Ceilyn could not tell whether she was asleep or not.

"You see what is happening to her. You will have to mind her like a child." Prescelli sat in the weak sunlight by the door, doing up her own dark hair. "I suggest that you begin by combing out those tangles, or it will all be in rats by the time you reach Cacr Cadwy."

Ceilyn glared at her. But then he realized that what she said was true: Someone had to take care of Teleri, and rather than appoint Prescelli as handmaiden he would have to tend her himself.

He searched through Kelpie's saddlebags until he found Teleri's old wooden comb, then he woke her again and led her out into the sunlight. As always, she carried the bag containing the iron pot that was really the Crown of Celydonn.

He took her to the well, where he washed her face and hands, then sat her down on the rim. Her skin had acquired a strange translucent quality, like wax. With her silvery fair hair hanging loose over her shoulders, her grey gown and cloak, Ceilyn thought she looked as cold and colorless as water.

He teased the tangles out of her hair one by one. While he worked, the herdsman and his wife came out of their cottage, to feed their pigs and geese, and to rake at a meager garden plot beside the house. Under their stony regard, Ceilyn self-consciously braided Teleri's hair into a clumsy plait.

She was so quiet and passive that Ceilyn thought he might try again to take the crown from her. He put his hand over hers, began gently to pry her fingers loose from their grip on the sack. "Let me carry it for a while—the burden is too much for you to bear. I will give it back to you whenever you ask," he said softly.

"No," said Teleri, just above a whisper.

Ceilyn gasped in pain. An icy hand reached into his chest and clutched his heart, squeezing so hard, he thought the organ must burst. Driven to his knees, Ceilyn released his hold on Teleri's fingers.

As suddenly as it had come, the pain was gone. Weak and shaken, he knelt there a moment longer, then staggered to his feet, torn between frustration at his own helplessness and a cold relief that Teleri had not, after all, struck to kill him. In that much, Prescelli had been wrong.

When he led Teleri back to the goat shed, Prescelli was waiting for him, standing in the doorway, watching him with hungry eyes and a bitter smile twisting her face. "Is it true what you told me last night—are you and Teleri betrothed?"

Ceilyn was uncertain how to reply. He had asked and Teleri had accepted, and neither of them had exactly taken back their words. And all those days when he believed that Teleri had turned away from him, she was already under the baleful influence of the sidhe-stone. "God knows, I regard myself as irrevocably pledged to *her*."

"And no matter what happens you will go on loving her, and there will be nothing left over for me?"

Ceilyn shook his head slowly. "No," he said, as gently as he could, "I don't believe there will be."

Her eyes became harder and brighter than ever, her smile more painful to look upon. "You really are a fool, Ceilyn mac Cuel— did no one ever tell you that?"

"I think it has been mentioned a time or two before," he said.

When it came time to saddle up the horses, Ceilyn saddled first Tegillus, and then Duir, the black stallion. Duir stood quietly while the young knight buckled the girth and adjusted the stirrups, but when Ceilyn led him out of the hut and climbed up into the saddle, the stallion began to act up, worrying at the bit, shaking his head, and refusing to stand still.

"God Almighty! You don't intend to take Teleri up on that wild horse, do you?" said Fflergant.

"I do," Ceilyn replied grimly. "Prescelli informs me that animal heat is what Teleri lacks, and here is Duir full of fire and spite. It may be that the two of them might do each other good."

Whether or not the stallion communicated any of his fire to Teleri after Fflergant helped her to mount up in front of Ceilyn, it was evident that her proximity had a favorable effect on Duir.

He became calmer almost immediately, and Ceilyn had no difficulty managing him after that.

But the taming of Duir—formerly Twrch—was the last good thing that happened that day. All morning and well into the afternoon, the travelers were plagued by one mishap after the other.

The girth on Tryffin's saddle broke as he cantered across a smooth stretch of road, occasioning an ignominious but harmless fall. Tryffin switched places with Fflergant, who was driving the wagon, but the incident, somehow, depressed everyone's spirits.

The road they followed led them between two hills, then ended at the site of a recent landslide, forcing them to go back and take a longer and more difficult route.

"I *told* you your fire would bring us bad luck," Prescelli whispered to Ceilyn, but Ceilyn only scowled at her.

When they stopped for dinner, they learned that a wineskin, a knife, and a packet of food were missing, whether lost along the way or left behind at the goat shed there was no way of telling.

And in the late afternoon, Prescelli's mare went lame. Cursing the mischance that had allowed this to happen when Teleri was incapable of treating the injury, Ceilyn dismounted and squatted down to examine the dun mare's leg.

"I am sorry," he said to Prescelli, who stood anxiously looking over his shoulder. "This is very bad—beyond my skill to treat. We will have to lead her for now, and leave her behind at the next place we come to."

"No," said Prescelli, in a hard, stubborn voice, though she looked very close to tears. "I don't want to give her up. Oh, she isn't much, I know, but she is mine, practically the only thing that *is* mine except for the clothes I wear on my back. And it isn't fair. There was no talk of leaving your stallion behind when he hurt his leg."

"That wasn't nearly so serious. If your mare is forced to keep on walking, she will be permanently lamed. As you say you are attached to her, surely that is the last thing you will want to happen.

"I will buy you another mare when we reach Caer Cadwy," he offered. "One much prettier. You did say once—didn't you?—that you always wanted a nice little coal-black mare. Find one that you like, and I will buy her for you."

Prescelli sniffed. "Much use I will have for a riding horse after we reach Caer Cadwy. Not much exercise she would get, while I'm in prison or a convent."

Ceilyn shook his head, unwilling to argue the point. "You can ride Tegillus the rest of the way."

"A fine fool I would look mounted up on a hulking great warhorse. I would rather take the sorrel mare," said Prescelli. "Tegillus can carry her load—or Tryffin's beast can—they both look strong enough."

Ceilyn frowned, unwilling to subject either charger to the indignity of acting as a packhorse. But Prescelli was adamant. "I won't ride him. I am certain he must be vicious."

So Ceilyn reluctantly complied, shifting the baggage to the chestnut's broad back and putting Prescelli's side saddle on the sorrel mare. By the time he had accomplished all that, his annoyance had dissipated.

"I am sorry about your mare," he said, as he helped Prescelli to mount.

"I have never known you *not* to be sorry," said Prescelli, gathering up the reins, "but what good has that ever done me?"

That evening, camping outdoors again, Teleri sat up with the others while she ate. Though she seemed more alert than she had during the day, she still refused food and remained as silent as ever.

Studying her by the dim glow of the fire, Ceilyn thought that a little color had come back into her face, just the faintest tinge of pink beneath the translucent skin. But whether or not he was imagining it, Ceilyn was not minded to sacrifice any progress Teleri might have made during the day by allowing her to grow colder during the night.

He made up a bed, using his bedding along with Teleri's, and slipped in beside her, under the blankets and the sheepskin covering, determined to offer her what heat he could. This was no time, he told himself, for observing the proprieties.

Teleri fell asleep almost instantly, lying on her side with the sack in her arms. Ceilyn slid one of his arms under her head, put the other around her, and buried his face in her hair. Sleep eluded him, just as it had the night before, his thoughts chasing each other in restless circles.

Added to all his other questions was a new and troubling one: Supposing he *could* keep Teleri alive—by one means or another—until they reached Caer Cadwy . . . what if the King was not there when they arrived? Would Teleri be willing to relinquish the crown into Sidonwy's keeping? Or would she insist on clinging to it until Cynwas finally returned?

The next morning at breakfast, a meal that Ceilyn neither tasted nor enjoyed, he was uncomfortably aware of Prescelli's curious scrutiny, equally self-conscious in the face of Tryffin's and Fflergant's studied disinterest. On an impulse, he took the gold ring off his smallest finger—the ring the Queen had given him in gratitude so many months before—and slid it onto Teleri's fourth finger.

An exchange of rings before witnesses was a binding ceremony, legally equivalent to a marriage. Even the Church recognized such unions, albeit grudgingly, insofar as the legitimacy of any children that might result, so long as a proper wedding before a priest eventually followed. Although this was half a marriage at best, the gesture satisfied Ceilyn's sense of propriety.

Whether or not his kinsmen noticed or approved, Ceilyn did not know. But Prescelli gathered her things together with uncharacteristic haste, and saddled and mounted the sorrel mare without waiting for his assistance.

Gold is universally acknowledge to be the perfect metal, for in it the four elements are united in due and perfect proportion. Fire gives gold its yellow color, the aerial element its purity. From moisture, gold derives it mallibility, and from its earthy components weight.

Only gold is perfect, but all other metals have a tendency toward perfection, differing only in their accidental rather than essential forms. Therefore, it is possible for the Alchemist to rectify these accidents in metals, and gold may be obtained by transmutation.

This art, Philosophers have named The Work of the Sun.

—from THE MIRROR OF THE ANCIENTS

24.

The Work of the Sun

Ceilyn stood on the eastern bank of the River Arfondwy, with one hand on Duir's bridle, staring across the placid face of the water, to the rolling green hills of southern Camboglanna. Only four more days, he thought. Weather permitting, four days of travel on reliable roads through civilized country.

He looked up at Teleri, huddled in her cloak atop the black stallion's back. Four days during which Teleri might slip further and further away from him, four days for the Clach Ghealach to continue drawing off her life force.

But his ring still glimmered on Teleri's finger, a spark of living gold, in bright contrast to the dead white of her hand. More than an empty gesture for the sake of propriety, Ceilyn was certain that the ring served as a symbolic link, binding him and Teleri together.

Signs, symbols, rituals . . . these were the tools of magic, whereby the magician directed and amplified his will. Ceilyn was not a Wizard, no trained talent like Teleri, but he knew he had a strong will, and all the bits and pieces of wizard-lore that Teleri had bestowed on him since first their friendship began.

"A perfect circle . . . there is power in that." So Teleri said when she gave him the iron bracelet meant to suppress his shapeshifting powers. And the silver bracelet she had later accepted as a token of friendship . . . that was a perfect circle, too. Men and women had been exchanging such tokens since time out of mind, as public pledges and private, at weddings and betrothals, at secret lovers' trysts, and Ceilyn thought of all the vows made and the rituals performed, and he knew there was power in them, the power of custom and belief, and that was a power he could draw on to save Teleri.

There was also the power of prayer, which Ceilyn had not abandoned.

The river was broad and shallow, the current slow. Taking a firmer hold on Duir's bridle, Ceilyn waded across. On reaching the far bank, he looked around to see if the others had crossed safely, and discovered that one of his party was missing. "Prescelli . . . did she cross before or after the rest of us?"

Fflergant and Tryffin exchanged a sheepish glance. "Ah well . . . I don't know that she crossed at all," Fflergant admitted. "We parted company with Prescelli at that last little village, the one we passed through after dinner."

Ceilyn looked from Fflergant to Tryffin, then back again, in outraged disbelief. "Parted *company*? Do you mean that Prescelli ran off and neither of you attempted to stop her?"

Tryffin cleared his throat. "It seemed to us that she was exerting an unhealthy influence, and that her departure would be scarcely unwelcome."

Ceilyn glared at him, wondering whether Prescelli had chosen to go off, or had been convinced that it was all for the best. "Welcome or unwelcome, we had a duty to take Prescelli back with us. Not a pleasant duty, perhaps, but—"

"As to that, *we* never felt any call of duty where Prescelli was concerned, not one way or the other," said Fflergant, bristling up in the old way. "It is just because she once meant something to you that you feel a perverse obligation to bring her to justice now. Oh, you have a fine time playing the martyr, but why should Prescelli offer herself as a willing sacrifice to your damned principles?"

"Prescelli was no sacrifice," Ceilyn retorted. "She asked to come along with us, begged me to stand as her champion—"

"—and then changed her mind," said Tryffin. "Or never truly intended to travel with us the whole way. An escort from Mochdreff to more civilized country, that probably suited her purposes very well. But either way, she is gone now, and you have more important things to do than go chasing off after her.

Ceilyn continued to glare at them both, for Prescelli was a responsibility he could not so casually shed. "God knows what will happen to her now," he said.

But even so, he felt a guilty surge of relief.

The weather had been gradually growing milder. Now they rode through familiar country, and Ceilyn's mistrust of inns and innkeepers faded. When evening came, he was glad to stop at one of the many comfortable inns and guesthouses that dotted the countryside. With the warmer days, and a fine fire and a big warm bed to sleep in for two nights running, Teleri began to brighten and take some notice of the world around her. Ceilyn felt his spirits rise.

But then the weather turned on them. The wind rose and a light snow began to fall. The sky grew dark at midday. Fflergant and Tryffin lighted lanterns and Ceilyn wrapped Teleri in blankets and cloaks, desperate to keep all the heat she had gained from escaping. It was no use. In a matter of hours, she grew cold and withdrawn again. She would not eat, she would not speak, and when Ceilyn tried to gain her attention by calling her name over and over again, not a flicker of interest or recognition could he arouse. Only when he tried to take the sack containing the disguised crown from her did she react, with a tightening of her fingers on the cloth.

When they stopped at an inn, Ceilyn carried Teleri into the common room, cold and limp and apparently asleep in his arms. The innkeeper informed them that he had only one bedchamber available.

Tryffin looked at Fflergant, and Fflergant nodded his head. "We have no objection to sleeping down here, while you and Teleri share the bedchamber," said Tryffin.

Ceilyn hesitated at the foot of the stairs. "You think that I should do as Prescelli advised, don't you?" he asked softly.

"You are the only one who knows what has passed between the two of you in the past, and you are the only one who knows—

or can hope to guess—how Teleri would feel about being saved in that particular way," said Tryffin.

"And if I don't know . . . if I can't guess?"

Tryffin shook his head. "Why then, I don't doubt you will still sleep easier without the inconvenience of our presence."

In the morning, when Ceilyn led Teleri down the stairs, neither Fflergant nor Tryffin asked what had occurred during the night. There was no need to ask questions, because the answer was all too discouragingly evident.

"You followed your conscience . . . a man can't do any more than that." Fflergant tried to comfort him.

"Can he not? I wonder." Ceilyn appreciated his cousins' loyalty, but he knew that it did not matter whether they condemned him or not. He knew that if Teleri died between the inn and Caer Cadwy or even afterward, because she was beyond any cure by the time she reached the castle and yielded the crown—it would not matter what anyone thought. He would never be able to forgive himself.

The day was wet and windy, their progress heart-breakingly slow. Ceilyn thought he could feel Teleri slipping away from him, hour by hour and minute by minute.

The sun was a tarnished gold disk sliding into a silver sea when the irregular towers of Caer Cadwy finally appeared on the horizon. "Tegillus is the freshest. Shall I take him and ride ahead to prepare the way?" Tryffin asked.

At a nod from Ceilyn, he changed mounts and spurred on ahead. The last few miles seemed to stretch on forever, but at last Ceilyn and Fflergant arrived at the castle. The gate stood open to welcome them.

It was Fflergant who climbed out of the wagon and took Teleri down from the black stallion's back, but it was Ceilyn who carried her past the horsehide hanging in the doorway and into the guardroom.

"Is the King in residence . . . or the Earl Marshall?" Ceilyn racked his brain to think of anyone else whose authority Teleri might recognize. But the Captain of the Guard assured him that the King was in residence and that Tryffin and several guardsmen had gone in search of him.

Ceilyn put Teleri down on a bench, sat beside her, supporting her with an arm around her shoulders. There was a sound of running footsteps, and the King burst into the guardroom, accompanied by Tryffin and Manogan fab Menai.

"The crown and the sidhe-stone . . . you have them safe?" Cynwas asked breathlessly.

"Yes, but carrying the sidhe-stone has made Teleri ill, and she would not allow anyone else to share the burden," said Ceilyn. "We are not certain that even now . . ."

But at the sound of Cynwas's voice, Teleri had opened her eyes. She moved against Ceilyn as though she were trying to sit up straighter.

The King went down on one knee. "My child, you have done me a great service," he said softly. "Will you not yield the crown to me now?"

There was a long pause. "Yes," Teleri breathed. It was more a sigh than a word. She allowed Cynwas to take the sack out of her hands and loosen the drawstring.

"We believe she has disguised it as—as an iron pot," said Ceilyn. The King and the Earl Marshall exchanged a startled glance.

"I have it," said Cynwas, and he drew it out of the bag. It was not an iron pot at all, but transformed by the King's touch, once more a heavy silver circlet with a frosty blue-white sidhe-stone set in its highest point.

Everyone watching heaved a mighty sigh of relief. The crown passed from the King's hands to the Earl Marshall. "Take this to its old place in the treasure room."

But with the transfer of the stone, Teleri's last strength deserted her. When the King turned back to thank her, she had already gone completely limp in Ceilyn's arms.

Teleri was in a cold, cold place, wandering down long glittering corridors and through high white chambers. She climbed a narrow spiralling staircase to the top of a crystal tower.

Where was she going? She could not remember. What was she seeking? She had no memory of that either. But the halls were chill and comfortless and she found no place to rest.

Once, she had been oblivious to the cold, impelled by a single purpose of diamondlike clarity, before which all doubt, all discomfort, all weakness receded—once, she had carried a precious something with her, encased in a glass box which she held close against her heart. But that something precious was gone, and with it all comfort, all sense of purpose.

She was in a room at the top of the tower, a many-sided chamber, with walls as clear and glittering as the facets of some great jewel. Somewhere, very distant, very thin, she could hear a voice calling her name.

Where was it coming from? She could not tell. The voice echoed on all sides, now a little louder, a bit more insistent, now growing weaker, with a note of desperation. She moved in what she thought might be the right direction, and found her way blocked by a solid, glittering wall.

"Teleri . . . Teleri . . . Teleri." The voice was stronger now. She knew its source was somewhere on the other side of the wall. But the wall was opaque, like clouded ice, and she could not see through to the other side. "Teleri . . . Teleri . . . Teleri." The wall of ice reverberated with every repetition of her name.

Suddenly, she wanted out, out of the cold crystal shell that encased her. She felt panic rising inside of her, a claustrophobic pressure. Out . . . out . . . she must get out. In desperation, she made her hands into fists and beat against the wall.

The ice began to crack, the cracks began to spread, the wall broke into splinters, into shining shards that fell away, leaving a ragged gap. On the other side of that gap was light and warmth and sound and color—a riot of sensation that drove her back. She hesitated, uncertain whether to advance or to retreat, whether to step forward into chaos, or back into peaceful oblivion.

But the voice came clearer than ever, and this time she was able to recognize it, to give it a name: *Ceilyn*. And clutching that name like a talisman against her heart, she found the courage to make her decision.

When Teleri opened her eyes, the first thing she saw was Ceilyn's face, very white and strained, very close to her own. She realized that he was cradling her in his arms and speaking her name, very softly, over and over again.

"Ceilyn," she said, in a small, weak voice, and watched his face light up with surprise and relief.

"Thank God," he said. "Praise Jesus Christ and all the Saints in Heaven . . . I never thought to hear you speak my name again."

He carried her across the room, sat her down in a high-backed chair near a blazing applewood fire. Teleri looked around her: The fireplace was decorated with a frieze of scallop shells and sea-trows worked in white plaster; bundled herbs hung from the ceiling; and the room was lined with shelves crowded with books and bottles and curious brass instruments. A little earthen pot of spiced wine was simmering on the hearth, and the kittens, Sulphur and Mercury, were curled up together on a rug by the fire. She had come home again—home to her little stillroom in the Mermaid Tower.

Ceilyn knelt down beside her chair. "Do you feel that you could eat something?"

"Yes, please." This time, her voice sounded stronger.

"Fflergant and Tryffin have gone to the kitchen . . . likely they'll come back bearing a feast, for you know they judge everyone's appetites by their own." Ceilyn spoke lightly, but when he reached out and took her hand in his, she could feel him trembling.

Tryffin and Fflergant arrived soon after, bearing platters of steaming food, which they laid out upon the long table in the center of the room. Teleri took a few sips of soup, nibbled at a piece of roast fowl, and drank half a cup of spiced wine from a goblet which Ceilyn held out for her. That was all that she could manage.

As she sat back in her chair, the glint of a gold ring on the fourth finger of her left hand caught her eye. "But what is this?" she asked.

Suddenly, the room was very quiet. Ceilyn went down on one knee again. "Do you remember consenting to marry me?"

Teleri nodded, then a look of pain crossed her face. "Yes, I remember. But you said—"

"I spoke hastily and in great bitterness of spirit, but I meant nothing that I said, nothing. Can you believe that and forgive me?"

Teleri examined the plain golden band, the single large gemstone. "But I have no ring to give you in return," she said at last.

Fflergant cleared his throat. "Allow me the honor of providing this." He drew off one of his own rings and dropped it in her lap. "Entirely appropriate, since we are now to be cousins."

Teleri picked up the heavy circle of gold and cupped it in the palm of her hand. Everyone watched breathlessly to see what she would do.

The ring slipped easily onto Ceilyn's fourth finger. Then Fflergant and Tryffin withdrew, leaving the newly pledged couple to settle the rest in privacy.

In the little bedchamber behind the stillroom, Ceilyn gently helped Teleri out of her cloak and gown. She spoke only once, as he drew the dress over head. "Ceilyn . . ." His heart lurched painfully, and he stopped breathing. ". . . I am still so *cold*."

He let out his breath slowly. "That will be better—I promise that will be better soon."

She stood shivering in her thin shift; her fine hair hung loose around her shoulders, pale gold by candlelight. When Ceilyn reached for her, her cool white arms slid around his neck; when he kissed her, she melted like water into his embrace.

Trembling with excitement, he lifted her and carried her over to the bed.

In another bedchamber on the floor above, Gwenlliant slowly opened her eyes. "I am hungry," the little girl said plaintively. "Please, may I have something to eat?"

There was a sound like a gasp of indrawn breath on the other side of the room, and a scuffle of footsteps. Fand appeared at the bedside and took Gwenlliant's hand in both of hers.

"She spoke—praise the Virgin, she *did* speak." The older girl burst into tears. "Gwenlliant, do you hear me? Are you truly awake?"

The child struggled to sit up. "Of course I am awake. Why are you crying, Fand?" Gwenlliant felt weak and strangely lightheaded. "Was I sick? But I think I am better now. And I missed the feast—can I *please* have something to eat?"

"You can have anything you like," Fand said, smiling through her tears. "Only lie back and rest, and I will send word to the Queen that you are better, and then down to the kitchen for some bread and soup."

Ceilyn woke to a loud, insistent knocking on the stillroom door. Reluctantly, he unwound himself from Teleri's sleeping embrace and climbed out of bed. He pulled on enough clothing to satisfy decency, and went into the next room to answer the door.

"A pity to wake you," said Gofan, stepping into the room. He carried a pile of clean clothing: linen shirt and breeches, parti-colored hose, and a long green wool tunic trimmed with miniver. A page bearing a basin of steaming wash water followed him in. "But the King and Queen were growing impatient. Well, Tryffin and Fflergant *told* them the entire story, three times over already, but—"

"No, I am the one who should apologize," said Ceilyn, yawning and stretching. "Keeping everyone waiting while I slept until—what time is it?"

"Well past noon," said Gofan.

Ceilyn washed and dressed, then he went back into the bedchamber and sat down on the bed beside Teleri.

Bright sunlight, coming in through one of the high, narrow windows, fell in a bar diagonally across the bed, shining full in Teleri's face, but she slept on, smiling in her sleep, undisturbed by either the light or Ceilyn's movements. The color had come back into her cheeks and her lips. Her silvery pale ash-blond hair fell across her breast, and the golden ring he had given her gleamed on her finger—it took his breath away to realize that she was really his wife now, finally and undeniably his, after so many months of aching and wanting.

He leaned forward and brushed a kiss across her cheek. She opened her eyes, smiled drowsily, and put her arms around his neck. Ceilyn wavered for a moment between duty and a sudden sharp desire to begin the night all over again. But then he remembered that Gofan and the other boy were waiting in the next room.

"I have to leave you for a little while," he whispered. "The King has summoned me. But I will return just as soon as I can."

As he and the boys descended the stairs, Ceilyn asked: "What news of Gwenlliant?"

"She woke this morning early. Brother Gildas has pronounced her fit physically and spiritually," said Gofan. "But she is not to have any visitors until after your lady has determined whether she suffers any magical effects."

They arrived in the small audience chamber where the King and Queen awaited his coming—along with the Earl Marshall, the Lord Constable, and other knights and officers of the court. There were also a number of ladies present.

Ceilyn paused on the threshold, looking back at Gofan. "You didn't tell me this was to be a formal audience."

Gofan grinned at him impudently. "I was told not to. If you have a complaint, you can present it to the King."

Self-consciously, Ceilyn crossed a great expanse of polished floor, and made his bow before the dais. "And not before time," said Cynwas, though his smile belied his impatient words.

"Permit the boy some small indulgence—last night was his wedding night," said the Queen, gently scolding. "And let us not begin the inquisition until after he has had something to eat and drink. He looks famished near to death."

A chair was instantly provided and two pages brought in a small trestle table which they set up upon the dais. Gofan ran down to the kitchen to see what the Cook had on hand, and Fergos went down to the cellar for a flagon of malvoisie. In a surprisingly short time, the table was laid and Ceilyn's dinner was served. While he ate, the King and Queen drank wine from silver cups.

Between bites, Ceilyn looked around him curiously. He spotted Fflergant and Tryffin talking to their uncle. He scarcely recognized the Earl Marshall, for the man looked fifteen years younger. His old lazy elegance had been replaced by a youthful vigor and enthusiasm that quite transformed him. At his side stood the Lord Constable, sun-browned and healthy-looking, for all that he wore one arm in a sling and a half-healed scar slashed his jaw from ear to chin.

"Would you believe it—Ysgafn was injured rescuing a young woman from bandits," Sidonwy whispered in Ceilyn's ear. "Nine men and he and the King vanquished them all. You must ask them to tell you the tale sometime, and the other knights as well . . . some of their exploits were quite exciting."

Ceilyn could well believe it. Everywhere he looked, all of the men had that same keen, bright look: Scilti mac Tearlach, Branach and his brother Dianach, Dillus, Rhodri, even the King himself. "It seems," said Ceilyn, "that the Princess's spell which sent them out adventuring did them more good than harm."

"And the Kingdom shall benefit as well, for the King and his officers have awakened to their responsibilities. They have grand plans, which you shall hear of before long," said Sidonwy.

But now the King was growing genuinely impatient, and Ceilyn was obliged to put aside his dinner, and begin to relate his own story. As he was able to furnish details of the quest for the crown which were unknown to Fflergant and Tryffin, everyone in the room listened eagerly.

But during the second telling—given at the King's request—his audience began to fall away. And when Cynwas would have had him repeat the whole thing again, Sidonwy intervened. "We have kept him from his bride too long, and see . . . she has come in search of him." She indicated the other side of the room where Teleri, in a blue gown, stood talking to Fflergant and Tryffin. "Let him bring her to us, and present her formally."

The King gave his assent. Ceilyn crossed to the place where Teleri was, kissed her, and led her back toward the dais.

The audience chamber had suddenly gown very still. "Kneel down," the Queen whispered helpfully.

Taken entirely by surprise, Ceilyn and Teleri did as they were told. The King cleared his throat impressively. "Cousin," he said, "I am well pleased by your deeds during the recent crisis. Therefore, I am minded to bestow on you certain lands out of my own demesne, and with them the title and the dignities pertaining thereto, as Lord of Regann."

Everyone cheered vigorously. But Ceilyn was stunned—he had been so intent on the adventure itself, first to last, that he had never thought there might be rewards involved.

"As for your lady," the King continued, when the cheering had died down, "there is a position on the Council, Glastyn's old place, that is waiting to be filled. It is past time that his apprentice—an apprentice no longer, but a Master Wizard in her own right—took that place. The Council meets in three days' time, and I shall expect to see you both in attendance."

Ceilyn felt Teleri's hand tremble in his. "My lord," she said softly, "I know . . . nothing of statecraft."

Cynwas smiled down on her indulgently. "A sad defect in the King's Wizard, but one which may be easily remedied. You shall learn as we all did, by watching and listening."

While Ceilyn and Teleri accepted the congratulations of the court, Tryffin slipped out of the audience chamber and headed across the courtyard toward the Mermaid Tower. Fflergant followed him out, catching up with him just as he entered Sidonwy's heraldic garden.

"You spoke for a long time with the Lord Constable," said Fflergant. "What was it all about?"

Tryffin shrugged. "You heard most of it, I think. Ysgafn will be warranting some new deputies; he is looking for volunteers, young men to help him dispense the King's Justice. I have volunteered, asking Ysgafn for a post which I think no one else will want.

"I asked him . . . to send me to Mochdreff."

"Mochdreff!" Fflergant stopped beside a topiary lion, and stared at his brother in disbelief. "A Prince of Tir Gwyngelli acting as Deputy Constable in Mochdreff? You must be mad. You couldn't even *live* in such a place, and as for the people—"

"Calchas lived there—our Cousin Calchas, no more Mochdreffi by blood than you or I," Tryffin pointed out. "I can't say that living there did him any good, but the air did not poison him nor the earth open and swallow him up. Bron lived there, too. If they could endure the place then so can I."

Fflergant followed him across the garden. "Yes, I see. This is some kind of a penance, isn't it?"

"In some sense it is a penance, yes," Tryffin admitted as they entered the Mermaid Tower, nodding politely to the guard at the door. "But there is more to it than that.

"You remember what Teleri said, what Glastyn told her? In order to understand the Mochdreffi you must first understand the land that bred them. I want that understanding—and I think I owe Calchas that much at least. I want to know if the Mochdreffi are born men like other men, and how the land shapes them. I want to know what part the land played in shaping Calchas. And if that understanding is something a man—an outsider—can gain in a single lifetime, if I have any time left afterward . . . why then I think I would like to go someplace else: to Cuan, or Draighen, or Gorwynnion. I have never been to any of those places."

They climbed the stairs to Gwenlliant's bedchamber. "Well . . ." said Fflergant, after considerable thought, "as penances go, it does sound better than joining a monastery and beating yourself with iron hooks every day."

"But not much better?" Tryffin suggested.

"Not very much . . . no," Fflergant admitted. "Oh, Cuan and Draighen and Gorwynnion sound well enough to me, and I may just have a talk with the Constable myself. But as for returning to Mochdreff . . . no, I think not."

Fand met them in the corridor outside the bedchamber. "She

remembers nothing that happened after we put her to bed before the feast. Oh, she knows she was ill for several days, but not how long it really was. We plan to break that to her gently, along with her brother's disappearance.''

Fflergant and Tryffin nodded solemnly. ''We will take care to say nothing to disturb her,'' said Tryffin.

Gwenlliant was sitting up in bed, propped up by pillows at her back. Despite Teleri's assurances, they had expected to find the child looking white and worn after her ordeal; so they were entirely unprepared for the blooming little face that turned up to receive their kisses.

''I missed the feast and the second day of the tournament,'' she said. ''And now there is something . . . some celebration. They hurried Teleri away and everyone was excited. I do think it hard I should miss that as well—I don't feel ill at all.''

Tryffin knelt down beside her bed. ''Cynwas has announced another tournament and a grand ball to follow, in place of the tourney that was ruined,'' he said. ''With your favor, Cousin, I will be your knight and escort you to the ball.''

Brightening at the prospect, Gwenlliant offered him her hand to kiss. And watching the two of them together, Fflergant thought he saw a softening of the pain in his brother's eyes.

When the Queen and her young ladies whisked Teleri away to plan for ''a proper wedding in the Chapel of St. March,'' Ceilyn went to the Mermaid Tower to visit Gwenlliant. When he walked into the Solar an hour later, he found Sidonwy and the other women there, but not Teleri.

''I am afraid we frightened her with our grandiose plans,'' the Queen admitted ruefully. ''I see it will have to be a simple ceremony in my private chapel, or your poor little bride will be too shy to attend.''

''I meant to thank you for the land and the house at Regann—that was your doing, I believe, as much as the King's,'' said Ceilyn.

''My suggestion, but only when the King asked me where you might like to live. You may remember there is a charming manor house there—an excellent place, I thought, to raise a family of budding wizards and sorceresses.

''It may be some time,'' she added seriously, ''before your father is willing to welcome you and your bride to Caer Celcynnon. He had great respect for Glastyn, but somehow a woman wizard is always suspect. I do not know why that should be so, and yet we both know that it is. We must hope that her position here and her place in the King's confidence will in time invest her with sufficient respectability. As for the difference in birth— any objection to that will certainly be overcome by the size of the dowry Cynwas intends to bestow on her.''

''A dowry?'' Ceilyn was not entirely pleased. ''I had no expectation of a dowry when I—''

''Naturally, you would prefer to take her penniless and friendless,'' the Queen said agreeably. ''We all know your fantastical notions of chivalry, but you will see that this way is better for everyone, and no more, truly, than Teleri deserves. Were the King to bestow on her only a tenth part of the value of the sidhestone, she would be the richest bride in Celydonn.

''Though out of respect for your principles I will urge the King to restrain his generosity,'' she added reassuringly, ''and only dower her sufficiently to satisfy your family's pride.''

Ceilyn found Teleri in Glastyn's garden. There was snow on the ground outside, but it was late spring in the garden where the earth kept its own seasons.

Teleri sat on the stone bench, which perched on four clawed feet by the mossy pond. All around her, the ivy, and the mint, and the roses ran riot. Ceilyn took a deep breath of the sparkling air, and felt a sense of homecoming.

As he crossed the garden to join her, the earth throbbed beneath his feet—but he recognized the rhythm now; it was his own heart and Teleri's beating as one. When he sat down beside her, the old, sweet, silent sympathy passed between them, as sharp and piercing as an arrow.

''It's been so long since I was here . . . before I left for the wilds last autumn,'' he said. ''Thank God it hasn't changed.''

''But I think that it has changed,'' said Teleri. ''Just as we have. I suppose we will go on changing each other . . . and the garden changing with us . . . gradually, a little at a time.''

Ceilyn smiled at her. ''Like the Alchemist seeking to change base metal into gold. . . . What was it Glastyn told you?''

''He said that it was a process of many months or years, and so expensive that the wise man undertakes it not for gain, but purely for joy in the discoveries he makes along the way.''

Ceilyn took her hand in both of his, thinking of what those months and years might bring. They had a lifetime before them

. . . a lifetime full of transformations and discoveries, magic, adventure, joy and sorrow . . . all to be shared together.

Just contemplating the years ahead of them filled him with a deep satisfaction.

And the lad slept that night with the giant's daughter, and she was his only wife as long as he lived.
—*from* THE BLACK BOOK OF TREGALEN